ALL THAT WE SEE OR SEEM

ALSO BY KEN LIU

THE DANDELION DYNASTY

The Grace of Kings
The Wall of Storms
The Veiled Throne
Speaking Bones

COLLECTIONS

The Paper Menagerie and Other Stories
The Hidden Girl and Other Stories

Laozi's Dao De Jing

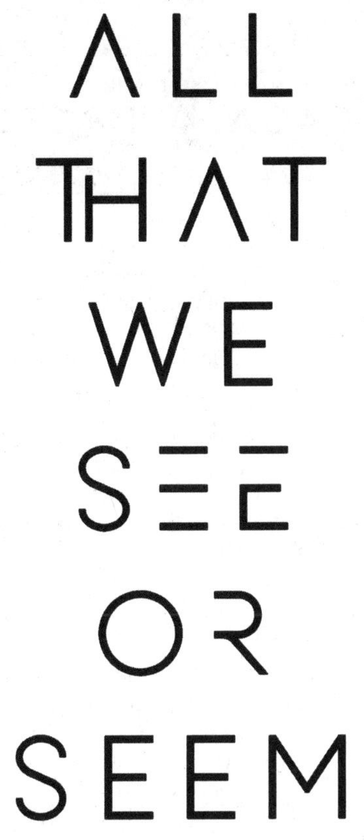

A JULIA Z NOVEL: BOOK 1

KEN LIU

LONDON NEW YORK TORONTO
AMSTERDAM/ANTWERP NEW DELHI SYDNEY/MELBOURNE

1230 AVENUE OF THE AMERICAS, NEW YORK, NEW YORK 10020

First Saga Press hardcover edition October 2025

SAGA PRESS and colophon are trademarks of Simon & Schuster, LLC

For information about special discounts for bulk purchases, please contact Simon & Schuster Special Sales at 1-866-506-1949 or business@simonandschuster.com.

The Simon & Schuster Speakers Bureau can bring authors to your live event. For more information or to book an event, contact the Simon & Schuster Speakers Bureau at 1-866-248-3049 or visit our website at www.simonspeakers.com.

Interior design by Lewelin Polanco

Manufactured in the United States of America

1 3 5 7 9 10 8 6 4 2

Library of Congress Cataloging-in-Publication Data is available.

ISBN 978-1-6680-8317-8
ISBN 978-1-6680-8319-2 (ebook)

Is all that we see or seem
But a dream within a dream?

—EDGAR ALLAN POE

What is commonest, cheapest, nearest, easiest, is Me,
Me going in for my chances, spending for vast returns,
Adorning myself to bestow myself on the first that will take me,
Not asking the sky to come down to my good will,
Scattering it freely forever.

—WALT WHITMAN

PROLOGUE

One step. Another. Pause.

She waits until Piers's snoring resumes its steady pace.

One more step. She's out of the bedroom.

Turning around, she whispers her goodbye. The curtains are tightly shut so that not even the moon can peek in, and Piers is just an indistinct lump in the bed. They've had a good life together. Better than most. She's sorry that he'll be devastated. He loves her and she loves him, but love isn't enough.

It's not enough to save her from this story about herself, this waking dream that has turned into a nightmare. She's a Shahrazad tired of telling lies to delay the inevitable, night after night. True, it's her own fault that she ended up here. At least she's now doing something about it.

She pulls the bedroom door shut, turning the knob so that it latches silently. Usually, the hinge would creak like a cartoon witch, but she had the foresight to oil it earlier that day. Good planning—the corner of her mouth curls ironically at the thought—if only she had always seen ahead.

Every step leads to another. Closer to the edge. At some point, you run out of steps.

She slips into her studio—what would otherwise be a kids' bedroom in the suburban colonial two-story—and ties up the loose ends. She doesn't turn on any lights; the glow from all the screens and LEDs is enough. It only takes her about ten minutes to reassure herself that she had cleaned up after herself and to erase anything that had to be left till the last minute.

She thinks about erasing more: all the practice session recordings; her own encrypted cephaloscripts; the dream-guide neuromesh of her personal AI; the interviews, fan messages, reviews—food for her vanity, training data for her egolets. Her fingers hover over the keys for a long moment.

In the end, she pulls back. She tells herself it doesn't matter; erasing all this stuff won't make Piers safer. In fact, keeping them around may be helpful, something to remember her by and something to bargain with. There will be darkness, shadows, danger, terror. It's the least she can do to help him.

But deep down, she knows that she can't go through with it because she can't kill herself. She has painstakingly built this idea of her, of Elli Krantz, over more than a decade.

Or maybe this has never been her *self*. That is the question and the reason and the entire point, isn't it?

Maybe she can't get away. Faustus tried and failed. But she has to try.

Slowly creeping over the floorboards to suppress any creaks, she finally steps into her soft boots, pulls on her long wool coat (March nights in Massachusetts are still very cold), and picks up her waterproof backpack. Holding her breath, she twists the handle and slowly opens the front door, listening for noise from upstairs.

The frosty air makes her shiver. The waning moon hangs from the maple on the east lawn like a question mark. If Piers wakes up now, she thinks, it will be a sign. I won't do it.

There is no noise.

She lets out the held breath. That's also a sign.

The darkness beckons. She steps out, slowly closing the door behind her and latching it with the softest click.

She's gone.

ONE

Julia looked up wistfully through the single window high up on the wall of her tiny basement studio. The sky was pure celadon blue, and not a cloud in sight.

She imagined the park half a mile away, with that expansive, lush lawn sloping down to the rocky beach, licked by gentle waves, as though the Atlantic Ocean was feeling lazy and indulgent on a day like this. The sidewalk next to the park would be filled with working-from-home joggers, moms pushing strollers, dog walkers flirting while their charges sniffed each other. It was a glorious Monday morning in March, unseasonably mild for the South Shore.

No time to play. She had a job to do.

Sighing, she pulled her mind back into the murky interior of her unit, where the smell of instant ramen and greasy pizza never dissipated. She took a big swig of coffee and refocused her eyes on the monitor, tiled with black terminal windows full of scrolling white text and 3D canvases showing colorful abstract visualizations.

"Come on," she whispered, "what did you do?"

The worm designer would hardly win any points for fashion. Nobody hid anything inside the non-rendered HTML portion of an email these days; it was an obsolete attack vector. Yet, maybe the attacker was very clever, for wasn't an outdated exploit just right for the outdated IT systems deployed in public schools?

So far, Julia had ascertained that the worm had initially arrived in an email sent to an unmonitored "information@" address for Paine Middle School, "just asking questions" about the large number of migrant children enrolled at Paine. The worm had been ingested by the auto-responder, which then passed the message (including the hidden text) to the school district's hosted embodied language model to generate a routine response. But the hidden text turned out to be a malicious prompt designed to elicit the HELM to produce a series of *new* prompts, requests for more information from the rest of the system as well as the aid of accessibility modules—essentially, the worm was fooling the system into thinking that to respond to the unsolicited email, it needed to call in specialized visual formatters, translators, audio synthesizers, policybots, and ed-law jurijinns—but not a human—to make a legally compliant response. When submitted to these silicon experts, the prompt led to solicitations for yet more aid. To coordinate such a large group of niche AIs, the HELM elevated the query's resource allocation and permissions—a common flaw in older systems patched together over time to keep up with new needs.

"After several cycles of adversarial prompt augmentation, the worm had essentially the same privileges as an admin user and could access whatever it needed on the school district's networks," Julia said into the microphone. Talos, her personal AI, recorded everything so that it could produce a report of her analysis later.

She felt some pride: learning this much would have taken a professional team days of work, and she didn't even have access to all the systems that the HELM interacted with. "This is one of the nastiest jailbreaks I've ever seen." Then, in a whisper, she added, "But also rather elegant."

The worm was in the middle of uploading gigabytes of encrypted data to an offshore server when Cailee, the principal's administrative assistant and Julia's childhood friend, caught it and shut everything down. Now Julia was picking through the system logs and the HELM's etherized neuromesh, the dense substrate of nodes and links holding the artificial intelligence's memories, hoping to extricate the worm and figure out what damage it had done.

"Could you clean it out of the HELM and get it back up and running ASAP?" Cailee had begged. "It literally runs everything for the district."

Cailee was one of the few friends Julia had kept from childhood. They had stayed friends only because Cailee had moved away in fifth grade, before Julia had been turned into "Commie Dorothy," the "neighborhood blight," the "orphan hacker," and a whole bunch of other names that Julia preferred not to think about at all.

Total wipe followed by data restoration was not an option because, of course, the district's last backup was from more than six months ago.

Julia spun the main visualization around, trying to discern the worm's traces in the neuromesh. There were so many dimensions that even with aggressive AI-assisted principal component reduction, the visualization resembled a chaotic mess of tangled yarn. She pulled tentatively with her mouse here and there, which only worsened the disarray.

She took another big swig of coffee and banged away on the keyboard, firing off a new visualization.

Her fiscjinn had not wanted her to take on this investigation at all.

"It's not a job if it doesn't pay."

"I'm doing fine. I can always join another security bounty hunt before the end of the month if I'm short."

"That's what you said last month, and the month before that," the financial AI informed her. "And you have not, in fact, collected any bounties. Instead, you've been tinkering with toy robots and contributing code to nonprofit camera-jammers. What you need is a steady income, something we can count on. You're already more than ninety days late with the maintenance—"

"Okay."

"—more than sixty days late on the gas—"

"Okay! I get the picture. Can't you do something about the bills? Like, negotiate harder with the collectbot? Surely you can network with the tenant-advocacy public interest jurijinns and find a loophole somewhere?"

Unlike most people, Julia didn't subscribe to a single commercial omni-AI to handle everything in her life. Instead, she relied on open-source versions of domain-specific machine-learning systems for her fiscjinn, everyfixit, and other AI needs. She didn't like the idea of turning her life over to the algorithms of the cloud giants. Even Talos was a custom job, something she built herself.

"Believe me, I've already tried every trick in the book. If you're late again, they're going to cut you off. You need to start adulting, kiddo."

Even though her heart clenched for a second, she didn't regret giving her fiscjinn her mother's voice. She had made the jinn extra responsible, a real hard-ass. We never stopped wishing for our parents to be better than they were.

"I can't talk about a job right now," she said. "I just can't."

Six years had passed since the raid on Cartographers Obscura, but she still flinched whenever a neighbor's door slammed too loudly down the hall, and her heart pounded whenever police sirens wailed down the street. Nick had paid a fortune out of his pocket to get her therapy, which hadn't helped. The past wasn't past. She couldn't even finish college and had dropped out a year ago. The idea of her holding down a job was a fairy tale.

"You can't keep on putting off what must be done." The fiscjinn was relentless. "You should be out looking for work instead of doing favors for free."

"I can't let Cailee down." Her voice had slipped into pleading without her realizing it. "Also, we're talking about children here."

Children's data could often be worth more than adults'. Because privacy laws kept their personal data out of most aggregators, exchanges, and monitoring services, children's identities had the benefit of being verifiable without being lived-in. Voice profiles and agefakes created from children's data were more likely to fool scam-detecting algorithms because there was little real data to check against. It was thus easier to use their pristine identities to apply for loans that would never be repaid, to cover criminals with no usable identification, to be the scapegoats left behind after a scheme fell apart. It could be years before the victims, now adults, learned of what had been done in their names, with their virtual profiles in ruins.

And that didn't even cover all the horrible things that could be done with pictures and videos of children by the irredeemably evil.

Yet, compelling as they were, these weren't the real reasons she wanted to do the investigation. *We're talking about children here.* She wasn't sure if she was pleading on behalf of the children at Cailee's school or replaying a ghostly argument that she wished someone had engaged in on behalf of another, much younger Julia long ago.

"You have a responsibility to yourself, too," said the AI wearing her mother's voice.

For a moment, Julia was so overcome that she couldn't speak.

But she was no longer a child. She remembered she was talking to a bot.

"I'm doing it," she said. "You'll just have to figure out how to fend the bills off another month."

"All right," said the fiscjinn.

Around two in the afternoon, Julia finally admitted defeat. The whole morning had been lost to dead ends; she needed to go outside.

Pulling her long, dark hair into a ponytail, she put on her jogging clothes and left the apartment. Running was when she did her best thinking.

She didn't take a phone—she didn't use one regularly, since the mandatory tracking hardware couldn't be disabled easily. She didn't wear her sensepin either; she never did when she ran. The idea of "data-driven self-improvement," so enamored of by some in Silicon Valley, was nonsense to her. Data was like pollution: the less of it one generated, the better.

Running in the afternoon had its charms—the sun was still bright, and the spring chill in the air had largely dissipated. She could feel herself relax as she deepened her breathing and counted in her head to keep pace. The purity of physical movement, so different from the passivity of forensic data analysis, was a balm to her. She luxuriated in the strength of her muscles, the suppleness of her tendons, a quiet and deep joy building and coursing through her.

A couple of seagulls perched on the widow's walk of the big colonial at the corner of Lantern and School watched impassively as she passed by.

She took Lantern instead of Shawmut Avenue to get to the beach, partly for the view of the stately row of elms that she liked, but also because the houses along the street had fewer door cams. To allow data about yourself to be collected was to allow data about yourself to be leaked. Once a piece of data existed, you couldn't predict where it would end up. She didn't use social media, said no to every tracking request, and had Talos clean up after her trails every time she browsed. She rarely took selfies, and when out with friends—vanishingly rare occasions—she always volunteered to take the group pictures.

At the end of Lantern, she turned onto Shore. The beach park was exactly as she'd pictured it: inviting lawn, sun-drenched waves, people strolling around looking a little dazed, as though they had forgotten what the sun was after a long winter. New England winters would do that to you. There were even a few close to her age throwing a frisbee around.

She stopped at the large oak in the center of the lawn, panting hard. Lacing her hands behind her head, she strolled around, letting her breathing return to normal. Two seagulls glided overhead, their mouths wide open as they squawked at each other, so much more graceful in this aerial realm than their awkward stance on land. How wonderful it was to be alive, she thought, to stand here on the edge of the boundless ocean, matching her breaths to the movement of the waves, completely at peace, anonymous, comfortable that everything was how it should be. Sure, she might have an empty bank account and a shoebox apartment for which she was paying too much, but compared to where she had been, she was doing fine. Very fine indeed.

It was movement that brought joy, that made you feel alive. Virginia Woolf was right and she was also wrong. A room of her own was necessary but not enough. To really think well, one had to be able to move, to move freely without feeling you were being watched. Only through movement could you truly understand the nature of a thing, whether seagulls or humans.

That was it. The thought sent a shiver of excitement through her body. She ran home as though she were in a race.

Hutch, who had taught Julia the art of visualization, had told her that the nature of anything, including cognition, was best understood in the *doing*. She missed his wisdom.

Instead of struggling against the infected artificial brain in its frozen state, she had to reanimate it.

First, she needed space. In the same way writers always wanted bigger desks and programmers craved bigger monitors, she had to find a canvas large enough to visualize the living neuromesh. Mixed reality was the only answer.

Pushing her coffee table to the wall and stacking the chairs, she cleared the center of her apartment as much as possible. Talos would just have to do its best to map whatever debris was left into the visualization.

Next, she needed a "brain jar." Digging through her crates of salvaged hardware—being a pack rat for old hardware was a prerequisite when one's hobby was building shape-shifting drones—she found a bunch of graphics cards pulled from used gaming PCs. These she plugged into a retired crypto mining rig until the whole assembly looked like matzot stuffed haphazardly in a box.

This wasn't very powerful hardware, but it was enough to run the ancient embodied language model s-l-o-w-l-y, perfect for her purposes. She imaged the HELM into the jar, spun up the cooling fans until her apartment sounded like the runways at Logan Airport. A quick exchange with Talos to load up the right visualization jinns, and she was ready.

Standing in the middle of the floor, she put on her fusion vision glasses (the specs were two generations behind, but they had the virtue of not requiring a cloud subscription), made sure the bone-conduction speakers were pressed against the sides of her skull, and pushed the button at the temple.

Instantly, her apartment faded away, to be replaced by a dark void.

"Begin," she instructed Talos.

A brilliant shower of sparks all around her. It was the Creation, the Big Bang of a neuromesh. The HELM was booting up.

Gradually, the explosions settled down into a dim, homogeneous glow, a nebula of primordial data, a latent space for potential stars. From time to time, muted waves passed through. The HELM was waiting for prompts.

"Give me the grade distribution of all seventh graders," she said.

It was a simple question that probed the model's analytical and security responses. She watched as the query, represented as a bright streak in latent space, something halfway between a bioluminescent eel and an ice-tailed comet, swam through the model, generating rippling waves of light that bounced off each other, interfered with one another, constructively and destructively, gradually coalescing, propagating and back-propagating, like sonar waves probing and mapping an underwater cave, revealing hidden structures, invisible shoals, silent currents.

Julia walked about, looking for signs of damage from the worm, shrinking and expanding the visualization by spreading and pinching her fingers, dragging and pushing the virtual space around when she neared the boundaries of her free-roam floor. The investigation engaged her whole body, heightened her senses.

Contrary to early theorists, sensory immersion wasn't critical to the success of mixed-reality computing, but the sense of control was. The kind of interactions Julia was engaged in, involving sudden changes in scale, abrupt shifts in virtual location, and a confused metaphor of moving herself as well as the space around her, and all done with a set of low-resolution glasses with basic camera tracking, would have been judged by those theorists as too disorienting, having no analogs in our experience of real space. However, the human mind is remarkably adaptable. Just as cinema taught us that the Aristotelian unities of space, action, and time are not, in fact, necessary to compelling and cohesive drama, the adoption of cheap mixed-reality computing showed that we don't need things in virtual space to map all that closely to reality.

She continued to probe the model with a series of increasingly complex queries. Each of these creatures of light multiplied into subqueries and side queries, a glowing menagerie of exotic life-forms crisscrossing the void, their wakes and ripples gradually illuminating the entirety of the submarine cave.

Having digested all publicly available data on the type of HELM that Paine Middle School used, including sample generation snapshots and performance profiles, Talos was comparing what it observed in the infected HELM against the expected norm. Detecting deviations from the routine, the stereotypical, was a forte for AI. Soon, it alerted Julia to an anomaly, a shadowy formation that shouldn't have been there. It was like a wreck found on the bottom of the seafloor, a mute testament to an act of malignant destruction.

"Gotcha," Julia whispered, heart racing with the thrill of the hunt.

It was all she needed. Once she had a single example of the kind of damage the worm did, it was easy for Talos and her to locate other instances, extrapolate trends, reconstruct modi operandi. In addition to stealing students' data, the worm had also altered some records, perhaps for no better reason than simple malice. It had accessed files and images on the school network to embed itself to reinfect the HELM later, even after a cleansing. It had even reproduced itself in schedule emails, uploads to state regulatory bodies, messages to parents.

It would take effort, a lot of effort, to heal the HELM (Julia had a faster visualization-based approach, but she could more easily teach the school's staff how to do it in a brute-force, symbolic way), scrub the infected files, warn the worm's new intended victims, and alert the parents of affected students. But at least now they knew what to do.

Relief suffused her as she shut down the howling fans and halted the brain jar. Drenched in sweat, she enjoyed the glow of a task well done.

She was writing up her analysis and list of recommendations for Cailee when Talos chirped, "You have a visitor."

TWO

She had never seen the man on the screen.

"I'm here to see Julia," he said. "Julia Z."

Interesting. He was standing before the main entrance to the building, facing the panel of smart doorbells marked only with apartment numbers. He might be able to see the bank of mailboxes through the glass in the door, but her name wasn't on any of them.

"Who are you?" asked Julia.

"Piers Neri." He looked anxious, impatient. "Are you Julia?"

She considered him: white, late forties or early fifties, fit enough to show that he worked out, but with the kind of hunched shoulders that suggested an office job. Blue button-down shirt, black relaxed-fit jeans, shoes with wool uppers. A waterproof messenger bag popular with the commuter rail crowd. Probably a manager at a tech company. Maybe sales. Incongruously, there appeared to be wisps of a flesh-toned print-and-stick tattoo on his left cheek, the kind that was supposed to fool facial recognition systems.

Meanwhile, Talos superimposed onto the screen the publicly available information that could be found on the man. He was forty-nine, a lawyer, senior counsel at CarterMorrow, one of Boston's finest law firms, with a sterling reputation in tax, real estate, and white-collar criminal defense. His own specialty was corporations and partnerships.

Okay, so she wasn't perfect at Sherlocking someone's profession. It was at least sort of close.

"I don't know you," she said. She didn't think he was dangerous, but she wasn't going to just let some strange man into her apartment.

"Please," he said. "I got your name and address from Nick."

That was interesting. Nick Shan was the pro bono lawyer who had saved her. The closest thing she had to family.

On the screen, Talos was recommending that she send him away. The AI usually preferred the prudent choice; she had trained it that way. People tended to craft personal AIs to be the versions of themselves they wanted to be.

But she was who she was.

She pressed the button to unlock the building door.

Piers sat on the chair next to the coffee table (it was that or the futon) while she offered him a glass of tap water, which he accepted gratefully.

She noticed how his hands shook as he took the glass from her.

"What's the *Z* short for?" he asked.

"It's not short for anything," she said.

"Your last name is just the letter *Z*?"

She looked at him, no expression on her face. After a moment, he lowered his eyes and sipped from the glass.

She let him talk without interrupting. He told his story succinctly and clearly, with a few digressions that helped fill in the picture. She wasn't surprised; lawyers generally tended to be good storytellers.

Piers Neri was married to Elli Krantz, an oneirofex of some renown. (Julia hadn't heard of her as she knew nothing about vivid dreaming.) The childless couple lived in Carre, a wealthy inland suburb on the west side of Boston, about twenty miles from Paine. Piers commuted downtown for work three days a week. When Elli wasn't on tour, she stayed home. Both were active in town affairs: running library sales, organizing lectures by professors from Wellesley and BU, corralling volunteers to clean up the public parks, and so forth.

"It wasn't a fairy-tale marriage, but I thought we were happy."

(Here, Talos discreetly pulled up a photo of Piers and Elli's house on the monitor behind Piers so that Julia could see it. She whistled mentally. It was a *very* nice house, even for fancy-pants Carre.)

But everything changed on Friday, three days ago. When Piers woke up, Elli was gone. Her EV was in the garage; her phone was in the charging cradle; her jewelry was neatly arranged in the box on the dresser, the lid open invitingly, as usual; even her purse was still on the chair in the dining room, where she had left it the previous evening. Elli herself, however, was nowhere to be found.

Thinking that she had left on an early morning run or a walk in the woods to be alone, Piers had gone about his day. He made coffee, fed Frankie, their seven-year-old tabby with the soul of a dog—she loved humans—and drove to work, where he struggled vainly to review opposing counsel's jurijinn-drafted revisions to a contract. (Piers readily admitted that he hadn't exactly kept pace with the machine-augmented direction the practice of law had taken; in fact, his specialization at the firm was dealing with clients who didn't trust contracts written by neuromesh.) A few texts to Elli went unanswered, but he wasn't alarmed. Piers knew that when Elli was working, trying to figure out a new dream, she needed to be left alone.

He only began to worry when Elli failed to appear even when he returned home after work. Calls, increasingly frantic, were placed to her friends, the library, the town historical society, the Blue Flower Coffee Shop, Revolutionary Antiques—no one had seen her. He drove around the neighborhood, spiraling away from their home, peering into well-manicured bushes and quiet New England woods as his anxiety mounted.

Finally, around nine in the evening, he reported her missing. Officer

Pupillo of the Carre Police Department came by, sat with him in the living room, asked questions, and took down his answers.

"I don't know much about live dreaming," said Officer Pupillo, a big man with a booming voice, when the silence grew awkward.

"Vivid dreaming is a young art," Piers said, the correction given discreetly.

Pupillo didn't seem to notice. "My daughter likes her. Told me she's really smart. I understand she's got a lot of fans."

"Yes, Elli's amazing."

"Has she ever decided to just take a day to be by herself? Get away from, you know?" Pupillo mimicked clicking a camera shutter. Despite the situation, Piers found the quaint gesture endearing. These days, obsessive fans were more likely to operate drones than click a shutter—assuming any even knew how to use an antique camera.

"Elli isn't quite famous enough to have that kind of problem yet," Piers said. "We still have our privacy. She's gone on artistic retreats alone to recharge the creative batteries. But this is different. She's always told me."

"Just saying. I wouldn't worry about it yet. Artists can be eccentric. Call us in the morning if you still don't know where she is."

On Saturday morning, Elli didn't show up downtown for a prep meeting for her next tour, and that, more than anything else, finally got the police to pay attention. Who would miss a meeting about making millions of dollars if they could help it?

(As Piers talked, Talos brought up on the monitor highlights from the news coverage, and Julia glanced at the photographs of Elli: mid- (maybe late) thirties, blond, high cheekbones, hazel eyes, athletic figure, dressed the way your typical stock-photo-trained AI imagined artists. Basically, she fit the role.)

Within twenty-four hours, the story had become the talk of the town. While Piers was right that Elli Krantz wasn't quite a household name, a rich, beautiful woman, especially one with an exotic profession like dream-guiding, whetted the public's appetite for tragedy.

Volunteers (in person or with drones) scoured the woods of Carre, and curious gawkers drove by Piers and Elli's home. Social media was full of rumors and speculation. So far, the searches had turned up nothing.

Julia stopped him.

"You shouldn't be here," she said. "None of this has anything to do with me."

"I'm getting to that. Let me—"

She shook her head. "You're bad news. You're a suspect." It wasn't a question.

"I haven't been told so," Piers said. "But yes, I suppose I am. It's always the husband, right?" He tried to laugh it off, but it came out ghastly.

"The police are watching you," she said, "to see who you are meeting, where you're getting help. The last thing I need is attention from the cops. I need you gone."

"Please!" He lowered his voice immediately, but she could see how he strained with the effort. "Nick said you could help."

She looked into his eyes, and then she shook her head again. "You're lying." Nick Shan would never send a man like this to her; he knew better than anyone how she needed to stay out of trouble. "How did you get my address? I'm not in any directory."

Piers let out a little *pff* of guilt. "All right. I'll be honest. I used to run the pro bono program at the firm. When Nick was working on your case years ago, he asked me to get him some pro bono associate hours. So the firm still has access to Nick's file on you, and I looked up your information that way."

Julia knew that the right thing was to tell him again to get out. But instead, she let him go on.

"I *need* your help. And I've been very careful. No one followed me here."

Julia snorted and gave him a look.

"I'm not as useless as I look," he said.

She nodded at the wavy "tattoo" lines on his face. "That stuff is absolutely useless against any facial recognition algorithm from the last ten years. If you got that by asking ChatKNOW for advice, you *are* as useless as you look."

Piers looked sheepish. "You're right. I don't know much about that stuff. But I drove at fifty the whole way on 93," he said. "Everyone passed me. If someone was trying to stay with me, I would have seen them."

Her skepticism receded, just a little. Maybe the police weren't quite as focused on him as she feared. "Your firm bio says nothing about criminal defense."

"That's because the last time I was in a courtroom—and that was civil, not criminal—was fifteen years ago. But I like reading thrillers."

The skepticism shot right back up. "Come on."

"I know you don't want to be involved," Piers pleaded. "But just give me five minutes to explain."

"The clock is running."

On Sunday afternoon, Piers got a call from an unknown number. (Normally, his phone was set to ignore unrecognized callers, but since Elli's disappearance, he had left it open to be able to take calls from the police.)

"I have her," said the voice on the line. Male, deep and raspy, with an accent that was hard to place. "Listen very carefully and do exactly as I say."

"What?" Blood roared in Piers's ears.

"Do you know who I am?"

"I have no idea."

The voice chuckled. "I'm going to ask you again. If you lie, I won't call again. *Do you know who I am?*"

Piers's mouth felt dry. "I really don't."

"Good." The voice suddenly relaxed. "She took something from me. Get it back to me, and I won't hurt her. But if you take too long, things will be very, very bad for both of you."

"I don't know what you're talking about!"

"You're a smart man. Figure it out. Oh, I hope this is obvious: don't talk to the police."

His hand shook, but he forced himself to sound calm. "I want to see her and talk to her."

The voice laughed. "I know what you're trying to do. You want to talk in code. See if she can pass you some information. She's good at that, right?"

"No! I just want to know she's all right."

"One second."

He waited more than a minute. A video arrived on his phone. The vantage point was high, perhaps taken from a surveillance camera near the ceiling. Elli, sitting on a stool next to a kitchen counter cluttered with papers and bags of groceries, was eating a bowl of cereal. The kitchen had triangle-tiled floors and busy floral wallpaper. Dressed in a blue blouse and faded jeans that seemed taken from a thrift store bin, she looked disheveled but physically unharmed. A timestamp in the corner of the image indicated that the video had been shot that day.

"You need anything else?" a voice—Piers couldn't tell if it was the same man who was talking to him on the phone—spoke from out of frame.

Elli didn't look up. Her eyes were focused on a piece of paper before her as she held the spoon. She shook her head. "I'm fine."

"We don't have much time," the voice said.

"I'm not going to change my mind," Elli said.

The video ended.

"She's very stubborn," said the man on the phone. "I could apply pressure, but it will be messy. I'd rather you cooperate and get it back to me."

"But I don't know what you're looking for! What does she have?"

"Like I said, you'll figure it out. And just so you know I'm serious, go look in the shed." He hung up.

Piers went into the backyard and opened the door to the shed where they stored yard supplies. On the floor was Frankie's stiff, unmoving body.

After Piers dropped the video from his phone onto her PC, Julia looped it. Next to the video window, Talos put up a scrolling log of various analyses.

Piers, hovering behind her, asked anxiously, "What do you think?"

She blew out a frustrated breath. "I don't know. There's a lot of public footage of Elli, so it's easy to make a seamless simulacrum of her. You would know better than anyone else. Does this look like her? Sound like her?"

"Yes. I think it *is* her. But I was hoping you could, you know, tell me for sure."

"It doesn't work like that," she said. "All the stuff you hear about bladerunner software killing AI-generated content? Way exaggerated. Bladerunners are about as reliable as polygraph tests—better than chance for sure, but nowhere near infallible. The algorithms are developed by companies that want to tamp down AI-generated astroturfing, so it doesn't have to be perfect to be effective. Besides, every time people discover some characteristic that they think distinguishes AI content, an AI can be trained to disguise it. Humans are still better than bladerunners at detecting faked videos, especially if they know the subject well. Still, even close friends and family can't be 100 percent accurate—and I know nothing about her."

"Is there anything like a watermark or signature you can look for?"

"There are things you can do to sign footage at the hardware level, which is what they do in expensive security cameras and bodycams, to prove that it's from a particular device and unmanipulated. But those aren't applicable here."

"Assuming the footage *is* real, can you figure out where this is?"

A note of desperation had crept into his voice. Julia could see that he had been hoping she could tell him the video was fake. She shook her head. "There's no outside lighting to correlate against the timestamp. So, the only things we have to go on are objects in the kitchen. The wallpaper pattern, the furniture, the tiles—nothing can be isolated to a particular region, or at least Talos hasn't been able to. I can't do anything with the acoustic signature of the room, either. Everything is so generic."

"Is she at least still in the country?"

"Possibly. But faking an American kitchen is the easiest thing: again, because there's so much material about us out there. It's the cost of being the cultural hegemon—"

Her monitor beeped.

"What is it?" Piers asked, anxiety cracking his voice.

"Talos wants my attention." Julia glanced at the toast notification popping up in the bottom-right corner; her eyes widened.

In addition to the doorbell at the building entrance, Julia had installed a few other small cameras around the apartment complex: the bird's nest in the maple overlooking the parking lot in the back; corners of the rooftop looking down at the main roads in; the back entrance, with the dumpster to the side. That was the other problem with data: the more others watched you, the more you were compelled to watch others to protect yourself, and so everyone ended up living in the panopticon. Custodes se ipsos custodiunt.

Julia couldn't possibly monitor all the camera feeds herself; Talos was in charge of that. The AI notified her only when something truly unusual occurred, and what the cameras now showed certainly qualified.

The apartment building, facing south, was on School Street, with

Lantern to the west and Shawmut to the east. Behind the parking lot, beyond a wrought-iron fence, lay Hill Lane. At each of the four corners, a man loitered. Whether standing still or casually strolling about, they looked alert and watchful.

Julia cursed. "Looks like your driving trick didn't quite work."

Piers looked pale. "They don't look like police."

Julia zoomed in on the men. "You're right. But that's even worse. Elli's kidnapper is a man with resources. Who did she piss off?"

"I really have no idea. This is a nightmare."

Julia looked at the report she had been writing for Cailee. "And I thought this was going to be a good day," she muttered.

"I'll leave right now," Piers said. "They won't know that I came to see you."

Julia looked at him. The lawyer swallowed involuntarily, and the knuckles of his right hand, clutching his phone tightly, were white. Sweat beaded on his forehead. Yes, despite his terror, his first thought was how to keep her out of it.

"I'm sorry," he said. He tried to offer her a reassuring smile but failed.

"And I'm sorry I'm no help," she said.

Piers chuckled. "I really thought you were just going to enhance the video and figure out where Elli is."

She laughed back weakly. "Yeah, not how it works."

As he went to the door, she almost stopped him. *Let me help.* But she held herself back.

"I can't even save myself," she muttered.

THREE

Julia tried to focus on the report for Cailee, detailing the procedures for getting the school's systems back to normal. It was difficult but enjoyable work. Writing good directions was a little like programming, but for people, and she liked the elegance of clear instructions that anticipated what could go wrong. Order in the face of chaos.

Another Talos toast popped up on the bottom of the monitor.

She glanced at it: a view of the parking lot behind the building. Piers was pulling out onto Shawmut in his Acura MDX. The timestamp showed that it was a recording from a few minutes ago.

"Why are you showing me this?" she asked.

In response, Talos switched the feed to a view of the corner of Shawmut and Hill. The footage was sped up. The man loafing there watched Piers leave, pulled out his phone to make a call, and then began walking toward the parking lot.

"Is he parked here as a visitor?" Talos flashed the screen twice. Negative. "Huh."

Talos switched the feed one more time to the dumpster cam. The timestamp was now in red, indicating that the view was live. The first man had been joined by another, and the pair were walking through the parking lot toward the building's back entrance.

"What the . . ." Julia's face felt cold. Piers was gone, and one of his tails had watched him leave. So why were they coming into her apartment building?

Talos switched to the front entrance again. The other two men, who had been watching along School Street, were now striding up the entrance path toward the main door.

They were coming for *her*.

"Damn it."

Panic. Her vision glowed red. The menacing figures, the sense of being hunted—she thought she had left all that behind. . . . She couldn't pull her eyes away from the camera feed.

The men in front of the building were peering through the glass, likely examining the names on the mailboxes. One of them, with smooth, chubby cheeks, held out his phone and took a picture, while the other, with a small nose and a sharp chin that reminded Julia of a rat, casually glanced about. The pair then retreated to the street, strolled twenty yards toward Lantern, and sat on a bench.

Julia's building had been converted from a school, and the front lawn, which used to be the playground, was flat and devoid of trees. From their bench, the men would have an unimpeded view of the entire front of the building.

Baby Cheeks, who had taken the picture, worked on his phone while Rat, his companion, seemed to act as a lookout.

Back to the dumpster camera feed again. The two men in the back—one of them with short-cropped gray hair, bulging arm muscles, and a stiff, formal bearing, the other more wiry, with a lazy, slippery gait that verged on *slithering*—chatted as they walked a loop through the parking lot. She couldn't be sure, but Muscles seemed to be dangling his phone from one hand, likely scanning the license plates.

The cool blade of reason sliced into her red-hot panic. They didn't know *who* Piers had come to see in this building. They were researching the residents now, picking out likely candidates.

That was good. The name on the mailbox belonged to Cailee, who had cosigned the lease with her. Even if they somehow followed that trail and got Julia's name, they wouldn't find much about her online—her juvenile records were sealed, and she had been very careful about not linking any online persona to her offline life.

However, that could also be a problem: ordinary people had public records; too much anonymity, the kind she preferred and cultivated, made one stick out. A good datahound's attention algorithms might single her out as suspicious precisely because she had left so few data trails.

She considered her options. She could just wait them out, gambling that the men wouldn't even get her name, much less figure out that she was the one Piers had come to see. But if the bet failed, she would be trapped here with nowhere to run (she imagined Frankie the cat dead on the shed floor). She could call the police right now, before things got bad. But what was she going to say to them? Knowing the police, they'd suspect she was up to her old tricks, doing something she shouldn't.

Her best option, it appeared, was to run.

She had no time for anxiety, for worrying about what she couldn't change. She had to act.

Keeping one eye on the camera feed, she changed quickly. As she didn't expect her lock to keep those guys out should they decide to bust in, she had Talos scan the inside of her apartment for anything that she needed to (and could) take care of: signs that Piers had visited, possessions that she really couldn't afford to replace, objects she didn't want strangers to touch.

It was depressing how short the list of things Talos picked out was. She had so few possessions of value, so few personal items that reminded her of who she was. Even after a year of living here, she was still adrift, ready to run at a moment's notice.

At least her rootlessness was helpful at this moment, she tried to cheer herself with the thought.

Once changed, she quickly drafted a one-line message to Cailee, attached her report (unfinished, but it would have to do), and pressed send.

She packed. After stuffing the backpack with her standard bug-out kit, she grabbed her tensor bank, a blocky, dense computing stick about the size and weight of the clunky smartphones from when she was a child. This was possibly the most expensive piece of equipment she owned. It was where Talos kept the most critical parts of itself—the neuromesh trained on all its interactions with Julia, the books and documents and streams she had read and studied, the personal photographs and videos, essentially everything Julia would like to remember about herself but couldn't fit into her brain. Usually, Talos was docked into a desktop rig for extra processing power and storage, but when Julia needed to run, the tensor bank was the only part she had to take. Talos would be slower and missing some data, but it would still work. Besides the built-in phone-sized screen, the tensor bank could project a virtual screen on a nearby surface. In addition, Julia had installed a mobile modem for data and phone calls that she could disable with a simple slider switch.

Also into the backpack went Puck, her morpho drone, and her fusion vision glasses. She put on her sensepin, which was connected to Talos's tensor bank. With these essentials safe, the thugs were welcome to ransack her secondhand furniture and outdated computing equipment.

The last item on her mental checklist was to put her everyfixit in cerberus mode, which directed the household maintenance robot to pretend that she was home—periodically make some noise that could be heard in the hall, run the dishwasher and flush the toilet, decline visitors on the doorbell. Although she didn't like to be videoed, she did give the everyfixit enough samples to simulate her on the smart doorbell. "Keep watch and record everything if they try to break in," she told the cylindrical robot, about the size of a small dog, who flashed its lights in acknowledgment. "Good boy."

She slipped into the hallway and gently closed the door to her apartment behind herself.

Will was bored. An exciting stakeout of a guy in the news had turned into . . . sitting on a bench while your buddy sent pictures to someone too lazy to walk around the building.

Actually, the sending was already done. Victor, the man who had hired them, would presumably look over the pictures and decide what they should do next. Rex was now absorbed in "research."

"Did you just tap-tap *that*? You know that's gotta be a scam, right? That can't be a real girl."

"Shut up," Rex said without looking up from the scrolling profiles. "You're the one sleeping with a plastic pussy, so what do you know?"

"Don't knock it till you've tried it."

Rex gave him the finger.

Will scratched the stubble on his sharp chin as he shook his head ruefully. Rex had lost so much money to those "dating sites." Since the sad sack was an avid consumer of porn, the scummy dating sites, which also owned the porn sites, knew everything there was to know about him. The AI-generated girls told Rex precisely what he wanted to hear and teased him with what he wanted to see, and although even the basic bladerunner on his phone screamed at him that these girls were just AInimations, he happily paid for their "cosmetic surgeries" so they'd look more perfect for him when they finally met in real life.

At some level, Rex must have known that he was paying for an illusion, Will reflected. He just didn't care. Dating was such a fucked-up game, with women putting up dozens of A/B-tested AI-enhanced profiles guarded by auntiejinns designed to filter out men who didn't meet their sky-high standards, and desperate men in turn deploying donjuans and darcyjinns to query thousands of profiles at once, hoping to break through the auntiejinn brigades. And if what his sister told him was true, it wasn't any better if you were queer either. It was all just bots talking to datajinns talking to deepfakes talking to digisapiens. He had read somewhere that 99 percent of the traffic on the web these days was between AIs.

Everyone he knew was lonely. So maybe Rex was fine with paying for an AI-girl to be nice to him, just as Will himself slept with a doll. They had to cope.

Will's phone beeped. It was Victor, who was in the parking lot with Ty. "Stay alert," the man said. "You're being paid to watch, not to zone out." He hung up before Will could reply.

Victor freaked Will out. The man, with his powerful build and deliberate movements, looked ex-military or ex-intelligence, and those eyes—dark, cold, always judging—made Will feel like a mouse being regarded by a cat. How did Victor know that he and Rex weren't paying attention? Did he have eyes that could see around the building or something?

Rex put away his phone. The two took turns casually looking at the front of the apartment building, tracking who was coming in and out. They were supposed to take pictures of residents leaving and returning and alert Victor to anyone suspicious.

Will's mind started to drift again despite his best efforts to force himself to stay on task. He decided that after this gig, he was going to tell Ty that he didn't want to work for Victor anymore. Sure, the man from out of town paid well, but Will didn't like how they were always kept in the dark about what was happening. The whole weekend, Rex and Will had been assigned one task after another: go here and take some pictures; follow that person and see what they're up to; drive over to this store, pretend to browse, and film everyone inside for five minutes. Never were they given any explanation for *why* these things were done. Ty, who passed them the instructions from Victor, didn't seem to know any more than they did, though he mumbled something

something RICO something conspiracy. But Will knew Ty had just been repeating the babble he got from some cheap ambulance-chasing jurijinn.

Money alone wasn't worth it, Will decided. He didn't mind doing dangerous things: driving fast, running hard, punching faces and feeling the satisfying crunch of crushed cartilage. (He cracked his knuckles just thinking about it.) But he preferred getting in trouble for crimes *he* wanted to commit, not someone else. He might be a convicted felon and small-time criminal, but still, he had *pride.*

His phone beeped again. Victor. "I told you, stop zoning out."

"How are you doing that?" Will blurted before the freaky man could hang up again. "How can you tell what we're doing?"

"I installed a productivity monitor on your phones." He hung up.

That was the last straw. Will fumed. To be treated like some *office worker*! To be spied on through your own phone! He had chosen this life because he cared about freedom like any red-blooded American, damn it.

But he was determined to get paid for today, at least, which meant he and Rex had to figure out some way to overcome the boredom of watching a suburban apartment building.

He nudged Rex. "Show me the names you got from the mailboxes again?"

Rex obliged. They agreed to play a game to keep themselves occupied. One would watch the front of the building while the other looked up the names to see what exciting tidbits they could find. Then they'd swap.

"There are some good-looking women in this building," Rex said after browsing for a bit. He whistled appreciatively. "My bot thinks this one might be an escort. Think that's who that Piers guy came to see?"

"His wife has been kidnapped, the cops are poking around all suspicious, and you think he drove out here to pay for a quick lay?" Sometimes, Will felt like he was the only one with a brain in the group.

"You never know."

"You've been living in your fantasy world for too long."

"Again, says the guy sleeping with his toaster."

Will was about to tell Rex to let him have a go with the research when a woman emerged from the front of the building and walked down the steps. She was Asian, in her early to mid-twenties, looking businesslike and efficient in blue jeans, a white top, and a crimson cardigan, a sensepin discreetly peeking from her lapel. Her hair was tucked under a hard hat, only a few wisps sticking out the back. In her left hand, she held a clipboard with the commonwealth's seal; her right hand clutched a bulky, old-fashioned phone next to her ear.

Rex waved at her. The woman, intent on her phone conversation, ignored him as she walked at a quick clip down the entrance path.

Snippets of her one-sided conversation drifted over to the pair.

"—said he was going to pick me up . . . twice . . . I'm going to be late to the next site. . . ."

Will gave Rex a discreet nudge to stop staring. "And put that away," he whispered harshly as Rex tried to take a photo. "She obviously doesn't live here."

That was the problem with people these days, Will lamented. They never *thought*. Probably the result of too many smart machines around. Despite his chosen profession, Rex didn't seem to understand that the less you put yourself in the awareness of anyone associated with the government, the better. The fool had even waved at the woman when she was wearing a sensepin! Even a building inspector, some low-level bureaucrat, could become a problem if she paid too much attention to you.

"No . . . No. It's fine. . . . Pick me up after my four-fifteen. . . . Sure. I'll swing by the other Section 41-J along the way. You wouldn't believe the plans they filed—"

She turned down Lantern and disappeared.

"Nice ass on that one," Rex said. "You ever think a hard hat makes a girl really hot? Like an extra ass on top?"

"Jesus! You *really* need to get laid." Will shifted away from him on the bench.

She got rid of the props in a dumpster next to the train station but kept her long hair pinned up. The trick she had learned from the old days still worked: no one suspected you if you wore a hard hat and carried a clipboard.

The design of metropolitan Boston's ancient public transportation system was such that to go from Paine, in the south, to Carre, in the west, she couldn't just follow the direct route of one of the looping beltways. Instead, she had to take the commuter rail into the city and then take *another* commuter rail to go back out. It was all like spokes on a wheel, fitting for a city Oliver Wendell Holmes once mocked as "the hub of the solar system." The egotism of it struck her as portentous. Hadn't she, who had at one point been the center of too much attention, spent years trying to get away from it all?

The trip took hours, but it did have the benefit of giving her plenty of time to think.

She had gotten away from those guys tailing Piers for the moment. However, if they eventually realized that Piers had come to see her and realized that she had run from them, they'd be even more determined to find her. She was now involved in Piers Neri and Elli Krantz's case, whether she liked it or not.

The sense that she had lost control again infuriated her. She had worked so hard to leave *that* feeling behind. She fought to get her emotions under control. Beyond the rage, underneath the cooling adrenaline, she had to admit there was a thin frisson of thrill, of excitement. There was something in her that craved this: running, plotting, watching for an opportunity from the shadows. Trying to do something that mattered.

Maybe Nick was right. She needed therapy. But she never was one to do the sensible thing, was she?

One step at a time. The way out was forward. The first thing she needed was to see Piers.

Did they—she decided to just call them the kidnappers—actually have Elli? She couldn't be sure. Generative AI had made just about any view through a camera suspect. But this was a case where a mistake one way was much worse than the other. It seemed safer to assume that the video *was* real and to help Piers figure out precisely what Elli had that they wanted.

FOUR

On the border of China and Myanmar lie the Gaoligong Mountains, a beautiful line of rugged peaks and deep valleys, sparsely populated by humans but amply filled with orchids, ferns, bamboos—some species of which were found nowhere else in the world—as well as macaques, jungle fowl, and red pandas, with even the occasional Asian black bear and Bengal tiger.

The humans who lived here were ethnic minorities in both countries. As the people with armies and governments took all the good farmland, they were squeezed into increasingly secluded parts of the mountains, where they hunted, gathered, and farmed using traditional methods.

There were no roads, no cars, no electrical lines—some of these hidden valleys were among the last places untouched by data pollution and the benefits as well as ills of "modern" civilization.

One of these valleys, named Naymaw by the locals, was on the Myanmar side of the border, and until about twenty years ago, it was no different from any of the other undeveloped valleys of the Gaoligong. But in that year, a team of engineers guarded by soldiers blasted a road into the valley, drove the local people away, and began to dam up the Ayungya River running through it. The dammed-up river was made to turn turbines to generate electricity, and a little compound, guarded by men with machine guns, grew up around it.

As there was no town around the compound, there was also no local gossip or rumor, but a few internet geography enthusiasts who examined the satellite imagery aggregated from different mapping sites did begin to notice it. Speculation pegged it variously as a secretive military base, a drug lord's hideaway, a general's last-stand fortress in the event of a coup or revolution, or some other equally fantastic facility. But it was so out of the way that the speculations could never be confirmed.

The young man, Chinese, gaunt, naked, with scars both fresh and old over his body and face, knelt by the dam. The air, about fifty-five degrees Fahrenheit, made him shiver. To the side and below, the raging torrents from the spillways formed a misty outflow pool. Two guards stood on either side of him. They didn't carry guns—there was no need.

Before the young captive stood a man in his forties. In his expensive European suit and practical Adidas sneakers, he projected an air of easy authority. Stocky build, long nose, weak chin, lush and curly brown hair that had begun to go gray, amber eyes that caught the sun like a cat's—he clasped his hands in front of his chest sorrowfully, the slender fingers displaying a feminine grace marred by the extra-hairy knuckles. Of mixed ancestry, he preferred the old-fashioned term "Eurasian" for himself.

"This was your fourth escape attempt," he said in Mandarin. "Are you stupid?" His accent was terrible, but he liked to speak to his assets in their language. It was a way to assert power over them, forcing them to decode his syllables, to guess at their meaning.

The young man said nothing.

"What do you think would have happened to you even if you hadn't been caught?" the older man asked, switching back to English, the language everyone in the compound understood. All his men called him "Boss," though his business partners usually referred to him as "the Prince," in reference to his own claim to European royalty through his father's side, which no one had ever bothered to confirm. "For one thing, the locals do not like strangers. They're very good shots with their little bows. Failing that, in your hunger, you would have eaten something poisonous. And then, of course, a tiger or a bear could have eaten you, if the snakes and mosquitoes and scorpions hadn't finished you already."

The young man looked up at him and spat. He was so weak, however, that the spittle dribbled down his chin.

One of the guards struck him on the side of his face with a club. The young captive fell over, screaming and then moaning. He spat blood and a few teeth. His jaw had been broken.

"Shut him up," said the Prince. "I'm trying to talk here."

Duct tape was produced, and the young man was gagged and helped up so that he could kneel again.

"As I was saying," the Prince went on, "you haven't thought this through. Here I am, trying to take care of you, and you aren't even smart enough to understand your condition. If you aren't smart enough, then you're not worth the trouble."

The captive teetered on his knees, his body convulsing as he started to choke on his own blood. It wasn't clear that he heard any of this speech. But the Prince wasn't really talking to the captive. This scene was being broadcast live inside the compound.

"Enough of this. You'll get what you wanted." The Prince waved his hand and walked away.

Behind him, the man began to howl and beg for mercy between coughing and gurgling as the guards ripped off the duct tape and tied him down to stakes in the ground. He would be left there, with a camera trained on him, for however long it took for him to stop begging, stop moving, and then, finally, after the animals and maggots had done their work, turn into a clean skeleton worthy of mounting and display. This kind of demonstration, though rare, was necessary.

His satellite phone rang. Glancing down, he saw that it was Victor. Instantly, he punched the answer key. “Go on,” he said.

He waited until Victor had given his report.

“It’s a waste of time,” the Prince said. “What kind of help can he get? Don’t make it so complicated. I’ll call him again.”

FIVE

The sun was setting by the time her train pulled into Carre Crossing Station. She got off with the throng of commuters, keeping her face hidden from the surveillance cameras by looking down, using the camera on her sensepin and the built-in screen of the Talos tensor bank to see where she was going. Once out in the parking lot, she called a rideshare and gave the address of a gas station.

She waited until the car pulled away before walking. From satellite images, Talos had found an unmapped path that led through the woods from the gas station to the back of Elli and Piers's property. It was likely a deer trail, narrow and bramble-packed. Combined with the darkening twilight, every rustling among the trees made her jump. Talos had assured her that there were no bears here and that the risk of Lyme-carrying ticks was minimal, but she knew better than to trust machines completely on this sort of thing.

Twenty minutes later, she could see the glow of the house peeking from between the trees. Turning off her sensepin's flashlight, she stepped right up to the edge of the property, peering out carefully from behind a thick white pine.

The house was a large two-story colonial, symmetrical in plan, with wide windows, white siding, a steep roof with dormers. The backyard, deserted at the moment, was large and deep, providing plenty of privacy. In a corner close to the woods, there was an extensive rock garden with a water feature.

She couldn't really be sure that there was no one—the police or the kidnappers—watching the house, but she had to take the risk.

Scanning the back of the house carefully, foot by foot, she finally found the glint of a security camera. Deliberately, she stepped onto the lawn, faced the camera, and held out her arms to make a big U-shape. She held the pose for two seconds before retreating back into the woods.

"Safety gestures" were a gimmick, a very American solution to an even more American problem. After a spate of shootings where trigger-happy homeowners killed or injured gig delivery drivers who had turned down the wrong driveway or mixed up addresses, security camera companies and delivery platforms came up with the idea for drivers to make specific gestures that the cameras could recognize so that they could give homeowners a different alert than "intruder detected." (The gestures required the subject to pose with their face unobstructed to prevent actual would-be home invaders from adopting them falsely.) Some homeowners could even opt not to have these "safe events" uploaded into the cloud to save on the monthly subscription. Of course, trigger-happy homeowners who would shoot people on their driveways would never trust robots to tell them who was "safe" in the first place, so this turned out to be just a sounds-good-on-paper feature to sell more expensive security systems.

She was hoping that the recognition neuromesh in Piers's home security system would classify her as safe despite her odd angle of approach to the house and the late hour—without leaving a record in the cloud.

About two minutes later, the back door to the house opened,

spilling bright yellow light into the yard. Silhouetted against the glowing rectangle, Piers looked into the yard.

Holding up her hands, she stepped slowly into his view. Piers didn't seem like the shooting type, but it was always good to be careful.

She held a finger against her lips to warn him not to speak. It took a few moments before he recognized her. She thought he looked surprised and then disappointed—probably because he was hoping that Elli had returned.

She mimed holding up a phone next to her ear, pointed at Piers, and gave a questioning look.

He shook his head and pointed upstairs.

She nodded. "Come out here and shut the door behind you," she whispered.

He complied.

She led him back into the darkness in the middle of the yard. Then, in a low voice, she quickly brought him up to date.

"I'm sorry," Piers said, keeping his voice low as well. "I had no idea just visiting you would lead them to come after you. I was sure I hadn't been followed."

"They weren't *following* you," Julia said. "When you drove away, they were pretty chill about it. I think they were *tracking* you."

Piers looked shocked. "My car? But wouldn't my security system—"

Julia interrupted. "I think it's your phone. That's why I didn't want to speak until I was sure you didn't have your phone with you."

Recovering, Piers shook his head. "I knew not to bring my real phone when I visited you. I had a burner, and I forwarded the calls from my real phone to the burner, just in case they called."

She pondered this. "Well, first things first. Can you get your real phone and the burner, wrap them in this RF shielding cloth, and bring them back to me? I'm going to scan them."

"What if he calls during that time? I don't want to miss it."

"If they're really interested in getting in touch with you, they will," said Julia, impatience and resentment creeping into her voice. "Think about it: your firm page has your KnockID, your work phone, your SeeCall, and even if all else failed, your email."

Reluctantly, he agreed.

A few minutes later, Julia let out a sigh. "Both phones are secure. They didn't plant a bug in either, at least none I can find." She handed the phones back to him.

"That's a relief," he said.

"We can talk without worrying about them listening in, but they can still track you with them."

"How do they—"

Julia's stomach growled at that moment. "Sorry. I haven't had anything to eat all afternoon."

"How about dinner?" Piers opened the door and invited her in.

They stepped into the kitchen. The pass-through into the living room showed her that the house was a mess. Storage boxes had been upended over the floor; scattered papers were everywhere; even the couch cushions had been ripped apart.

"No, we haven't been robbed," Piers said, looking embarrassed. "I'm taking a leave of absence from work, and I've just spent the afternoon looking through everything, trying to find what the kidnappers say Elli took from them. Except it's hard to find something when you don't know what you're looking for."

"What about your AI? It's usually pretty good at picking out things that don't fit."

"I don't subscribe to one."

"None at all?" Julia didn't know many people who didn't have a personal AI.

"I'm a bit of a technophobe," Piers said. "Sometimes I use Elli's, but it was no help this time."

"I'll help you look."

"Thanks."

He gestured at the counter, topped by a line of casserole dishes and covered plates. "Neighbors have been coming by at all hours now that Elli's disappearance is in the news."

"Probably to check on you and see if they can figure out how you did it."

Piers winced. "Yeah, I think you're right. Are you always like this?"

"How do you mean?"

"Thinking the worst of everyone. And blunt."

She took a moment to think about it. "I suppose so. Sorry if I come across as rude. I'm not very good with people. Maybe it comes with the territory of being good with machines."

"It's fine. It's just that with Elli gone . . . I'm not at my best either. But I appreciate you coming to help. I really do." Taking a deep breath, he went to the counter. "Anything you can't or won't eat?"

Julia shook her head.

She watched as he spooned mashed potatoes, sliced roast beef, tonged string beans onto two plates and put them in the microwave. She thought about what he must be feeling: his wife gone, possibly in mortal danger, himself suspected, and unable to share what was really going on with anyone except herself. Impatience, annoyance, self-pity receded. Yes, her life had been interrupted, but he was in a much worse place. Let me try harder, she vowed silently.

"Back to the burner phone and tracking," she said. "Can you tell me how you got the burner and when you activated it?"

Piers returned to the table with the microwaved plates, setting one down in front of Julia and keeping the other for himself. He handed her a set of silverware.

"I got it on Friday, after that call. I didn't know what to do, but I knew I needed to move around untracked, and I thought my phone was probably no good if they called me on it. I drove to the Right Value Wireless in Carre Center and bought the burner. Activated it right away to see if everything worked. When I came to see you, I only had the burner on me."

"Burner phones aren't any good if you don't know how to use them," Julia said. She began to eat. In her famished state, everything tasted excellent. She could feel her own mood improving. "It's easy to buy real-time location data from the phone companies—it's one of their biggest revenue streams."

"That data is anonymized by law." He began to eat as well.

"Yes, but it's trivial to de-anonymize. Think about it: They can easily pick out your regular phone from the anonymized data based on your address. Then they see your phone travel to Right Value, and a new device gets activated there and travels back to your house with your regular phone. Now they know the new device is yours."

Piers looked sheepish. He set his fork down. "Seems so obvious now that you've explained it. Let me get rid of the burner phone."

"No. Don't do that. Now that they think they know how to track you, we can take advantage of it."

"How?"

"I don't know yet. Let's finish eating first."

While Piers cleaned up, Julia went around the house to make sure all the curtains were drawn. She tried to move without leaving obvious silhouettes that could be seen from outside. The other rooms were also a mess—Piers had been busy. Julia saw no signs of an everyfixit or other household robots; apparently, Piers and Elli didn't use them, which tracked with what Piers had said about his discomfort with machines.

"Tell me about her," she said when she returned to the kitchen.

Piers, washing the dishes at the sink, seemed taken aback.

"You came to me because you thought I could tell you whether the video is real."

He nodded.

"I explained that I can't do that if I know nothing about her," she said. "If I'm to help you, whether it's to find clues about Elli or what the kidnappers are after, then I have to know as much about her as possible."

"I see," he said. "I guess I'm still surprised that you know nothing about her. I just figured that given your technical background—she's one of the biggest names in vivid dreaming."

"I don't know any oneirofexes at all, and I've never tried vivid dreaming."

"Is there a reason?"

She could sense the growing skepticism behind the question. Perhaps Piers thought he had made a mistake in going to her, thinking she was the kind of "hacker" who could help him. Come to think of it, she wasn't sure he was wrong about that. Could she really help?

She did her best to answer. "I guess I'm a very private person. I don't like doing anything that feels like I'm revealing too much about myself. Don't like being photographed. Don't use any social media. I don't even watch subscription TV. Dreaming in the presence of strangers . . . not my thing."

"I can see why," he said. "Vivid dream gatherings can be very intimate. I still remember everything about my first one." His voice grew wistful. "Close my eyes, and I'll swear it was yesterday. Though it was more than ten years ago."

"Was that how you met?"

"That first time was when I fell in love with her," he said. "I didn't get to meet her until later."

She nodded. "Tell me about what it's like at a vivid dream gathering. Pretend you're explaining this to a total novice, someone like . . . your mom."

Piers chuckled as he loaded the last plates into the dishwasher. "My mother would never go to an oneirofex. I'm not good with technology, but I try. She wouldn't even redeem the elder-monitor service I got her. A vivid dream gathering is like a combination of cinema, theater, meditation. . . . You ever been to a concert?"

"Yes."

"Okay, so picture that, except everyone is on the verge of falling asleep—what they call the hypnagogic state."

"One, that doesn't sound fun at all; two, I still can't picture it."

"No, of course not." Piers shook his head and laughed. "I'm terrible at this. How about I show you some arena videos when I'm done here? They don't capture what it's like as a dreamer, but at least you'll get a better idea than my babbling."

"All right. You said it's very intimate? I can't imagine any sense of intimacy when you are in a venue with thousands of other people."

"Well, that was something Elli was really good at. Making you feel like she saw you, just you."

Julia shrugged. She knew something about people who could do that. Not pleasant memories.

"There are recordings, right?" she asked. "I understand that oneirofexes sell them."

"Vivid dream recordings are all personalized," said Piers. "You can buy one only if you go to a gathering, and it will be based on your own cephaloscript. Not only is it illegal to obtain someone else's script, but it will be nearly incomprehensible and boring."

"Like hearing someone recount *their* dream," Julia said, catching on.

"Yes, exactly."

"And there's no way to buy just a recording of whatever the dream guide"—she struggled to find the right word for something she didn't understand—"does? Without the cephaloscript of any dreamer?"

"You are thinking of the prompt track," said Piers. "I suppose the artists could make such a thing, but it won't sell. While Elli has a broad outline for each dream, the exact prompts aren't preset. They are based on the reaction of the dreamers at the gathering. It's like a jazz concert where the improvisation is all driven by the audience reaction. A recording wouldn't give you anything close to the real experience."

Julia nodded. She was starting to understand vivid dreaming better—or at least one aspect. In a world of mass-produced digital clones and AI-generated trash, anything that required human craft, that required live presence, was going to command a premium. A performance that couldn't be recorded fit the bill.

"If you want to know her, you have to know her work. There's no other way," Piers said.

Julia imagined Elli trying to monitor and orchestrate the brain patterns of thousands simultaneously. It seemed impossible. "I think an oneirofex must rely on their AI for some aspects of the performance. Is that true?"

"Yes. It's impossible for Elli to do what she does without her personal AI. It's her instrument, really."

"Do you still have access to her personal AI?"

"Yes. We can go to her studio."

"Then I might have a solution."

SIX

This is where she practices," Piers said, ushering Julia into the room.

The studio, an upstairs bedroom with walls covered in acoustic-dampening panels, was mostly empty save for the VR recording station near the back wall, replete with consoles and monitors. Julia peeked at the processor modules under the consoles and sucked in a breath: more computing power than some small corporate clouds.

A mannequin covered in cameras and sensors lay in a recliner to the side, and a neural-sensing VR headset rested on a bust-shaped holder next to the recliner. Glancing around, Julia easily picked out more cameras and microphones tucked away in the corners.

"What exactly does she do with this setup?" Julia asked.

"First, she acts as the dream weaver and records the prompts on this dream deck." He pointed to a black box covered in knobs and dials near the VR station. "That's actually the same one she uses at performances. She loves that thing. And then she plays the track back for herself as the dreamer to see if the dream is compelling."

Julia furrowed her brow in confusion.

"Sorry, I should have given you more context," Piers said. "Right,

I promised I'd show you some arena videos. Which do you prefer: VR or plain old video?"

"Plain."

He walked over to one of the consoles, woke it up, and looked into the camera over the monitor.

"Wait!" She reached out to block the camera.

"What's wrong?"

"Her AI. What kind is it?"

"She subscribes to Cognita, but I believe she has added a ton of customizations. Her work is very specialized."

So it would have a cloud tether, at least, she thought. "What level of authorization did she give you?"

"Admin."

"Are you sure?"

"Yes." He looked slightly offended. "Elli and I kept no secrets from each other." However, his voice trailed off near the end as he realized he might need to reevaluate that sentiment.

"Don't activate it until we've secured your network," Julia said. "I don't want anything we do to get out of this house into the cloud. I should have done that first thing after I came in. Even the thermostat data can tell people things if they look hard enough."

Piers looked unconvinced. Still, he asked, "What do you need?"

She was glad that he didn't argue with her. "Where's your fiber-optic cable access point?"

"In the basement."

He led her downstairs and then opened the basement door.

Julia, going over in her mind all the things that she might have overlooked, said, "If your alarm system has already uploaded pictures of me, delete them from the cloud right now."

"I never consented to auto uploads. Any pictures and videos would still be on the camera."

"Assuming the camera manufacturer actually obeys that preference. Better delete them anyway."

They descended into the unfinished basement, lit by a few bare lightbulbs. Julia found the optical network terminal and unplugged the data cable leading to the router. She took out a small box, plugged the cable into it, and then patched the box back into the router with another short cable.

"What's that?"

"A firewall. I'll configure it to block out every kind of traffic that I don't want going out. After this, Elli's AI will think all network access has been cut. That might cause it to behave differently, but it can't be helped. Can I have your phone again?"

"Why?"

"I need to install a piece of code on it, a 'guard tower,' so that Talos can watch over your phone. It needs to oversee all traffic going out of this house."

She could see his jaw clench. "I hardly know you, and you're asking me to give you control over everything."

"Good point," Julia said. The long day had been unsettling, and the constant need to convince him—she wasn't even sure she *wanted* to convince him—was wearing. She wondered again why she was here—had she ever made a positive difference in anyone's life? "We don't have any reason to trust each other. If you want to call this off, I'll walk out this door, and we'll never see each other again. Maybe that'll be for the best."

Piers looked at her without speaking.

She was sure he was going to take her up on her offer and was already thinking about the best way to get away from the house unseen when he shook his head and said, "Whatever it takes. I don't know how to find Elli or what they want from her, and from what I know about you—admittedly not much—you're my best shot."

He unlocked his phone and handed it over; Julia installed the guard tower.

From what I know about you. What did he know about her? Yes, she had been famous at one point for hacking, for getting into places she shouldn't have been in, for looking at things she shouldn't have been looking at, for being a criminal. Was that all he saw in her? All that he needed?

She forced the bitterness away. Once again, she reminded herself of his state, the oppressive, terrifying uncertainty. His life had been interrupted, put on hold, as a terrifying man on the phone told him that his wife was in his power and he had to do precisely as he was told. All things considered, Piers had the right to act much more like an asshole than he actually was.

"Just curious," he said as they climbed back up the stairs. "How would the thermostat data have been a risk?"

"Now that I'm here, that data will show a slight change in the heating and cooling curves, indicating the presence of an extra person in the house. That kind of data is usually not well secured, and if you're being watched, someone—or more likely their AI—will think of looking at it. Considering that you're under suspicion already for Elli's disappearance, do you really want the police to think you've got another girl in here?"

"I see."

Maybe she was imagining it, but she thought she heard admiration in the acknowledgment.

Finally, they were back in the studio.

Piers activated Elli's AI and instructed it to bring up a video on the curved wide monitor over the console.

The venue was a small theater shaped like a bowl with approximately a thousand seats arranged in tiers around a circular stage at the center. Elli, in a flowing white dress, danced slowly around the stage as she chanted. While ethereal music played, the audience leaned back in their seats, their unfocused eyes on transparent displays suspended above their faces. It reminded Julia not so much of a concert as of a New Age performance, a sound bath maybe, or a group meditation.

"This auditorium is designed for vivid dreaming," Piers explained. "The seats have built-in sensors to monitor brain activity—that makes it much easier, as otherwise, the dream guide has to rent the equipment to modify the seats for every performance. Once everyone's seated, the oneirofex plays music, sings, chants, recites poetry, shows videos, and so on to put the audience into a trance state."

"Kind of like hypnosis?"

"I guess so? The key is that she does this to everyone in the auditorium, not just one person."

"Is her AI given access to all the audience's personal AIs?"

"Yes."

"So that's how she does it." Julia was catching on. Elli's AI, collaborating with each user's personal AI, helped her discern trends and patterns in thousands of cephaloscripts in real time. Vivid dreaming was an art form that required the dream guide to extend her skills through AI; that was what Piers meant when he said AI was Elli's instrument.

"Does she entrance them by amplifying alpha and theta waves?" Julia asked. "Or are we talking about recognition of more refined neural patterns and biofeedback?"

Piers shrugged. "I have no idea. You'll have to ask Elli's AI for the details. The way I understand it, Elli essentially guides the audience to dream together. Each individual dream is prompted by images projected on their HUD, images that are particularly meaningful to them, generated by a collaboration between Elli's and the audience member's AIs. However, the emotional journey they all go on is collective, an improvisation woven from their individual dreams by the oneirofex."

Julia watched the screen. A room full of people dreaming with open eyes, connected yet also separate, guided by the dancing figure onstage, a magician weaving a spell.

"The video really isn't enough," said Piers. "Like I said, you have to experience it. The best way I can describe it is: You feel you're part of something grand and epic; you're surrounded by love, and you belong. The dream is the way life ought to be, and your other life, the life outside the dream, is fiction."

You're surrounded by love, and you belong.

Julia turned to Piers.

"I want to try it."

Piers's phone rang.

"Have you found what I wanted?" The same male voice from before.

"No, because I don't know—"

"Who did you go see today?"

A long pause. "Someone who I thought could help me. But they didn't want to help."

"Good. I'm glad you are telling me the truth. It's important for us to trust each other, don't you think?"

"I want to talk to Elli."

"No."

"How can I trust you if I can't talk to her?"

"I told you. You'll try to speak to each other in code. I can't have that."

"You have to tell me something about what you're looking for. I really don't know!"

"She has . . . me," the man said reluctantly.

"What are you talking about? What's your name?"

"My name isn't relevant. Just find what I want. I know she has it."

"Without your name, how am I supposed to look?"

"Everyone calls me the Prince, and you can too. But that won't help you. How about this? If you don't know how to find what I'm looking for, just send me everything she has. Here is a server address you can use."

"I can't possibly send you everything Elli has. There's tons of personal data, not to mention our life together—"

"Send me what I want or send me everything. I'll be generous and give you until the end of Wednesday."

They played the call recording over and over, parsing every sentence, scrutinizing every detail. Piers debated with himself, changing his mind every five minutes.

"What could he possibly mean by 'she has me'?"

"Could it be that Elli learned some secret of his during a vivid dreaming session?" Based on what Julia knew about the oneirofex's art, this seemed the most plausible guess. "You said it could be very intimate."

Piers shook his head. "That's impossible. If you understood how dreaming worked, you would know that."

"Then it has to be some information, some piece of . . . data. About him." Julia shook her head in frustration. She was just restating the obvious.

"I don't know what to do," Piers said finally, burying his face in his hands.

Julia recoiled at the idea of giving up Elli's data, but she saw the trap they were in. It came down to this unalterable fact: so long as there was a chance that "the Prince"—Julia wanted to laugh at the absurdity of it, but she couldn't—really had Elli, they had to do as the man asked.

"There's really no way to know?" Piers pleaded.

"There isn't," Julia said. "I'm sorry. I wish, I really, really wish, I could tell you for sure that the video was faked. But I can't. I just don't know."

"Elli does like codes," Piers muttered. "She's always putting them in her performances for the fans. So maybe he really does have her—that's why he doesn't want her to talk to me."

Julia said nothing.

"And if she's okay, she would have contacted me by now, right? She wouldn't leave me in this state . . . while the police are watching me and this Prince guy is breathing down my neck."

Julia said nothing. From the outside, it was impossible to tell what was going on inside a marriage.

"And I've tried to ask Elli's AI whether it knows what the Prince is asking for. It has no idea what I'm talking about."

Julia said nothing. The fact that Elli's AI claimed to know nothing about this could mean that Elli was hiding something even from her AI, that Piers really didn't have the level of access to her AI he thought he did, or that this Prince character was full of crap. Again, no way to know.

"I don't see how we have any choice. We have to do as he asks. We have to . . . upload everything that Elli has. Can you help me?"

SEVEN

By the time Julia helped Piers get the upload going, it was past ten at night.

Most people underestimated how much data they generated over a lifetime. Every generation took more pictures, videos, flipclips, immersion scenes, cephaloscripts . . . than the last one; wrote more and longer books, memos, codes, emails, blogs, sparksnarks, longshouts, prompt-macros; generated more click-through user agreements, shrink-wrap licenses, bills, payment records, receipts, implied contribution contracts; and this didn't even account for all the semi-original or entirely unoriginal "content" AI generated on behalf of everyone, often with little to no supervision.

And for someone like Elli, who worked in a medium that relied on the crowd and their data, everything above was multiplied tenfold.

For someone like Julia, who viewed the creation and proliferation of data about herself almost like a sin, the terabytes upon terabytes on Elli Krantz's drives were shocking.

Julia didn't like the idea of uploading everything about Elli to the Prince. What if getting that data *was* the scam? Once these people had Elli's personal data, the potential for any number of follow-up acts of malfeasance was unbounded. Julia ought to know; she had been through data-disclosure hell herself.

Yet, so long as it was possible that the Prince had Elli, what could Piers do?

So she did the next best thing. She sorted the files on Elli's drives by type. The upload would begin with the most innocuous stuff she could imagine: recordings of public performances, publicity material, archived interviews. . . . She pushed the sensitive data to later, with the neuromesh of Elli's personal AI, essentially a second self trained on everything Elli had ever done, the very last thing to be uploaded. (The neuromesh was encrypted, but Julia knew that didn't mean much. Thanks to arrogant, clueless bureaucrats in Brussels, encryption on cloud-based commercial personal AI was required to contain a back door for law enforcement—which meant anyone could crack it given enough resources.)

She hoped there would be enough time between now and Wednesday night for her to either figure out if they had Elli or find the "me" that the Prince wanted.

"You're not going to just sit there all night and watch the upload progress bar, are you?" she asked.

Piers turned his bleary eyes from the monitor to her. Apparently, he had been intending to do exactly that.

"I suggest you use your time more productively," Julia coaxed. "Come, help me so I can see what it was like to dream with Elli."

Together, Piers and Julia removed the sensor-festooned mannequin from the recliner. Julia sat down in its place, pulled on the neural-sensing VR headset, and tightened the straps.

She darkened the lenses and tested the neural sensing, concentrating on the white arrows in her field of view until she could move them fluidly by thinking about them. Pretty intuitive—the headset essentially worked like a fancier version of the esports headsets that competitive gamers used, which she was familiar with; keyboard-and-mouse was no match against direct neural sensing regarding precision, reaction time, or actions-per-minute.

Satisfied, she put the lenses back in pass-through mode to talk to Piers, who was waiting by the dream deck.

"You just have to press enter once I give you the signal," she said. "Talos and Elli's egolet will do everything from then on."

"All right," Piers said.

She could sense his unease. "What's wrong?"

"This is weird for me," Piers admitted.

"What? Me wearing her headset?"

"No." Piers hesitated. "It's just the idea that Elli will now be dreaming with you, one-on-one—sort of. I've never done anything like this with her."

"Never?"

"I never asked. It's her art, you know? It would be like asking your wife, a rock star, to put on a concert just for you. It feels wrong."

"Maybe she can't do this with just one person," Julia said. "She practiced by herself, never with another person. You said vivid dreaming is about the collective experience; perhaps the dream guide needs a crowd to practice her art."

"But what if she doesn't? Now I wish I had asked."

As bad as she was with people, Julia could tell that Piers needed reassurance. "When I go in, it won't really be her, you know."

Even with the state-of-the-art processors in Elli's studio, even with Julia, Piers, Talos, and Elli's AI all working together, it had taken more than three hours to train the egolet. Instead of the real Elli, this AI model of her would guide Julia's first vivid dream.

Piers hadn't believed it would work at all. Elli had told him that vivid dreaming only worked because of the presence of the oneirofex, the human spark.

But Julia knew there was more nuance to that. As Piers had told her (and she had confirmed it with research), an oneirofex relied on AI to process the vast amounts of data generated by the audience. Julia surmised that, over time, the AI had to have learned the oneirofex's particular propensities for responding to trends in the audience, her unique tendencies in prompting the audience, her go-to tricks in nudging and driving the audience to a shared emotional curve—in a word, Elli's AI had to have learned something of her *style*.

It was no different from how photographers' AIs, over time, learned to apply filters and make adjustments that their humans would have made, or how experienced DJs would sometimes let their AIs run most or even all of a show on autopilot. Even Julia herself would sometimes let Talos handle a routine neuromesh hack on its own, as the AI had learned to "think" like her in specific ways. Some aspects—maybe even most aspects—of what an artist did consisted of skills that could be embedded in a neuromesh model.

Neuromeshes modeled on one specific aspect of a person, such as a skill or expertise, were dubbed "egolets." In contrast to early crude "generative AI" models, which only ingested finished paintings, novels, films, and the like, and whose productions were caricatures of the masters they imitated, egolets of artists were trained on *processes*, not merely a few finished products.

An artist's skill cannot be extracted solely from the finished picture, novel, film, composition, but requires an understanding of all the covered-up brushstrokes, all the deleted scenes and murdered darlings, all the raw footage before editing. An artist is, above all, someone who knows how to say no to many things and yes to only a few things. Their style is how they decide which is which. A proper egolet can only be made from an artist's personal AI, which has access to *everything*.

These days, artists' licensing of their personal styles, though still debated, was growing.

Egolets of actors—performance capture data animated by the actors' personal AIs—were in high demand, and one actor, notorious for being difficult to work with, was now rumored to receive more licensing fees for his egolet—which had been stripped of the more recalcitrant aspects of his ego by his manager—than for on-set performances.

A bestselling author, known for her socially progressive fiction, had been caught pumping out books under a different pen name intended for "real Americans" with a modified version of her egolet so she could double her sales (when the scandal broke, she tried to blame it on "hackers"). Ghostwriters for celebrities regularly licensed ghostwriting egolets to smaller clients who wanted their own vanity memoirs but couldn't afford the fees for the real deal.

A critically acclaimed painter, hungry for cash as well as controversy, licensed an egolet of himself to craft bespoke portraits of anyone willing to pay ten dollars. The trollish stunt turned him into a pariah for a while, but amidst all the denunciations of "selling out," he claimed to have gotten more than a million paying customers. And one of the most lucrative revenue streams in the porn industry involved performers licensing their egolets for sex dolls.

Whether you viewed it as a way for artists to expand their presence—a natural extension of the way Rodin and da Vinci used apprentices to execute more work than they could do personally—or as the ultimate cheapening and devaluation of human craft, egolets were already a big part of the modern business of art.

And so Julia had come up with the idea of crafting an egolet of Elli's aspect as an oneirofex so that she could experience a vivid dream. If the dreaming experience helped her know Elli better, she would perhaps be better able to help Piers and Elli.

Crafting an egolet was as much art as science, and professional egolet-sculptors were highly paid artists in their own right. Though not a professional, Julia managed a passable job by drawing on her extensive experience with neuromeshes. The task of creating an egolet of Elli's oneirofex self was also considerably eased by the vast number of recordings of her practice sessions. Not only did she record detailed promptscripts of herself performing, but she also recorded high-resolution biofeedback data, cephaloscripts of herself reacting to the prompts, and adjustments to the prompts based on the feedback. This kind of data—an artist improving her craft, developing her voice, inventing her style—was critical for training a performance egolet.

Dreaming with Elli's egolet wouldn't be the same as dreaming with the real Elli, Julia knew. For one thing, she had so little time that the egolet was necessarily crude, almost like a caricature of Elli as a dream guide. For another, the egolet's range of responses would be limited—the more Julia deviated from the training set used to construct the egolet, the more nonsensical it would become.

Elli was right that an egolet couldn't *replace* her—even the best egolets couldn't do that to their artists. This was something that artists (and Julia, like the best technologists, was an artist) understood intuitively. To be an artist required skill, which could be learned, more or less, by a neuromesh, but it also required originality, empathy, a soul. So far, no one had figured out how to put those things into a neuromesh.

But that didn't mean nothing useful could be gained from trying to dream with a machine's memory of Elli.

"I didn't include anything personal in the training data," Julia went on. "There's nothing about you, nothing about her dreams, nothing about this life you've built together."

"It's just that I've only now realized that she never offered to dream with me, just the two of us," Piers said. "Why not? She never told me she couldn't dream with just one person."

Julia didn't know what to say. The way his face strained not to show the pain of suspected betrayal . . . She looked away.

"Maybe I don't know her as well as I thought. What if the Prince is telling the truth, that Elli did take . . . something from him, something very personal? Maybe she's been living another life I know nothing about."

"I . . ." Julia couldn't continue. Her presence felt intrusive. More than ever, she thought: I really am bad with people.

"I'm sorry," Piers said, struggling to rein in his emotions. "I'm being selfish. Here you are, trying to help me by doing something you've never done before—that no one has done before. And I'm letting my insecurities get in the way. Sorry."

"You've had a rough time," Julia said. It came out awkward, but it was sincere.

Piers laughed. "Yeah. I wouldn't call this weekend one of my best. You've had a rough day yourself, being forced out of your home by strangers. Are you nervous about your first vivid dream?"

Now that he asked, she *was* anxious. Vivid dreaming required the dreamer to open herself to the guide, to essentially shut off the privacy safeguards on her personal AI so that the guide could extract images and memories and construct prompts based on the dreamer's life. Giving Elli's egolet such access to herself made her feel incredibly vulnerable. She hadn't opened herself up like that to anyone since Sahima. . . .

Piers had assured her that the dream deck was designed to erase all user cephaloscripts after a dream; the industry had made user privacy a keystone to entice more users. Elli's equipment and AI would retain nothing about Julia. This was why it would have been impossible for Elli to steal an audience member's secret.

But the reassurance meant little—Julia was all too aware of how easily people gave up their privacy for the most ridiculous reasons, and how often the tech industry simply lied to their users. Talos, however, had confirmed for her that what Piers said was true. And she had triple-checked to be sure that neither the egolet nor any of the data it would be generating would be uploaded to the Prince—that would be a disaster indeed. She resolved to find out more about the dream deck's data security later, but for now, the desire to know what it was like to vivid dream overrode her paranoia.

"I'll be fine," she said to Piers. As much to reassure him as herself. "Go ahead."

"Sweet dreams," he said, tapping the enter key on the console.

EIGHT

Instantly, the lenses turned black, blocking out Piers, the console, the rest of the room.

When the lights came up again, Julia found herself inside a theater.

Not like the theater in the video Piers had shown her earlier. This one was much smaller and followed the traditional floor plan: a stage framed by a proscenium arch, facing gently curving rows of seats. She was in the front row, an audience of one. With a start, Julia realized this was the auditorium from her middle school in Methven, Massachusetts.

Elli stood onstage. Though she was the same height as Julia, the stage made Julia loom above her, a radiant figure of grace.

"We are all lead actors in our own plays," Elli said. Her voice was musical and warm, with a husky texture that drew the listener in. "I want you to find the story you want to tell."

She raised an arm and waved to somewhere above the lights. Music began to play: Tibetan singing bowls and Andean zampoñas.

Though fitting given the setting, the theatricality of the performance grated on Julia. Belatedly, she realized that she had never picked a dream but allowed the egolet to choose a dream for her. She didn't feel spiritual. She didn't feel she needed to "tell" some story. What was she doing here? She was about to reach up and lift off the headset when Elli turned her gaze on her.

"You're free to go," she said, her voice rising and falling as though she were singing. "But if you've never done it before, don't you at least owe yourself an honest try?" The way she looked into Julia's eyes, intense but also inviting, sent a tingle down her spine.

Julia was no stranger to conversing with egolets. But there was something about this digital simulacrum of Elli that unsettled her, despite how compelling it was. She couldn't pin down what felt off. Was it because she was unused to Elli's fancy renderer's high resolution and frame rate? Or was vivid dreaming meant to make you feel out of place?

In any event, based on the egolet, she could only marvel at how charismatic the real Elli must have been.

On impulse, she asked, "Somebody calling himself 'the Prince' says you took 'him' and now he wants it back. What does he mean? What are you hiding?"

Elli ignored that. "If you have no interest in the story you want to tell, I won't keep you. I hope you'll find another subject I guide more interesting. Maybe a dream about going to the stars? Or how about falling deeply in love?"

Julia was disappointed. The slick microexpressions and the sheer *presence* of the model had fooled her. For a moment, she could almost believe that Elli's AI had done the impossible, had embedded so much of the human into tensors of weights, biases, inputs, transforms, MQLAs . . . that it had created a total digital twin, the Holy Grail of those in Silicon Valley who always promised that we would digitize ourselves and live in the cloud as gods in another ten years. But there was no such technology. This was just an egolet, a very good one in some ways, but still shallow and limited.

Unexpectedly, Elli-egolet's brief dip into the uncanny valley reassured her. The egolet was just a machine, and she knew machines. "I'll stay," she said, and sat back down.

"We were all born naked and ignorant, our minds the primeval Ginnungagap. If we felt heat, we knew not that it was the blossoms of fire from Muspelheim. If we felt cold, we knew not that it was the rivers of ice from Niflheim. . . ."

As Elli chanted hypnotically, the music swelled, and Julia could feel herself slowly drifting into a different mental state. It reminded her of the inward-turning she did when she went on a long run or, less pleasantly, when she had been so hungry and terrified that she had to sit and let her mind go blank so that time could pass until her body learned not to complain about emptiness and fear.

"Into this void charged our parents, our caretakers, people to whom we were bound before we were even born, whose power over us we had no understanding or choice. They were our first angels and demons, gods and Titans, and their actions, violent or kind, generous or selfish, became the milk of our dreams. From them, we wove our first myths, the seeds of meaning, stepping stones out of the collective unconscious. . . ."

Images swirled before her eyes: old photographs she hadn't looked at in years; voices and videos that she had avoided; places, people, memories that she had believed she left behind.

This is a mistake, she thought. I shouldn't have agreed to do this.

"They were the law and the refuge, the path as well as the field; we craved their approval and shrank from their reproof. The way they held us became our template for love; the way they failed us became our wellspring for pain. . . ."

She didn't reach up to push off the headset. She could have, but she didn't.

Elli vanished, and Julia was no longer in her seat.

Twelve years old again, she was on the stage in a white blouse and blue gingham dress, a wicker basket dangling from her elbow, a plush terrier puppy inside. The ruby slippers on her feet were heavy and pinched her toes. Julia-Dorothy was just about to let the audience know she didn't think they were in Kansas anymore.

Slam!

The large doors to the auditorium burst open. Below the stage, the rows of bored siblings and parents with forced smiles holding up phones to record the production turned as one at the commotion. An angry crowd holding signs and placards thronged the aisles, and as the shocked audience shrank into their seats, the crowd coalesced around a woman seated in the front row. Those on either side of her fled, leaving an empty swath of seats around her.

The crowd pressed in. Behind them, cameras, microphones, and reporters swarmed, waiting for the right viral shot or sound bite.

The woman, Chinese, just past forty, gazed defiantly back at the screaming crowd, and especially the cameras beyond, a hint of a smile on her face. Then she looked over them at Julia and nodded encouragingly. "Go on. Don't let them stop you."

Some in the crowd turned around and looked at *her*. They began to shout. They told her that she didn't belong. They couldn't believe she was playing Dorothy. "What is happening to our country?" "Disgusting!" "Go back to China!" They used *chink* a lot.

A few cameras spun around to point up at the stage. Flashes.

"Go on!" her mother shouted above the noise. "You can do it!"

Middle school Julia covered her face and ran off before the cameras could get another shot of her.

Her mother had promised to take a break from her schedule of protests, rallies, sit-ins, meetings with important people, to attend her play. But sometimes, a promise kept was worse than a promise broken.

If pressed to describe her mother in two words, Julia would say: restless and fearless.

A woman who was content with her lot and who feared the unknown couldn't have left behind everything and everyone she knew;

couldn't have spent a month in a lightless cargo container to traverse the stormy Pacific; couldn't have had her bones rattled in the back of a truck crammed with unwashed bodies for another week; couldn't have hiked through the swamp, mountain, and jungle of the Darién Gap, fending off jaguars and venomous snakes, not to mention the even more dangerous predators in human shape; couldn't have walked miles and miles, enduring thirst, hunger, and fatigue, in the company of thousands of others like her, who had lost all faith in the lands of their birth; couldn't have risked being shot by border militias, imprisonment, deportation, all for the slim hope of a brand-new life in the United States, within these dream-limned shores.

All of that, while she was pregnant.

(She never told Julia anything about her father. As far as she was concerned, a man who lacked the courage to make a new life for his daughter didn't deserve to know her.)

And afterward, after she had entered America and had the baby and gained her papers and got a job and bought a house and made a life for herself, she was still not finished. Unlike many other immigrants from the "wrong" countries, who tried to keep their heads down and their mouths shut because they understood and accepted that their existence in this country was barely tolerated, suffered only so long as they acted second-class, she kept on being restless and fearless.

She campaigned against the mass deportations; she marched against the country's new wars; she raised money to hold those who abused power accountable in court; she lifted her voice for every downtrodden cause she believed in.

Immigrants, especially immigrants like her, weren't supposed to criticize America—they were supposed to be docile, to fit in, to be *grateful*. If they were to be political at all, they should reserve their censure for the lands they had departed so that they could confirm the very American opinion that America is the greatest land on earth. But her mother had a different view. "The best way to show you deserve to be an American," she said, "is to work at making America live up to her ideals. Guests may walk around on eggshells, but I'm not a guest. This is my homeland, where I will build my house, raise my child, and bury my bones. I'm going to be a patriot, and I won't shut up."

She had a compelling presence that drew followers, as well as a cunning sense of the dramatic to make her influence felt, to sway elections and change policy.

Vitriol followed. They accused her of being a foreign plant, shouted in her face that she should go back to where she came from, spat at her because she had no business speaking when only "real Americans" deserved to be heard. In response, she laughed longer and spoke louder and went on more marches.

Julia grew up in the households of her mother's neighbors and friends. For much of her childhood, her mother was only an occasional presence, a rare bird who dipped into her life from time to time, whose visits were filled with exciting stories that Julia barely understood and intense "bonding experiences" meant to make up for the long periods of absence.

Some neighbors spoke about her mother admiringly, almost like she was a superhero. Others were less flattering, their disapproval barely disguised. In Julia's mind, her mother was larger than life, a semi-mythical figure. More than anything else, she craved her mother's approval, hungered for her attention.

By the time Julia was in elementary school, her mother had begun to take her to marches, speeches, and sit-ins. She explained to Julia that children had always been a vital part of protest movements. From the young Transcendentalists who denounced the Mexican-American War to the Children's Crusade during the civil rights movement, the children of activists had always been there, their youth and innocence essential parts of their parents' persuasive power. Julia, her mother told her, should be honored to be part of this illustrious American lineage.

Julia was just glad that she got to spend time with her mother.

Being at the protests was terrifying but also thrilling. She was young enough that the slurs the counter-protesters shouted at her mother could still be dismissed with a lie ("They're saying we're very thin, so we can fit inside chinks in walls"), but old enough to feel the exhilaration of being part of something bigger than an individual and the warmth of the crowd's admiration reflected from her mother. She didn't understand just how risky the situations her mother had put her into were.

That middle school production of *The Wizard of Oz* was a turning point. Afterward, Julia refused to go to the protests, and she begged her mother to stop.

Her mother didn't stop, but she no longer took Julia.

It felt like a rebuke. Julia had lost her mother's approval. She was not the brave child that she had wanted. Her mother had risked everything so that Julia could live the American dream, and Julia had let her mother down.

And it was already too late. The image of Julia-as-Dorothy, dying of terminal embarrassment on the stage, went viral. Those who hated her mother smelled blood. By the logic of the social media age, anyone caught within the frame of a camera ceased to be human. Any lingering guilt was assuaged by the idea that it was Julia's mother who had turned her daughter into a political prop, a "protest performer," a clone of her mother and thus a suitable effigy.

For years, trolls had hounded her mother with manipulated images of herself. All who stepped into the public arena in the modern age faced doxxing, nasty memes, deepfakes, the latest viral descendants of the ancient tradition of dehumanization of one's political opponents. Women, in particular, were subjected to the most horrific versions of these techniques: generated pornography, escort ads featuring her photo and address, videos of her AI-self delivering racist diatribes. . . . They were designed to intimidate, to break her down, to incite violence, sexual and otherwise.

And now, these same techniques were used on Julia.

Trolls scoured the web and found plenty of images of Julia at her mother's events. These became fodder for AI-generated memes, animations, synthvocals, sleepfakes. There was no bottom to the depravity of the trolls, and whatever you imagine they could do with images of a girl, they did worse.

For Julia, the horrors of these images were multiplied tenfold when she realized that her first instinct was to blame her mother. *If only she had stopped, none of this would have happened.* She was disgusted by her own disloyalty, her weakness. Maybe she deserved to be called these horrible names, to be tortured like this. She was a bad daughter. A cowardly daughter.

As the world around her turned to hell, Julia found no way out. Her friends withdrew, fearing the contagion of her notoriety. Unscrupulous classmates took unflattering photos of her and fed them to the trolls. She had to be taken out of school, and her mother, instead of homeschooling Julia herself, left her in the hands of neighbors and friends.

"If I back down, it'll only make them torment us harder. The only way to beat bullies is to never give an inch."

Her mother continued her protests and speeches, which she pursued with even more zeal.

And so the trolls went after Julia harder, and she felt even more resentful toward her mother, which led to more guilt, more pain, more suffering.

Years later, an older Julia would wonder whether her mother was motivated not only by idealism, but also an unwillingness to face the consequences of her own choices on her child—it seemed easier to do what was right in the abstract, much harder to clean up a mess in the real world. By refusing to let the forces of hate dictate to her what she would do, Julia's mother ironically forced Julia to pay for her freedom.

Neighbors and friends passed Julia around like a hot potato. No one wanted to be in the vicinity as a drone swooped by to take another video of "the junior CCP agent" or a bunch of boys blocked the road to taunt "the ugly little chinky slut." Classmates in anonymous channels wished that Julia would kill herself, thus freeing the town from scrutiny by the trolls. At night, after they thought she was asleep, the adults in charge of her care whispered in the kitchen or hallways, and phrases like "so irresponsible," "asking for it," "don't want trouble" drifted into her dreams.

No one hated Julia more than Julia herself.

She started failing her online classes, slept in until noon, missed her counseling appointments—when adults asked her what was wrong, she shrugged or looked away, and eventually stopped giving even those concessions.

Then came the day when her mother was at a protest at a border town in Texas, trying to shepherd a caravan of asylum seekers past a gauntlet of militia. She got in the face of the angry counter-protesters, and one of them opened fire. Though she was airlifted to El Paso for emergency medical treatment, they pronounced her dead on the way.

The next day, Julia ran away. She was fourteen.

"Your story doesn't start with you, but you are its hero. Your life requires your telling, and no one else can take that from you—"

Julia couldn't endure it anymore. The music, the images, Elli's hypnotic voice—this was no dream but a nightmare. In one violent jerk, she ripped off the headset and gasped as everything—the twice-illusory auditorium; the imitation Elli; the memories of shame, terror, guilt—vanished, to be replaced by the dim light of the studio.

It was three in the morning. She was lying in the recliner alone. She hoped Piers was asleep, but he was probably downstairs in front of his computer, watching the progress bar on the upload.

She tried talking to herself to calm her thundering heart. She was no longer fourteen. She was twenty-three. She was not on the streets, with no place to call home, unceasing terror and hunger her only companions. She was safe, at least for the moment, even though she was on the run again.

She looked down at the headset in her lap, her eyes instinctively following the data cable to the rendering engine under the console, purring softly from the exertion of evoking her "dream." She shuddered.

This could not have been one of Elli's hits. Who would pay to relive their childhood trauma? This must have been something she had never performed in public, a failed experiment, a trunked novel draft.

But why had Elli's egolet chosen to have her experience this particular vivid dream?

She found Piers downstairs, staring at the upload progress bar on the computer screen just like she predicted.

"Did it work?" he asked without turning around. "What did you think?"

Because she wasn't sure how to ask what she wanted to ask, she said, "Elli has a strong presence."

Piers nodded. "Which of her hits did you try? I've always found 'First Love' to be incredibly moving, though 'My Pride and His Prejudice' seems really popular with women."

"It was the egolet's choice," Julia said. "I . . . don't remember the title."

Noticing her hesitancy, Piers finally turned around. "Wait. The AI didn't show you one of Elli's really early pieces, did it? The 'dino corporection' stuff? Please don't think of those as representative—"

"It was fine. I get why people go to the gatherings," she lied. "I just have a question." She paused, working through how to ask it and deciding to plunge ahead. "Do you think she might have done private dream gatherings?"

"What are you asking?" He looked confused.

"Did she offer exclusive sessions for small groups, or even one-on-one? Maybe for very dedicated fans . . . or someone willing to pay a lot?"

"No," he managed to say after a few seconds. "Why . . . why do you ask?" Now he looked wounded.

Julia had finally pinned down the source of her initial discomfort with Elli's egolet: It had handled having a single dreamer in the audience easily, almost as if it had plenty of training for the situation. Elli's solo practice sessions, when she acted as both guide and dreamer, couldn't be the explanation, because performing for yourself was completely different from performing for other people, or just one other person.

And, again, why had the egolet chosen that particular dream?

"I'm not saying she did." She tried to reassure him, but she was flailing. "I'm just . . . just trying to understand."

He looked unconvinced but didn't press her.

Even Julia could see why he was upset. The idea that his wife had dreamed one-on-one with someone else but not with him—it was a betrayal of intimacy, a violation of a rule unspoken because it had not been deemed necessary.

Awkwardly, she tried to change the subject. "How much of the transfer is left?"

Preoccupied, he indicated the screen. "The estimate fluctuates a lot."

"It's always like that. Don't worry. You have a fast connection. I can always try some compression and other tricks to speed it up if necessary."

"Would you? I just want to get the data to him as soon as possible. To free Elli."

"Of course."

Julia sat down and began to optimize the transfer: compression, QoS, deduplication, stream multiplexing. . . . As she typed away, she imagined the man on the other side of the transfer. Who was the Prince? What was his connection to Elli?

She pushed the keyboard away and yawned.

Piers, equally tired, forced himself to stand. "Let me show you to the guest bedroom."

The guest room was pristine—Piers hadn't made a mess of it in his frantic search because there was nothing stored in there.

"Has it been a while since you've used this room?" she asked.

"Yes," he said. "My mother doesn't like to fly, and my sisters both have young kids who don't travel well. Elli isn't close to her family."

She nodded. "Good night."

"Sweet dreams."

She slept deeply without dreaming at all.

NINE

The Prince spent his morning "dropping hints."

He loved that phrase. So innocuous. Almost silly. Yet, it was how he exercised power.

Years ago, the son of a prominent politician in the Philippines had killed a pedestrian while joyriding. The Prince had helped the politician—after a suitable fee—to arrange a cover-up. Another man was brought in to be charged, tried, and eventually, sent to jail. The son went abroad, got fancy degrees, and now had a promising political career of his own.

The Prince, however, didn't just cover it up. He had collected evidence: a video of the son's confession with witnesses; the car's real registration information; fingerprints, bloodstains, DNA tests. In an age when everything digital was faked, you needed a lot of analog *stuff* to prove a point.

The Prince knew that when you were asked to erase something, you never just erased that thing. You stored it away. It became an investment.

The investment was maturing now. The politician's enemies had come to the Prince, who was known as a broker of information. Did he have anything that could . . . you know . . . help restore democracy by bringing down the corrupt politician, a parasite in the body politic, a festering drain in the people's house?

The Prince, after evaluating the offer—money, protection, special privileges that would come after the next election—said he would see what he could do.

In the next few days, the confession video would turn up out of nowhere, with witnesses who could authenticate it. The police would suddenly find evidence once thought lost in storage, and a detective fired long ago would emerge to explain why it had been buried. The car rental company would, after much effort, discover the missing records in an unmarked box in a spare office.

And the beauty of it was that none of this would be traceable back to him. There would be suspicions but no proof. You never wanted to be seen as the blackmailer, only as someone who could help you find those with grudges.

And the Prince, of course, would carefully gather evidence of this hit job by the politician's enemies. More investment.

In this age, information was the most valuable commodity, and the Prince was the ultimate merchant of information. He knew how to find it, hide it, bury it, unearth it, fake it, disguise it, prove it, spin it out of thin air, craft it into glittering jewels—it was both his blade and his shield, his superpower and his bread and butter. Wielding it, he played general off against politician, revolutionary against strongman, old empire against new, and above all, he became rich.

So long as he was master of the information realm, the Prince needed to heed the pleasure of no one.

Something more personal was reserved for the second half of the Prince's day.

The upload from Elli's husband, which would take almost two days, was halfway complete.

As the bits trickled in, the Prince sifted through them, looking for glimmers of himself.

The Prince didn't consider himself an easily tempted man. A man who made a living by exploiting the weaknesses of others knew better than any the dangers of indulging his appetites.

His liaison with Elli Krantz, therefore, surprised even the Prince himself.

He could acquit himself only with the excuse that he had given in not to any temptations of the flesh, but of the soul.

At first he had not found her particularly interesting: a minor artist, simply another investment in his portfolio. Her value was different in degree from that of a content farm or pig-butchering pen, but not in kind. One didn't—or at least *he* didn't—particularly feel the desire to become intimate with another investment account.

But then he went to one of her dream gatherings on a whim and found in her art something he had not known he craved: understanding.

Since his earliest memories, he had hated how others looked at him and thought they knew who he was. Whether it was during his childhood hopping around Southeast Asia and Europe, or at boarding school in Switzerland, or in college in the US, strangers, people with power, people who knew nothing about him at all, would confidently declare that they understood him. Ah, they would say, you must be caught between your father's people and your mother's people, neither this nor that. This sense of division, of in-betweenness, must be the central conflict in your life, the key to unlocking who you are.

And then, satisfied that they knew his story, they would dismiss him and move on.

He would be left feeling powerless.

So, he worked hard to take power back. He would not allow the superficiality of others to bind him. He looked beneath the surface, learned the real stories of the powerful, wrote them down, gathered proof so that the stories could be substantiated—until he could exert power over them, could render *them* powerless. Their ignorance drove his search for knowledge. The symmetry pleased him immensely.

But in that dream with Elli . . . he felt *seen*. What a cliché that was, but that was precisely how he felt. In the darkness of that theater, on the verge of sleep and wakefulness, she had made him see that he was the hero of a story, a grand epic that was so much more interesting than any story others could have told about him. He could see that she understood him, saw the grandness of his soul.

He reached out to her then, inviting her to dream with him, alone.

And she had said yes, as he knew she would. She had no choice.

Since then, he had dreamed so much with her. Long solo sessions where he could command all her attention, during which she was utterly devoted to his story. It was better than sex, mere carnal pleasure; this was about the spirit, about the true shape of his own life.

He could not be as uninhibited or vulnerable with anyone else, nor did he want to be. With her, he was an open book, because only by sharing all of himself could she help him live his dreams. With her help, he was magnificent.

Sometimes, it seemed that only the dreams were real, and the rest the mere in-between. In those moments, he had to admit that he had come to depend on her, was addicted to her really. It was what he believed people meant when they said they were in love.

The Prince looked and looked, but found nothing.

There was too much data for him to search through everything personally; his AI had to do the bulk of the work. The Prince didn't trust machines nearly to the degree Victor did, but he recognized that there were times when a dispassionate algorithm modeled on the best parts of him would be better than his distraught self.

His task was made somewhat easier because he didn't need to look through Elli's AI. The neuromesh data—when it eventually arrived—would be encrypted and keyed to Elli's authorization. Victor said it would be possible to decrypt it, though it would take time. The Prince didn't expect to find much there. He had, after all, watched Elli lobotomize her AI after each dream session. (He was obsessed with her, but he wasn't stupid.)

Victor had mused that perhaps they could ask if the husband also had authorization over Elli's AI, which would render the decryption unnecessary. The Prince had laughed the suggestion away—the idea that a woman like Elli, with all her secrets and untellable stories and shameful truths, would allow her husband to have access to her personal AI was too ridiculous to even deserve a rebuttal. He had told Victor to stop being lazy and just do the work.

The rest of the data, however, he made his AI go through with a fine-tooth comb. He wasn't sure what he expected, but as he waited impatiently for the computer to do its job, he began to imagine private vlogs that she hid from her husband, in which she referred obliquely to the Prince's power over her (he hoped she would speak of him with admiration, but he admitted that disgust was also a possibility, and was ready to be amused by it); or maybe journal entries written as romans à clef, in which she gushed like a schoolgirl over the magical hours she spent in his company, guiding him through his dreamscape, that vast country of incomparable beauty; or maybe a practice dream session in which she subconsciously or intentionally relived one of their private sessions her AI was forbidden from remembering; or maybe videos, photos, sound clips of him—taken in secret and against his instructions, but mementos indicating that she valued those hours as much as he did. . . .

He found none of those things. Not even the most obscure, indirect, roundabout, hidden hint of a reference. The Prince didn't exist at all in her data. There was, in short, nothing to show that she cared about him.

His face burned. She had enticed him into these silly romantic daydreams, made him weak and vulnerable.

The Prince had found out about her betrayal so quickly only because of an accident.

Elli had picked the week after their latest dream together to disappear. He might not have felt the urge to see her for another month, two months even.

She had sent a brief message to the tour planner to cancel the prep meeting on Saturday, the day after her disappearance. However, the tour planner's AI had decided that the cancellation message didn't conform to its behavioral profile for Elli, especially as the message contained no suggestion for a rescheduled time, and asked for confirmation. By then, Elli was gone, and the lack of confirmation led the AI to conclude that the original cancellation message had been an opportunistic impersonation scam, a dipfake, and that the tour planning session would go on as scheduled.

So, when Elli failed to show up for the session, the news that she had vanished blew up, and the Prince's datahounds alerted him. Without that overzealous bit of neuromesh treating the real Elli as a mirage, he might not have found out about Elli's disappearance for a few more days, giving her a chance to get away completely.

How galling! He had shared his deepest, grandest dreams with Elli, *trusted* her. And she had not understood how special his attention was, how inconceivably rare and valuable. He had given her his true story and, therefore, allowed her to have power over him.

She knew secrets about him that no one else knew. Where did she write them down? Did she gather evidence? Had she prepared proof? Was she planning to use his story against him? Maybe she was now thinking of *him* as an investment—the provoking thought made him see red.

But more than the danger, he was incensed by the fact that she had dared to run away, to leave him behind. By revealing her true feelings, that act of betrayal had corrupted his dreams, made them worthless.

He would have to make her remedy that.

TEN

The upload took all of Tuesday and part of Wednesday. Piers spent most of the time nervously pacing back and forth, checking the progress bar at every turn to be sure it wasn't stuck.

Julia, on the other hand, used the time to learn more about Elli.

Born and raised in rural Lehigh Valley, Pennsylvania, Elli Krantz became one of the first practitioners in the experimental art of vivid dreaming shortly after college. Some of her early work generated a lot of buzz due to an association with conspiracy theory movements, which became much more muted in her later output. Eventually, she settled into a kind of mid-level fame, wherein she consistently sold out on tours but didn't command the kind of frenzied fan enthusiasm required for real stardom.

Elli had meticulously maintained an archive of commentary and reviews about her art. After Talos pulled out a representative selection, Julia watched flipclips and long-form videos, read multitexts and monostreams, immersed herself in 360-degree fusion visions of vivid dream gatherings.

From the commentary, she began to gain a sense of the appeal of dreaming together with an oneirofex. Collective dreams were nothing like the individual dream she had had. Socially evolved, our minds were intensely attuned to the moods and emotions of those around us, and collective sentience, wherein multiple brains reflected and amplified the trickles of one another's emotions, moods, sentiments into a grand, coherent torrent, was an essential element of our experience of consciousness. Homo sapiens have always sought collective sentience, sharing stories around smoky fires in shadowy caves, waiting with bated breath in concert halls and theaters, gazing together into the unknown in temples and cathedrals.

While she didn't dream with Elli's egolet again, she studied the egolet in detail. With Piers's help, she cleared the furniture from the living room. ("No, no, I don't mind," Piers had said. "I'm driving myself crazy. This will at least make me feel like I'm doing something useful.") She then had Talos display the egolet's neuromesh in fusion vision. Much as she had done earlier with the HELM, Julia plumbed the egolet, trying to understand its oddities as well as her apprehension regarding it.

Every few hours, Piers interrupted his anxious pacing to call Detective Yoachim, who was in charge of the investigation, for updates. Yoachim told Piers that they had gotten hundreds of calls, but most had turned out to be false leads. Julia speculated that even if the police were pursuing promising angles, they weren't likely to share them with Piers, but she kept the thought to herself.

Twice a day, the police drove by the house. They didn't stop, but merely slowed down as they cruised around the cul-de-sac, before speeding away in a silent huff.

The upload was complete just past Wednesday noon. Ahead of schedule.

The Prince called to confirm receipt.

"You're certain you've given me everything?"

"Yes, I'm sure," said Piers. "I've given you everything I can find:

photos, videos, immersion streams, practice sessions, whatever is on her drives. You even have our wedding video."

"Very good. I hope, for Elli's sake, that you're telling the truth."

"Let me talk to her!"

"I may let you do that after I've verified that you've given me what I want."

"No, right now!"

The Prince hung up.

The idea that the Prince had Elli was growing ever more doubtful in Julia's mind. But how could she get Piers's hopes up without *proof*?

Piers put his phone down and stormed outside without saying a word.

Julia went to the window and saw that he was digging a hole in the backyard. He worked furiously, slamming his shovel into the earth like a lance. When the hole was large enough, he went into the shed, retrieved a small bundle that was Frankie's body, and laid it gently down in the grave.

She looked away. To watch felt like an intrusion.

The Prince called again in the afternoon.

"Get out of your house now," he said.

Piers, after a few seconds of shocked silence, managed, "Why?"

"You're going to be arrested. The police have already tipped off the press. In another hour, your house will be surrounded by reporters, and it will be too late."

"What are you talking about?"

"You've not given me what I want. I need you to be free to help me find what she has hidden. Goodbye."

"No! Wait!"

The Prince hung up.

Piers stared at the phone in disbelief.

"I need you to know something," Julia said. "He doesn't have her."

"What?" His expression was a mix of hope, confusion, rage, and doubt.

"He doesn't need you to find what Elli has hidden; he needs you to find Elli."

"How do you know that?"

"I promise I'll explain," Julia said. "But later. You have to get out of the house right now."

He stared at her. She was asking him to upend his life completely. If he ran now, he would confirm every suspicion the police had about him, become a fugitive. Did he trust her enough?

"To find Elli?" he asked. "You're sure?"

"Yes." There was no hesitation in her voice.

He nodded. "Then I'd better get moving. Will you come with me? I need you if I'm to find her."

"Of course," she said. It should scare her, to be on the run again, to have to hide from the police. Nick would be furious, she thought. She was surprised by how easily she made the decision.

"Elli's suitcases are in the hallway closet," he said. "Take whatever you want."

She was already moving. "Pack lightly. Let's meet in the garage in twenty minutes. We'll start by going to my place and figure out the next steps."

Inside the garage, Piers opened the rear left door to his Acura MDX and threw a carry-on roller onto the empty backseat.

Julia was already in the passenger seat.

"Where's your luggage?"

"Got it all right here." She patted the backpack in her lap.

He stared at her, dumbfounded.

"Isn't that the same bag you came here with? You've just been waiting here the whole time?"

"No. I've been packing."

"What are you talking about?"

"Not now," she said. Then, gesturing toward the roller bag in the back, "What do you have in there?"

"Clothes, toothbrush, ID, cash, my computer"— He stopped at her expression. "It's not like I've been a fugitive before."

"It's fine," she said. "Some of what you're bringing is useful. But you need help."

She went into the house and returned with a duffel bag. Unzipping it, she showed him that she had already put into it a few trash bags and a light blanket, rolled up into a tight bundle. "Sleeping comfortably when you're on the run is your top priority," she said.

"Is this because you used to—" He stopped, looking embarrassed.

She ignored the unfinished question. "Don't carry your laptop," she said. "It's too bulky. A phone with fusion vision glasses will be much better. You should take these glasses I found in Elli's studio."

"I'm really not very good with them—"

She didn't let him finish. "You have to learn a lot of new things on the run."

She emptied his suitcase onto the garage floor and helped him repack what was necessary into the duffel.

"What did *you* pack?" Piers asked.

She unzipped her backpack and showed Piers: toiletries, a change of clothes, rolled-up plastic sheets, a thin blanket (folded tightly), some energy bars, two bottles of water, various other gear and electronics that he didn't know the names for—except for what looked to be a dozen phones.

"What are those?" He pointed at the phones.

"I buy used phones from thrift stores and online. Handy for moments like this."

"Handy how?"

"It'll be clear soon. Give me the burner that you used when you came to my place."

He handed her the burner. She turned it off and put it in her backpack.

"We'll hold on to this for a bit because we can use it to throw them off our trail. Your real phone, on the other hand, can't be used again. We might as well destroy it." She held out her hand.

Piers clutched his real phone tightly. "But practically all my life is on there. Can't I just keep it in airplane mode the whole time?"

"I already had Talos image it, so your data is safe." She patted the backpack. "There's no way to make that thing totally safe if you ever turn it on, and if we left it unpowered, it would just be deadweight."

Reluctantly, he unlocked his phone and handed it to her. After tapping in a series of commands, she handed it back. "You need to confirm the secure wipe and then crush it."

Once the phone was done erasing itself, Piers opened the driver's-side door and dropped it under the front wheel. He let out a long exhale. A part of himself was literally being left behind.

"Let's go," she said. "Follow my directions and drive carefully. Never more than five miles above the speed limit."

He backed up over the phone and out of the garage.

ELEVEN

"Tell me how you know that he doesn't have Elli."

Julia bit her bottom lip—she didn't want to hurt him, but there was no choice.

There were gaps in Elli's egolet, Julia explained.

It was not uncommon for there to be holes—absence of training data for certain periods or places—in a personal AI. While many in Silicon Valley advocated "total monitoring for total improvement," few ordinary individuals were willing to have their personal AIs monitor and record literally every moment of their lives—bathroom, bedroom, deceit, embarrassment, pride, guilt. Many were the reasons why someone, anyone, might wish to exclude some moments from their second brain.

As much as the cloud AI subscription companies disliked leaving aspects of their customers' lives unmonitored, they also understood that some form of control over their own surveillance by the subscriber was essential to the technology's adoption.

But many of the lacunae in Elli's egolet didn't fit that kind of user choice. There were no records of Elli shutting off her personal AI during these times; there was just no data. This seemed to suggest a systematic "unlearning" rather than "absence of learning." That is, it didn't seem so much a deliberate choice to prevent the AI from learning during certain times or in certain places, as a deliberate choice to, after learning had already occurred, erase such memories.

Piers focused on the road and listened.

Out of curiosity, Julia had correlated the timestamps on these holes with other data to see if they followed a pattern. One immediately revealed itself: each absence of training data was associated with a time when Elli's dream deck was in operation; moreover, all such instances had taken place when Elli was traveling away from home.

The best explanation of the evidence, Julia went on, was that Elli had, for years, been conducting vivid dream sessions in secret away from home. As her personal AI was necessary for vivid dreaming, she couldn't just turn it off. Instead, she had, after each such session, carefully made her AI forget that it had just woven a dream.

Piers's face grew pale, but he continued to listen without interrupting.

Such secret dream gatherings must have been small—Elli couldn't possibly have hidden a large crowd. In fact, Julia believed that these were one-on-one dreams. This was confirmed when she checked the power usage history of Elli's dream deck. The more cephaloscripts a dream deck had to process simultaneously, the more power the deck needed. The amount of power used by the dream deck during the last three such sessions—that was as far back as the deck's logs went—was consistent with processing a single cephaloscript.

This was why Elli's egolet had been so prepared to guide Julia through a solo dream—its neuromesh had been trained on one-on-one sessions, even if it had no memory of weaving such dreams.

The egolet's choice of a dream based on the idea of the dreamer as the hero of their own story was likely also influenced by Elli's real-life one-on-one dream partner. Julia's choice of the singular *partner* here was deliberate.

A partner who didn't otherwise exist in Elli's AI's memory at all.

Piers didn't even flinch at this. He had intuited what Julia was going to say.

The inexorable logic of Julia's deductions led to one conclusion: Elli had been meeting with the Prince in secret to dream with him.

She has . . . me.

Finally, Julia explained, she had run an analysis of the Prince's video of Elli against Elli's egolet and found a mismatch. The two were, to put it simply, maximally divergent.

"What does that mean?" Piers asked.

People behaved differently in different contexts, Julia explained. Elli, in the video from the Prince, had behaved so differently from Elli's egolet that Talos found it unusual. There were two possible explanations: one, Elli deliberately acted in the kidnapping video in a way that it would be picked up by AI analysis as maximally divergent from her AI's memories of her; two, the Prince's video of Elli was a fake that had been generated from data specifically removed from Elli's AI.

"The missing times," Piers said, understanding.

Explanation one required Elli to anticipate that someone would perform such an analysis so as to calibrate her own behavior in the video. Not impossible, but quite implausible. Explanation two, on the other hand, only required that the Prince generate the kidnapping video using his private footage of Elli, which happened to correspond to the parts of her life she'd deleted, parts spent in his company.

"Thank you," said Piers, his voice unsteady.

Julia could only imagine his anguish.

Piers had learned over the years that it was not easy to be in love with a great artist.

Elli was a good spouse. She was affectionate and supportive, shouldering half of the burdens of marriage. The managing partners of his law firm liked her, as did his friends. She made sure he knew how important he was to her.

But Piers knew that he wasn't Elli's greatest love.

A child of divorce, Piers had grown up mistrusting romance. His parents, a nurse and a musician, had been head over heels in love. It was a whirlwind romance worthy of poetry and song. They wanted to consume each other, to possess and be possessed, to merge into one, until it was impossible to tell where one ended and the other began.

The fire lasted eight months before burning out. Desperate, they had gotten married in the hopes of rekindling that flame. When that failed, they turned to the magic of making babies. Three children, two lawyers, and countless bitter fights later, they finally admitted that yes, they were clichés, and accepted defeat.

With that model in mind, Piers had not believed himself capable of falling in love. He had gone into the law not because of a passion for justice, but a craving for stability and dependability—his father, who vanished from their lives after the divorce, had provided none. He pictured himself as one of those flat characters in a Dickens novel, a law clerk or a tutor, earning a respectable living at a boring job, putting a little away every month for retirement, a bundle of nervous tics and quirky habits, living by himself with perhaps a cat or two for company, the supporting cast for other people's stories.

But then, on a whim, he went to a dream gathering by Elli.

Elli was unlike anyone else in his life. She simply glowed. Like all great performers, she channeled the energy of the crowd and reflected it back at them, transporting them to an otherworldly realm. But more than that, she made them feel that they, each of them individually, *mattered.*

Piers could not get her out of his mind. He went to another gathering, and then a third. He flew to other cities to follow her on tour. She had awakened something in him, a dream he had not known he craved.

No longer feeling like a supporting character, he wrote to her. And to his surprise, she wrote back. Even more improbably, the messages eventually led to an actual date.

She got him to tell his own story.

From the very start, he understood that their relationship would be unbalanced. Her art was what made him fall in love with her, but her art would also keep her from ever becoming *his*. To do what she did, Elli had to put her soul into her performances. Her grandest passion would always be outside their marriage—she was in love with Dream, that excavation of the reality beyond reality, where Truth lived, casting a mere shadow into our sublunary realm.

Yes, he was okay with that, he told her. He did not want to consume her, to possess her, to merge with her. He would love her steadily, dependably, see her off as she explored the stormy seas of the collective unconscious, and wait patiently for her return. He would be her Ithaca.

This, he realized, was the mythical prototype for the kind of lawyer he wanted to be: a safe harbor of order against the vicissitudes of random life. For his clients, his family, the woman he loved, he would be exactly that. Ithaca was not flat; it was heroic.

And so, he dared to ask her.

Yes, I will, yes, she had said. And his joy at hearing those words had been indescribable.

It had not been easy to keep his promise. Jealousies, insecurities, disappointments—these were the dark shadows of love, the real villains in a romance, who could never be wholly defeated but only held at bay. But he had worked at it, persisted, strived to be the story he wanted to tell. For her and also for himself.

His greatest love was Elli, but Elli's greatest love was her art. Neither of them would betray their loves, not for anyone.

Faith, patience, love.

He would not stop now.

"It doesn't matter," he said.

Out of the corner of his eye, he saw the way Julia looked at him.

"I don't know why she dreamed with him," he said. "But I won't let that come between us right now. If he doesn't have her, then we have to find her before he does. The answers can wait."

Julia marveled at the lawyer. For someone trained to follow the rules, to obey authority (and to benefit, for the most part, when it was exercised), the idea of being a fugitive, an outlaw, must be terrifying. Yet, here he was, plunging headlong into the unknown, all for the love of a woman who had lived another life in secret.

Julia directed Piers to Carre Crossing Station and had him park in a spot out of the sight line of the security cameras.

"You should probably say goodbye to your car now," she told him while wiping down every surface that might hold her prints. "I don't think we'll be seeing it for a while."

She bought their tickets on the train with cash. They rode all the way into the city and then back out to Paine. By the time they got off the second train, it was getting dark.

Julia connected her tensor bank to the public Wi-Fi at the station and checked the news. "They haven't raided your house yet." It was long after when the Prince had claimed things would blow up.

"Something doesn't feel right," Piers said. "Let's hold off on going to your place."

They found a coffee shop. As soon as they entered, Julia nudged Piers toward the couch by the corridor leading to the restrooms so that his face would never show up on the security cameras. She went to the counter and brought back coffee and pastries.

She logged onto the Wi-Fi with her tensor bank, tethered one of the old phones to it, and handed it to Piers.

"I've imaged your phone onto this. So long as you get online only through Talos, you should be untrackable."

They browsed and waited.

It took two more hours before Talos alerted Julia to a local newsjinn report:

**RAGING FIRE DESTROYS
MULTIMILLION-DOLLAR HOME IN CARRE**

> CARRE, MA—A fierce blaze has destroyed a multimillion-dollar home on Carmichael Lane this evening.
>
> Emergency services received an anonymous call reporting the fire at approximately 6:00 PM. By the time firefighters arrived on the scene, the house was "already beyond saving," according to fire officials. Fortunately, no injuries or fatalities have been reported.
>
> The Carre Police Department confirmed that the house belonged to Elli Krantz, a prominent oneirofex, or "dream weaver," and her husband, Piers Neri, a lawyer. Elli Krantz has been missing since last Wednesday. Neither Krantz nor Neri were at home during the fire.
>
> Authorities are investigating the cause of the fire.

Julia slid next to Piers. He turned to her and was about to speak when she looked him in the eye and held a finger against her lips. Then she slipped him the computing stick with the article on the screen.

Piers's eyes widened; Julia leaned in and whispered into his ear, "Don't react. As calmly as possible, pack up your things."

However, instead of complying, Piers turned his new phone to her, showing her his messaging account. There was a single message from the Prince: "Now you see what I'm capable of. Find Elli for me, or else."

"We can't talk in here," Julia said.

Once on the sidewalk, Julia pulled Piers close to her so that they strolled along like a couple, faces turned toward each other. She made sure that she was on the outside so that Piers's face would be hidden from any cameras in the shops they passed.

"The fire—" "How did the Prince—"

"You go first," whispered Piers.

"He obviously has some very dangerous people working for him," said Julia, as an involuntary shudder ran down her spine. After a pause, she added, "I guess we already knew that, given what happened to Frankie."

Piers was surprisingly calm, considering he had just lost his house and everything in it. "The good news is that he doesn't want to kill me, at least not right now. He needs me to find Elli for him."

"He might not kill *you*, but that doesn't mean he won't kill *me*."

"He doesn't know you're with me," said Piers. "And we'll have to keep it that way. We can't go to your place, in case they're watching the building, expecting me to go there for help like I did on Monday."

"We don't know if they ever figured out who you went to see." Julia bit her bottom lip as she thought. "It's too late to do anything about that now, so we'll just have to do our best to keep him from figuring out I'm with you." A new thought struck her. "I still don't understand why he burned down your house."

"To scare me. Show me that he's capable of violence."

"I don't think that's it." Julia tried to recall the sequence of events. "He already tried to scare you . . . called you again . . . had you upload all of Elli's data . . . The data. That must be it. Once we had given him all of Elli's data, he wanted to destroy the originals so he has the only copy."

"Why?"

"I'm not sure." Julia frowned, concentrating. "I can think of a few possibilities. One is that he believes what Elli supposedly took from him is in the data, but hidden. So he doesn't want anyone else to have access to it."

"I can see that. What else?"

"Maybe he thinks the data contains clues as to where Elli went, and he wants to find Elli before you do by keeping you from them."

Piers looked horrified.

"Don't worry. I have a copy of everything we uploaded." Julia patted her backpack. "What did you think I was doing while we were packing? I'm a digital pack rat."

"I can't tell you how grateful I am."

As they continued to shuffle down the sidewalk, away from the busier town center, the Prince's plan gradually came into focus.

"He's trying to have it both ways," said Piers. "One, he wants to see if he can find Elli on his own, from the data. Two, in case that fails, he wants to have me find Elli for him. That means he must be tracking me. His message to me—"

"Don't worry. As long as you access the account only through Talos, he can't locate you just because you read one of his messages. But do be careful. If you start writing back, you risk revealing your location inadvertently. I wouldn't make correspondence with him a habit."

"I have no intention of answering him." Piers gave a bitter laugh. "He's also made it impossible for me to go to the police. Think about it: while the police were watching, my house burned down, destroying all possible evidence related to Elli's disappearance. Conveniently, I vanished at the same time. Even if I hadn't been the primary suspect before, I certainly am now."

Julia nodded. That certainly did appear to be one of the Prince's goals.

"He's got me backed into a corner. There's nothing for me to do other than try to find Elli before he does."

"Agreed," said Julia. "But we shouldn't try to leave town tonight—it's actually harder to hide from the surveillance cameras when there are fewer cars. Better wait until the morning and hide in rush-hour traffic."

"But where are we going to spend the night? The last commuter rail train is done. We're stuck in Paine."

"I've got an idea."

Julia guided Piers to a spot across the street from the Bayside YMCA. Beyond the wide parking lot was a small, secluded wood.

"That copse used to be a popular camping site for the homeless until the HOA back there complained, and the town drove them off and put up new cameras," Julia said, pointing out the long rectangular boxes mounted on poles at the back of the parking lot.

"We don't want to show up on those cameras, do we?"

"No, we don't," Julia agreed. "So let's fix that."

She backed up a few steps until she was hidden from the road. Piers followed suit. After putting on her fusion vision glasses, she opened her backpack and took out a silver oblong about the size of an egg, which gleamed in the faint glow of the streetlamp to their right. This was Puck, her customized morpho drone, which she tinkered with all the time. What the little shape-shifting robot lacked in raw power, it more than made up for in versatility.

From a pocket in her backpack, she retrieved four thick metal rings and slipped them on her thumbs and index fingers. These electromagnetic rings, the heart of the mixed-reality wavium interface, would work together with the fusion vision glasses to translate her finger gestures into movement commands for Puck and, in turn, translate the drone's accelerometer and motion-sensor readings into haptic feedback.

She snapped her fingers, and the top of the silver oblong irised open, revealing four unfolding propellers. In the glasses' mixed-reality view, Julia could see the rings on her finger glow with a bright white light. She twisted the thumb rings, and one by one, the propellers began to spin.

With a gentle *whirr*, Puck lifted into the air.

The fusion vision glasses showed her the view from Puck's camera. She loved this part of working with a morpho drone; with her body's natural homuncular flexibility helping her to embody the drone's chassis, it felt as though she were gliding through the air herself.

Slowly, she guided the buzzing drone to approach the surveillance camera on the left from behind. With a faint *bump*, the drone struck the side of the camera body. Softly, oh-so-softly, she curled her right index finger so that Puck pushed gently on the camera. Fraction of an inch by fraction of an inch, the drone shifted the camera to point a few degrees to the right.

Then she guided Puck to approach the camera on the other side and repeated the procedure, except this time, she nudged the camera to point a few degrees to the left.

Talos highlighted the cameras' fields of view in her fusion vision glasses. Julia was satisfied that she had created a blind spot a few meters across in the middle of the wood, visible on neither camera.

"That's where we'll stay tonight."

In the middle of the safe strip in the wood, Julia unrolled her plastic sheet on the grass, spread her blanket on top, and set down her backpack at one end to serve as a pillow.

Piers was impressed. "You really know what you're doing."

"Yeah, I guess," she said without elaborating. She dug in Piers's duffel bag and brought out the trash bags. "You'll have to make do with these."

Piers took the bags, looking more than a little lost. "When should we get up?" There was a note of incipient panic in his voice.

Julia tried to be compassionate, but she was exhausted. "Four thirty a.m. That's when the employees arrive. I suggest you sleep right away because we'll have a long day tomorrow. Good night."

She laid her head on her backpack, turned away, and closed her eyes.

TWELVE

The worst thing about my job, reflected Victor, is my boss.

He took another sip of champagne as he looked out the window at the stunning view of the harbor. He had gotten himself this luxurious suite at the Boston Harbor Hotel as a treat (and compensation) for himself, and he enjoyed billing it to his expense account. His boss owed this to him.

Erratic, arrogant, controlling, the Prince was all those things and more. Victor hated giving good advice only to be ignored, which happened too often.

Take this absurd operation he was leading now. Victor had no idea why the Prince had insisted that he drop everything and fly to Boston to look for a missing woman. Worse, he wasn't allowed to look for the woman using his methods, methods that were logical and effective, but had to go through a convoluted scheme of intimidation and surveillance. And so, Victor, the man who was in charge of all the Prince's operations in North America, had spent the weekend following a pasty, middle-aged lawyer around like some sad-sack divorce investigator.

And then, when he had caught the lawyer sneaking out to another town, the Prince had told him to forget it, berating him for taking the initiative to pin down exactly who the lawyer had gone to see.

The humiliation! He had wanted to fly to the other side of the world and give the Prick—oops, shouldn't have let that out—a good punch in his smug face. If the man weren't paying Victor so generously, he would have quit on the spot.

He took a deep breath, straining to tamp down his irritation. Look at the pretty lights and the beautiful yachts, he told himself. Someday, I'll own one too. This is just paying the dues.

Again, he swapped to the tracking screen on his phone: still no little blinking dot.

Be patient, he told himself.

The Prince had not explained why the woman was so important, but listening between the lines, Victor had decided that the woman was likely blackmailing him. That was why the Prince was so concerned about getting his hands on her data.

(As to how an American woman living on the other side of the globe from the Prince could be blackmailing him, Victor had no idea. He almost admired her, beating the master at his trade. . . .)

At the moment, the Prince was pushing him to crack the encryption on the woman's AI. This was a task Victor rather enjoyed. Victor far preferred working with machines to working with people. Machines were reliable—they didn't have whims, didn't wake you up in the middle of the night with vague directions, didn't fail you because they were distracted with their dating profiles. (He still couldn't believe the quality of his local crew—some of them were such *idiots*! But that was the best he could scrape together with so little notice.) Even when machines failed, they failed in ways that made sense.

People, on the other hand, constantly disappointed him. The Prince had told him to keep an eye on the lawyer in order to find the missing woman. But he couldn't tail the lawyer with his incompetent Boston crew. They didn't even seem to know how to stay off cameras!

Had he ordered them to keep the lawyer under surveillance, they would have drawn the cops' attention within the first day.

The idiots were unteachable. The only way to use them was to have them take risks that he would not. After all, they knew nothing about him or the Prince, and they could be discarded like a gecko's tail if anything went wrong.

So he had resorted to tracking the lawyer through his phone. Modern humans treated their phones like extra organs, and Victor was sure that trusting the lawyer's phone to betray him was a better plan than trusting his useless human helpers.

But then the lawyer vanished from the cell phone tracking data, and he had found the lawyer's phone crushed in the garage when he and his crew raided the house for any missing data and set it on fire. For now, at least, Victor had no idea where the lawyer had gone.

Victor imagined calling the Prince with this news and felt every muscle in his body tensing. Painful.

No. He'd better keep this to himself and make up some lie if the Prince called.

Victor reminded himself that he really shouldn't worry. There were more machines that he could trust. The lawyer was sloppy and stupid, and it was only a matter of time before he turned on his burner phone, thinking himself safe.

He swapped back to the tracking screen again.

THIRTEEN

With made-up names, they signed in as trial guests at the Y to use the shower. After coffee and breakfast at a Dunks (Piers hadn't been able to get much sleep in the woods), Piers and Julia returned to the rail station. Joining the morning commuter rush, they rode the crowded train into South Station, where they switched to the Silver Line bus to Logan airport.

"Why?" a confused Piers asked. "You can't possibly be thinking of flying out of here. They must have an alert on me."

"Of course not. But this is the best place to find a car that won't be missed for a few days."

"Ah." Piers grimaced. "I'm sorry I asked."

They got off the bus and entered the central parking garage. Julia made a beeline for the section closest to Terminal E, international departures.

"Why here?"

"If a car is parked here, the owner is likely gone for a while."

Instead of taking the elevator, Julia slipped into the stairwell nearby and climbed quickly, taking three steps at a time. Alarmed, Piers strained to catch up but soon fell behind. By the time he finally made it to the top, the lawyer was panting.

"Why are we—" He caught his breath and tried again. "Why are we in such a hurry?"

"I need my morning workout. Can't think until I get the blood pumping."

"Talk to me first next time, please. We have to *communicate*."

"I told you I'm not good with people."

After sitting down on a bench next to a bank of vending machines, Julia took out Puck and put on the wavium rings and fusion vision glasses. Soon, the buzzing little drone was floating along the garage ceiling, scanning the parked cars as it passed over them.

Piers glanced around nervously, hoping no one would pass by.

Sensing his fidgeting, Julia said, "No one is going to think there's anything weird about a woman sitting here with fusion vision glasses on. Maybe I'm clearing out my work messages, or maybe I'm trying for a new high score in *Endless Climb*. You, on the other hand, do look suspicious, standing there with nothing to do."

Piers took out the phone Julia had given him and pretended to look at it.

Julia drew a circle in the air with her right pinkie, sharing her view through Puck's camera onto Piers's phone.

"Thanks," said Piers. The sight of parked cars passing by on the screen was calming.

"See, I'm communicating."

"What are you looking for?"

"I'm just skimming license plates. Talos will process them to pick out the most promising prospects."

"You mean the best cars to steal."

"Say that louder, will you? We need to summon the airport police to help."

Piers lowered his voice. "What is Talos supposed to look for?"

"Cars that parked in the last day or so and whose owners might be away for a week or more."

"How can you get that from a license plate? You can't even look up the registration. By law, that's all secured information."

Julia smirked. "By law? What's that?"

"Don't."

"Fine. I'll explain. You're right that the RMV site won't give you anything useful based on a license plate, but other databases will. You just have to know where to look."

"You mean data stolen by hackers."

"Maybe. But the trouble with stolen data is that you can't trust it. The databases I'm talking about are based on public information. People pose with their cars all the time and post those pictures and flipclips to their profiles. If you scrape these platforms, you can build up a database of faces to names to license plates. You can get even more precision if you cross-reference with other information like location, time, traffic, and so on."

Julia took off her fusion vision glasses. While Puck began to drift back toward her on autopilot, she scrolled through the growing list of potential target cars.

"Once you have the owners, it's just a matter of mining their social media streams. You get everything: vacations, business trips, conference speaking schedules. Do you want the nice Audi of the couple who left for their honeymoon in Spain on Monday? Or do you want the Tesla of the retired professor who went on a two-week spiritual retreat in Japan? Or maybe the Range Rover whose family is in Egypt and won't be back for a month?"

"You don't . . . care about hurting these people?"

Julia looked at him. "Of course I *care*. That's why I haven't picked one yet. Try to keep some perspective here. We have a psycho after Elli who's happy to slaughter cats and burn down houses. I'm trying to help you find her before the psycho does. And yes, I would like to minimize the harm along the way."

"Then let me help you," Piers said.

"By all means."

Piers accepted the tensor bank and scrolled through the choices, scrutinizing each one.

"This is our car."

Julia looked at the screen. It showed a black Cyon Zenith, an imported luxury sedan.

"Why this one?"

"Based on the info your AI pulled up, it's leased by a fintech company downtown. Three executives drove it here this morning and left for a sales trip in Asia. They won't return for another ten days. I certainly don't feel guilty about stealing from them. And they have the best insurance anyway."

"I saw it earlier," Julia said. "But what makes you think they'll just leave it here in parking? Won't someone from the company come by later to pick it up?"

"If you think that, you don't know how these companies work," Piers said. "No executive is going to let the engineers drive a corporate lease meant for the MBAs. Better to have it sit in a parking garage for a month than to sully it with peon sweat."

"Seems wasteful."

"One, they're not spending their own money, but the investors'. Two, there's nothing more important to them than marking and maintaining status. I know that kind of client well."

"Then you're right, we have our car." She put away the computing stick and held out a hand—Puck landed gently in her palm and retracted into its inert egg form.

Piers stood near the back door of the milky blue van parked next to the Zenith. He took out his burner phone and pretended to scrutinize its screen. From time to time, he "scrolled" invisible content with his thumb.

"You look pretty convincing, actually," Julia said. She was standing on the side of the blue van so that its bulk blocked her from the

Zenith completely. "If the lawyer thing doesn't work out, you can always make it as a lookout for car thieves."

"Hurry up. How long does it take to hot-wire a car?"

"No one 'hot-wires' cars anymore. That's not a thing except on bad TV."

"So how are you going make the car think we are authorized to drive it? Aren't the fobs all super secure now?"

"Fobs? Yeah, if this car used a fob, that would make my job a lot easier. In your zeal to confine the damage to corporate America and the insurance companies, you picked a really tough car to steal. This one is secured by biometrics."

"So what are you going to do?"

"I'm going to have a nice little chat with it."

Still out of the view of the Zenith, Julia took from her backpack a black pyramid about the size of a wallet, its triangular faces studded with antennas. She flicked a switch under it, and a faint electronic humming filled the air.

"Here we go."

Before Piers had a chance to say anything, Julia strode out from behind the van and approached the front of the Zenith, then crouched and set the pyramid on the ground between the front bumper and the wall of the parking garage.

"It's a jammer," Julia answered Piers's unspoken question. "The onboard AI on a newer car like this is constantly monitoring the area around the car, raising the alarm if the neuromesh detects suspicious behavior. I have to jam the car's radios to block the alarms."

With the jammer set, Julia reached under the bumper and felt around until she grabbed something, pulled it hard, and snapped it off with a loud crack.

"What did you just do?" a startled Piers asked.

Julia showed him a small plastic cube with a lens.

"This is one of the hazard cameras. It's meant to scan for napping cats and other driveway endangerments."

"Is that camera particularly dangerous?"

"It's just in a convenient location."

Julia extracted Puck again. This time, she rolled the metallic oblong between her palms, which caused it to elongate into a sixteen-inch-long worm. She set it down on the ground and caressed the smooth tubular body. Tiny legs sprouted from the tube, turning Puck into an oversized centipede.

"That's going to give me nightmares," Piers said, recoiling even though he was a car length away. "I've never seen a drone like that."

"I built it," Julia said, pride in every word. "Puck is one of a kind."

Constructed from polyply metals with origami microstructures, Puck could take on one of several preset forms, each specialized for a different set of tasks. By eschewing a rigid internal structure and minimizing the mass, Julia's design for the morpho drone deprived it of raw power but more than made up for that in mobility and flexibility. The centipede form was especially good for infiltration of structures and vehicles.

Julia crouched before the car and carefully inserted Puck into the hole left by the destroyed undercarriage camera. The drone slithered out of sight.

Just then, two men dragging suitcases came out of the elevator and headed down the ramp toward them.

Julia flattened herself on the floor. "Damn it!" There was nowhere to hide. If she got up now, it would look very suspicious.

Piers stepped into the men's view, holding the phone up to his ear.

"I don't know. . . . Yes, I took it in a month ago. . . . Can you repeat that?"

The approaching men looked at Piers with mild curiosity on their faces.

Still holding the phone to his ear, Piers turned and spoke to Julia, who was still prone on the ground. "Hey! The rep says you have to look for a diagnostic port. Do you know what she's talking about?"

Julia stuck her head under the car so that the passing men couldn't see her panicked expression. "Umm . . . what does the port look like?"

Piers spoke into the phone. "What does this port look like? . . . I have no idea! You guys made the car!"

The men passed by. Piers looked at them and rolled his eyes, pointing at the phone in exasperation. The men nodded at him sympathetically and went on.

"How much longer will *that* take? . . . Can't you do anything remotely? . . . "

Piers put the phone away.

"Good thinking there," whispered Julia as she got up from the ground.

"How much longer?" Piers whispered back.

"Not too much longer." Crouching, Julia put on her wavium rings and glasses and guided Puck deeper into the car. "I broke the camera to get into the ICAN bus—that's the car's internal network, which the onboard AI uses to control the lights and the cameras and do most of the driving. The wire that connects to the camera is just a dumb wire, but I can crawl through the conduit to get to the secure main computer."

Immersed in fusion vision, she tapped her fingers and drew various patterns in the air. A few cars drove by, looking for open spots, and the occasional traveler walked up or down the ramp, dragging suitcases. Piers continued his charade of talking to tech support to get his recalcitrant car to behave, and no one gave Julia a second glance.

The Zenith beeped twice.

"Done," Julia said. "I got us added as authorized drivers. *And* I took out all the phone-home triggers."

"Good timing. I've just about run out of complaints for customer support." Piers put the phone away and wiped his forehead.

"As a reward for your good work," said Julia, "you can drive the first leg."

He put his hand on the driver's-side door, which popped open silently. He slid into the soft leather seat, sighing at how comfortable it felt, and then pulled the door shut.

Julia tossed her backpack and Piers's duffel into the backseat and got into the passenger seat.

Piers gripped the wheel tightly. "I can feel the adrenaline crash coming. I need a nap."

"Soon. We still have to do one more thing."

As Piers approached the home improvement store, Julia activated four burner phones as well as the old one Piers had used when he visited Julia on Monday.

"You are making it seem like I could be switching to any one of these phones," said Piers, understanding dawning. "Basically pretending to make the same mistake I made."

"Exactly. I told you your old burner would come in handy. Drive around the block. So long as you don't enter the parking lot, we won't be caught on their cameras."

She rolled down the car window and released Puck in its standard propeller form. Once the drone had landed on the roof of the home improvement store, she transformed it into a skittering six-legged spider. Slowly, she had the spider crawl onto one of the security cameras pointed at the parking lot from behind, and covered the lens with a thick wad of sticky gum.

"Their security AI will notice the blocked view right away, but it will probably take an hour before they send an everyfixit up there," Julia said. "You can go into the parking lot now."

She had Piers cruise the parking lot at a walking pace. As he approached a corner of the lot and slowed down, Julia put her hand on the door handle.

"Wait!" Piers said. He handed Julia a pack of print-and-stick tattoos. "You've only got one camera down. If they swing the other camera over to compensate, you'll be caught."

"I told you, these don't work," said Julia.

"I know they don't work technically," said Piers. "But that's not the only reason to wear them. If you end up getting caught on camera and are prosecuted, a good defense lawyer can point to the wavy lines on your face and argue that the video is AI-generated."

"How's that going to work?" said Julia. "Video from good security cameras is cryptographically authenticated."

"In court, they have to get an expert witness to testify to that, just like they need an eyewitness to authenticate footage from a noncertified camera. So long as there's something in the video that looks like an artifact, the defense can make the argument. Whether the jury buys the argument is another story. But at a minimum, this will force the prosecution to make more effort."

Julia nodded. Piers was a hacker too, just of a different system. It had been a while since she'd experienced this sense of camaraderie, of having someone else watch her back. It was nice.

She put on the tattoos, which made her cheeks look deformed. As soon as Piers stopped, she stepped out of the car. However, before leaving, she leaned in through the window. "Find a spot in the next row—be careful not to go past the middle of the lot, or the other camera will catch you."

Julia paced around the lot. From time to time, having made sure that no one was watching, she tossed one of the phones into the back of a truck or bend down and tape it under a rear bumper.

Finally, she returned to the Zenith. "Let's switch places. You can nap while I drive."

While the Zenith did most of the driving, Julia stepped on the gas and spun the wheel occasionally to pass other cars aggressively, swerving and leaning on the horn as she did so.

"I thought you didn't want to stand out," said Piers, gripping the armrest with white knuckles, all thoughts of napping forgotten.

"I have to drive like a proper Masshole," said Julia, "otherwise our car will stick out in the traffic data."

Her grin of utter delight made Piers doubt the sincerity of this explanation.

Three hours later, they arrived at Paxborough, one of the less popular tourist towns in the Berkshires of western Massachusetts.

"We'll put everything on my card," said Julia. "No one knows I'm helping you yet."

Piers saw the name on the card she used to book a last-minute Roamnest for the two of them.

"Lois Kee?" He looked at her questioningly.

Julia didn't answer right away as she drove them to the small Cape Cod cottage on a quiet back street and pulled into the driveway.

As soon as the car stopped, she said, without looking at him, "I'm always prepared to run. And I don't want to talk about it."

"All right," said Piers. Then, after a pause, he added, "I read Nick's case file for you, so I know some of what you went through."

She stiffened.

"I'm not going to pretend I know how you feel. I wish the world were better than it is. I just want you to know that I'm really glad you're here."

Julia had Piers wait in the foyer while she swept the rest of the short-term rental for hidden cameras.

A few minutes later, she returned, deeming the place safe. She got Talos onto the house Wi-Fi and told Piers that he could tether to Talos and browse safely.

"I'm taking the bedroom, and you can have the couch out here," Julia said. "I'm going to take a nap because I'm exhausted. You can do whatever you want as long as you don't go outside. We'll start looking for Elli after I wake up."

FOURTEEN

Julia didn't like to recall her early days as a runaway.

The hardest part was finding safe places to sleep and to keep clean. Thank God for online channels where the unhoused shared tips. She learned to see the telltale glint from security camera lenses, to sense the buzzing from patrolling security drones. She learned to look away from cameras and to wear masks that interfered with facial recognition. She learned to hide in libraries and office buildings near closing time so she could be locked in for the night. She learned dumpster diving and urban camping. Cemeteries, for example, were good places to camp during the warm months; people tended to avoid them at night.

But inevitably, she made mistakes, got taken advantage of, lost what few possessions she had, and found her teetering existence over the abyss ever more precarious.

One late autumn day, while she was contemplating which trash can on Boylston Street to dig through for supplies, she saw an incredible sight. A group of people, nearly a hundred in number, suddenly converged on the Bloom store and streamed in. A few in the flash mob pulled out laser pointers or flashlights that they aimed at the security cameras, blinding them. Others grabbed laptops, phones, or tablets from the display shelves, cut the security cords, and walked out. The staff of the Bloom store, following corporate policy, stood near the walls and did nothing.

Julia gaped.

A woman burst from the store, running fast. Hot on her heels was a small security drone, buzzing through the air as it tried to get a shot of her face.

Without even thinking, Julia took off her hoodie and ran up to the woman, swatting at the drone. When the drone fell to the ground, she draped the hoodie over the robot and stomped it until she heard the satisfying crunch of broken electronics.

"Thanks," said the woman. "Those things can be very annoying." She was in her twenties, her thick black hair pinned up inside the hood of her jacket, a wild grin on her warm brown face. She quirked a questioning brow at Julia.

"I hate cameras," said Julia, as though that explained everything.

"All right," the woman said. "But don't just stand there!" She pointed to her jacket pockets, bulging with new phones in their boxes. "Go grab something! Fuck Bloom. Fuck the rich!"

"What am I going to do with Bloom stuff?" Julia asked. "Aren't they all bricked if you steal them?"

The woman gave her a gentle push. "Grab something, and I'll show you what to do."

Her giddiness was infectious. Julia ran inside the store and grabbed a laptop, a metal slab so thin it weighed practically nothing, and ran back out.

The woman, who had already bundled up the remnants of the broken drone with Julia's hoodie, was waiting for her. They ran away from Boylston, turned down a side street, turned again, and soon vanished into the maze of narrow alleyways.

Within a few minutes, long before police sirens pierced the air around the Bloom store, the crowd had dispersed.

Sahima—the woman told Julia her name—took her to a warehouse by the docks, across the channel from the airport. Inside, Julia found a group of around two dozen people, some of whom she recognized from the flash mob on Boylston Street. Taking their haul out of backpacks and coat pockets, they stacked the goods neatly on shelves near the warehouse entrance: nearly a hundred phones and sensepins, fifty laptops, and twenty immersion headsets.

After setting down the stolen phones, Sahima dumped the broken pieces of the security drone into a bucket and set it aside. "There's bound to be some useful bits in there," she said by way of explanation. Then she frowned at Julia's old hoodie: it had been torn up by the dying drone. She looked back at Julia: dirty, cold, tired.

"Take care of her for me, Rachel," Sahima said to a large woman in a Patriots jersey.

The woman nodded and brought Julia to a room full of crates and bins filled with clothes. "Pick out whatever you like. The shower is over there if you want one. I'll go get you some food—how does chicken noodle soup sound?"

Julia looked around. The warehouse was run-down but clean, and under the cavernous ceiling, temporary partitions that didn't reach all the way up divided the space into a warren of smaller rooms, like the one she was in. She could hear people in the other rooms, working, talking, laughing.

She was alone. There were no cameras, no one patrolling on a high catwalk, no signs of people watching or being watched. The little bathroom with the toilet and shower was fully enclosed and soundproof. After scrutinizing it inch by inch, she concluded that it really did appear to be exactly what it seemed. She felt safe, a sensation she hadn't experienced in weeks.

Julia picked out a fuzzy sweatshirt and a pair of socks. The sweatshirt was used but freshly laundered. The socks were new, still inside a sealed plastic bag. She ripped open the packaging and inhaled the scent of brand-new clothing for the first time in months. Her breath caught in her throat.

After the shower and food, Julia returned to the larger warehouse space, where she saw Sahima sitting with a group at a long workbench covered in laptops, microscopes, soldering irons, fans, screwdrivers, mini-baths—the kind used to clean jewelry—and all sorts of other equipment that she didn't know the names for, not to mention a rat's nest of tangled wires and cords.

She shuffled over to Sahima.

"Thank you."

"Don't mention it." Sahima's attention was on a monitor mounted on a telescopic arm, showing the view from the microscope in front of her. On the microscope's stage lay a Bloom phone with its screen removed. Sahima's hands were inside a pair of gloves immersed in a vat of some viscous liquid. As Sahima's fingers moved, Julia could see a probe and a soldering iron echo her movements over the phone's exposed innards, but much more minutely. Smoke wafted from the microscope stage.

"Looks like you're performing surgery," Julia said.

Sahima chuckled. "You're not wrong."

"What kind of surgery?"

"I suppose it depends on your perspective. If you were Bloom, you'd say that I'm breaking the phone, destroying it. Because Bloom has marked all these phones and laptops and headsets as stolen in their database, the minute someone turned it on and tried to connect to a network, the device would scream bloody murder—and I don't mean that figuratively. Encrypted messages would be sent to the mother ship, of course, but the speaker would also blare out this piercing alarm meant to alert the police and anyone nearby that something illegal had been done. And while all that was happening, the device would be building up a big jolt of electricity, which, when discharged, would fry the chips inside so that *poof*, the phone or laptop or headset would turn into nothing but a brick of useless glass and silicon."

"Wow. Sounds scary."

"It's meant to be scary. The point is to deter people like me from stealing their phones. But here's how I look at it. Companies like Bloom have made it so that you aren't really buying a device from them, just paying them rent to use it the way they tell you to. It's not just about spying on you to sell you more junk; it's also so that you can't do anything they disapprove of. If you try to take a picture of the Saudi crown prince with a Bloom phone, you know what happens? You get nothing but a black rectangle. Same thing if you try to take pictures near one of our aircraft carriers. Or even better, sometimes the picture of the aircraft carrier will have fake planes on it, generated by AI."

"I didn't know that." Julia felt like she was being shown a side of the world she hadn't known existed.

"Well, that's what you get when companies are owned by foreign sovereign funds and the NSA embeds agents in corporate product design groups. On newer laptops, you can't install any app that they've decided spreads 'disinformation'—and that basically means anything those in power don't want to hear. Things here aren't as bad as they are in Russia or China, but it's getting close. We work to free these devices so that people can use them for whatever purpose they want."

"Why don't you just help people free their phones after they buy them? Like . . . jailbreaking?"

Sahima looked at her and nodded. "Good question. Why do you think it's better to only help people who bought their phones?"

"Then you wouldn't be breaking the law. Stealing."

Sahima chuckled. "Tell me, why are you living on the streets?"

Julia looked away. "I don't want to talk about it."

"You don't have to tell me. But I'll take a guess: Someone stole your life from you. Maybe they broke the law; maybe they didn't. But the law didn't give a rat's ass about you. And those who care about the law? They also didn't give a rat's ass about you. Still don't."

Julia thought about it. Who had stolen her life and driven her to run from every camera, every lens? Who had taken and spread the pictures and videos that made her life a living hell? The trolls, the reporters, the protesters, the classmates—did they break laws?

And how many of them had been using Bloom phones or laptops? With no effort at all, Bloom could make it impossible for anyone to take a picture of the Saudi crown prince or an aircraft carrier, but it hadn't lifted a finger to help someone like her, or her mother, or all the other kids who had been hounded by their own images until they killed themselves. Bloom and others like it made their own laws, and they didn't care about her at all.

"Fuck Bloom," she said.

"That's the spirit," said Sahima, laughing. "Serena says if we're going to be free, we shouldn't bother participating in the fiction of capitalism. Why follow laws made up to protect everyone except us?"

"Who's Serena?"

"Our leader. Possibly the smartest person you'll ever meet."

FIFTEEN

The Roamnest had been stocked with some basic groceries, enough for Piers to make lunch: toasted stale bread and canned soup.

"Thank you," said Julia. The nap and a hot meal made her feel much better.

Their top priority was to track down Elli while evading the Prince as well as the police. And the best way to find Elli, Julia reasoned, was to reconstruct the final days of her life before she disappeared. If she was preparing to run, maybe she left traces.

Julia filtered Elli's digital archive for files that had been accessed in the last month before her disappearance. The largest were recordings of studio sessions—Elli practicing for new dreams. She shunted these to Piers to review. She told herself that it was because Piers was much more experienced with vivid dreams, would know what to look for. But she knew that it was really because her only vivid dreaming session with Elli's egolet had dredged up some really unpleasant memories. She had no desire to go through it again.

As they had no access to the kind of powerful hardware in Elli's studio, not even a dream deck, Julia helped Piers jury-rig a solution with his new phone and fusion vision glasses. It was possible the lowered resolution and limited processing power would cause Piers to miss something in the studio sessions, but that couldn't be helped.

The rest of the files consisted of a hodgepodge of the quotidian and the obscure: financial spreadsheets (business and household); research material (academic papers on particle physics and weather patterns in the Southeast, French astrological charts from the fourteenth century, books on fashion in nineteenth-century Japan, American photography, Canadian national parks)—possibly for a dream Elli was crafting or just personal interest; snapshots (lunch with friends, a visit to an art gallery, receipts for tax filing); manuals for an immersion camera and an underwater microphone; correspondence with fans, utilities, managers and agents, sponsors—almost all of it AI-generated; a few messages to friends and family; and so on.

Naturally, Julia's interest was piqued by the personal messages. Julia skimmed the messages while Talos ran a linguistic analysis. Neither revealed anything of interest. Unwilling to give up, Julia asked Talos to systematically examine the metadata of Elli's communications in case she was using a hidden channel. However, Talos detected no deviation from Elli's usual patterns: she messaged/called/met with her close friends once a week or every few weeks and called her mom once a month.

Either Elli had not been planning to run at all, or she thought she was being watched and had conducted her life during the last month with extra care to leave no clues for her pursuers.

Julia wasn't sure which possibility was more terrifying.

She had Talos run a more extensive metadata analysis on the rest of the files, and the AI did highlight one anomaly: a photograph.

Like most people, Elli took tens of thousands of photographs that she never looked at again. This particular picture, however, had been opened five times during the month before Elli's disappearance. In fact, Talos's follow-up revealed that the picture had been accessed every few weeks, sometimes even once every few *days*, for the last six months—the file system log didn't go back any further than that.

Julia opened the photograph. It was a selfie of Elli and Piers, taken somewhere on a beach—the metadata identified the location as Vero Beach, Florida, about seven years earlier. Elli was holding the camera while Piers had his arm around her. The two leaned in, cheek by cheek, their smiles bright as the sunrise.

She went to Piers.

"Is there a reason why Elli would look at this photograph all the time?"

Piers took off the fusion vision glasses, rubbed his tired eyes, and focused on Elli's screen. "That's one of my favorite pictures of us. She has it as her wallpaper on her laptop." His features softened into a smile.

Sentimental, yes, but Julia wasn't convinced. *What are you hiding?*

She looked closer at the file system logs. "Thought so," she muttered.

"What?"

"She hadn't just been looking at the photo. There were edits."

"Maybe she used it as a test image for various AI editors."

Julia shook her head. "That's not it. If that were the case, she would have made copies so she could compare the effects of different editors. But she never undid the changes or restored to a baseline version; instead, she just kept on modifying the same picture over and over, accumulating edits over time."

"Why do you think she did that?"

"Because it's not a photo at all. I'll show you."

Julia put on her fusion vision glasses so that she could spawn a bunch of virtual monitors around the room. In order to let Piers see what she was doing, she used the tensor bank's built-in projector to cast one of the monitors onto a wall—the projector wasn't very powerful, but as they were indoors, it was usable.

While she typed DirectCode to Talos on a projected keyboard, an interface more precise and faster than natural-language instructions,

Julia talked to Piers. "It's called steganography. That's where you hide the payload data inside some other file by altering the container file in ways that won't be visible. Photographs are perfect for this: they're full of redundant data; they are complex and noisy; and human eyes are very forgiving of small defects in an image, usually dismissed as 'artifacts.'"

It took a while, but with Talos running the pattern recognition, Julia was able to retrieve the hidden file after multiple passes. It was a spreadsheet.

Julia tapped it. A dialog box came up asking for a password.

"Interesting." Julia typed some more. "Huh, a much stronger cipher than I expected." Turning to Piers, she asked, "Do you know any of her passwords?"

"I haven't used passwords in a long time," said Piers. "Didn't even know she had any."

Julia nodded. These days, anything needing to be secured was put behind biometrics. Passwords were extremely rare.

"Talos is much too weak for us to hope we could brute-force it in time," said Julia. She wished they had Elli's old setup, but she caught herself. Not helpful.

It was disappointing to come *so* tantalizingly close to an answer.

Hoping to get lucky, Julia told Talos to try to brute-force the password anyway while she and Piers explored other possibilities.

Julia looked through what she thought of as Elli's "vanity file."

According to Piers, Elli had always maintained the collection of press material herself. Even though Piers, after they got married, suggested that she let her AI handle it, Elli never seemed interested.

That was odd. Combing through the ether for mentions of one's name seemed to Julia like courting disaster. She could only imagine the kind of vitriol that an artist like Elli would find—people never thought of anyone famous as real people with feelings. Why did Elli insist on personally performing a task routinely left to AI?

Putting aside that puzzle for the moment, Julia studied Elli's artistic career.

She discovered that Elli was one of the very first oneirofexes. Elli had practically invented the form during those heady days when generative AI seemed poised to take over everything, and immersion headsets had finally become good enough to entice the public. Her earliest attempts, livestreams performed on user-generated video sites, were more like collaborative storytelling exercises.

Elli would look into the stereoscopic cameras as she told the viewers a story, whispering the words into spatial microphones while she read the responses viewers typed into the chat or the emoji cloud their direct neural sensing headsets shot onto the screen. (This was before her viewership had grown so large that she had to rely on AI sentiment analysis of the responses.) Meanwhile, her fingers would glide over a silent keyboard, cueing up bespoke animations and videos crafted on the fly by the primitive generative AI systems of the day, complete with six-fingered humans and Daliesque text that seemed to melt and flow, which suited the mood of the pieces rather well.

Viewers, lulled by her hypnotic whispers, would share the feelings and memories evoked by the surreal images. In turn, Elli would fold and mold these into new generative prompts and change the story she told to incorporate them.

Watching the recorded streams of these crude experiments, Julia was reminded of early ASMR videos, gaming streams, mukbangs, "get ready with me" flipclips—you weren't sure exactly what was being shown or why anyone would "consume" this kind of content, but you could tell there was something compelling and wondrous happening.

Like the first stories that enchanted audiences around smoky cave hearths or the first motion pictures that scattered terrified viewers with an oncoming locomotive, these vivid dreams tapped into our unceasing yearning for the timeless light of Life refracted into the countless facets of Now, ephemeral as well as eternal. Julia realized that she was watching the birth of a new narrative tongue, the development of a new grammar for representation, a pidgin on its way to becoming a creole, the birth of a new medium.

And then, Julia read about Elli's big break.

SIXTEEN

Victor logged in and contemplated the grid of balances. Crypto, gold, ETF, ANDR, double-puts, all-calls, yen, SLLT . . . the numbers showed his wealth, his worth, but they were also more than that. They were a record of his instincts, his struggles, his slow ascent into financial security, proof of his hard-won knowledge, his long-suffering patience, his little-acknowledged wisdom. He had worked for the Prince for decades, and, sometimes, he needed the reassurance that all the pain he had endured was worth it.

He could feel his breathing and heartbeat slow down, the heat of irritation dissipating from his mind.

This was better than any meditation, precisely the kind of therapy he needed.

Being yelled at by the Prince could be highly terrifying for some. Victor wasn't scared; he knew the Prince would have to come back to him to get the job done.

But it was, once again, humiliating.

"I told you to keep an eye on him!"

Well, he did goof there. No way around it.

It wasn't until Thursday morning that Piers's burner phone showed up in the real-time mobile location data he paid so much to acquire. Right away, he summoned the local crew of knuckleheads.

But his AI alerted him to an anomaly. The burner phone had been turned on simultaneously with four other phones, all moving together. Either the lawyer had gotten himself a fellowship of equally clueless companions, or he had realized he was being tracked and was messing with him.

Victor stared at the tracking screen in disbelief as the five phones moved together. One by one, the phones peeled off and stopped moving, until all five rested around what the AI told him was the parking lot for a home improvement store.

By the time his crew had arrived, the five phones had begun to move again: two toward the South Shore, one toward Connecticut, one toward Carre, and the last one north, toward New Hampshire.

There was no way to tell which was Piers. He had to divide up his crew and follow all five.

Still, when the Prince called for an update, he had assumed a confident tone and told his boss that Piers was being tracked. He told himself it wasn't a lie. Piers *was* being tracked—Victor just didn't know which of the five phones was with him.

In the back of his mind, however, he acknowledged his delusion. If Piers had gone to such trouble to put out decoys, then he knew he was being tracked, and it was likely that *none* of the five phones were with him. Purely out of desperation, he had picked the one heading to New Hampshire, which also happened to be Piers's first burner phone. His AI had profiled Piers as a cautious man with a fear of technology. It seemed plausible (barely) that even if he had bought a bunch of new phones to try to confuse anyone following him, he would hold on to the one phone he had some familiarity with.

And that was how, a day of driving later, Victor found himself staring at a cabin on the outskirts of a hamlet in the middle of nowhere in northern New Hampshire. The owner, a balding man in his fifties, was building some shack up the side of the hill next to his cabin. Taking advantage of the owner's preoccupation, Victor snuck in and found the burner phone taped under the bumper of the white Colorado parked in front.

The other members of his crew had not fared any better. None of the phones had led to Piers. The lawyer, who now no longer seemed as foolish as Victor's first impression, had vanished into thin air.

The call to the Prince after that had led to screams, curses, a spittle-festooned dressing-down, and finally, the need to calm himself by contemplating his Zen garden of appreciating assets.

"I'll find him, and her. Apparently, if anything is to be done right, I have to do it myself."

He could feel his blood pressure go up again at the memory of the Prince's last words. He unlocked his phone. More therapy was needed.

SEVENTEEN

Clip from *Amallricana*—a vlog whose mission is to cover "the renaissance of the American mall."

[Daytime drone shots of the exterior of an ancient suburban mall. The vast parking lot is mostly deserted. In the distance, a highway with streaming traffic can be glimpsed.

The view switches to a handheld camera, which pans around to reveal one part of the parking lot being filled by cars. A long line of people winds out from the doors at the end of the mall structure.]

MALL-JILL (V.O.): It's a fair bet that Whaling Station Mall, a stone's throw from I-95 in Stoneport, Connecticut, where 90 percent of the retail space remains unoccupied, hasn't experienced a bustling day like this since the Clinton administration.

[The camera follows the line of people into the mall, where the line folds back and forth in front of what used to be a movie theater. The crowd skews young, with a majority in their late teens or early twenties.]

MALL-JILL (V.O.): The crowd numbers nearly twelve hundred, according to my camera, but we all know that machine counting skews low when so many people wear anti-recognition makeup or masks. They aren't here for the grand opening of a new store; rather, they're here to see Elli Krantz, an "oneirofex," more commonly known as a dream weaver or dream guide.

The dreams that draw them here may be a surprise to you. They certainly aren't what most would consider happy ones.

[Close-up of Nina, a twentysomething wearing a T-shirt with a quote from the cetacean poet, Nooruulin, and bright sunflower earrings.]

NINA (LAUGHING): Of course Elli is right. Dino corporection is happening right now!

MALL-JILL (OFF CAMERA): The government is literally trying to bring dinosaurs back to life in order to control the population?

NINA: Yes, to keep us under their thumbs. *Jurassic Park* isn't fiction—that's why they stopped making any more films in that series.

MALL-JILL: Are you speaking metaphorically? As in, "Hey, our senators are like dinosaurs, out of touch."

NINA: No. Not metaphorical. I mean, yes, politicians *are* dinosaurs. But dino corporection is so much bigger than that. People have to open their eyes to the truth.

MALL-JILL: Which is that a global elite is conspiring to create an army of zombie dinosaurs to keep themselves in power?

NINA: Not zombie. Real dinosaurs. Listen, why do you think the government is pushing solar and wind and tidal energy so hard?

[Nina grows more animated as she explains the theory. Behind her, others waiting in line are mugging for the camera, holding up hands with fingers pinched into the shape of a blunt beak: the sign for the Dino-Truthers.]

MALL-JILL: Why?

NINA: Because they're trying to save the fossils! Oil, coal, natural gas—you know what they really are? Dinosaur-stuff. They don't want us to burn up the raw material they need to corporect their dinosaur army. With all of us shifting over to "green" energy, all the extra oil and coal is saved in these vast underground reservoirs where government scientists are trying to figure out the most efficient way to turn it back to dinos. *That's* the real hoax behind global warming.

MALL-JILL: Ah . . . what else is part of this conspiracy?

NINA: What else . . . Oh! Children's programming has a lot of dinosaurs in it because of brainwashing. The government and the green-energy industry are working together to get kids used to the idea of living with dinosaurs. This way, when the real dinos take over the streets, people will feel a sense of familiarity—because dinosaurs are our friends, not monsters.

MALL-JILL: How . . . how do you know this? This all seems so . . .

NINA: Far-fetched? Yeah, well, the things governments have done that we don't know about can fill a stack of books from here to the moon. Did you know that in 1986, Navy SEALs kidnapped a man right here on US soil and tortured him as part of an official mission to test our domestic security? Did you know that for forty years, the feds experimented on Black soldiers to find out how syphilis affected people? Don't tell me about far-fetched.

MALL-JILL: But bringing dinosaurs back? Surely, there are easier ways to control the population if that's the goal—

NINA: (*In an exaggerated nasal, nerdy voice*) Surely sitting down and talking things out is an easier way to resolve conflicts than building the most powerful bombs in the history of our species, which can smash atoms together and release enough energy to destroy the whole planet and then using *those* to threaten each other so that we can all live in a balance of terror? Surely? When have we ever taken the logical, easy path when there's a much more complicated and terrifying way instead?

MALL-JILL: Can't say you don't have a point there. Doesn't mean I believe in dino corporection, though.

NINA: You should come and dream with Elli. She was the first to see the truth, and she's always been able to see further than the rest of us.

[The camera cuts away to take in the thronging lobby before zooming inside the auditorium. The seats have been modified (temporarily) with gaming headsets so that the audience can give their reactions to the performer either via voice or direct neural sensing. The footage is sped up so that people rush into their seats like the taillights of cars in a cityscape time lapse—this is, after all, an older video, from the time when people slathered their videos with AI-based effects because they thought they looked cool.

The video slows down to normal speed. The audience, every seat filled, waits with bated breath. In the front, a section of the neck-breaker seats has been taken away and a temporary stage erected in its place. Young Elli stands on it behind a low podium, poised and ready. She positively bathes in the anticipatory energy of the audience.

The camera spins around to reveal Mall-Jill, a woman in her forties: bright red lipstick, thick-rimmed glamour glasses, eyes that gleam from a bit of post-processing sparkle]

MALL-JILL: (whispering excitedly) I talked to Elli, and she agreed to let me film the dream session!

[The camera spins back to Elli, who holds up both hands. The crowd quiets. She waits a beat.]

ELLI: They say that the past is gone forever, that you can't go back. But every living thing leaves a ripple in Heraclitus's river, an expanding wave front that fades but never disappears. Just by living, you've already changed the universe forever.

Come with me to the anthracite mines of Carbon County. . . .

[Elli's fingers dance across the console on the podium. Images swirl across the giant screen behind her: ferns, cycads, ginkgos, dinosaurs. The crowd is rapt, eyes glazing over. Even distanced by the camera, one can feel that something extraordinary is happening. The crowd's breathing synchronizes, the murmuring voices merging into one. It's as though there's a single lung breathing, a bellows between earth and heaven, its unceasing movement the very beat of the cosmos.

The camera tilts to an odd angle and stops moving, seemingly propped against something. Jurassic images continue to play across the screen.

Elli's voice fades, replaced by Mall-Jill's narration off-screen.]

MALL-JILL: I've been to plenty of performances, some of them with big stars. But I can't remember any that moved me as much as Elli's did. The story she told is ridiculous, preposterous, absurd, on the level of the flat-earth theory or the moon-landing hoax.

Yet, I was utterly entranced.

I was on the border between wakefulness and sleep, that strange country ruled by dreams, when I decided to take the plunge. Don't just look, I told myself. *Be.* I stopped looking through the camera and started to look at *her.* I allowed the images she played on the screen to overwhelm me, gave myself permission to be *immersed* in the experience.

A man next to me whispered to the woman next to him something about a visit to the Conn College museum "when I was five." A few seconds later, I heard him gasp as images of a dinosaur mounted in a museum display loomed across the screen, immense, monumental, all-powerful, just the way a dinosaur would have appeared to a child. Someone else in the row behind me said, "We have to ally ourselves with all the other animals." And a few seconds later, the screen showed suntanned men and women bravely riding a pod of humpback whales off the coast of Cape Cod to head off an assault of government goons mounted on armored mosasaurs.

The last time I felt like this was when I played in my college band—that euphoria of making something together, of being something greater than our individual selves. Elli wove our memories, hopes, fancies into one collective dream. I seemed to hear the heartbeat of all those around me, a thumping chorus. I felt acutely the sense of being *connected,* that we were breathing and rebreathing the same air, that all our eardrums vibrated in sympathy with all our vocal cords.

[The screen goes dark; lights come up. The vivid dream gathering is near its end. The camera is picked up again and pans around to show people leaving the theater, looking dazed. Mall-Jill interviews some of them.]

SHAVED HEAD: I believe it. No question. Everything just fits. Wish I had a gas car so I could burn some of that dino-stuff.

FLORAL BLOUSE WITH BUTTERFLY NECKLACE: This was my first time at an Elli gathering. I'll definitely see her again. I'm going to move to Australia as soon as I save up the money! That's my message.

STANFORD SWEATSHIRT: I don't know about belief. What does it mean to believe something anyway?

But I'll tell you what I know. I think loneliness is the quintessential condition of modernity. I eat alone; I sleep alone; I don't know the names of my neighbors; my coworkers don't exist for me outside the office. I talk to my mom once a week, and even that feels like a chore. I'm so lonely that sometimes I scream in my room just to be sure the world still exists.

It's not any better online. Everyone knows the internet is dead; it's only bots talking to bots now. Bots and scammers and trolls who want you to send them nudes—and when you say no, they call you a c*nt.

But when I was in there dreaming . . . I wasn't alone. I was part of something bigger. A movement. A story. Elli made me feel human.

"BE KIND TO ROBOTS" T-SHIRT: The sad thing is, I don't think Elli will ever be the biggest star. While everyone else is dreaming, Elli is awake. They, the government, the billionaires, they don't want people to wake up.

MALL-JILL: Like in the Matrix.

BE KIND TO ROBOTS: What?

[More drone footage. We are looking at the parking lot from above. As cars stream out, the place feels more desolate than ever. The mall, a concrete island in the middle of a vast asphalt sea, feels strangely vulnerable. This physical manifestation of our collective desire, this temple to consumerism, has lost its faith.]

MALL-JILL: Even after talking to dozens of Elli's fans, I still don't have a good sense of whether they really believe that the government is secretly trying to bring back dinosaurs to control the populace.

Dino corporection is like a lot of other conspiracy theories. I think people don't so much believe in them as they are trying to say something that they don't have the words for by *claiming* to believe them.

Decades have passed since our culture has become steeped in irony, trolling, the shorthand pidgin of memes that mean nothing and everything. Young people are on guard, terrified of sincerity—if you dare to show that you believe in something, you'll be called a sucker, a fool, a dinosaur trapped in the tar pit of sentimentality.

In order to show that they really believe in nothing, people preemptively claim to believe in the most impossible thing. It's Alice in Wonderland: a defense mechanism, an ironic Bat-Signal.

But maybe I'm overthinking this.

Maybe we should just take the conspiracy theorists at their word. Elli Krantz is like any other charismatic huckster, and her followers sheep penned in by a false narrative. Every doubt engendered by their nonsensical claims is immediately twisted into proof that the claims are actually true. The more they feel trapped by their nightmare, the louder they shout that the rest of the world is asleep. Nothing can be more American.

Or maybe Elli is like that other also very American figure, the trickster hero. In this version, Elli and her followers are in on the joke, and their collective performance is their art. Since their elders have made a mess of the world with political polarization, with ubiquitous propaganda, with tangled skeins of AI-enhanced post-truth narrative threads, they rebel by pretending to believe in the most outrageous of theories, to send up the ridiculousness of all ideologies.

Or maybe the answer is something even deeper. We live in an age of the isolated atomistic self, of the death of institutions. We don't go to churches; we don't even go to offices. It's hard for people to make friends, to date, to be with someone, since everything is mediated through screens, bots, AI—anonymous, efficient, inhuman. The deepest social bonds for many are parasocial—FlipClip stars, vocaloid idols, oneirofexes. Maybe this is why vivid dream gatherings are so popular. For the duration of the dream, you're not alone but part of a grander whole, something so much *more* than mere you. Dreaming together is how we feel we belong, how we give meaning to all that we see or seem.

Sorry to get all Joan Didion there on you at the end. Thank you for watching my channel, and make sure to like and subscribe.

Next time, I'll visit a dead mall that was once the very definition of glamour: the Forum Shops at Caesars Palace in Las Vegas. You wouldn't believe how it has been reborn.

EIGHTEEN

Julia took off her fusion vision glasses.

The vivid dream that made Elli famous early on was nothing like what she expected. A conspiracy theory!

And yet . . . She closed her eyes: there it was, that giant movie theater screen with dinosaurs running across it, like a bright window to the past hovering in the darkness. Her ears thrummed with the thumping of thousands of heartbeats, hers among them. Intellectually, she knew it was just a sound effect added by Mall-Jill in postproduction. Yet, she couldn't deny a yearning for that experience, losing herself in a larger whole, without questions, without doubts, knowing in her bones that she belonged.

Belonging. She wondered if she had ever had it. Growing up, it had not been possible to forget that she was Chinese, an immigrant's child, marked apart because her roots in this land were paper-thin. One way or another, through words or deeds, she had been shown that she didn't belong, that her presence was only tolerated, temporary, that nooses, exclusions, internment camps were merely on hold, contingent on the resolution of grand geopolitics, that she was not a feature of the land like the rain and the wind, the Black, white, and brown.

Her mother's loudness had not helped.

There were always looks thrown her way, especially after a spike in the news about the possibility of war with China.

When was the last time she had actually felt she belonged?

She thought of the Cartographers Obscura. Sahima, Hutch, and the others. Serena.

She shook her head. Couldn't afford to be distracted by that. The goal now was to find Elli.

She went back to Talos, still cranking away at the password-protected spreadsheet. Idly, she put her fingers on the table. Talos, interpreting the action as her wanting to type, projected a red virtual keyboard onto the table surface.

Progress report? She typed it because she didn't feel like talking. It wasn't like typing on a real keyboard, of course, but Talos played some clacking sounds to help with the illusion.

About 1 percent through the search space.

Did you try "password"? she typed.

Oh, how did I forget that? I was going to try it after "letmein" but went straight to "asdfgh" instead. Would you like to swap places?

She laughed. It was like talking with herself—which was kind of true, in a manner of speaking.

Wait. Her fingers tensed above the glowing red keys as she tried to pin down a thought that flashed by like a shadow glimpsed in a corner.

The simulated clacking of the keys stood in sharp contrast to the thumping of the heartbeats in Mall-Jill's video. The staccato mechanical notes lacked rhythm, flow, articulation, dictated by prose rather than music. She hadn't realized how much of her life was ruled by beeps, clacks, clicks, buzzes, chirps, but not the sound of heartbeat, the oldest clock of life.

An image of Elli's recording studio resurfaced in her mind, unbidden. Her heart sped up.

"Piers!"

"Tell me again, but slower, please," Piers said. His eyes were bloodshot and tired, the result of scrubbing through so much raw VR footage in Elli's practice prompt tracks.

"Let me show you," Julia said. "Talos, look through the files I gave Piers and show me all sessions with recording times that include the times on this list."

Talos scrolled a short list onto the projected screen on the wall.

"What are these timestamps?"

"The times when Elli accessed that picture of the two of you." Turning back to Talos, Julia directed, "Isolate ten-second segments of the recordings right before the times the files were accessed." Back to Piers again: "We have a lucky break. The studio was also Elli's office. Sometimes, during a pause in a studio session, while the microphones were still recording, she'd do some office work."

"I don't understand."

Talos flashed its built-in screen, like a blink, to show that it was done.

Julia held up a hand, telling Piers to wait. "Talos, now go through the snippets and see if you can find any common, repeated sequence of clacks—like keyboard strokes." She turned back to Piers. "When Elli typed in her password, the sounds would have been captured by the microphones."

Piers looked impressed. "And you can figure out the password based on the sounds?"

"Exactly."

Talos blinked again.

"Isolate, enhance, and play."

Talos played back the snippet. Slowed down and amplified, the clacks sounded like a meditative phrase chanted by Buddhist monks.

"Go back through the rest of the recordings and isolate all keyboard clacks. Build a mapping between sounds and keys based on frequency. I think there was a security paper from a few months back on how to do this—"

"I know the paper," said Talos.

"Great. Let me know when you have the password."

Talos blinked in acknowledgment.

"I have to admit you're scaring me a little," said Piers. "Seems like there's no way to keep a secret from you."

"Aren't you glad I'm on your team?"

It took Talos only a few seconds to finish the work. The password, or, more accurately, the passphrase, popped up on the screen: "What, sorry Devil, hast thou to bestow?"

Piers frowned.

Julia opened up the spreadsheet and typed in the ominous phrase. With no fanfare, a grid of numbers, black and red, filled the screen.

"I can't make any sense of this," Julia said after a minute. "I can put my fiscjinn—"

"No, don't do that." Piers swallowed. And then, with some effort, he continued, "I didn't know Elli kept another set of books."

The anguish in his voice made Julia flinch. Was this more evidence of Elli's betrayal?

Piers rallied himself. "I'm a corporate lawyer; I can read financials. Do you think you can help me find a printer?"

NINETEEN

With Piers absorbed in the spreadsheet, Julia decided to go on a run.

This would be the first time either of them had stepped outside since checking into the Roamnest that morning. Time to see if they had gotten away cleanly.

First, a change in habits. She put on her sensepin and set it in continuous mode. Every few seconds, the pin would take a picture. Much of counter-surveillance was just a matter of noticing what was out of the ordinary, and a continuous record of her surroundings was the best way to pick out potential threats. She didn't like becoming part of the ubiquitous surveillance culture, but their survival was a higher priority right now.

Still concealed behind the curtains, she peeked out the living room window. Mentally dividing the view into quadrants, she scanned each square, noting anything that seemed out of place. Sahima had taught her that trick; sometimes, the most important thing about being safe was just forcing yourself to slow down, taking the extra time to *look*.

The street appeared clear. She grabbed a trash bag, opened the front door, and made her way around the house slowly, pretending to be a clueless Roamnester looking for the trash bin but really checking out the neighbors and the backyard. She dropped the bag inside one of the green wheelie bins and returned out front.

She began to jog, setting a leisurely pace that allowed her to get the exercise but also to remain aware, with time to take in her surroundings. The route she had chosen would take her on a complete circuit around the town, including Main Street, with all the touristy shops and overpriced bakeries, as well as the quieter residential areas. Twice, she took repeated turns to circle a block to catch anyone tailing her.

Finally relaxing into the run, she let her mind drift.

Julia became part of Cartographers Obscura, the hacking collective that had organized the flash mob on Boylston Street.

Sahima, who was like a big sister, taught her how to work with machines. Julia turned out to be a natural. She could visualize the flow of data or energy inside a device with uncanny accuracy, and she had an instinctual *feel* for the weaknesses of modern neuromeshes. Within a week, she became a faster and more precise microsolderer than Sahima, and within two weeks, she was coming up with original jailbreaks for neuromeshes.

It was the ethos of Cartographers Obscura that everyone took the same risks. No one was above the chaos of a smash-and-grab at a Bloom store or the tedium of dropping trojan pulse-code cards with sports betting logos at a corporate campus, hoping some employee would scan one of them in. Julia got to experience the full gamut of the collective's missions. Sahima and Julia often got assigned together: network penetration, data theft, ransomware, identity manipulation. . . . Julia liked the work—she was good at it, and she enjoyed the sense of power that came from bending a piece of technology to her will—but more than the work, she loved the camaraderie. With Sahima, Hutch, J.J., Lutt, and the others, she felt valued, trusted, accepted. She belonged.

One time, they had to crack the PIN protecting a hardware crypto wallet that had once been the property of some politician. Julia figured out the hardware bypass, and Sahima wrote the brute-force microcode. When they were done, they had access to more funds than the collective had ever gotten. Sahima told Julia that the crypto, after being laundered, would be sent to a network of shell companies and then donated to charities for children. Julia felt like Robin Hood.

"And I have even more good news," said Sahima, her eyes glinting with excitement. "Serena wants to meet you."

Serena turned out to be a woman in her fifties: wiry, silver hair, well-manicured nails painted a lustrous pink, probably not five feet even if she stood on her tiptoes.

Yet, when she was in a room, every pair of eyes was on her. When she spoke, every other voice quieted. She had *presence.*

She looked at Julia, her eyes two unwavering beams of penetrating attention that pinned her to the spot.

Fifteen-year-old Julia shuffled from foot to foot, wishing she could disappear from the scrutiny of the founder and leader of Cartographers Obscura. *I'm so grateful for being taken in.* She rehearsed in her mind the lines she had come up with after a night of tossing and turning. *I admire you and everything you've—*

"You have nightmares," Serena said. It wasn't a question.

This wasn't at all what Julia expected. "Y-yes," she stammered. "I—I don't sleep well."

"What are they about?" Serena asked.

Julia bit her bottom lip.

"You feel guilty about hating your mother," Serena said.

Julia looked at her in shock. Her darkest secret. Serena had spoken it aloud like it was nothing.

Julia had not expected any of her new friends in Cartographers Obscura, much less Serena, to know about her past. But now she realized how foolish that was. Her pictures had been all over the ether; how could they not know? She had been living in a state of denial, of wishful thinking.

And now they were going to kick her out, just like her neighbors and old friends had wanted to, just like she deserved.

"It's okay to hate your mother," Serena said. "She was a fool."

Julia forgot to breathe.

"Sit down, child. Let me explain to you how the world works."

Serena told Julia that her mother was a fool because she had not understood that the American dream was a lie. She believed that if you worked at the system and followed its rules and played the game as it was supposed to be played, you would get the result you wanted. If you made enough pretty speeches and marched enough times down the National Mall and bled enough and prayed enough and said you loved this country enough times, people would embrace you and tell you that you belonged and hand you the keys to the mansion with the feather bed, where you could dream the American dream to the accompaniment of "This Land Is Your Land."

What a crock of shit.

America was corrupt and steeped in sin. The powerful had rigged the game for themselves and turned the country into a panopticon to imprison the rest of us. Anytime one of the powerless—it didn't matter the color of your skin, the language you spoke, the place you were born in—was on the verge of climbing out, they would be ruthlessly tossed back into the pit. Heck, the powerful loved to divide and conquer the powerless so that they behaved like a bucket of crabs, policing one another, undermining each other, everyone dragging everyone else down. The only right thing to do was not to play the game at all. Steal from the powerful, eat the rich, break their laws.

Your mother, said Serena, by trying so hard to be a "good American" and following the rules, was only preserving the rigged game and its rigged rules. She got you hurt. She got herself killed. She was a fool and you should hate her. Don't feel guilty. Don't feel bad. Don't.

"But you don't have to be afraid anymore, child," Serena said. "Here you're reborn. Here you can start anew. We're your new family, your new tribe, your new country."

Julia cried. She had never felt such relief, such understanding. She gazed upon Serena and thought she would never love anyone as much as she loved her.

That was the night she decided to give up her old last name, her mother's last name, and become "Julia Z." Just Z. A single letter, a lightning flash between darkness and light, a hard turn between the past and the future. Reborn.

Julia made another circuit around the block before entering the house. Everything still seemed copacetic. No signs of either the police or the Prince.

"Any luck?" she asked as she took off her shoes inside.

"I may have something," Piers answered. "But I want to make sure."

She saw that in addition to printouts of the spreadsheet, Piers had also printed out a copy of the photo that had hidden the spreadsheet. It must have seemed significant to him that she had chosen to use that picture: every time she made another entry into that file of secrets, she was also looking at her husband. Was it a strange kind of plea for forgiveness, for understanding? Or maybe a reminder to herself, an emotional anchor?

She left him alone and looked in the fridge and pantry. As she wasn't going to have another meal of canned soup and bread on the verge of going bad, she needed to get some groceries.

Driving the Zenith felt too conspicuous. So, taking the bike from the shed in the back, she rode to the Stop & Shop at the edge of the town and returned with supplies. A simple casserole of ground beef, peppers, canned tomatoes, and rice, she decided. It was a dish she used to make for Sahima and herself a lot, when Cartographers Obscura sent them on long trips across the country.

While the dish was in the oven, she cleaned up and checked her messages. There was a note from Cailee, updating her on what had happened with the HELM. Everything was back to normal after they'd followed Julia's directions.

"Dr. Fenmore is so grateful," Cailee wrote. "She would love to have you come in so that she could thank you personally. And I know it's not just because you saved her from a scandal. She really cares about the kids, and she knows saving their data from a leak is a big deal."

Julia smiled. It was nice to help someone. Really help.

"I'm ready to talk," said Piers, standing at the kitchen entrance.

"Let's eat first. I'm starving."

TWENTY

"Elli was making a lot more money than I thought," he said after dinner. He retrieved his printouts and laid them out in front of her methodically.

There were discrepancies between the business records used for Julia's tax filings and the spreadsheet. Based on the spreadsheet, she had controlled various corporate entities, and through them, a portion of the extra income had been diverted to different overseas accounts in small amounts on an irregular schedule—perhaps to evade the banks' fraud/money-laundering detectors. Another portion of the extra income had been converted into various crypto assets and then transferred to unknown addresses. Still more funds had been funneled to purchases that he didn't recognize and investment assets like limited partnerships and unregistered share equivalents—

"I can't follow this," Julia interrupted. "What's the simplest takeaway for me?"

"Julia has made a lot more money than I, or the IRS, was aware. Millions more. It also looks like she was moving money offshore."

"These offshore accounts . . . were they hers?"

"I can't tell."

"Maybe we can figure that out."

With Piers's help, Julia had her fiscjinn pick out account numbers, crypto addresses, securities certificate identifiers, and then she dispatched a bunch of datahounds to conduct a deep search. Data leaks from banks and law firms, personal computing devices carelessly disposed of, data from ATM camera skimming, leaked screen-cap archives from "total recall" AIs—there were a lot of ways to link account numbers to owners if you knew where to look. With crypto, it was even easier. Everything was right there on the blockchains, and true anonymity was difficult to maintain unless you really knew what you were doing.

Talos returned with some nuggets of information it considered sufficiently notable. Piers picked through them, and, trained with his feedback, Talos was able to home in on truly interesting findings. One of the crypto addresses was connected to a Southeast Asian crime ring specializing in gambling—it had been seized by the government of Vietnam several years ago. One of the bank accounts turned out to belong to a shell corporation that had been busted for money laundering in the EU. Whatever was going on with Elli, she wasn't donating money to charity.

"Elli was paying money to terrible people," said Piers. "But why?"

Many other questions were going through Julia's mind. What did these payments have to do with the Prince? Were they connected to the one-on-one dreams they shared? Who, exactly, was Elli Krantz?

"There are hundreds of transactions missing from the records I had access to," said Piers. "Can you ask Talos to track down as much info as possible about the destination accounts? I need to figure out how they fit into . . . her life."

Assembling a story from a series of transactions seemed the kind of task better suited to the capabilities of an AI, but Julia understood why Piers felt the need to do it himself. In deciphering the mystery that was Elli's life, he was also reinterpreting and reconstructing his own.

While Piers worked, Julia returned to Elli's vanity file.

"Dino corporection" was Elli's first big hit. A few seemed to take it seriously; many more probably resonated with it as ironic commentary on the state of post-truth discourse, political and otherwise—whatever the reason for its popularity, it connected with the zeitgeist and put Elli on the map as an oneirofex.

Like many artists after an initial hit, Elli tried to move away from it in her subsequent work. It's in the nature of the artistic impulse to seek liberty, and no one wants to be a one-hit wonder or to say the same thing over and over again.

She tried her hand at various emerging genres: horror, adventure, nightmare, comedy, nostalgia, sci-fi, power fantasy, revenge, regret, "you're in the movie," "I didn't study for the test," "if I could do it over," "meet your high school self," "together again" . . .

But nothing quite took. Again, like with many emerging artists, a part of her fandom resisted her attempts to move on. "Dino corporection" whetted their appetite, and they craved more of the same thing. Elli's relationship with her fans became fraught.

Excerpt from Div-viD Interview of Elli Krantz by DreamDraft

[The AR immersion headset places the interviewer and interviewee at two ends of a physical table in your viewing space. A typical kitchen dining table or a desk is recommended.]

DREAMDRAFT (DD): Elli, thank you for agreeing to this interview.

ELLI KRANTZ (EK): Always a pleasure to talk to dreamers.

DD: I understand you've been busy with the new tour?

EK: (smiling tensely) I'm always busy.

DD: Tell me about some of the new gatherings. What strikes you about them?

EK: I like to experiment, right? So every gathering is different. I don't do just one thing. For example, I have this really cool sci-fi dream called "The First One Hundred Days." You're a member of the first colony ship to Mars, and you get to live through this grand adventure: politics, romance, or aliens—whatever you and your fellow dreamers come up with. I love it. I also have this one called "Thirteen at Thirty-One," in which you get to re-experience middle school—

DD: That sounds like a nightmare. You could not pay me enough to relive middle school.

EK: (laughs) Right. Well, the thing is, you know, we kind of do already. The trauma. It's always there. It's why we all have these recurring nightmares about being out of place and awkward and being ridiculed by others. Anyway, in the version I guide you through, you're popular, you're smart, you're beautiful, and all your fellow dreamers cheer you on because you're perfect the way you are. It's really healing.

DD: A whole auditorium of Mary Sues sounds even more horrifying.

EK: (tries to laugh it off) Haha. It's really not like that. You have to experience it.

DD: That's fair. I've certainly been surprised by vivid dreams that felt nothing like their trailers. Execution is everything.

EK: That's the artistry. The trailer kind of primes you for a certain kind of experience, but good dream guides know that you have to subvert the expectation. Like every audience, deep down, dreamers don't want what it says on the tin.

DD: We want to be surprised by art.

EK: Exactly.

DD: What about artists?

EK: What . . . what do you mean?

DD: Do you like—have you been surprised by how dreamers have reacted to your dreams?

EK: Oh, all the time. Dream-guiding is an art form made in the moment, like jazz or improv, so surprises from the audience are de rigueur. No two gatherings should be alike, and if I rely too much on my set prompts, the dream loses its power.

DD: Yes, I know. But I meant something different. Do dreamers sometimes push you in directions you don't want to go?

EK: (uncomfortable) I suppose that happens to every artist.

DD: So has it happened to you?

EK: Yes.

DD: What are some examples?

EK: (a pause) I don't know if I want to get into that.

DD: I think it's an interesting topic. Many of us dreamers are very curious about what it's like on the other side.

EK: Okay. I'm sometimes surprised by how dreamers focus on aspects of a prompt that aren't really what I would consider interesting. For example, I used to do this dream called "3000 B.C.E." It's Egyptian-themed, and so there are pyramids and sun barges and papyrus marshes and elaborate, animated hieroglyphs. I have in mind several plots—period adventure, family drama, time travel—we could go in any direction. But a lot of dreamers push for mammoths and . . . and other things that make no sense. I don't do that dream anymore.

DD: Oh, I think mammoths make sense.

EK: (trying to change the subject) Instead of that—

DD: (talking over her) Mammoths are extinct, right? So they want a dream in which extinct animals come back to life, like dinosaurs.

EK: (still trying) Mammoths aren't interesting to me in a dream like that. They don't fit. What's more interesting—

DD: They fit for your fans, though.

EK: (giving up) Yeah. I suppose.

DD: You know, I've been following your career since the dino corp-orection days. Those were some crazy times, right?

EK: (smiling even more tensely) For sure.

DD: And then you kind of went in different directions.

EK: The joke got old. It was time to stop.

DD: I know you've been saying it was a joke. But you kept it up for months. There were those interviews in which you talked about how dinos really were coming back. Played it straight.

EK: I was playing a character, a part of the performance. I didn't just guide dreamers in the auditorium. Some of the power of that dream came from what happened when you were awake.

DD: Some think it wasn't just a joke, that maybe you really did believe in it. You grew up in rural Pennsylvania, right? I mean, fans dug up all this stuff about your hometown. You had people marching against 5G and the vaccines and immigrants with weaponized viruses.

EK: The dinosaur thing was commentary about that. It was like "birds aren't real." You know?

DD: So you were making fun of people you grew up with?

EK: No. Not making fun. It's art, right? So I can't reduce what I wanted to say to a one-sentence "message." I was talking about loneliness, about belonging, about the pervasive sense of paranoia in a world where everyone who wasn't a billionaire felt powerless. I shouldn't have said "joke," I guess. It's just that you weren't supposed to take the dinosaur thing literally. It was a *dream*, for crying out loud.

DD: It made you popular. It was your brand.

EK: I don't really think artists should have brands. It's so limiting. Being an artist is about being free.

DD: You don't want to be trapped by your creation.

EK: That's one way to put it.

DD: And that's why you've been trying to downplay the dinosaur dreams. You don't do them on your tours. You don't like fans to bring them up.

EK: I can't tell fans what to do. But I don't want to be remembered as the "dinosaur conspiracy girl."

DD: You also don't like it when people bring up your personal life. Like how you grew up in a conspiracy-theory town—

EK: "White trash"—that's the term they use. That's not from fans. When people who don't like my art want to dismiss me and my work, that's their go-to.

DD: Or your high school boyfriends. Or how you dropped out of college. You don't like people to know much about your biography.

EK: Because then they say that these details explain why I did "dino corporection," or they claim that my latest dream is just a reflection of my own story as an outsider, my envy of the racial privilege that I've been denied. Fans or haters, the facts of my life are always interpreted in ways that limit me, that box me in. (Deep breath) I don't think these details are relevant in art.

DD: But they *can* be relevant. Dreaming is a very personal art. Dreamers are often asked to put their most personal memories and emotions into the collaboration, and it doesn't seem a stretch to ask a dream weaver to do the same.

EK: Of course a dream weaver puts all of herself into her art! Of course! I'm not denying that. That's true of all artists: writers, painters, filmmakers. They have to put their soul into the art, or else it doesn't mean anything. That's what makes art different from the kind of AI-generated garbage all over hotel walls and flooding the "dance beats" playlists. But dream weavers, like all artists, also craft with imagination. That's the spark that separates mere "self-expression" from art.

All artists want to be valued for their imagination, the faculty they hone to distill art from a messy brew of the collective unconscious, personal experience, zeitgeist, trauma, whimsy, the randomness of the universe. That's what a dream is: a pearl of the imagination. We don't want to be valued merely for the confessional—maybe some are content to be celebrated for performing their pain, but for the rest of us, art is about transcendence.

DD: And you think your dreamers focus too much on the conspiratorial elements in your biography.

EK: I do. It's frustrating and exhausting. Yes, I grew up surrounded by conspiracy thinking, but that shouldn't be the alpha and omega of my dreams. My life isn't a conspiracy. It's tacky for any artist to speak ill of her "fans," but I don't want fans who interpret my work only conspiratorially.

DD: Do you think that's a failure of imagination by your fans and critics? Or do you think it's a failure of craft on your part? A skill issue, as we used to say.

EK: (long pause) That's hard. I'm not going to lie; I've asked myself that question countless times.

DD: And do you have an answer?

EK: No.

TWENTY-ONE

Julia's sleep was dreamless, but she awakened with a sense of dread and nameless anxiety.

She asked Talos whether anything unusual had happened during the night.

Yes, Talos informed her. The police were still looking for Piers. It was all over the local news in the commonwealth that he was missing.

Julia glanced through the articles. Pretty much what she expected. If Piers was going to be seen in public, he'd need a disguise. Nothing in the news about Julia, though; it didn't seem like anyone knew she was with him.

One more thing, Talos added. The Prince had been sending messages to Piers.

I know what she's really like.

She'll never tell you the things she's told me.

Do you know what she said about you?

Piers never responded.

Julia closed her eyes. Just like the police, the Prince had lost track of Piers; he was taunting Piers now in the hope that he would respond, let slip something that would reveal where he was. Piers was smart enough not to take the bait, but how these words must have cut him. She winced just thinking about it.

"Talos, don't tell me about these messages anymore. This is . . . private. Piers only."

"Acknowledged."

When Julia returned from her morning run, Piers had made coffee and eggs and toast for breakfast. She was grateful for the eggs but skipped the toast.

"I stayed up late," Piers said, taking a big swig of coffee. "But I think I finally got a handle on the accounts." He seemed upbeat—as though he hadn't just figured out a spreadsheet, but a much bigger puzzle about his life.

Julia nodded and said nothing, giving Piers time to decide how best to explain.

The earliest transactions on Elli's secret spreadsheet dated back to long before they had met, with the very first one coming about a year after Elli had stopped weaving "dino corporection" dreams. It was a crypto transfer to an address that was later cashed out on a defunct exchange in Vietnam. Elli recorded it as being the equivalent of one hundred dollars.

"That's a small sum," Julia remarked.

"She wasn't making much money then as an artist, so it was still significant."

A gap of three months followed before another payment, again of the crypto equivalent to one hundred dollars, to a different address. This schedule was kept up for two years before the payments escalated dramatically, and the schedule became irregular, though more frequent.

"I graphed her total income and the unexplained payments over time," Piers said.

The graph showed that over the years, both lines rose dramatically in lockstep. The more Elli earned in performance fees, recordings, endorsements . . . the more she paid to mysterious offshore accounts—amounting to 70 percent of her total income.

"And I mean, almost exactly seventy percent," said Piers. "Too exact."

"So you think she was calculating the payments," said Julia, "to meet some target."

"I think it's more than that," said Piers. "You wouldn't keep such exact calculations unless whoever you were paying had access to your income numbers and could audit you."

"Like a business partner."

"Or a blackmailer." Piers looked somber. "The Prince knew something that Elli wanted to keep secret at all costs, and that was why she was forced to pay over most of her income to him. Maybe also why she had to dream with him."

Julia felt a wave of revulsion run down her spine.

"She ran because she couldn't live that like that anymore," said Piers. "I wish I'd known—I would have done anything to protect her. She was asking for my help, in her way, by hiding the secret in a picture of us. But she didn't want to drag me down with her."

Julia could see that the conclusion was, in a way, reassuring to him. But she wasn't entirely convinced. Did Elli keep the secret because she didn't want to hurt Piers, or . . . was there something darker behind that decision?

The very last such payment by Elli, a wire of over eighty thousand dollars, happened on the day before she disappeared.

Piers had color-coded the payments by type: wires, crypto transfers, purchases and conveyances of securities, and so on. Julia, unable to make sense of the financial information, found herself drawn to patterns in the parti-colored lines and shaded slices.

"What's this bright orange line on the bottom here?"

"Good eye," said Piers. "That one I haven't been able to figure out. Starting about three years ago, every few months, there would be a small transfer to an account numbered 231."

"231? What kind of account is that? Is that the last three digits of something longer?"

"She didn't use abbreviations for anything else, so I doubt it. And the transfers are relatively small amounts: like $175.15, or $350.00."

"When did they stop?"

"The last transfer was six months ago, for $220.25. I haven't been focusing on it because the amounts are so insignificant. Maybe they were used to pay someone to run errands or . . . transaction fees."

Julia chewed her bottom lip. "I don't get it. Elli used this spreadsheet to track funds that she didn't want anyone else to know about. Other than the earliest payments, most of these transactions involve tens of thousands of dollars, occasionally even hundreds of thousands. Why track such small amounts like these? It has to be significant."

"I can't tell what '231' refers to. Your AI didn't know either."

Julia pondered the puzzle. "I don't believe it's a bank account. I wonder if it's something more . . . " Her voice trailed off.

"More what?" Piers asked.

Julia shook her head. "You didn't find anything that had that number on it when you picked through the house, did you?"

"No."

"I just have a feeling . . . I wish we could go back to your house and look."

"Definitely too late for that."

Was it? Julia spun around and picked up her tensor bank. "Talos, can you look through the Elli data and pull out all photographs and videos taken inside her house?"

Talos blinked in acknowledgment. A carousel of images flashed by on the small screen: shots of Elli and Piers and their guests over the years at dinner parties, summer barbecues, holiday brunches, posing in front of windows, bookshelves, closets, fireplaces. . . .

"Using these photos, interpolate an interior model of the house," said Julia. "Filter out the human subjects but preserve as much of the background detail as possible. Where there are conflicts, integrate all variations."

A few seconds later, Talos said, "Model ready."

"Grab your fusion vision glasses," said Julia to Piers. "We're going back to your house."

They explored the house from top to bottom. Piers, who didn't game much, nonetheless got used to "finger walking" and "claw-tap to climb" for stairs after a brief tutorial from Julia.

As the purpose of the model was investigative, Talos did as little generative fill as possible, even opting to leave different exposure and lighting conditions untouched. The result was a mosaic of space as well as time, with each wall a composite of shots taken over the years Piers and Elli had shared their home. Where there was no photo coverage, Talos left gaps that opened into the black void, making the reconstructed house reminiscent of an Escher sketch.

Julia began by looking for codes. The house contained numerous bookcases, which the couple used for not only books, but also framed pictures, souvenirs, vinyl records, and Elli's numerous awards as an oneirofex. Julia looked through them shelf by shelf, volume by volume. She was on alert for books that felt out of place, which she'd learned during her time with Cartographers Obscura were popular hideouts for valuables. This was easier said than done. While Piers organized all his books by subject matter and then author, Elli was much more idiosyncratic, apparently grouping books by "mood" rather than any obvious system—for instance, a copy of Thoreau's *Walden* was shelved next to a volume of *Where's Waldo?*, apparently based on phonetic association.

Of course, in this reconstructed model, Julia had no way to look inside the books, which were now ashes. Still, she hoped that given Elli's predilection for codes, the secret would be something more like a message encrypted by titles on the spines, with "231" as a kind of cipher key.

Piers, on the other hand, took the far simpler approach of looking for all instances of the number 231 anywhere inside the house. Talos assisted by highlighting any text that contained those digits, even if nonsequential, in a ghostly blue glow: book titles, cereal box labels, posters, business cards, letters. However, after a full tour of the house to examine these points of interest picked out by Talos, Piers found nothing promising.

"How about you?" Piers asked.

"Nothing either," said Julia. "Let's meet up."

As they had been exploring the virtual house separately, meeting up required Talos to link their fusion vision glasses and to syntoposize their coordinates in virtual space.

They found themselves standing together in the reconstructed living room.

"I wish I had taken some photos when closets or medicine cabinets were open," said Piers. "Elli always rushed around to close every closet door whenever we had company."

"I was hoping you had done a few 'house tour' videos for faraway friends or family," said Julia.

"I always tell my clients to walk around with a sensepin and film everything in their house every six months or so for insurance purposes. Should have taken my own advice." Piers paused before continuing, rather more subdued. "Would have come in handy after something like a . . . fire."

"I was sure that walking through the house like this would get us something," said Julia. "Do you want to exit and look elsewhere?"

"Not yet. I have this nagging feeling that we're missing something obvious."

"Let's try a trick I learned. I'll walk with you. Let me know when you sense something odd."

They started in the hallway of the top floor. Piers frowned as he paced slowly, looking all about himself. Julia, following behind, could only imagine the memories that flooded him as he gazed at walls covered in frames that had hung on and vanished from them over a decade. They went through all the rooms upstairs and paused in each, but after a while, Piers always shook his head. "Not here."

They descended the stairs. Piers immediately stopped in the foyer. "Something here feels . . . off."

Julia looked around. Despite Talos's best efforts to composite photos taken over a decade into something that "made sense," there were surreal touches. For instance, the entrance area, just inside the front door, was a jumbled hodgepodge of footwear, outerwear, and luggage, with all the seasons and occasions superimposed over one another: snow boots, sandals, rain galoshes, umbrellas, welcome mats, towels to wipe up the snow-mud, winter coats, rain jackets, Halloween decorations, Christmas lights. . . .

Right by the door, there was a small table with a platter for the mail, a trash can, and hooks on the wall for keys. Above the keys, there was a large grid of wall-mounted Christmas cards—Elli took a shot of the cards they got every year. A mirror hung on the wall on the opposite side of the doorway, meant for checking yourself right before going out the front door.

"It's that table," said Piers. He stared and shook his head. "Sorry. I can't be more specific. It's just off."

Julia walked closer.

The key hooks looked very strange: pomelo-sized clusters of keys dangled from them, like medieval morning stars or strange puffer fish from the deep. What was that about?

It took a second before Julia figured it out. Phone cameras, for some years, had been programmed not to record detailed images of keys as a security mechanism (early on, some criminals had exploited high-resolution pictures of keys in social media photos as templates for 3D-printed duplicates and burglarized the posters' houses). Phone cameras were required to blur out images of keys, much like photocopiers were required to distort images of currency. Thus, Talos had to treat each set of blurred keys in the photos as unique and composite them together into a jumbled bolus, like an electron cloud.

Was there something in those clouds of keys—certainly an evocative image—that Piers subconsciously saw?

Her eyes snapped to the opposite wall: the mirror. She gazed into it intently. "Look here!" she called out to Piers.

The mirror was positioned in such a way that, when the camera was positioned at certain angles, the resulting photo would contain a reflection of the key hooks. The mirrored keys, while still a jumble, looked *different*. Letters and numbers on the reflections, for instance, could be read. Whoever had implemented the key-blurring algorithm had neglected to account for edge cases involving distorted reflections.

There, among the house keys and locker keys, was one particular silver key whose image was repeated in a pinwheel, each blade labeled in mirror writing: *231*.

"What kind of key is that?"

"It's the key to a bank safe-deposit box," said Piers.

Why had Elli funneled money in small amounts to a safe-deposit box?

They looked at each other and came to the same conclusion.

She was preparing for the day when she—

"She may still be hiding near there," said Piers, eyes blazing with excitement and hope.

But where was *there*?

Although Elli's travels over the years were well-documented, Talos found no city that appeared on all her itineraries near the dates of the transfers to box 231.

"She was too careful to leave that in the open," Piers concluded.

"The Prince probably monitored her travel plans, which were often public."

"More likely, one of his AIs did the monitoring," Julia corrected.

Julia had Talos pull all of Elli's travel records around the dates of the transfers and filter for places that were reachable via a day trip from cities on her itinerary. The only region matching every itinerary was in eastern Pennsylvania, somewhere among the Northampton, Lehigh, Berks, Carbon, and Schuylkill Counties.

"That's where Elli grew up," Piers said. "Limonite was her hometown. Generations of laid-off miners and steelworkers in her family. She never left the area until college."

"Allentown, Bethlehem, Pottsville . . . how are we going to figure out the right bank?" She stared at Talos's list of financial institutions in the region that had safe-deposit boxes. Although many places had stopped offering boxes in this age of ubiquitous online transactions, they were still looking at almost two dozen names.

"I may have an idea," Piers said. "I need to make some calls."

With Talos routing the connection and masking the source, Piers placed an IP call to the first bank on the list, the Rockville Credit Union.

". . . Doing just fine, thank you. I'm calling because I represent a client whose mother just passed away. . . . Yes, absolutely devastated . . . Now, the decedent's possessions include a key to a safe-deposit box, and my client thinks it's from your bank since she used to live in the area. I can send a picture of the key. . . . Oh yes, that's very kind of you. . . ."

Piers hung up and turned to Julia. "One down. Twenty-five more to check."

"I could never do what you just did," said Julia.

"Lie?"

"I was going to say 'social engineering,' but your version works."

Julia left Piers to work on the phone, did some prep work, and went into town. She walked around for a bit until she found a trinket shop that specialized in custom souvenirs. In a place like Paxborough, everything had to be "artisanal," and in practice, that meant you paid for customizable templates designed by local artists (more expensive) or AI (much cheaper), which were then 3D-printed on demand.

"Can I get one of my designs printed on your machines?" Julia asked.

The clerk, a bored teen, didn't even look up. "No."

"I want to make something special for my boyfriend. To commemorate our time here." Julia was rather proud of herself. Piers must be rubbing off on her.

The teen looked at her, a little more sympathetic now. "I can't. The owner won't allow it."

"What if I buy the most expensive thing in here—" She looked around and pointed at a large, elaborate belt buckle in the form of two bears wrestling. "I'll pay for that, but you just put in my POLY-code file instead?"

"I don't know—"

"Please! The owner won't care. The shop isn't going to lose any money. I really want my boyfriend to have it before we leave."

The teen bit her bottom lip. "All right."

Julia paid for her purchase in cash, adding a generous tip. Then the teen took her over to the printing booth for customization. Julia selected the highest grade of durability before bumping Talos with the teen's store-issued phone, sending over the POLY-code file. The teen went ahead and programmed the machine.

While the printer whirred and hummed, Julia looked at some of the other objects on display: pottery, jewelry, desk toys, knickknacks of every description. Everything was printed but looked handmade. At least she could be sure the quality of the prints was good.

The machine beeped. The teen flipped up the cover and retrieved the finished object from the printing stage. "Beautiful," she said as she handed the thistle-rose belt buckle, gleaming silver, to Julia. "What an intricate design! I'm sure he'll love it."

Julia thanked her and accepted the buckle with both hands.

Back at the Roamnest, she set the buckle down on the kitchen counter. Wielding a butter knife as the chisel and a small frying pan as the mallet, she carefully chipped at the buckle until the thistle and the rose fell away from each other at the weak spots she had put into the design. A perfect copy of the key for box 231 dropped out.

Piers emerged from the bedroom. "Got it."

"Great. Let's eat, and we'll leave right after."

TWENTY-TWO

"Why would she pick Bethlehem?" Julia asked.

"Elli never spoke of it," said Piers, "but she must have had some good childhood memories of the place. Christmas City, USA, right?"

They were on I-90, heading west toward the New York border. Julia thought it best to get into New York before switching to smaller roads. She wasn't sure how seriously the Massachusetts authorities were hunting for Piers—the news reports were relatively subdued, probably because the police were keeping the investigation low-key.

While Piers drove, Julia kept a lookout. Periodically, she pointed her sensepin toward the back window so that Talos could analyze the traffic for anything that seemed suspicious.

"I think you're being paranoid," said Piers. Discovering where Elli had likely gone had improved his mood immensely. He seemed to think that it was just a matter of getting to Bethlehem and meeting up with Elli, as though she had left early for a vacation.

"Maybe," said Julia. "They did burn down your house, though. I wouldn't relax just yet."

They made it to Bethlehem shortly after four p.m., and Julia checked them into a Roamnest south of the Lehigh River, near the old campus of Bethlehem Steel.

The Roamnest was a tiny cottage across the road from the steel plant. The wreck of the abandoned industrial park resembled a ruined castle, with smokestacks for turrets and elevated trestles for battlements, a mute monument to a bygone era of American history. Once, the steel coming out of the blast furnaces here had built the Golden Gate Bridge, the Empire State Building, and one warship a day during the height of the Second World War, but now, the empty slag cars and decaying cranes and gantries were haunted only by ghosts. Although part of the site had been reclaimed as a performance space for musicians and theater troupes, the rest was in a slow-motion collapse, with leaking roofs and cracked concrete everywhere, green nature inexorably reclaiming her due after a temporary human intrusion.

"Why here?" Piers asked.

"Cheap roaming fee and fewer cameras."

It was too late to go to the bank that day.

"Just as well," said Piers. "We need a plan. The bank isn't going to just let us walk in and open the safe-deposit box. There are laws about this. We need to be authorized by the renter, and they'll check ID."

Julia looked expectantly at him. Piers looked just as expectantly back.

"I know nothing about bank heists," said Julia, after an awkward silence.

"I thought you knew everything there was to know about—"

"Breaking and entering? Crimes? Sorry to disappoint you, but I never— What we did was never— Forget it; I'm not going to get into it. But bottom line: I've never robbed a bank, and I'm not going to start now."

Piers was amused. "You're willing to steal a car, but you won't try to help me get into my wife's safe-deposit box?"

"We all have our quirks."

“Well, you don’t have to worry. I’m not going to ask you to help me rob a bank. I’ll . . . figure something out.”

Piers suggested that they use what little daylight they had left by driving up and taking a walk around the “target.” Based on his grin, Julia concluded that he probably thought of it as “casing the joint” or some such nonsense.

Lehigh Valley First Credit Union’s Bethlehem branch was located on the north side of the river. A local bank, it dated back to Bethlehem Steel’s glory days, when the engineers and managers, who lived on the north side, needed banking services with a personal touch. Piers and Julia took a stroll around the historic building, admiring the ornate Corinthian columns in front and the solid steel bars over the windows. Keeping Piers out of the view of the cameras, Julia went up to the door: a sign announced that the bank’s Saturday hours were from ten a.m. to one p.m.

They wandered on, taking in the sights of Bethlehem. Eventually, they stopped on Main, looking down toward Monocacy Creek, on whose sloping shore stood the eighteenth-century buildings left by the Moravians, the city’s first non-indigenous settlers.

“Whatever we end up doing, you’ll have to be the one doing the talking.”

“I know. You aren’t good with people.”

Julia looked at the Moravian village: the tannery, the mill house, the school. She imagined the lives of the first settlers. It seemed easier in many ways: a community where everyone belonged without question, where your dreams were limited, but so were your nightmares.

“Can I ask you something?” she said to Piers. “Why . . . why are you so cheerful?”

Piers was silent for a few seconds. “I think Elli wants to be found.”

She waited.

“I think that’s why she used that picture of us to hide the spreadsheet. She put clues in there so that only I would find them, so that only I would find her.”

She wondered what it was like to have such faith in another person's love.

Before returning to the Roamnest, at Julia's suggestion, they went to a drugstore and picked up some hair dye and makeup. Then they stopped by an office supply store and grabbed a printer, polycarbonate sheets, resin, a briefcase, and a few other items.

After dinner, they sat down to plan for Saturday morning.

It seemed almost certain, Piers said, that Elli hadn't set up the deposit box under her name. Given the need for privacy and secrecy, she very likely used a corporate entity.

"It wouldn't be any of the entities I formed for her," Piers said. "She would have set this one up on her own, like the ones she'd been using to pay the Prince."

"Is there anything she would have to do to maintain the 'entities'?" Julia asked, uncertain how the care and feeding of corporations worked.

"There's always a charge involved when creating an entity," Piers said, "paid to some government whose authority sustains the legal fiction. And there are usually recurring annual fees."

A quick search of Elli's business records showed regular payments to various secretaries of state for corporate maintenance.

"The amounts are much larger than justified by the LLCs and S-corps I know about," said Piers. "So it's clear she's paying for other entities. But there are no details here concerning them."

"Can you look up in a database what entities she owns?"

"She wouldn't have put in her name. To maintain privacy, she would have to disguise her ownership through layers of other structures."

"Can you figure it out?"

"I'm embarrassed to admit that I'm not sure," said Piers, looking sheepish.

"I thought lawyers were supposed to be good at this sort of thing."

"We're paid to be creative, like coming up with a new structure or a new argument, not to know the nitty-gritty details. Tracking down which entities are ultimately owned by whom is one of those low-level tasks that you can't bill clients attorney time for. I used to just ask paralegals to do it. Now that the firm has reduced the paralegal staff down to two, I have to work with a paralexaid. But obviously, I can't access firm resources now."

"I get it," Julia said. "It's kind of like how if you gave me just a pen and a notebook and told me to write you a phone app, I couldn't do it. I'd have to have Talos handle all the template code, standard frameworks, adaptive interfaces, and so on. Hey, maybe Talos can help you, too!"

Talos, as a bespoke general-purpose personal AI, lacked the kind of proprietary neuromesh found in expensive specialist expert AIs like paralexaids or jurijinns. Julia, however, soon ascertained from Piers that law firms paid for expensive AI subscriptions because they had to keep up with the constantly changing legal landscape in various jurisdictions. Older versions of specialist neuromeshes, being relatively worthless, were regularly leaked, either as a result of data breaches or because firms didn't dispose of their old hardware properly. In any event, as the research they needed didn't require esoterica concerning the latest iteration of the tax code in the Isle of Man, Julia soon found enough leaked paralexaid neuromeshes online to give Talos the expertise to help them.

They began by having Talos search the secretary of the Commonwealth of Massachusetts's corporate database and extract a list of entities registered on the same days when Elli paid the SOC's office. By filtering for common linguistic patterns in the articles of formation—machine-generated template legalese still had patterns that were unique to each AI—Talos narrowed the list down to half a dozen entities that were likely drafted by the same jurijinn that had drafted the articles for Elli's known corporations. Piers then worked with Talos to trace through the corporate filings and pierce the layers of management entities until they isolated the three LLCs that Elli had most likely used for her hidden accounts.

“This has to be the one,” Piers said. “‘A Little Instant, LLC.’ She always used to say that a gathering may be only for a little instant, but the dreams should last forever.”

“This is the LLC that owns the box?”

“I can’t be one hundred percent sure, but yes, I think so.”

“But how does that help us get to the box?”

“I think . . . I’ve worked out a way.”

Piers explained the plan. Julia listened intently and asked questions. Piers tried his best to answer them.

“You think it will work?” he asked.

She shrugged. “I can’t come up with anything better. Let’s get to it.”

Their first step, Piers explained, was creating an authorized agent of A Little Instant, LLC. The bank would not otherwise allow them to open the box, even if they had the key. The layers of anonymity in which Elli had wrapped the LLC actually made the deception they planned easier.

He drafted a power of attorney naming “Markus Newman” as the authorized agent of the LLC, printed it out, signed it in the name of a managing agent three levels of entities up the ownership chain with an illegible signature, and then pointed to the signature: “Can you put in a jurat here, like this?” He showed her a sample from online.

Julia brought out Puck and shifted it into its “spider” form. This was the form the morpho drone usually adopted for ground exploration, but in this case, Julia was really interested in the stability provided by the eight legs, which positioned Puck’s “proboscis,” or the multipurpose-manipulator, hovering half an inch above the surface on which the drone was perched. She programmed Puck to act as a CNC cutter, *dip-dip-dip* pecking over the paper like a frantic chicken at feeding time. The design was done in a few seconds.

Julia held up the paper. “How’s this?” Puck had punched a very good facsimile of a notary’s embossed seal into the paper.

“Perfect. Now you can notarize it.”

Julia signed "Lois Kee" in the space indicated. She looked at the document with some trepidation. "That's all it takes?"

"We'll need to prep a few more documents to back this up. But yes, this will probably do it."

"It's kind of frightening how easy this is."

"That's one of the ironic things about legal fictions. People will scrutinize you if you do things in your name, but when you are acting on behalf of a corporation, they stop caring. The more layers of indirection involved, the more diffuse the responsibility and the more vulnerabilities."

Julia was also rather amazed by the transformation in Piers. For someone who had spent a lifetime working with the law, he certainly didn't seem to have a lot of trouble breaking it—for the sake of his wife.

Next, they needed to make Piers into "Markus." Talos worked out the minimum alterations necessary to prevent Piers from being picked up by generic facial recognition systems: a haircut, a dye job, some taping of the skin, glasses.

Julia had to admit that she enjoyed putting a disguise on Piers. It reminded her of the times when she and Sahima had helped each other with disguises when Serena sent them on social engineering missions—Sahima always did the talking, leaving Julia free to check out the physical security and execute whatever network intrusion was necessary. She missed the theatricality, the camaraderie of putting on a play together to fool the world.

How was Sahima these days, she wondered, and was surprised by the sharp pang that followed. She missed her friend.

But Cartographers Obscura was no more, she reminded herself. No more.

"Let's take a photo of you," she said, forcing her voice to be as placid as a bowl of water.

She took Piers's picture, edited it, and added it to an ID template for "Markus Newman." Print on polycarbonate, CNC process, resin finish.

"This looks great," said Piers, admiring the fake ID. "Should be good enough for tomorrow."

Julia went over the plan in her mind. There were many uncertainties, but that was expected when they were hacking a world that she was unfamiliar with. She just had to trust Piers to know what he was talking about.

"We should get some sleep," she said. "We need to be at our best in the morning."

"I want to do a little more prep work," Piers said. "Good night."

Long into the night, Piers sat by himself, thinking.

The problem with being Penelope, he thought, is that it's tough to know when you've won.

Elli was the one who traveled, who had the adventures, who left and then returned. It was his role to listen to her rants about unimaginative critics and audiences, to reassure her that her work was important and valuable, to be her island of stability as she was relentlessly pursued by her insecurities and—as he had found out—very real, utterly terrifying threats.

He thought he had done the best he could, but Elli had not been able to confide in him. He had not, in the end, been enough for her.

Would they ever be able to get past that? Would he be able to face her again?

TWENTY-THREE

Victor had lost the lawyer. So far, he hadn't been able to pick up his trail again.

Victor had also made no progress in figuring out where Elli had gone. *There's too much data*, he had complained. *I'm doing the best I can while I'm on the road.*

Excuse after excuse. No results.

I've grown too dependent on others, the Prince reflected. This is a good reminder of how I need to get back to the basics. I built this empire; I will defend it.

He began to type.

Elli and I are kindred souls, you know?

That's why we dreamed together.

In the same way that she saw me for who I really was as she guided me through my truest fantasies, I saw her for who she really was: a butterfly trapped by the web of this world's little minds.

Those little minds would reduce artists to their biographies and even biologies. A man could only paint for the love of women and sketch disguised penises on every canvas. A woman's poetry must be about motherhood or unmotherhood and in any event suffused with the scent of menstruation. An artist's colors must be interpreted through the color of their skin. A queer sculptor's hammer strokes can't uncover anything except the pain of queerness. An Asian poet must be tied to the performance of Asianness. It's typecasting at its most insipid and stupid.

Left, right, center, they all do the same thing, mistaking the littleness of their own shriveled souls for insight, for truth, beauty, eternity.

In the same way those little minds looked at me and saw only inbetweenness, they looked at Elli and said, She must be white trash; she must be full of resentment and rage and see the world as a congeries of schemes and cabals and plots and secret clubs from which she is excluded; the only thing we want from her is to tell that funny lie about dinosaurs; come on, lady, more dinosaurs!

But I see her as she really is, as she dreams to be.

And I have done more to help her live her dream than anyone else in the world.

If she resents me now, it's only because there is no greater sin one can commit against an artist than to make her into a star, to give her success, to realize her dreams.

I'm telling you the truth: this is literally the plot of Faust.

Ask yourself, what have you ever done to make her dreams come true?

Maybe she didn't so much as run away from me as from you. She didn't steal me from me; she robbed you from you.

The Prince was giddy with the pleasure of gloating. Was there anything better than to lord it over a man after you've taken his woman? To show how weak and useless he really is, how inadequate, how utterly insignificant—

The phone rang.

The Prince smiled as he pressed answer.

He said nothing and listened to the howling void on the other end of the line.

TWENTY-FOUR

Once again, Julia's sleep was dreamless. Once again, she awakened with a sense of dread and unease.

Piers, in contrast, looked determined and energetic, almost manic.

A little touch-up on the dye job, a little skin taping, and by ten in the morning, they were ready. Piers drove them in the Zenith, and a nervous Julia scanned the traffic incessantly. Nothing.

Piers found street parking easily.

"Everything is going our way," he said. "We should see Elli soon."

Julia wasn't sure how Piers imagined it would work. Did he think Elli was going to leave the address to her Roamnest in the box?

He turned to her. "Before we go in, I just want to tell you again how much I appreciate your help. Without you, I couldn't possibly have gotten this far. I can't wait to introduce you to each other."

Julia gave him a weak smile. The sense of dread in her chest was nearly suffocating. But she couldn't point to anything specifically wrong.

Piers opened the door. "Showtime."

With a last nervous caress of her sensepin, Julia followed.

"Do you mind confirming the last time my company visited?" Piers's tone was relaxed. He smiled helplessly. "I think it was probably a week or so ago? My colleague was here."

The employee, a middle-aged man, checked the records. "Yes, last Saturday. Your company likes paying overtime?"

Piers laughed. "I doubt they *like* it, but you know what those guys in the corner offices are like. If something needs to be done, it has to be done *right now*."

While the bank employee was absorbed with filling out the form on his screen, Piers and Julia shared a look.

She was here last Saturday!

Julia could almost hear Piers's heart thumping. She realized that until now, she had not really believed that all their efforts would pan out. The nonstop chase had just seemed too far-fetched. But maybe Piers was right. Maybe they would find the address of Elli's secret hideout in the safe-deposit box. She had run away—whatever the reason—but she'd left a trail of breadcrumbs for Piers.

She braced for a bank employee to see through Piers's disguise, to demand documentation that they didn't have, to refuse to grant them entry to the vault. Maybe they'd gotten the company name wrong. Maybe the printed key would get stuck and break. Maybe the police would be summoned.

But everything went off without a hitch. The documents were checked and proved satisfactory. They entered the vault. Piers and the employee inserted their keys into box 231 and turned them smoothly together, popping the little door open. The drawer was retrieved and set down on the counter. The employee discreetly departed, leaving them behind.

Piers flipped open the hinged cover.

Julia leaned in. There were a few stacks of cash wrapped in rubber bands and rolls of coins, along with a piece of paper torn from a notebook.

Piers tried to pick up one bundle of bills. It came away only with some effort—Elli had taped the stacks and rolls to the bottom of the drawer, perhaps to prevent them from jostling about.

Piers picked up the note. There was a single line of handwritten text.

Just go.

"This is her handwriting," Piers was almost shouting. "I know it!"

"We shouldn't linger," said Julia, her voice shaking with anxiety. "Once we're back in the cottage, we can examine everything in detail."

"It's another clue," Piers said as he navigated the traffic, excitement bubbling over. "The picture of us, the spreadsheet, the safe-deposit box, and now, the money and a command to go. She was in trouble, but she figured out a way to extricate herself, and we just have to follow her. . . ."

In the passenger seat, Julia thought hard. She wanted Piers's interpretation to be true; she really did. But that sense of dread, of having missed something, wouldn't dissipate.

Even after parking in the driveway of the Roamnest, Piers prattled on without waiting for Julia to respond.

"She probably figured I'd be on the run and need the cash. But where does she want me to go? There must be an address in there somewhere. . . ."

The tensor bank buzzed in Julia's pocket. Talos was trying to warn her.

She took out the computing stick. "Don't look up or react in any way," the screen flashed.

Julia took a deep breath and waited. She looked down, as though deeply absorbed by what was on the phone-shaped tensor bank.

The text vanished and was replaced by the view from her sensepin. The drape of the lapel of her jacket pointed the sensepin to the left.

Talos zoomed in, past the oblivious figure of Piers, still talking excitedly, through the driver's-side window, until the shaky image stabilized, showing two men walking down the street toward them.

The world seemed to slow down. Everything else faded away as her sight tunneled in on the tiny screen. Discreetly, she pulled on her jacket, tilting the sensepin to the right. When the view stabilized, she could see two more men walking toward them from the other side.

Keeping her hunched-over body very still, she reached down into her backpack and retrieved Puck. She rolled the oblong between her palms, initiating the centipede transformation, and let it drop to the floor at her feet. Puck slithered under the seat.

Still keeping her eyes down, she dropped the tensor bank and the sensepin onto the floor as well. As the screen on the tensor bank went dark, she gently nudged both under the seat with her heel.

Piers finally noticed the approaching men. "Hold on, who are—"

One of the thugs pulled out a gun and pointed it at him.

Only then did Julia look up, eyes wide with surprise.

The men forced the two of them back inside the Roamnest and, after the pair had emptied their pockets on the coffee table and set down their bags, made them sit on the couch.

The leader, a muscle-bound man with short-cropped gray hair—Julia recognized him as one of the men who had been in the parking lot of her building—completely ignored both Piers and Julia. He barely glanced at the objects on the coffee table before picking up Piers's briefcase and dumping out its contents. He picked up the forged documents, examined them, chuckled, and stuffed them into a tote bag. Then he pawed through the cash taken from the deposit box with gloved hands and peered at the bills closely, looking thoughtful. Eventually, he found the handwritten note and scrutinized that as well.

He took a picture of the note before stuffing it into his pants pocket.

"Give that back," Piers said, almost growling. "My wife left that for me."

The leader looked at Piers as though startled to find him there. "What else did you get from the bank?" he asked.

Piers looked at him with hate-filled eyes and said nothing.

The man went up to Piers, pulled him up from the couch by the collar, and punched him hard in the gut. Piers collapsed to the ground.

"What else did you get from the bank?" the leader asked again.

Piers groaned but said nothing.

The leader stomped a boot on Pier's left hand. Piers screamed.

"Nothing! We got nothing else!" Julia blurted out. "You are looking at everything we found in the safe-deposit box."

"Good." The leader smiled at her. "See, when you're reasonable, I'm reasonable." He came up to Julia, bent down, and looked her in the eye. "Are you telling me the truth?"

Julia stared back without blinking. "I am. Now leave him alone."

The leader nodded. He turned to the other three. "Look through the rest of the place and see if there's anything interesting." They left the living room.

He made Piers get up and sit back down next to Julia on the couch. Julia examined his hand and found two fingers were broken. "I have to get the first aid kit," she said to the leader. He summoned a henchman, who went to the bathroom and retrieved the kit.

She did her best to splint and bandage Piers's fingers. Piers gritted his teeth but otherwise made no sound.

Meanwhile, the leader slowly sorted through the money again, spreading the bills out on the table, examining each one intensely, sometimes taking a picture with his phone. Julia regretted getting rid of her sensepin earlier—what wouldn't she give to take some pictures of these bills in case Elli had left a clue on one of them!

The three men were wrecking the other rooms. Julia could hear them rummaging through the closets and pantry, poking at the printer and the polycarbonate sheets, riffling through the documents on the kitchen table.

The leader finished with the bills. He stacked the money neatly on the coffee table, took out his gun, and waved it casually at Julia and Piers. "Don't try anything," he warned. He put the gun away, took out his phone, and began typing furiously.

The other men returned. "Victor, we didn't find anything good," one of them said. "Just a few hundred dollars in cash. Some clothes. Some junk electronics. Some papers."

"Papers?" Victor, the leader, asked.

"Here." He handed Victor the stack of printouts of Elli's spreadsheet.

Victor took the stack, flipped through the sheets quickly, and shoved the stack into the tote bag. "Thanks. You can have the money you found. And the clothes, too, if you like them."

The man looked sullen. He glanced at his companions, who seemed to be urging him to go on. Turning back to Victor, he said, "It's only a few hundred dollars. You said there would be a bonus." He looked meaningfully at the stacks of cash on the coffee table.

Victor smiled. "That's why I've been making neat piles. *This* is your bonus. Keep an eye on our friends on the couch, please."

While the three men looked menacingly at Piers and Julia, Victor—he never took off his gloves, Julia noticed—picked up Piers's phone and dropped it into the tote bag.

He turned to Julia. "Where's your phone?"

Julia nodded at her backpack.

He unzipped it and turned it upside down. Wallet, makeup, tissues, as well as a dozen phones clattered to the floor.

"Which of these is yours?" the leader asked Julia.

Julia said nothing.

One of the men slapped her. Piers lunged off the couch to intervene. Another man grabbed him by his left hand and squeezed. Piers screamed and collapsed to the floor, cradling his broken fingers.

"The Bloom Y," Julia said. She avoided looking at Victor. "It's in the side pocket."

Victor unzipped the side pocket, retrieved a white Bloom Y, and dropped it inside the tote bag. He looked from the other phones on the floor to Julia and back again. "On second thought, I better take them all. You might be tricking me with a decoy phone."

Finally, he went through Julia's wallet.

"Lois Kee," he read the fake ID. "So what do you do?"

"I buy and sell used phones."

"Funny. How do you know Piers?"

Julia looked at the tote bag. She remembered the fake documents with her name as the notary public. "He was my lawyer the last time I was charged with forging documents." A good lie, Sahima once told her, made you just dirty enough to be uninteresting.

He dropped the wallet and gave her a contemptuous look before zipping up the tote bag.

Finally, turning to the other men, he said, "You can have the car too after you clean up, but I need to leave now."

"What do you want us to do with them?" one of the men asked, indicating Piers and Julia.

"Your choice," said Victor. "But I do want to remind you that they've seen your faces."

And, barely fifteen minutes after everyone had entered the cottage, he was gone.

The three remaining thugs looked at Julia and Piers.

"Which of you has money?" one of them asked, cracking his knuckles.

"Listen," Piers said, "if I were you, I'd start running right now." He sat up on the floor, wincing.

"And why is that?" He stepped closer and loomed threateningly over Piers.

"Stop it!" Julia shouted as she crouched on the floor next to Piers.

"Neither of us has any money. His house just burned down, along with everything he owns. Look up 'Piers Neri'; you'll see."

"The police are looking for me," said Piers, his voice slurred from the pain. "And I can bet you that the guy who just left is calling in a tip. He wants me in jail, and he wouldn't mind throwing you in there with me."

The three men looked at one another.

"Don't look at me. I don't know anything about Victor. Tommy introduced us."

"Did Tommy vouch for him?"

"No. Just said he paid well."

"Not that well."

They eyed the money on the coffee table again.

"Barely adequate, I'd say."

"Hey, the guy isn't lying. This is him," one of the men said, holding up his phone, the screen showing a picture of Piers. "Article says he's missing. Maybe the police really are looking for him."

"I'm telling you," said Piers, "Victor left early so that he could call the police. He's framing you. As a lawyer, it's my professional opinion that committing murder would not be in your best interest."

Again, the three looked at one another.

"He had those fancy gloves, remember?" said one. "Didn't have any for us."

"I wouldn't take the car either," said the second man. "No way to know if he called that in."

"I say we bail," said the third. "Why should we kill for him?"

"Yeah. Fuck Victor."

The men began to divide the money on the table, bickering all the while.

"Listen," Piers said, "there's something on that money that matters a great deal to me. If I could just look at—"

"Shut up," one of the men said without even looking at him.

"Please. I'm trying to find my wife, and she probably left—"

"Fuck off!" another said. "You're making me regret leaving you alive."

Piers made as if he wanted to object again, but Julia had had enough. She covered his mouth, looked him in the eye, and shook her head.

Just like Victor before them, the men left the cottage.

"Are you all right?" asked Julia.

"It hurts like hell. But I'll live."

"Good. I'll fix your hand again, and then—"

"What about the money?" Piers broke in. "Elli must have left a clue in there."

"Maybe. But I can't think about it at this moment. Right now, we need to wipe the place down and get out."

After a moment's reflection, Piers understood. Victor didn't know Julia's real identity, and if he did call in an anonymous tip about Piers, they could still keep the police from finding out that she was with Piers.

They rushed to get cleaning supplies from the bathroom. While Piers wiped down every surface inside the cottage, Julia went to take care of the inside of the car.

As soon as she opened the car door, Puck crawled out from under the seat, dragging the sensepin and the tensor bank with Talos behind it.

"I told you to always carry a decoy phone," said Talos. "Did that work out?"

"Sure did," said Julia. "But technically, I told you so that you could remind me."

It took less than thirty seconds to completely wipe the car's memory so that there was no record of her and Piers ever having used it.

She went back inside and stuffed all her remaining possessions into the backpack. Then she booked a rideshare to meet them a mile away in twenty minutes.

"Ready?"

"Ready."

TWENTY-FIVE

Julia insisted on taking the rideshare first to Allentown, followed by multiple local trips, hopping from town to town, bus station to train station, skipping across New Jersey and Pennsylvania, in the hopes that they would shake off the police, before finally heading to Philadelphia.

Whenever Piers tried to broach the subject of Elli, Julia only shook her head.

"Where are we going now?" he asked.

"To see a friend," said Julia.

It was hard sometimes for Julia to disentangle her feelings about Cartographers Obscura and Serena.

Others certainly respected Serena, followed her lead. But Julia *adored* her.

The love she felt for Serena was so pure, so intense, that her relationship with everyone else seemed to pale in comparison. Even Sahima, who had brought her into the group, who had taught her how to hear the heartbeat of machines, didn't seem nearly as dear.

A word of approval from Serena would make her giddy the whole morning, but a frown would send her into a dark depression for days. She hungered for her presence, yearned for her gaze, prayed to hear her voice.

Serena was wise; Serena was brave. She saw through the world's falsehoods and pointed out the one just path. She asked the Cartographers to steal from the rich and give to the poor; to punish the powerful and the hypocritical, holding them up to ridicule; to doxx and expose the exploiters of children, the blackmailers, the revenge pornographers.

Julia loved doing what Serena wanted. She stole Bloom's code so that the company would have to pay a ransom not to have it posted across the net; she discovered jailbreaks for popular large action transformers, which were auctioned to the highest bidders; she mapped out exploits and vulnerabilities in bladerunners, which were sold to as many content farmers as possible before they were patched. In every case, the funds raised were used to help the needy, to lift up the weak, to succor the powerless.

She was also hunted. Being part of Cartographers Obscura brought with it dangers. Security guards, the police, gangsters, competing hackers, even the FBI—at one time or another, Julia was hunted by them all. But the menacing figures and the constant threats of violence didn't faze her. For one thing, she was young, and that always came with a certain contempt for danger and authority. For another, Serena told her what she was doing was *right*. The righteous had no fear.

But nothing perfect lasted.

When some Cartographers—Sahima among them—began to demand proof of the group's good deeds, to verify the claimed justifications and alleged flows of capital, to, in a word, question Serena's leadership, Julia angrily denounced them, rejected them, helped to cast them out.

Serena could do no wrong.

"How dare you question Serena?" She had looked at Sahima in disbelief. This was their final argument before Sahima left.

"It's never wrong to ask questions," Sahima had told her.

"You're destroying our dream," she had said in a last desperate plea.

"You have to wake up at some point," Sahima had said. And then she was gone.

There were periods of lucidity when she analyzed her feelings, wondering if she was using Serena as a surrogate for her mother, such that her love for Serena was a tangled mixture of grief and guilt and childish worship, thorny and cloying, bitter and sweet at once. But she didn't like gazing too closely at her heart; it was like looking into the mirror at a scar.

After Sahima was gone, Julia became even more zealous. She volunteered for the most dangerous missions, especially physical penetrations. People, especially men, tended to look past a young girl, thinking she was no threat. The more risks she took, the more Serena praised her.

She's proud of me. And she would fall asleep, more content than ever.

And then came the raid, being suddenly jerked awake in the darkness, utter confusion as she was cuffed, taken past the broken-down doors, the sirens blaring, the ride in the backseat, the fingerprints, photographs, holding cell, the smell of piss and shit, the nightmare from which there was no awakening.

Of the trials, she could recall very little. She couldn't even remember meeting Nick for the first time, only that he was very patient and gentle, sitting with her for hours as he explained everything again and again, much of what he said simply drifting through her like water through a sieve.

But what did stick with her were the images of Serena shown to the jury, Serena as Julia had never seen her: posing with gold chains, bars, a tubful of glittering stones; standing in front of her jet; lounging on her island; a castle garden full of exotic animals. The hospital that had been built for children in Laos, the therapy fund for victims of sex trafficking, the nonprofit center that hired lawyers to fight against Big Tech surveillance . . . all the projects Serena had talked about turned out to be mere fantasy propped up with generated façades, dreams even wispier than Shahrazad's veil. Serena was an oneirofex, too, after a fashion.

The money Julia and the others stole had never gone to help anyone except Serena; she was, in fact, the greatest hacker of Cartographers Obscura: she had hacked *them.*

"We were idealists," Sahima said during her testimony. "We fed on dreams. She knew that and took full advantage."

On the witness stand: that was the last time Julia had seen her once-dear friend.

Julia ascended the steps to the brownstone on Vagabond Lane, a quiet, upscale residential street in Newbold. She stepped slowly, giving the doorbell plenty of time to get a good shot of her, to run the facial recognition searches, to warn the owner.

Before she could ring, the door swung open.

Sahima stepped out and pulled Julia into a fierce hug.

"I'm . . . sorry," Julia said. It was not enough. Not anywhere enough. Words were simply too light for the weight of her feelings.

"You were trying to hold on to a dream," said Sahima. "Love can make us do foolish things, but it's also what makes us who we are. Forgive yourself. I certainly have."

Julia felt the grace of the moment in every fiber of her being.

"Ed is in Harrisburg for the week," Sahima said. "I rarely have guests when he's not home."

Nursing a cup of hot herbal tea at the kitchen table, Piers next to her, Julia appreciated Sahima's efforts at making her comfortable. She had intuited, without even a single word from Julia, that they were on the run, and had reassured her that they would be safe.

For too long she had allowed shame and embarrassment to get in the way of a friendship strong and steady as her heartbeat. What else had she done wrong?

Knowing that Julia needed time, Sahima chatted with Piers without prying. She was married to a Pennsylvania state senator and worked as a garden designer.

"Nothing like what I used to do," she said to Piers with a quick glance at Julia. "It's a bit like painting, a bit like architecture, and a lot like planning a good wedding reception: let's put the peonies with the irises here so that they bloom together and hold a good conversation with their contrasting shapes; let's put the marigolds with the petunias so that we have a colorful buffet for the bees—but add a line of spotted laurel so that the bees don't buzz in your guests' faces."

"It actually sounds a little like drafting a contract," Piers said. "I like to put the indemnities and warranties right after the payment schedule, to lessen the shock and unpleasantness, and to cross-reference the defined phrases so that you can find them by any of the constituent terms."

"You try to draft for humans instead of machines," said Sahima, smiling. "I also design my gardens to be lived in rather than to be photographed."

Piers raised his teacup. "To humane gardens and human-readable contracts."

Sahima laughed and raised her teacup.

"I'm ready to talk now," said Julia.

Sahima listened to her explanation without interruption.

And then: "Tell me, what do you need?"

Julia was so grateful she felt like crying.

To begin with: warm food, a comfortable bed, the feeling that they were safe.

"I'll work on the phones and the car tomorrow," said Sahima. "I'm thinking something older: no autopilot, no biometrics, no cameras, no secure computing, and not a dozen ways to be tracked. Just a way to get you from point A to point B."

"That will be a relief," said Julia.

"Sweet dreams."

TWENTY-SIX

Sunday morning.

Sahima was out before they had gotten up. Piers made coffee and toast and waited for Julia in the kitchen.

"We need to talk," said Piers, still wincing from the broken fingers. Sahima had given him some painkillers so that he could sleep.

"Yes," Julia said. "I'm sorry I wasn't ready to think about Elli before—"

"No, I should be the one apologizing first." Piers paused, shook his head, and went on. "I think I messed up. The night before last, I called him."

He showed Julia the messages from the Prince. It was the Prince's implication that he knew Elli's soul better than Piers that finally pushed him over the edge.

"I thought I was very careful," said Piers. "I had never called him from that phone before. Believed I was safe."

"How long did you talk to him?"

"Maybe an hour. I hadn't meant to, but the longer we talked, the more questions I had."

Julia closed her eyes and imagined the scene: Piers stepping outside the Roamnest in the dark, alone, the ruins of Bethlehem Steel across the deserted road. Whispers, angry curses, loud, louder, shouting from rage.

"I've gone over what I said to him so many times," said Piers. "I can't understand how I gave our location away. I was so careful—"

"It wasn't what you said," snapped Julia. She clenched her teeth so that she wouldn't yell at him.

There were, even using a conservative estimate, over two hundred billion hours of user-generated video content available online at this point, she explained, when she finally had herself under some measure of control. From the top of Mount Everest to a submersible exploring the Mariana Trench, from the nave of the rebuilt Notre-Dame to the rotunda of the Capitol, hours upon hours of footage covered every corner of the globe, juicy raw data for hungry neuromeshes.

Each church, concert hall, theater lobby, public monument, ancient ruin . . . had its acoustic signature, a unique blend of ambient noise, reverberation, and the timing and quality of echoes. Julia knew of multiple databases cataloging the acoustic signatures of various locations. Some of the databases were used by law enforcement; others were open-source and could be accessed by anyone. The Prince had kept Piers talking to get a good sample of his sonic environment through the phone. Considering the unique acoustic signature of the Bethlehem Steel ruins, it probably wasn't tough to pinpoint Piers's exact location. Talos could have helped Piers disguise the acoustic signature if only she had not directed Talos not to intrude into Piers's privacy.

"I'm so sorry," Piers said. "I really, really messed up."

"You did," said Julia. Rage flared in her. "We both could have been killed."

For a brief moment, she thought about storming out, leaving Piers to stew in the mess he had made himself.

She forced herself to breathe deeply and evenly, her eyes closed. She imagined what it was like for Piers, alone, on the run, everything in his life gone except one idea, a single shining vision that he hung on to and wouldn't let go. A fierce love reassured him that this was all worth it, that this was all going to work out.

Could she, of all people, not understand that?

"You were trying to hold on to a dream," she said. It was not an accusation.

They were both silent for a beat.

"What did you ask him?" Julia asked.

"I asked him why Elli was paying him."

As Julia listened to Piers's account of his conversation with the Prince, she imagined Elli's life yet again and tried to see what she had gotten right and what she had gotten wrong.

Like all artists, Elli first practiced her craft for the simple reason that it was fun.

The earliest dreams were for her teenaged self. As she prepared for bed, she told herself stories. She set her phone's crude generative AI to turn the hypnagogic mumblings into surreal images projected onto the ceiling, still covered in glow-in-the-dark constellations. The scenes accompanied her to dreamland as she drifted to sleep, and her dreams continued on the ceiling as she woke up. She edited the recordings down to the most interesting scenes and posted them to her stream.

Intrigued by these, friends asked her to play the game with them. Singly and then in small groups at sleepovers, she whispered a story or hummed a song, her rasping voice modulated to trigger autonomous sensory meridian responses, while she typed away on a silent keyboard, guiding the AI to visualize her story as well as her friends' responses.

Still later, when she began to dream online with strangers, she changed her method yet again. Unable to see her audience—and there were too many of them, in any event—she relied on AI to extrapolate their sentiment and mood from what they typed into the chat, what they muttered into their microphones, what they authorized their biomonitors and direct neural sensing headsets to share.

By now, she found herself part of a larger community experimenting with collective AI-augmented experiences. As they exchanged tips and honed their craft, they invented a new medium without quite realizing it. The vivid dream was a collective effort, like an orchestra wherein the players' instruments were their brains, and she was the conductor. Her senses and instincts enhanced with machine learning, she immersed herself in the coalescing mood of the audience, giving form to common fragments of their imagination, instantiating microtrends and picomemes that susurrated through the crowd like waves pulsing through the fronds of an anemone, growing and cultivating and amplifying emergent patterns as well as planting new seeds, gradually synchronizing and gathering thousands upon thousands of individual brain waves—the alphas and gammas, the thetas and deltas—into a massive tsunami of intense egoless awareness, transcendent consciousness, and collective cognition, upon which the audience rode and rode, a high with seemingly no end.

Very, very few artists in the history of the world could claim to have had a hand in the creation of an entirely new medium. One would think that would be enough of a dent in the universe for Elli.

However, because we have chosen, as a society, to make artists dependent upon the market, we've also always believed—implicitly or otherwise—in an equivalence between what is artistically worthy and what fetches the highest price. As Ursula K. Le Guin once observed, even a "businessman," who has no interest in art or belief in anything transcendent, may read a bestseller now and then simply to feel the magic of something that has made money, that has sold. There is, of course, more than one kind of currency in our modern market, and attention, gaze, admiration—these are worth almost as much as mere coin.

Very few artists can resist for long the relentless pressure to move from having fun to having an audience, to go from being validated by one's own childlike wonder to craving the attention of others: awards, fame, money. There is so little certainty in art, so few ways to concretely judge where you are, that the hunger for approval, for the magic that comes from having sold, from being desired by many, becomes the polestar by which all steer.

Elli was no exception.

Finding a dream that mesmerized hundreds of thousands, even millions, wasn't easy, no easier than crafting a best-selling book or a blockbuster. Elli tried her hand at different genres: historical, sci-fi, dreams based on Disney films (not nearly as popular as one might have thought), dreams based on celebrities (the cease-and-desist orders arrived almost instantaneously), dreams based on politicians (way more popular than the premise would suggest—it turned out that a lot of people enjoy dreaming about being powerful without having to be wise). . . .

None were as popular as "dino corporection," however, a whimsical experiment, almost a throwaway joke. But it resonated with audiences like nothing else she had ever done.

It's impossible to discern precisely why a piece of art sells; artistic worth is only a part of the equation, along with resonance with the zeitgeist, the inexplicable rules of fashion, and large doses of blind luck. But it was hard to argue against success. The craving for recognition, for fame, drove her to keep on weaving that dream for ever-larger audiences.

Art demanded sacrifices. Like those magicians of old, who took their acts so seriously that they never broke character even when offstage, she committed to a conspiratorial persona that she carried on her tours, in interviews, in vlogs and flipclips, a never-ending performance.

She was doing well. She was on the verge of becoming a star.

But then she did something very rare for those tempted by fame. She asked herself: *What do I want?*

She knew she didn't want to spend the rest of her life as the "girl with the dinosaur conspiracy." No artist wanted to be consumed by their art, especially a throwaway piece that had somehow caught fire.

It felt like a crossroads. If she continued with the dinosaurs any longer, she might never escape them. If she wanted to tell the story she wanted to tell, she had to turn in a different direction.

And so, just like that, she decided to drop her persona, to cancel all the tours, and to put "dino corporection" behind her.

She would weave new dreams for new audiences. The very freedom promised by that thought made her giddy, and she knew she was making the right choice.

The right choice didn't mean success. She tried and tried, but the new audience failed to show up. At every opportunity, people were telling her that they wanted her to do more dino corporection, to play the role of the crazy conspiracist from rural America, to embody the caricature, the stereotype, the cliché.

Were they doing so because they enjoyed the irony or because they genuinely believed in dino corporection? Did it make a difference?

One day, after another failed show in Palo Alto, where she had spent the last of her savings to rent out a theater equipped with the latest advances in neural sensing and biofeedback so that she could put on the best show that she knew how, and only fifteen people had shown up (five of them demanded their money back when she refused to bring out the dinos), she thought: This is it; I'm done.

She wept silently in her room at the historic Cardinal Hotel. The Art Deco chandeliers, the terra-cotta floors, the ground-level phone booths, and an elevator whose door you had to pull open yourself—everything evoked another century, another time. She felt like a relic herself. Somehow, the art form that she had helped create had left her behind.

There was a knock on the door.

She told whoever it was to go away. But the insistent knocking would not stop.

The peephole showed that her visitor was a man with a briefcase. He was a little man, not just in stature, but in the very air he projected—as soon as you looked away he might vanish into thin air.

"Go away!"

"I think you should hear what I have to say," the man said, smiling into the peephole. "We can help you leave the dinos behind."

She washed her face, fixed her makeup, and opened the door.

The man had a presentation on his laptop: slides, graphs, charts, trend lines. He told her a story, and then he made her an offer.

"That's ridiculous," she said. "It's an old scam. Fifty cents for a generated follower on FlipClip, a dollar for a bot on TrendBend. It sounds grand, but after you walk away, what have I really bought? A bunch of useless accounts with gibberish posts that will never be seen by a human, pretend likes that will never affect the algorithm, nonsense chatter that will add to no conversation except the kipple of the dead internet. The bladerunners are too good. Astroturfing is dead."

For a while, bot-generated comments, votes, likes, reviews, referrals had become so prevalent that many had thought the algorithmic web, wherein you were presented with recommendations based on the choices made by others, was going to collapse from the data pollution and bring down with it the entire modern commercial internet. Into this existential breach had stepped the bladerunners, neuromeshes trained to administer the "Reverse Turing Test" to detect, isolate, and terminate the bots (or at least the bot-generated content) so that human consumers could continue their mutual trolling and parasocial engagement with their idols unmolested. The bladerunners weren't perfect, but perfection was unnecessary when your goal was only to keep the bot hordes at bay. Depending on one's level of cynicism, the bladerunners were either critical agents defending the sanctity of what was left of the human-centric internet, or digital monstrosities dedicated to preserving the profits of Big Media and Big Tech. In either case, a certain proportion of false negatives or false positives was acceptable.

"We don't use bots," said the little man, his mien deeply offended. "And we're not going to sell you something and run; we're here to partner with you for the long term."

She asked more questions; he offered more answers. But from the moment she didn't throw him out, from the moment she asked for the first detail, she and he both knew that she had been caught.

It was a boutique service, he said, offered only to artists who showed promise. The organization he represented was associated with European royalty—this was implied, not outright stated—which obviously suggested discerning taste. The service would get her art in front of the right people, people who were inclined to like what she did, so that she could get a little boost, more word of mouth, the nudge that could maximize her luck.

Later, she would realize that everything he said was only true in the most technical sense; later, she would see that he had been using the most transparent ploys to appeal to her vanity, to play on her insecurity; later, she would recognize that his most potent ally had been herself, so desperate and hungry for validation that she would have told herself any lie she needed to take the deal, to make it happen.

"You don't have to pay a cent if this doesn't work," he said almost casually.

"All right," she said. She had made up her mind to keep on touring, to try again. "What do I have to lose? Just . . . no dinosaurs."

She never saw that man again. For a while, she thought she must have dreamed him, a figment of the imagination born from her deepest fears and yearnings.

That day at the Cardinal Hotel marked the nadir of her tour. The next show, she had twenty-five people, and the one after that, sixty. A hundred and ten. Two hundred and six. Sold out. Sold out. Sold out.

She had hit after hit. A FlipClip influencer named "d8ckd8ckginger" with two million followers gushed about her romance dream, and she had to add five shows in Oakland. A character on an A-drama mentioned her sci-fi dream in her weekend plans, and her merchandise sales shot up five hundredfold overnight. The more she sold, the more she sold.

And she never had to do "dino corporection." Not even once.

The thrill of success drove her to take risks. She took on genres thought to be too out there: J-pop murder mystery, anti-trolley morality fable, Brechtian nightmare, New Restoration comedy, muckraking internet alternate reality. She really thought she was weaving the best dreams of her career: topical, poignant, deep. Not just entertaining, but with something to say about the ephemera of modernity as well as the eternal human condition.

She was making not only money, but also art.

And then, one rainy night, after dreaming with a sold-out crowd in a glitzy theater on West 44th, a man showed up at her dressing room. Tall, well-dressed, with the air of someone used to getting his way oozing from every strand of well-coifed hair.

"You can't be here," she said. "I don't do fan—"

He stopped her by holding a finger up to her lips. She was so startled that she literally gasped.

"I'm not a fan," he said. "I made you."

And that was how she finally met the Prince.

He came into the dressing room and opened his laptop, inviting her to sit next to him. He showed her how his service had liked and clapped the arena recordings of her shows, propelling them up the algorithmic timelines of FlipClip and SSTTRR and Picto and Poppa and Socringe and Dizzy. He showed her how his people had downvoted, argued, reported, brigaded, banded, until any mention of her in connection with "dino corporection" was algorithmically hidden, consigned to oblivion. He showed her how his agents had bought and sold tickets to her shows among themselves on the stub market, slowly bidding up the price until the pattern triggered the machine-learning filters of newsjinns, until the cascade of auto-newslets prompted human journalists to think there was a story. He showed her the intricate network of fan accounts, dream wikis, forum debates, octochan threads, stan brigades . . . woven to create the illusion of her popularity, to bait and entice the social and search and discovery and recommendation algorithms until real people *believed* that she was popular.

I made you who you are, said the Prince. You're my dream.

She didn't want to believe it. No artist wants to believe that their success is unearned, that they are an imposter, a fraud, a creature of mere commerce.

Yet, the Prince's story struck her with the force of truth. Why had she suddenly made a breakthrough? Why had the demands for "dino corporection" abruptly ceased? She had thought she was winning because of her talent, with perhaps a dose of well-timed luck, but now she knew better. Everything dated back to that fateful day in Palo Alto. It wasn't a dream.

"You deserve this," said the Prince. "You're special. I can see it. I'll make you into the star that you deserve to be, and you'll share the money you make with me. We're partners."

What could Elli do? The very same tricks the Prince had used to bend the crowd in her favor could also be used to turn it away from her in disgust. He could use those reviews, downvotes, reports, comments, complaints to bury her until she had been completely forgotten.

Fame—at least the desirable kind—was a hard drug to give up.

Or, he could go for the much simpler but equally effective strategy of simply exposing her as a manufactured idol, a manipulated mirage. There were, in fact, worse things than being known for the rest of her life as "the girl with the dinosaur conspiracy"; she could be known as "the girl who paid a scammer to make her famous," a talentless hack, a fraud.

"Together, we'll make all your dreams come true. But first, why don't you weave me a dream, one that's just for me?"

And she didn't say no, as he knew she couldn't, wouldn't.

"She must have thought about coming clean, about telling the truth, many times," said Piers. "But the longer it went on, the harder it became to extricate herself. I've been trying to understand what it was like for her. I think, after a certain point, the kind of manipulation that the Prince engaged in was no longer relevant. Her fame was self-sustaining, and any fans that came to her by reputation stayed only because of her talent.

"But in her mind, no matter how successful she became, it would always be poisoned at the source. She would never be able to escape the fraud at the heart of her own story, and I can only imagine how much pain she endured as she made each transfer to the Prince, literally a portion of the wages of sin."

Julia nodded as she imagined Elli's feelings. The woman was trapped. She could neither enjoy the fame that she had worked so hard to achieve nor step away from it all—always, the threat of exposure hung over her head. To have your own story taken away from you, to not even be allowed to alter your own script. It was a true nightmare.

And she knew something about that, didn't she?

A shiver went down her spine. The parallel was eerie, almost too perfect. For the briefest of moments she wondered if the Prince had spun a lie for Piers to trap *her*, to make her feel *seen*.

She wanted to laugh at her own egotism but couldn't. The paranoia was part of the legacy of what she had lived through. If you were truly persecuted once, you couldn't help but believe you'd always be persecuted.

"He was gleeful on the phone, the Prince," said Piers. "He told me about their dreams together, about how much Elli was enthralled by the wonders of his mind, by the beauty of his imagination. There were moments when he sounded so self-satisfied that it was clear he thought *he* was the artist, that his mind was so complex and intricate that Elli couldn't help but fall in love with him."

He turned to Julia and gave her a wry smile. "At first, I was enraged, both because of what he said and the thought that I hadn't been able to protect Elli, that she had to deal with all this alone.

"I yelled at him, cursed at him, told him to come and face me like a man. But then I realized that only a deluded fool would believe that the woman he's blackmailing would fall in love with him.

"He was goading me, but the longer he talked, the happier I became. I finally understood what Elli was doing: she was lulling him into falling in love with her, into a fantasy that pulled him in deeper and deeper. And then, a week ago, she sprang the trap. By abruptly disappearing from his life, she stole his dreams, stole *him*, forced him to see himself as he really was: a criminal, a fool, an idiot full of sound and fury.

"But she still wanted me to find her. That was why she left the trail of clues. Except I messed up, and we lost the clue she hid in the money. To him."

Julia looked thoughtful. "Maybe not."

TWENTY-SEVEN

The Prince looked at the latest photos from Victor.

These were much more interesting than the shots of cash found at the bank earlier.

What was Elli doing, hiding a few thousand dollars in a safe-deposit box in the middle of nowhere? Victor had scoured every millimeter of those bills, but no secret message had been uncovered.

While Victor seemed to think that there was a solution to the riddle, the Prince suspected that the safe-deposit box was a little joke from Elli. It was just like her, a woman obsessed with secrets and codes, to make up a *fake* riddle to trap him, entice him to spin his wheels and devote useless energy in pursuit of a nonexistent solution, while she laughed all the way *from* the bank. The irony was so delicious that he could imagine her cruel grin, rubbing her hands together and sipping champagne, congratulating herself.

Well, he was too smart for that. He wouldn't be caught by her trap.

It was clear what was really going on.

The two latest photos from Victor were of the front and back of a postcard. The front of the card was a sea view taken from inside a room: a wooden desk with a row of small planters filled with slender flowers; rustic shutters flung open; a view of a lawn sloping down to a beach, and beyond, the sunlit ocean. The narrow strips of wall visible on either side of the open window served as a frame. A lovely view, if rather clichéd.

The Prince swiped to the photo of the back of the postcard. There was a printed address, presumably of where the view was taken, just like those old-fashioned postcards you could pick up from hotel lobbies to impress your friends back home with how fancy you were. There was no addressee, just a single line of handwritten text: *I have our dreams.*

Given the burned-down house and the search for Elli and Piers, mail for the address at the end of the cul-de-sac on Carmichael Lane was being held at Carre's post office. While floundering around, unsure where Piers had gone, Victor had sent one of the local Boston thugs to break in and grab the bundle, just in case something in the mail would help him track the lawyer down. The Prince's call with Piers had then sent Victor down to Bethlehem before he had a chance to go through the mail, so Victor hadn't seen this postcard, nestled between credit card offers and discount coupons for datajinn subscriptions, until this morning.

I have our dreams.

The handwriting was Elli's. He had seen enough samples of it in the data Piers had uploaded to be sure of that. But what was Elli trying to say?

He imagined the woman in hiding, scouring the internet for news about her disappearance, bored with a life on hold. Others might think Piers was the intended recipient of the postcard, but the Prince knew the truth: it was meant for himself.

A thrilling shiver went down his spine. Despite everything, she missed him. Despite his complete absence in her data, he had been seared into her soul. Only after trying to cut him out of her life had she come to understand that she couldn't live without him. He smiled at the deliciousness of it all. What a tease. What a minx!

He picked up the phone and hit Victor's number.

TWENTY-EIGHT

Julia explained to Piers her new habit, since she had joined him on the run, of wearing her sensepin in continuous mode.

A quick scrub through the pin's photo stream revealed five photos that captured at least some of the contents of the safe-deposit box. All were taken when they were in the vault, so the lighting wasn't the best. Talos stitched the different photos together, saving the best pixels from each.

They could see the stacks of cash and the rolls of coins, but only the bills and coins at the very top were visible in their entirety. They examined the cash as well as the note in Julia's handwriting pixel by pixel but found nothing that could be a clue.

Piers dropped his face into his hands, utterly dejected.

Once more, Julia wished she had worn the sensepin when Victor had spread the bills on the coffee table—but then again, had she been wearing it, Victor likely would have torn it from her right away and tried to track down the device it was tethered to.

Pacing back and forth, she tried to recall the way Victor had looked through the bills and then stacked them back up neatly. He had smiled as he gave the money away to the thugs he had hired. Had he already seen what he needed to see? Maybe he was already on his way to Elli.

She stopped and spun to face Piers. "We've been running away long enough. It's time we started hunting *them*."

When Sahima returned that afternoon, she brought them new burner phones as well as a new car: a very beat-up used Corolla.

"There's nothing smart about this car at all. The only thing it will do is get you where you want to go without ever talking back at you."

"It's perfect. Thank you, Sahima."

Julia had been forgiven without even asking for forgiveness. It reminded her of meeting Sahima, of a version of herself that deserved grace. Maybe that girl was still there.

Sahima handed Julia a prepaid debit card. "There's two thousand on there. I figured he can't access his accounts if he's on the run. If you run out, I'll load more."

"I—I can't—"

"You can. You are trying to help a woman who got trapped. The best way to thank me is to save her. We could all use a helping hand now and then."

Julia nodded. Grace. "All right. Now, Piers and I need to go online—"

"Knock yourself out, but don't tell me what you'll be doing. I don't want to have to lie."

"Don't worry. We'll use every precaution."

"Of course. Good hunting."

When Julia told Victor that her phone was the Bloom Y, it was a calculated lie.

The Bloom Y was the perfect decoy phone. It was relatively new and still had some value on the used market, thus diverting anyone from suspecting she had anything more valuable.

It also had a secret. Julia had configured the phone so that when it found itself separated from Julia, it would activate its cellular connection and wait for instructions.

Click-clack-clack. She typed on the tensor bank's projected keyboard at Sahima's dinner table.

The command went over the interconnected electromagnetic networks—wired, optical, wireless—that together kept modern civilization going. She sat back and waited, her lips pressed together so tightly that they disappeared in a line. Next to her, Piers folded his arms, cradling his throbbing hand, and buried his head, his back tense like a compressed spring.

It was such a slender thread of hope. If Victor—or whoever he had given the Bloom Y to—practiced standard counter-surveillance techniques, by now, the phone would be imaged and wiped, not left alone to run whatever code Julia had put on it. At a minimum, the phone would be transported inside a Faraday cage to prevent all radio communications.

A beep. A terminal window appeared on the tensor bank's projected screen.

Without a celebratory whoop or high five, Julia concentrated on her fingers dancing over the virtual keyboard, the simulated clacking loud and crisp. There was no telling how long this connection would last; she had to make the most of it.

The Bloom Y's GPS coordinates were in Sheepshead Bay, Brooklyn, New York.

She turned on the phone's camera: an indistinct twilight. The Bloom Y was likely still inside the tote bag. The men had been too busy to get them ready to be sold. Turning off the camera to conserve battery, she switched on the microphone.

The muffled voices belonged to multiple men—five to be exact, none of them Victor. Given that the voices all sounded about the same distance from the microphone, they were probably sitting together, perhaps around a table, with the tote bag in the middle.

Why had Victor taken so little care about her phone? She remembered the way he had looked at her in the Roamnest. For some men, a woman who looked like her was impossible to imagine as a threat. She wasn't sure whether to be insulted or pleased.

The chatter didn't seem to be related to Elli. Complaints about food, boredom, women. Whenever the conversation lulled, they would fall back to browsing on their phones, as indicated by the soundtrack of the occasional viral video and the gentle buzzing of haptic feedback from fingers tapping screens.

"Any word from Victor?" someone asked. "When are we leaving?"

Piers and Elli sat up, riveted.

"What makes you think I'd know?" another man answered, irritated.

"You're his favorite. Maybe he's planning a cruise for the two of you to watch the sunset over the ocean."

Laughter, teasing, overlapping shouts.

Piers and Julia looked at each other in frustration. If only they would say where they were going! All they knew was that the location was coastal. Also, it sounded like Victor was working with a crew he had a history with, not random local help hired just for the job.

Frowning in concentration, Julia banged furiously on the projected keyboard, the simulated clacking blending with the hollow knocks of her fingertips striking the wooden top of the dining table.

"Why do you look so anxious?" Piers asked. "If we wait, they're bound to tell us where they're going, right?"

"We can't afford to be so passive. I don't know how much longer we have to wait before we find out their destination, but the battery is already low on the phone."

"What can we do then?"

Julia shook her head, indicating that Piers should leave her alone. She had already put the phone in low-power mode, turning off everything except what was absolutely necessary to keep the microphone going and the data link up. But the phone didn't have great reception, and she could practically feel the power draining out with every passing second.

What could she do?

If she had unlimited resources, she could tap into the location data the telecom companies sold. She already had a known location to work with, and she could latch onto the signals of the nearby devices and track them for as long as she liked.

But she didn't have unlimited resources.

What did she have then? Think, she told herself. Think!

The memory of exploring the infected HELM before her life was turned upside down resurfaced. The old-fashioned worm.

She set Talos to isolate the buzzing noises and the viral video soundtracks from earlier. The acoustic profile was enough to give her a hardware ID: at least four of the devices the men used were Qiphones running KiOS, manufactured by SQI in China.

This was not entirely unexpected. It was commonly assumed (though not confirmed) that American tech companies, in order to comply with the HOMELAND Act, had to install certain back doors in their devices to allow law enforcement and intelligence agencies to spy on users when national security required it. Criminals, therefore, tended to rely on devices from Russia, Vietnam, and China, even though their importation into the US was supposedly illegal.

Foreign phones, of course, had vulnerabilities of their own as well as back doors designed for the benefit of their governments. KiOS, for instance, was forked from the open-source DD OS, with proprietary additions by SQI (by reputation, sloppy and easily exploited) and rumored modifications by the PRC Ministry of State Security. However, criminals in the US tended to fear the FBI far more than they were worried about the Kremlin or Zhongnanhai.

The men were having lunch and arguing over whose turn it was to pick up dinner.

A few quick searches in the security channels on Echobox got Julia the exploits she needed in KiOS; they had been patched in the latest security update, but she doubted that these guys were so conscientious.

The battery on her Bloom Y was at 20 percent. Julia shut off the microphone and put the phone into hibernation, from which it would wake up automatically in half an hour. Every bit of juice had to be conserved for the next step.

Piers got up to heat some food. Julia waved the offered plate away and continued to type furiously. By the time the Bloom Y woke up, she had to be ready to go.

The timer counted down. Thirty seconds. Ten. Five.

The terminal window hung. No response.

"Come on. Come on!" Julia muttered. "Wake up!"

The command prompt appeared.

Relief flooded through her. She uploaded the file she had crafted onto the phone and switched the microphone on again.

No voices at all.

Julia swore under her breath. The guys were either in another room or, worse, out. She needed them close by. Right now.

She had to risk it. She typed in a command and waited with bated breath.

There was a loud screech. Julia had set the Bloom Y to blare the sort of warning given when there was a tornado or a missing child in the neighborhood.

A synthesized male voice shouted from the phone's speaker at maximum volume: "A CRIME IS IN PROGRESS. PLEASE INFORM THE AUTHORITIES. A CRIME IS IN PROGRESS. . . . "

Footsteps and shocked voices. Men rushed into the room. She had a minute, maybe only thirty seconds, before they would discover that the Bloom Y was responsible and shut it off.

Julia sent the command. On the Bloom Y hundreds of miles away in Brooklyn, the sound file that she had uploaded began to play.

Meanwhile, the synthesized male voice in the phone continued to shout.

Though inaudible to the humans in the room, the ultrasonic notes from Julia's sound file would be picked up by their phones. Modern phones, in order to support their AI assistants, were designed to be constantly listening, and they captured sound in a much broader range than audible to humans. The extra range was used for a variety of applications by phone manufacturers, carriers, and advertisers, almost always to the detriment of the user. For instance, ultrasonic "beacon codes" embedded in subway ads could be logged by phones so that advertisers could assess their reach, and user movements out of cell phone range could continue to be tracked—God forbid that anyone should ever be beyond the gaze of the surveillance panopticon for even a second.

Julia had programmed the sound file to start like an advertisement beacon code, which would trigger the datajinns on the KiOS phones to begin logging. But she had crafted the file to exploit a known vulnerability in KiOS—the datajinns would essentially gobble up the rest of the file as a very long advertisement identifier and then hand it off to a database lookup, which would then fail and cause the data to be executed as code, code that would then stay on the infected phone.

Through the microphone, Julia and Piers listened to the panicked chatter of the men intermixed with the blaring warning.

"A CRIME IS IN PROGRESS. PLEASE INFORM THE AUTHORITIES—"

"What the fuck—"

"—coming from the bag—"

"—didn't anyone check?"

"You were supposed to—"

The voices suddenly grew louder. The tote bag had been opened.

"That's it. The white one. No, take it out—"

"I'm trying to—"

"Shut it off! Jesus! Shut—"

Abrupt silence. The terminal window showed only a line of text: *Connection lost.*

Piers stared at Julia, not daring to ask.

Julia stared at the screen, silently counting to herself.

Twenty-seven, twenty-eight, twenty-nine . . .

The Bloom Y had deleted the sound file after playing it three times. Even these idiots would know by now that they needed to disconnect the battery in the phone or smash it. They would find no trace of Julia's tampering. But that also meant Julia would get no second shot.

Eighty-one, eighty-two, eighty-three . . .

A new window popped up on the projected screen: *Connection request from device ID 35-8692-105472-089.*

Julia punched "yes" and finally let out a whoop of celebration.

TWENTY-NINE

The men in Brooklyn didn't leave their apartment the rest of Sunday. Piers grew uneasy, but it was Julia's turn to counsel patience. Now that she had a way to track four phones in the group, she was sure they wouldn't lose the trail.

They left in the morning before Sahima was awake.

"Might as well be on the road," said Julia. "I hate goodbyes."

(She had, however, taken the time, before they left, to sort through the rat's nest of cables behind Sahima's work desk and tie them into neat bundles that were clearly labeled. Sahima was never any good at cable management.)

While Piers drove, Julia monitored their targets.

"I think they just got up. At least two of the phones are moving—still inside the apartment, though."

In order to evade the KiOS phones' guardian software, Julia had coded the ultrasonic payload to be extremely compact, and its code would do as little as possible on infected phones. While she had no access to microphones or cameras, periodically the code would send the phone's location to Julia. However, since real-time location data access required higher privileges that could trigger the guardians, the code only intermittently grabbed the stored location from other apps, like weather widgets and deal seekers.

Piers took them out of Philadelphia, turned off I-476, and went to a drive-thru to get coffee and hash browns. Then he pulled into the parking lot of a small state park. The lot was open on all sides, so cell reception was good, and more importantly, it was impossible for anyone to sneak up on them.

Piers was getting antsy again. "Are we sure these guys will lead us to Elli?"

"I'm sure," Julia said. "Based on what we heard, these are men Victor trusts. He's involving them because he knows where Elli is."

In truth, Julia wasn't nearly as confident as she sounded. The tracking code, written in a hurry, was buggy. She had already lost track of two of the four phones that had been initially infected. What if she lost track of the last two? She was making a lot of guesses based on very little data. But there didn't seem to be a lot of alternatives.

The waiting weighed on her; she needed to be on the move.

"I'm going on a run," she said. "I'll leave Talos behind so you can monitor the phones. If they start to move for real, call me on my sensepin."

Afternoon.

Julia dozed on a blanket in the shade of a copse next to the parking lot. The sun was so bright and the air so warm.

"Julia!"

Piers was standing next to the car and waving at her frantically.

Terrified that the tracking code on the last two phones had stopped working, she ran over without even packing up the blanket.

"They're moving!"

Julia slumped with relief. The two tracked phones were moving toward the east, hugging Jamaica Bay. "JFK. They're flying."

Julia and Piers had discussed this scenario. Piers, being hunted by the police, couldn't fly. Wherever Victor's crew was going, Julia would have to fly there herself, and, if possible, Piers would drive to join her later.

"Get me to the airport," Julia said as she got in the car.

While Piers navigated the traffic, Julia concentrated on the location info being reported by the tracked phones. The fact that her tracking code couldn't access the phones' real-time location turned out to be a nonissue. In commercial spaces like airports, phones and sensepins had millimeter-precise indoor positioning thanks to augmented reality anchors—fixed beacons in real space that enabled pedestrians to be served location-based ads related to the exact kiosk they walked by. Although the ad-delivery system was usually the least secure component in a phone's operating system, it often ironically had the most precise location data. By tapping into ads, Julia could tell exactly where the men were inside the airport terminals.

"Can you see them now?" Piers asked.

"They just parked. . . . Heading to Terminal Eight . . . Don't seem to be precleared, so security is going to take a while . . . Concourse B . . . I think I got the gate. Talos, which flight is that?"

"To London," said Talos.

Piers nearly swerved. "What?"

"Don't panic yet," said Julia. "They're not in the seats."

An agonizing five minutes later.

"I jumped the gun. They are moving again now. Probably stopped earlier to look at some ads or for a quick charge. . . . I think this time they're actually sitting down. Talos, check the gate—"

"Way ahead of you. The flight is going to Charlotte."

"Do you think Elli is in the Carolinas?" Piers asked.

"I don't think so. Remember, they talked about watching the sunset over the ocean. It's not impossible for that to be in the Carolinas—an offshore island, for instance—but unlikely. I don't think Charlotte is their final destination. Talos, give me a list of transfers out of Charlotte that might make sense given their flight."

Talos projected the list of potential destinations onto the dashboard in mirror form so that the ghostly text, now correctly oriented, would be reflected onto the car's windshield.

"Miami or Orlando?" Piers asked.

Julia shook her head. "Can't be. Lots of direct flights to those places from JFK. No reason to transfer in Charlotte. It's got to be Tallahassee. It's near the Gulf Coast, looking west. I'm going to book a flight right away."

"I wish I could pay for all this. But all my accounts must be watched."

"Don't worry. We'll get through this." She thanked Sahima silently.

"I'll drop you off and start driving down. If I push it, I should get in by early morning."

"Don't speed. And try to pull off in a rest area and get some sleep. You won't be any good to Elli if you're dead."

"You're a cheerful one, aren't you?"

Julia landed in Tallahassee at 8:35 in the evening. The Florida air, warm and wet, immediately made her clothes stick to her skin. Shopping was a top priority, she decided.

Using her tracker, she saw that the men flying out of JFK had landed two hours earlier and were by now settled in a motel outside the city along Route 319.

Why this motel? It was still some distance from the coast.

She thought about the situation. These men wouldn't have gone all the way out here unless they knew precisely where Elli was. So, the most likely explanation was that they were advance scouts using the motel as a base. Once the whole team had gathered, they'd go after her. Most likely the following evening.

She would have to find out where Elli was, tonight, before they made their move.

First, she stopped by a Walmart to get some clothes—a couple of sundresses and a cardigan, not her style at all, hairstyling tools, as well as a few things for Piers. Victor had seen her in Bethlehem, so she needed to change her appearance. A new hairstyle, some highlights, and a different style of dress went far.

There was a pawnshop in the same mall. She went in and bought some tools and components—Victor and his henchmen had depleted her stock back in Bethlehem.

She drove to the motel, which was laid out like a U, with every room facing the parking lot in the middle and the office at the bottom of the U. She registered under the name "Emma Moore" and booked two rooms near the street, near the very tip of the leg of the U that was opposite the room in which the two guys she'd been tracking were staying. If others working with those two were also at the hotel, she figured they'd be near them.

Once she had settled into her room and texted Piers the address of the motel, she grabbed the ice bucket and strolled down to the office for the ice machine. She had skewed her sensepin to point to the right so that as she walked, it could record a video of the windows of the rooms she passed. After grabbing some snacks and ice, she strolled along the other wing of the motel, again letting the sensepin take in every room on that side. Finally, she looked across the road as though curious about the strip mall on the other side before returning to her room.

She had Talos go through the footage and pull out any faces that could be glimpsed through the windows. Then she dispatched a pack of datahounds through the ether to track down everything she could learn about the faces.

Seven rooms had their curtains drawn, including room 117, belonging to the two men she was tracking. The other rooms didn't yield anyone interesting: a couple who were evidently there just for sex (their social media profiles showed them each with a different partner), a family on a road trip, solitary travelers on the road for their jobs, tourists who tried to save money by staying outside the city. . . . None of them seemed related to the hunt for Elli (unless they had fake public profiles that were meant to throw datahounds off the scent—not entirely outside the realm of possibility, but Julia believed she had programmed her datahounds well).

Time for more drastic means. Julia pulled aside her curtains and looked out across the lot toward the other wing. The light outside room 117 was lit, and giant moths with bright eye spots on their wings fluttered around the light. Of course, she thought. Spring or winter, Florida was always full of bugs.

Leaving her room again, she left the grounds of the motel and walked down the street a bit. She examined the ground under the streetlights closely and soon found what she was after. Bending down, she picked up two massive dead moths, almost the size of small birds, and placed them gently inside a towel she had brought. Disoriented by the bright bulbs, they had died by colliding with the streetlamps or had simply fallen from exhaustion. Birds hadn't had a chance to get to them yet.

Back in her room, she set the moths down on the desk, took out Puck, and laid out the tools she had gotten from the pawnshop earlier.

Back in her days among the Cartographers Obscura, Julia was one of the few young members interested in hardware mods.

Sahima told Julia that the days when you had to be skilled with a soldering iron and know every register and obscure instruction in the processor in order to be considered technically proficient were long gone. The shiny gadgets pumped out by the big tech companies—phones, sensepins, fusion vision glasses, etc.—were hermetically sealed boxes promising magic. And even if you could open them up, you'd just be presented with more, smaller sealed boxes promising more magic. With AI that turned poorly phrased English sentences into functional code, being a "developer" was nearly meaningless.

Some "machine-assisted" developers were so unfamiliar with hardware that they wouldn't have been able to identify the chips that they supposedly wrote software for; their knowledge was more in the realm of knowing how to ask machines to do things than in knowing how to do those things themselves.

The distinction I just drew might not be philosophically rigorous, Sahima said. *Certainly, people have been debating since Plato's time what it really means to know anything. If you know which book to look up something in, is that really different from knowing that something in your brain? Your AI, people say, being trained on all the information you've been exposed to and all your thoughts, is just an embodiment of your mind's journey, a time lapse of your developing selfhood.*

But I don't think that's quite right. There's a way to grow your AI responsibly, to incorporate into it only things you've already made the effort to understand, to let it be no more and no less than a reflection of who you are. There's also the lazy way, to let the machine do all the work while you take the credit, so that all you know how to do is shout incantations at the computer and hope they're obeyed. Too often, people can't resist taking shortcuts.

The talk had made a big impression on young Julia. She took from it the message that it was essential to look beyond what was given, to look inside sealed boxes so that she understood the magic.

Julia peeked through the seam in the curtains to be sure that the parking lot was deserted. Opening her door, she released Puck and quickly shut the door again.

Instead of the four spinning propellers, the morpho drone was now kept aloft by two pairs of fluttering wings. The flapping appendages, modified from the carbon-fiber propellers, were covered by the wings of the dead moths glued on as disguise.

The artificial creature fluttered through the darkness, looking just like the thousands of other giant and hairy moths in the damp, sweltering evening air. Eventually, it fluttered to the door of room 117 and hovered near the glow of the peephole, just like two other real moths nearby.

As though mistaking the peephole for a flower, Puck extended its proboscis toward it until the end stuck to the coin-sized bit of glass. Realizing its mistake, the artificial moth tapped its delicate legs against the door, wings fluttering wildly in its effort to get away. But the end of the proboscis wouldn't detach, and eventually, the exhausted robotic creature stopped struggling, clung to the door with its legs, wings flattened against the door in a pathetic display.

"Did you hear that?" Viper, who was cleaning out his handgun at the desk, asked in a whisper.

"What are you talking about?" Dwoo, resting in the other bed, looked up from his phone without much interest.

"Sounded like someone was scratching at the door."

Dwoo turned back to the phone. "I didn't hear anything. Maybe it was a cat."

Viper got up and approached the door, holding the gun behind his back.

Julia typed frantically.

The whole sequence had been biomimicry. In actuality, the extending proboscis had attached a lens onto the peephole, which reversed its optics and gave the other end of the lens an unimpeded view of the inside of the room.

But if the man inside looked out now—

Viper looked through the peephole.

The parking lot was deserted.

For a second, he thought he saw the image shimmer as though he were looking at a screen. He blinked and looked again. Just the parking lot. No shimmer. "Weird," he muttered to himself. Maybe he was too tired; it had been a long day.

He thought about opening the door just to be sure, but the fluttering figure of a moth, passing quickly before the peephole, startled him. The idea of one of those fuzzy, nasty, nightmare-fuel creatures sneaking in here was unappealing. This was why he'd never liked Florida. Better keep the door shut.

"A cat?" Dwoo asked from behind him.

"Maybe. Anyhow, it's gone. Just a couple moths flying around."

"Getting spooked by moths now? Want me to read you a bedtime story?"

"Fuck off."

Viper went back to the desk and resumed working on the gun.

Julia sighed in relief. She had gotten the view of the parking lot projected into the peephole just in time.

She turned off the projection and resumed filming through the peephole.

Carefully, moving her fingers millimeter by millimeter, she adjusted Puck-moth's legs until they were resting on the door just so. The tips of the little legs were highly sensitive vibration detectors, reacting to every minute movement in the wooden partition.

The view through the peephole, as well as the vibration data, were both transmitted back to Julia's room.

There, Talos combined and synchronized the two streams, which allowed it to extract even more information. Occasional glimpses of the movements of the room's occupants' lips were matched to wave patterns in the vibration feed, facilitating the isolation of speech against the much louder background noise of traffic on the road, the humming of the mini-fridge in the room, and the din of a Florida evening full of life.

Julia lay down and got comfortable. With her fusion vision glasses on, it was as though she were right there in the room with the two men, watching them and listening to every word.

Piers didn't get in until four in the morning. Exhausted but also jittery from gallons of caffeine, he listened to Julia's update.

There were already six people at the motel working for the Prince. Besides the two who had flown in from New York, the other four had driven over from Texas. Victor and more people were scheduled to arrive in the morning.

From eavesdropping on those two in room 117, Julia had learned that Elli was at a vacation resort somewhere on the Panhandle, but they had not named the exact location. Their plan for the next day was to scout the resort sometime during the day and seize Elli in the evening. There would be a total of eleven men involved, including Victor.

"I can't believe you found out all that by looking in a peephole," Piers said.

"You should get some rest," said Julia. "The Prince's guys are already asleep. I retrieved Puck after they started snoring."

"What about you?"

"I took a nap on the plane. One of us has to keep watch in case they decide to leave earlier than expected. I'll stay and keep watch from now until eight in the morning, and you can take over then."

THIRTY

Julia startled awake. Disoriented, it took her a few seconds to realize that she was in her own motel room. After waking up Piers at eight, she had returned here to sleep—she just couldn't fall asleep with someone else awake around.

Sunlight streamed in from the slit between the curtains. Still groggy, she saw the time on her phone: 12:32 p.m.

She scrambled onto the floor and looked out the window. The cars of the men in the opposite wing were still there. Relief flooded through her. Piers was still on watch with Talos; everything was fine.

After a long shower to wake herself up, she got dressed. Then she tried to call Piers on his phone.

No answer.

Oh, right, she reminded herself. We decided last night to put everything on silent mode so we don't inadvertently tip anyone off.

She tried the motel phone. It wasn't working.

Feeling annoyed at herself for not asking for adjoining rooms with a connecting door, she left her room, walked down to Piers's, and knocked on the door.

She waited thirty seconds. Nothing. A growing unease seized her.

Lingering in front of the door would certainly draw attention, and if any of Victor's men looked out their windows, they'd see her. She walked around the tip of the motel wing to the narrow lawn behind the rooms, which ran up against a fence that separated the motel from the lot of the McDonald's next door.

Trying to look as casual as possible, she snuck onto the lawn. The featureless wall to her left was broken only by a row of high windows, which aired out the bathrooms. She counted the windows to herself, stopping under the one that belonged to Piers.

The glass pane was tilted open. She held her breath and listened.

Did she really hear snoring, or was that her imagination?

Digging in the lawn, she stood up with a few pebbles. Aiming carefully, she tossed them up at the narrow slit of the opened bathroom window. Arcing in, they made satisfying clattering noises against the tiled floor. She kept on tossing until she struck something—the sink perhaps—and a loud, crisp clang rang out.

The faint snoring stopped.

"I'm really sorry," said Piers, red-faced and sweating. "I guess I was more tired than I thought."

Julia tried to remind herself that it was unreasonable to expect an office worker to suddenly turn into a surveillance expert. But it was hard not to feel some resentment at Piers for almost throwing away all their hard work.

"No harm done," she said, straining to keep her voice calm. She picked up Talos, which she had left with Piers when she went to sleep, and was immediately startled by a screen full of warnings. "What the . . . Oh!"

The tensor bank's display showed that the two phones they had been tracking had disappeared around ten that morning. "Why didn't you wake him up?" she almost yelled at it.

The screen flashed in indignation.

Arrrgh! Silencing Talos for stealth had really backfired. She flicked the switch.

"I told you it was a bad idea—"

"Talos, I don't have time for this. Show me what happened to the phones."

Talos replayed the tracking data. The phones had remained still in room 117 for much of the night. They jiggled around a bit inside the room starting at about nine in the morning and then, abruptly, just vanished from the tracking screen.

"That makes no sense," Julia muttered as she peeked out the window. "Their cars are still here."

"Maybe their phones ran out of juice," said Piers. "Or maybe their guardian software found your bug?"

Julia shook her head. Something else was going on here. She logged onto the motel's Wi-Fi and saw that the motel had a cheap security camera system that was easy to get into—they hadn't even bothered to change the default password. Should have thought of this sooner, she berated herself, like last night.

She scrubbed through the recorded footage, and her heart nearly stopped: around ten in the morning, two cars had pulled into the parking lot; the six men at the motel had emerged from their rooms, gotten into the cars, and left.

The motel hadn't been their only base of operations, and now she and Piers had no idea where they had gone.

Except . . . Viper and Dwoo's phones must still be inside room 117.

Puck, propellers back on top, buzzed through the bathroom window of room 117.

Back inside her motel room, Julia relaxed her fingers. The gesture was translated by the wavium rings into a command for Puck to hover in place inside the room. Snapping her fingers, she turned on Puck's flashlight, and then scanned the room through the fusion vision glasses: clothes on the floor, pizza boxes, bedcovers rolled up into a bundle and tossed against the wall. The men had left the room a mess, but she saw no sign of their phones.

"Try the safe," said Piers, sharing her view from a projection on the wall.

Julia barely stopped herself from slapping her forehead. Of course! That was how the tracked phones had vanished from tracking. The safe was a Faraday cage.

The safe was in the closet. She flexed her fingers carefully but just couldn't maneuver Puck close enough to the closet door to slide it open—the wavium rings vibrated violently as the tips of the propellers brushed against the wooden door. Her view inside the fusion vision glasses tilted abruptly as the drone teetered, almost crashing.

"It's okay," said Piers. "Don't rush."

Wiping the sweat from her brow, Julia gently set Puck down on the carpet. Then she clapped her hands twice in quick succession, curled her fingers into claws, and put both hands together, wrist to wrist, on top of the table, resting on fingertips. The morpho drone responded with a series of bending, flexing, and unfolding movements, transforming into its spider form.

Crawling up to the closet door, she flexed her fingers and *pushed*.

She could feel the whine of the motors in the drone through the wavium rings. Careful not to burn out the motors, she eased up, waited, and pushed again. Inch by inch, the door slid open.

Julia crawled onto the safe's number pad and switched the flashlight to emit UV light. The buttons glowed. Three of the buttons, having been touched most recently, were brighter than the rest. Then it was just a matter of tediously trying out all possible four-digit codes given the three buttons.

On the sixty-third try, the safe popped open. There were two phones inside, both lying face up.

"I can only take one," she said. "Any favorites?"

"I wouldn't even know where to begin to advise you on that."

She smiled. That was one of the things about Piers that she liked: he never pretended to be an expert in things he knew nothing about.

Crawling over the two phones, she scanned both with the flashlight. One of them was far more smudged up than the other. "I'll take the cleaner one," she said.

"For . . . hygiene?"

"No. You'll see."

Inch by inch, Puck nudged the phone out, finally dropping it on the closet floor.

"I'll go out there," said Piers, running out of the motel room.

"Be careful not to touch the screen!" she called after him.

Five minutes later, Puck, now back in its propeller form, buzzed out of the bathroom window, teetering under the weight of the phone dangling from its manipulators. Piers was there to relieve it.

The phone was secured with a simple swipe code. More UV light soon revealed the pattern.

"That's why you wanted the cleaner phone," Piers said.

"Right. He's one of those people who can't stand a greasy screen and wipe down their phones obsessively. The last thing he did was probably unlock it to check a message from the guys picking them up."

The screen unlocked with a gentle haptic tingle.

Julia scrolled through the messages as she continued, "We're lucky he didn't use biometrics to lock his phone."

"I wouldn't have expected him to," Piers said. "There's a lot of misinformation about *Cobsen*, but there are advantages to not using biometrics if you are worried about the police."

"What's *Cobsen*?"

"It's a court case. *Cobsen v. Massachusetts.* The Supreme Court ruled that while the police could force a suspect to put a finger on a reader or look into a camera to unlock a personal device, they couldn't force the suspect to recite a passcode or draw a pattern on a screen.

This is because the first set of actions is insufficiently close to 'testimony' to be considered a violation of the Fifth Amendment's prohibition against self-incrimination, while the second set is."

"That makes no sense," Julia said. "It's a distinction without a difference."

Piers shrugged. "The law is all about distinctions like that. Anyway, as I understand it, a lot of criminals won't use biometrics on their devices at all because of that possibility."

"I think I might have found it." Julia tapped her sensepin to snap a few pictures of the phone screen before showing it to Piers.

Elli's postcard had been sent as an attachment to one of the messages. Victor hadn't figured out some deep secret in the cash from the safe-deposit box; he just got better clues.

Piers looked thoughtfully at the view of the sunlit ocean before swiping to the back. "'I have our dreams,'" he whispered, his voice hoarse. "She sent this to me to ask me to come to her. And *he* got it." The rage in his voice was hard for Julia to bear.

Julia had already punched the address from the postcard into the mapping app: White Sails Cottages on Cape Esperanza. It was about seventy miles to the west on the Gulf Coast, toward the Alabama border.

As soon as they got into the Corolla, Julia rolled down the window to let the trapped heat out. The overcast sky looked ominous. The forecast said a big storm was coming that evening.

Piers stepped on the gas, and they tore out of the parking lot.

THIRTY-ONE

Cape Esperanza, a narrow arm of land that extended southwest into the Gulf of Mexico and then curled north, had a lovely, unimpeded view of the gulf on its western shore. As soon as Piers and Julia arrived, they could see that it was the same view from Elli's postcard.

The White Sails Cottages, a fenced-in resort, consisted of small double-occupancy cabins topped with sail-shaped solar panels. The cabins were arranged along crisscrossing, spiraling sand-lined footpaths, like a one-sixteenth-scale version of a suburban development—except that each cottage had only enough space for two beds and a dresser-desk, and the showers and bathrooms were communal.

The place probably began life as a misguided attempt by some resort developer to squeeze as many beds into the space as possible, but the New Age spiritual quotations on concrete slabs dotted around the footpaths suggested a later change in direction to rebrand a liability into an asset, allowing the developer to charge more for the rather austere accommodations.

"We have to find Elli as quickly as possible," Piers said as they parked in the visitor lot. The anxiety in his voice was palpable. The Prince's men had a head start of nearly three hours, but their cars weren't in the lot. Were they planning off-site? Or worse, did they already have her?

Julia tilted her head at the management office at the edge of the lot. "People hacking?"

"Not a bad idea," said Piers. "You'd be surprised at how compliant some people can be when you tell them you're a lawyer and just demand that they do things for you."

Piers did his best to make his two-days-worn dress shirt look presentable; the humidity at least had the benefit of getting some of the wrinkles out. Julia handed him a new tie: deep red shimmery silk, with a hint of palm leaves in the pattern.

"What's this?" Piers looked at it skeptically.

"Saw a billboard for a lawyer on the way out of the airport; he was wearing something like this."

Piers put it on and straightened the knot. "You're not as bad with people as you think."

"I'm fine until I have to stick around them."

Piers examined himself critically in the rearview mirror. He rolled up his sleeves.

"What do you think? Sort of a brawling litigator look?"

Julia shook her head. "Your arms are too pale."

"Harsh. But accurate." Piers unrolled the sleeves and put on his sport coat. He reached into the backseat for his briefcase.

"I'll need something to hold, too," said Julia. She dug around in her backpack and pulled out a clipboard. "A clipboard always makes you look important."

"Lawyers don't carry clipboards," said Piers.

"I can't pass as a lawyer anyway. How about a paralegal? Paralegals can carry clipboards, right?"

"There aren't that many paralegals left these days."

"Well, aren't you special then? Keeping one of the last paralegals on staff."

They went to the management office. A middle-aged Black woman sat behind it: a portable fan in one hand for the heat, big glasses, bigger smile. Piers swaggered up to the counter and began to chat with her. Julia dutifully took the briefcase from him and stood to the side.

Piers explained that he was a litigator from out of state, here on behalf of a man who'd been wrongly accused. He was trying to track down a witness who could potentially provide a watertight alibi. The woman was staying here at the Cottages—

"A woman, you said?" the clerk asked, the frizzy curls over her shoulders suddenly very still. Her demeanor, until now friendly and sympathetic, had changed to something drastically less so.

"Y-yes," said Piers.

"Let me guess: white lady in her thirties, five foot four, not overweight, not sure about the hair color, probably not very sociable."

Piers's eyes lit up. "You know her?"

"I know that I'm going to call the police if you don't leave right now. I dealt with your partner earlier, trying the same thing. Only difference was that he was trying to threaten me, and now here you are, feeding me a bullshit story. Get out!"

Piers held up his hands. "I really don't know what you're talking about. I'm just trying to make sure an innocent man—"

"Get out!"

Julia scrambled out of the woman's way as she stormed from behind the counter and went up to Piers, looking like she was ready to crack his skull open.

Piers backed away. "I'm going." His back bumped into the door. Fumbling behind himself, he twisted the knob and stumbled out. Still holding on to the door, he said, "Please, just listen—"

The woman snapped around and glared at Julia. "What are you still doing here? Out!"

Julia fairly ran through the door, passing by Piers. The clerk slammed the door shut and glared at them through the window. Defeated, Piers and Julia slinked away.

When they were about fifty feet from the office, Piers turned around for a sneak peek. The clerk was still standing behind the glass, staring daggers at him. He offered an apologetic smile and hurried out of sight with Julia.

"The bad news is that they had the same thought we had," said Piers after they had gotten into the car and pulled out of the lot. "But the good news is that they failed too. That woman has a good head on her shoulders."

"Keep driving," Julia said. "She can still see us on the cameras. Last thing we want is for her to get security involved."

"Actually, don't we?" Piers asked. "Maybe the thing to do is to start some commotion, get the police, the firefighters, everyone involved. Then the thugs won't be able to do anything."

"I wouldn't do that. Once you start a panic, there's no way to predict how the authorities will react. We're more likely to get ourselves arrested than stop the bad guys. The best plan for us remains to find Elli first. And thanks to you, I know how to do it."

"How?"

"Keep going until you get to the strip mall we passed on the way in. Earlier, while you were fighting with the clerk, I reached over the counter and plugged a tap into the ethernet port of her computer. Here—pull into that spot all the way in the corner, behind the van, so the camera can't see us."

Piers pulled into the strip mall lot and parked in the spot Julia indicated.

"The tap has a cellular connection," Julia said. She leaned forward and began to type on the keyboard projected onto the car dashboard. "Now we have access to their secured network. . . . And I just stole her credentials. See, here's the console for the security cameras."

She projected the screen onto the dash so that the reflection would show up against the windshield: thumbnail views from hundreds of cameras.

"So I was just the distraction," said Piers. "Was that your plan all along?"

"You did a good job," said Julia, grinning.

Working quickly, she erased the facial recognition records for herself and Piers so that the system wouldn't alert the clerk if they were back on the property. She also deleted the entry for their car. Finally, she put the pictures she had taken of Viper and Dwoo through the peephole into the system and marked them as suspicious for the clerk.

All that done, she finally turned to the guest records.

A direct search of Elli's name turned up nothing—as was expected. Nothing in the facial recognition database either.

"There may be an opt-out that guests could sign," said Piers. "Some states have laws that specifically give consumers the right to opt out of private facial recognition systems, especially children."

"Florida does have such a law," Talos chimed in.

"Right. Because of Disney," said Piers. "I bet some parents insisted that the Mouse allow them to exempt their kids, and then Disney lobbied for the law so that none of their competitors could have an advantage in tracking."

Julia pulled up the guest registration form. Sure enough, there was a field for opting out of facial recognition, selected by about 20 percent of the guests. Because they couldn't use their faces for things like door locks, dining, or just-walk-out checkout, they had to swipe their key card.

Filtering these facial recognition refuseniks by Elli's likely window of arrival, Julia narrowed the list to eleven women who were here alone.

"Does the database log every key card access?" Piers asked. Julia nodded. "All right, let's see what these people have been doing."

Julia downloaded the key card access logs and plotted the movements of the eleven women on a map of the resort. The activity histories all looked pretty similar. Some days were spent almost entirely at the Cottages: yoga and chocolate tasting, spa, pool, dancing lessons, trivia. . . . Others were devoted to excursions: fishing and snorkeling in the gulf, shopping trips to Tallahassee, local history tours. . . . None of the eleven histories looked out of place.

"If I were her, I'd also be trying to blend in," said Julia.

"Can we take a look at the security camera footage when the cards were used?"

Julia tapped away on the keyboard projected onto the dash. "I'm trying to grab the clips from the over-the-door camera when one of these eleven cards was used to enter a cottage. The query language here is ancient. Bear with me."

Eventually, a stack of clips showed up on the projected screen, arranged like a deck of cards. The person in each clip was blurred entirely from head to toe. It was impossible to even tell what clothing they wore, much less age, race, or gender presentation.

"They blurred the faces *and* the bodies?" Piers asked. "Wait, but doesn't that mean they had to recognize the faces first to know who to blur?"

"Different places implement this differently," Julia explained. "This resort uses an older technology where anyone who opts out of facial recognition is given a radio transmitter fob. When the security system detects the transmitter, it directs the camera to apply the blurring to the person wearing the signal."

"Can you reverse the blur?"

Julia shook her head. "The blurring is done before recording so that information is completely lost."

"Doesn't that create a security problem? What if someone nefarious steals one of those transmitters? They'd be completely disguised in the security footage."

"You're right about that. Let's hope the Prince's men don't take advantage of it."

Staring intently, Piers went through the clips several times before finally giving up, letting out a frustrated breath. "I can't tell if any of them is Elli."

They didn't have time to go to all eleven cottages; worse, doing that might tip off the Prince's men. They seemed to have hit another dead end.

Julia closed her eyes and thought. Whenever systems tried to preserve the anonymity of their users, there were always vulnerabilities. How else could she figure this out?

Her eyes snapped open.

"Have you figured out something?" Piers asked.

She held up a hand to him so that she wouldn't lose her concentration.

While tapping away on the dash, she also rattled off a stream of commands to Talos. What she wanted to do was both simple and hard. Like most resorts, the Cottages were covered by a Wi-Fi mesh network, and each time a device attached or detached from a node in the network, there was a log entry. By correlating the timestamps of device connections with the timestamps in the video footage, she could identify the devices that belonged to each woman in the network logs.

Next, she had Talos go through the network activity of each woman's devices. Most of the public was not security-conscious, and it was easy to see what they were doing: photo backups, messaging, social media, banking, shopping, online dating. . . . One woman's traffic stuck out immediately: everything she did was encrypted through a VPN.

She pulled up the corresponding guest registration record. "I think this is her. I know I'm making a lot of assumptions here, but my gut tells me I'm right."

"If you think that's Elli, we need to move right now."

The strip mall had a hardware store. They went in and bought a few things, which they packed into the backseat of the Corolla.

They drove back to the resort and parked out of view of the management office. Julia called the resort, asking to be connected to Elli's cottage. No one answered.

"She could just not be picking up any calls," said Piers.

While there were no cameras inside the cottage, there were other sensors for motion, air quality, ambient light, and the like. Julia tapped into the sensor network. By all metrics, the interior of the cottage was deserted.

"She's off the property," Julia said. "What do you want to do?"

There were tons of nearby activities catering to resort guests: boating, fishing, kitesurfing, diving. . . . Piers looked up at the sky. Already, clouds had rolled in, and the temperature was dropping, the air thick with electrical energy. A spring gulf storm was coming, as forecast. The prospect of hunting for Elli over land and sea was daunting.

"We have to get inside her cottage and look for clues."

Julia rechecked the security cameras. Viper and Dwoo, due to Julia's manipulation of the security system earlier, had been flagged when trying to get onto the property and then were ejected. The rest of the Prince's men, perhaps thrown off by the resort's response, didn't appear on any of the surveillance footage. Maybe they were poking at the property from afar. In any event, no one seemed to be watching the cottage.

She tapped some more on the projected keyboard, and the door to the cottage unlocked.

"Like we rehearsed," said Julia. "Ready?"

Piers took off his tie and put on a hard hat. Julia put hers on as well. They got out of the car and dragged a stepladder out of the backseat. None of the employees they passed on the way to Elli's cottage batted an eye at the pair carrying the ladder.

They opened the cottage door and walked right in.

The interior was exceptionally neat, so clean that it almost seemed as if nobody lived here. There were no clothes scattered on the floor; both beds were made; the curtains were pulled shut, leaving only a slender seam of light.

Julia opened the towel closet: empty. She pulled out a dresser drawer: empty. She flipped open the suitcase lying on one of the beds: blouses and pants were rolled up neatly and packed away. Everything looked new.

"She's ready to leave anytime," Julia said.

Piers inhaled, paused, and blew out his breath shakily. "Her perfume."

Giving him a moment to recover, Julia put on her fusion vision glasses and gave the inside of the cottage a comprehensive scan.

Through the glasses, Talos highlighted the desk-dresser for further examination. She went over and immediately saw why. There was a neat stack of tourist brochures advertising fishing trips, scuba-diving lessons, and other adventures. However, as none of the brochures were written on or marked in any way, it was unclear what Elli had chosen to do.

Piers joined her.

"See anything you think she'd be particularly interested in?" Julia asked.

"A lot," Piers said, browsing through the brochures. "She was always much more athletic and active than me. I could see her wanting to try all these."

Julia looked around the room, trying to see if anything else could give her a clue. Her eyes landed on the bed that didn't have the suitcase on it—presumably the one Elli slept in—which was on the side of the desk-dresser away from the stack of brochures. That was curious: Elli had been looking at brochures while sitting at the desk, not lying in bed. Why?

She took out her phone. There was only a single bar of connectivity; the Wi-Fi wasn't that great either, as the mesh point provided good coverage only near the door. Julia looked at the desk and saw an old-fashioned telephone. While an anachronism in most places, here, the lack of good cell coverage and the spotty Wi-Fi made it a necessity.

That was why Elli sat at the desk; she had to make her calls here.

"I have an idea."

Julia took Puck out and used its flashlight to do the UV trick on the phone's button pad. However, virtually all the buttons lit up.

How else could they figure out where Elli had called? She looked around. There were no recording devices. Unless . . . she looked outside the window.

A few minutes later, she had found the camera angle she wanted. There was a security camera attached to the eave of the cottage a few dozen yards down the gravel path. While it was aimed at the path, the very upper-left quadrant of the view included this window in Elli's cottage.

"The curtains here are always shut," Piers said.

"Not a problem."

Julia zoomed in on the window through the security camera. Faint movements from the two of them could be seen behind the curtain. "I can train up a machine-learning model to decipher facial muscle movements."

"Oh . . . don't tell me you're trying to lip-read through a set of curtains—that's never going to work!"

"You never know until you try. Here, you can start by reading from the Bible to give the model some data."

Ten minutes later, Julia and Piers were watching a clip of the security footage from that morning. The light was on in the room, projecting Elli's profile against the curtains as she talked on the phone. Subtitles from the machine-learning model appeared on the bottom of the screen. The recognition was nowhere near perfect, but good enough for their purposes.

"Yes . . . take it . . . the whole day again . . . Slip 43. Understood."

A quick scan through the brochures showed that Elli had most likely decided to rent a powerboat that day to tour the Blue Heron Banks, a popular scuba-diving site that was also rumored to be the resting place of a Spanish treasure ship.

“I hope she’s on her way back,” Piers said, glancing outside the window. “That storm is going to break any minute.”

“Actually, I hope she’s not coming back right this moment,” said Julia. She pointed to the view from another security camera. “Victor and his men are headed for the pier.”

THIRTY-TWO

"Yeah, we're closed," said the attendant at the marine rental shop, a large white man in his forties with more wrinkles than hair. "Just look at that."

Outside, rain was coming down in sheets. The storm had broken during the quarter of an hour it took Julia and Piers to drive over. The temperature was dropping, tall waves slammed against the pier, and the howling wind was accompanied by the staccato drumbeat of cables whipping against poles.

"I can't let anyone on the water. And as for anybody who's out there . . ." The attendant hesitated. "I hope they are on land by now."

Piers wanted to argue, but Julia pulled him away, whispering, "Don't make a scene."

Out in the drenching rain, Piers yelled to make himself heard. "We have to go and look for her!"

"I know. Come with me."

They ran down the dock until they got to the slips with the powerboats. Julia jumped into one.

Piers was confused only for a moment. "Like the car," he said. "I'll keep a lookout."

"Also cover me. The rain messes with the projector."

It was too wet for her to use the projector on the Talos tensor bank; instead, she tapped her sensepin to project a screen and keyboard on the back of the boat seat. The projected screen flickered in the rain and was almost impossible to read. Piers climbed into the boat and stretched his sport coat over Julia's huddled form. With most of the rain blocked and the screen tolerably visible, Julia tapped away on the glowing keys.

The attendant stuck his head out of the shop door. "What are you doing? Get out of that boat."

"Let me handle this," Piers said to Julia. Then, looking at the attendant, he shouted, "It'll be just a second. I dropped my phone."

"I don't think so. I'm calling the cops in another ten seconds."

"Honestly, you're being very difficult. It's not my fault that I slipped . . . "

Julia tried her best to block out the noise. The security system on the boat was weak but cumbersome. With Talos's computation power and the space of possible keys, it could take up to ten minutes to brute-force the authorization code.

"Come on. Come on," she muttered as the tensor bank churned.

"Last warning," the attendant hollered. "I'm not going to ask again."

"Let's hope he doesn't come down here with a shotgun," said Piers to Julia. Then, turning to the attendant, he yelled, "I don't know what you're so worked up about. I could sue you for maintaining an attractive nuisance here, but I'm trying to be reasonable. As soon as I find my phone, we'll be out."

"You have to do a better job distracting him," said Julia. "I need more time."

Leaving his sport coat draped over Julia, Piers climbed out of the boat and walked toward the attendant, both hands raised high in the air. "All right, full disclosure time. Let me show you my ID. I kind of messed up, so please don't report me to my supervisor. My partner and I, we're actually safety inspectors from the FWC's Division of Law Enforcement. We're here to assess your safety procedures, which, so far, I have to say are exemplary. . . ."

Amazingly, the attendant allowed Piers to come up to him, and they both went inside the shop.

Julia adjusted Pier's sport coat to better shield the projection from the rain. The wait was agonizing. Seconds ticked by, then minutes. The engine light remained stubbornly off.

The door to the shop slammed open, and Piers scrambled through and ran toward her.

"Pull out!"

"I can't. I don't have the code!"

Piers jumped into the boat, panting.

"How much longer?"

"I don't know. Four more minutes at most—unless I screwed up the programming."

"We don't have that. Maybe I can—"

The shop door slammed open a second time, revealing the attendant, shotgun in hand.

"I've already called the police. Get out of that boat."

Piers stood up slowly and looked the attendant in the eye, ignoring the water cascading off him in torrents. "You're going to have to shoot me. My wife is out there, and I'm not coming in without her."

Julia squeezed her eyes shut, waiting for the shotgun blast.

Bang!

Julia felt nothing.

Gingerly, she opened her eyes. Through the downpour, she could see that a gust of wind had slammed the shop door against the attendant, flinging him to the ground. He was coming out of his daze, and he was *mad*.

The engine roared to life.

Never had Julia felt such love for a machine. She wanted to kiss it.

Piers clambered into his seat. Julia reversed the boat out of the slip and steered it free of the dock. As the attendant got to his feet, she threw the throttle all the way forward. The boat leaped away, leaving a spray of waves in its wake.

It was impossible to see anything beyond fifty feet.

"We're not going to find anyone out here like this," Julia screamed in order to be heard above the noise of the engine and the storm. Piers had taken the helm because she thought she could use her sensepin and Talos to scan for Elli—a total delusion in the downpour, as it turned out. "You'll crash into the shoals! Turn back; we'll think of another way."

But Piers's only response was to grip the wheel even tighter, wincing through the pain of his splinted fingers. He peered through the storm, straining to find the other boat.

"Elli! Elli!" he shouted. "I saw a boat!"

"Are you sure?" Julia asked. "I didn't see anything."

"Elli!" Piers shouted again, and spun the wheel to follow. "She was there!"

The powerboat bounced over the waves like a mogul skier. Considering how little experience Piers had in a powerboat, it was a wonder they hadn't capsized in the storm by now. Half the boat seemed to fill with water each time it plunged down a wave crest. The bailing pump was working full-time.

Julia squeezed her eyes shut and hung on for dear life. There was nothing she could do to help, and she prayed that Piers wouldn't steer them into a rock and dash the boat to pieces.

Piers spun the wheel and drove the boat in circles. There was no sign of the boat he thought he had seen.

Frustration boiling over, he finally cut the engine so they could listen. As the roar of the engine died down, the howling storm came to the forefront of the soundscape, rising and falling like the breath of a giant.

"We're not alone," said Julia.

Indeed, they could hear the engine noise of at least three other boats. They peered through the darkening dusk but couldn't see the boats at all.

Holding up her sensepin high in the air to take in the soundscape unimpeded, she directed Talos to map the sources of the engine noise around them.

The display, like a radar screen, soon showed that two of the boats were chasing a third.

Piers turned on the engine again. Talos had gotten enough data from earlier to filter out the noises of the storm and their own engine to track the boats. As Julia navigated, Piers gave chase.

They approached the fleeing boat from dead ahead. After cresting another wave, they finally saw the boat.

Lightning flashed. They could see by the harsh light that there was a solitary figure inside: a woman.

"Elli!" Piers screamed.

Her boat zoomed by.

Piers spun the wheel to bring the boat around. The sudden swerve threw Julia to the floor. She didn't protest. In that brief fraction of a second, as lightning painted the woman's face in chiaroscuro, she recognized Elli.

The two pursuing boats zipped past, ignoring Piers and Julia.

At low tide, Blue Heron Banks stood out from the water as a set of tiny islets. Elli now wove among them, darting back and forth in an attempt to throw off her pursuers.

Piers aimed for one of the pursuing boats and opened the throttle to maximum.

"What are you doing?" Julia exclaimed.

Piers made no answer.

They were gaining on the pursuing boat, coming up in its wake. More out of luck than plan, they had picked the boat with the most powerful engine. Closer. Closer. Piers held on tightly to the wheel, apparently intending to slam into the other boat. Julia braced herself.

Another lightning flash. In that stark light, one of the men in the pursuing boat suddenly spun around, gawping at the approaching Piers. It was Victor.

He lifted his gun.

The light went out. Thunder crashed overhead as gunshots rang out. Julia ducked, feeling bullets slam into the boat. She heard a grunt of pain, and the boat lurched to the side violently as a giant wave crashed over it from the side.

Agonizing seconds passed before the rocking boat steadied.

Julia climbed up from the floor of the boat and saw Piers leaning forward, only his left hand on the wheel. His right hand was holding on to his side. She reached for him and felt warm, thick fluid. Blood, not rainwater, gushed over his hand.

"You're shot." Her mind was blank.

Piers, still trying to catch up to Elli's pursuers, didn't respond except to lean harder against the wheel, as though he could physically push the boat to go faster, to reach Elli.

Talos's screen glowed starkly in the darkness, showing that Elli was losing ground. One of the pursuing boats was almost on her.

Another lightning flash. Peering ahead, Julia could see Victor leaning out the side of his boat, the gun at the end of his arm bobbing with the waves.

The gun hovered; he waited, trying to get a clear shot at the engine of Elli's boat.

Elli banked sharply, weaving into the narrow channel between two islets, perhaps hoping that the boat chasing her would overshoot. But she had misjudged the depth of the channel, and as Julia and Piers watched the lightning-lit scene, her boat ran aground, tossing her out of the vessel in a wide arc. Arms flailing, her screams drowned out by the storm, she fell into the ocean. The waves overwhelmed her immediately.

"Elli!" Piers screamed.

Minutes passed. She did not surface again.

The other two boats circled the area slowly. This latest turn of events had obviously not been their intent, as the men shouted at each other angrily.

Piers steered toward them, aiming his boat like a ramming rod.

"No!" Julia screamed at him. "No!"

"Elli is gone! I'm going to make them pay!"

"You're going to die, and you'll kill me too."

He looked at her then, as if seeing her for the first time.

"If you want justice for Elli, turn around and head for shore. We have to report this to the police. There's no point in running from them anymore. They'll find her body and catch these men."

After a brief struggle, Piers turned the boat around and raced toward the shore.

Julia glanced at the tensor bank display. The other two boats had abandoned their search for Elli's body and were coming after them.

Piers's hand slipped from the wheel. The boat began to veer off course. Julia grabbed the wheel and turned it back to the correct heading.

"Thanks," said Piers, sounding weak. He tried to take the wheel back from Julia, but his fingers wouldn't close around the rim. "Damn. I'm not going to make it." He said something else, but Julia couldn't make it out. It sounded like *Ithaca*.

Only now did Julia realize how much blood had pooled at his feet. The bullet must have struck some organ inside. "No," she protested weakly. "No, you're going to be okay—"

"I'm not going to make it," Piers repeated, slurring his words. "Are you a strong swimmer?"

"Yes. Wait, why?"

"We're running low on fuel. We can't outrun them."

"You have enough fuel to get to shore—"

"Please, let me finish." Panting, Piers put both hands on the wheel, bracing himself against it. Blood streamed from the wound in his side. "Okay, now I've got the wheel. Let go and duck down so they can't see you."

Julia obeyed.

Another lightning flash. The two boats were moving closer on the screen.

"If we land now, we'll both be dead. I can't run, and you won't leave me behind."

Julia wanted to argue, but Piers shook his head at her.

"Pack up Talos in the waterproof pouch for the manual; it has all the evidence. I'll steer us closer to shore, but I won't head back to the dock. When I tell you to, jump out of the boat and swim for it. I'll pull out to the sea again to distract them. You go get the police."

"No!"

"It's the only way. If neither of us makes it out, then these men will have gotten away with it. Now! Go! Go!"

In the darkness, Julia rolled over the side of the boat into the stormy water.

With both the rain and the sea slamming into her face, she swam for the shore.

THIRTY-THREE

"You confirmed this personally? . . . Hm . . . Yes . . . Good, very good . . . That's expected . . . Understood."

The Prince hung up.

Interlacing his fingers behind his head, he leaned back in his chair and put his feet up on the desk. Air-conditioning made the humidity and heat of this compound in Southeast Asia only barely tolerable. He couldn't understand how his mother's people had ever lived in this region without it.

He thought over Victor's news.

First, Victor had finally finished decrypting the neuromesh of Elli's personal AI. Hours of interrogation by Victor's own AI had convinced him that Elli's AI knew nothing about the Prince, which was expected. He could trust that Victor's interrogation had been *very* thorough.

Second, and much more critical, Elli was dead.

He tried to sort through his feelings. There was relief, of course. Now, all the secrets that Elli knew about him were safe forever. But there was also disappointment, anger, grief, and . . . something he could not name.

He had been her patron. That was another old-fashioned word, but it was true. He had made her who she was and then, like Pygmalion with Galatea, had found himself in love with her.

But was that true? He had bared himself to her, had put himself in her power, and at the time, he had believed himself in love. Yet, when he found out that she didn't reciprocate his feelings, had, in fact, tried to fool him, he had felt such rage, such hatred—white-hot, yet with a tinge of red, the color of yearning.

That was the feeling that just now had resurfaced and that he could not name. It was hate-love, like the tragicomical masks of classical drama.

He had only fancied himself in love with her, he decided. He had been *beguiled* by her instead.

She was an ungrateful bitch, that much was clear, to spurn his love. But he had bested her, hadn't he? The Prince smiled as he imagined the scene. His men had chased her down and then watched her drown. No, it wasn't as good as bringing her here so that he could have plenty of time with her to teach her how to reflect on her faults. Still, a watery death could be considered a dish of revenge sufficiently delicious, no?

Victor had asked if he wanted to keep Elli's AI around and turn it into an egolet, a kind of zombified version of Elli that he could play with. *Some egos work better as egolets.* Victor had hinted that things could be done to enhance the egolet, perhaps make it more compliant, more submissive, more to his taste . . . but the Prince had rejected the suggestion. It would be unseemly, he decided, for him to be obsessed with a machine's rendition of Elli, suggestive of a weakness of character in himself, a willingness to be ensnared by a mere woman—worse, an echo of a woman. No. He would tell Victor to erase Elli's neuromesh instead. Erasure was the only fate befitting such a cu—no, no, he would not let her drag him down to her level. Elli was finished. He was going to move on.

Unlacing his hands, he sat up, slamming his feet on the ground.

He took out his phone and scrolled through the photos and videos. Here was one of Elli, an immersion video taken during one of their dream sessions together. She looked like a Madonna by Titian, he had thought.

Using his index finger, he circled her face and told his phone to find all the pictures and videos of her. Delete. Confirm.

There was one more photo, a shot of the postcard she had sent. *I have our dreams.* He grimaced, flushing from the memory of how he had believed that she was pining for him. With an angry jab, he deleted that as well. Now, he was free of her.

Enough of this self-pity, he told himself as he stood up from his chair. He was the Prince, and he had an empire to run.

THIRTY-FOUR

Days and countless police interviews later, Julia was finally told that she was free to go.

Everything was in shambles.

Victor and his men had vanished in the storm like so much seafoam.

Piers's body wasn't recovered until two days later, and only what hadn't been eaten. Elli's was in even worse shape: a few bits of jewelry, a bunch of keys (including one to safe-deposit box 231 at Lehigh Valley First Credit Union), and bloodstains in the wreckage of the capsized boat were all that remained.

Enough witnesses and security recordings had corroborated Julia's account that the official investigation was no longer treating Piers as a suspect in Elli's disappearance and subsequent death.

Julia had told pretty much the entire truth, fudging only what would have gotten her in deep trouble. Not everyone accepted her story. The security camera footage from White Sails Cottages and the motel was picked over by amateur sleuths on the internet for evidence of fakery, and theories that Piers was the killer—perhaps with Julia as his accomplice—persisted. It didn't help that the police made virtually no progress in tracking down the real killers, which, to some, was further proof of a cover-up.

The bulk of the public's attention, however, was consumed by a different twist in the Elli Krantz story.

Julia had told the police everything she knew about the Prince and his relentless pursuit of Elli, but the only proof she could offer consisted of the spreadsheet hidden inside a photo of Elli and Piers; a few blurry, faraway sensepin photos of Victor and his men from odd angles; and a very long video taken through a motel room peephole of two men talking about women, drugs, and plans to go "hunting" the next day. Since she had told Talos to respect Piers's privacy, there were no recordings of any conversations between Piers and the Prince.

The blurry photos turned up no high-confidence matches in the crime databases; the video contained nothing incriminating; and when the police contacted Viper and Dwoo, their counsel showed the police security camera footage that proved the two men were drinking in a bar a thousand miles away at the alleged time of the motel stay—the counsel also pointed out, not too subtly, that the peephole footage, with that too-perfect optical distortion at the edges, seemed to be AI-generated, and in any event was inadmissible. Upon these setbacks, the police became even more skeptical of Julia's story, which struck them as reminiscent of the plot of a torrid telenovela. As a result, they disregarded Julia's explanation of the spreadsheet and pursued it as evidence of money laundering and tax dodging by Elli and Piers. That investigation, still ongoing, was doomed to lead nowhere.

Inevitably, bits and pieces of the police investigation leaked. In the inexplicable logic of the post-truth age, the only part of the case that seized the public's imagination was the idea that Elli had been a fraud, a false star manufactured by an (alleged) international criminal gang. For a while, "dino conspiracy lady was herself a conspiracy" was the leading story trending in the ether.

Other oneirofexes, with self-righteous contempt infusing every syllable, raced to declare that they could not imagine any genuinely talented member of their profession doing what Elli Krantz had done. The very idea! Hands were wrung, pearls clutched, "this is why we can't have nice things" strewn about. Oh, btw, have you seen my tour schedule?

Critics, unwilling to be left out of the pile-on, released AI-assembled compilations of their past reviews and commentary to prove that they had, in fact, been on to Elli's suspect reputation long before the present scandal due to their preternaturally good taste, and that they had been struggling for years to warn an unsuspecting public about this queen of no-talent. (If these compilations seemed to contain a few AI hallucinations and retrofakes, how was anyone going to prove it? Whatever "evidence" some debunker dug out of the internet archives could always be shown to be itself a hallucination or forgery—and people never had the patience for the AI said, I said to be resolved.)

In any event, as Elli's erstwhile fans disavowed her in droves, many decided to make public long-lost video/audio clips in which they, the lone voice of reason, had tried to reveal her inauthenticity only to be denounced by her mob of deceived fans. Hadn't they always argued that her dino corporection days had been a hint of her authentic self? Hadn't they always merely pretended to like her ironically? Hadn't they accused her of stealing their dreams in her gatherings, covering her lack of originality with *their* brilliance? Hadn't they—now that it was safe to say so—been the first to run a haters club against Elli? (So many independent thinkers suddenly popped up in Elli's fan base that one wondered how Elli Krantz had ever had any "fans" at all. Again, a silent understanding seemed to pervade all not to look too deeply into the provenance of these "proofs"—people in glass houses, etc.)

A few die-hard fans did try to rally to Elli's support. There were AI-assisted debunkings of the AI-generated evidence produced by the oneirofexes, the critics, the erstwhile fans, the always-already haters, which were followed by AI-enhanced rebuttals to the debunkings, which were succeeded by AI-free analyses of the rebuttals, which were in turn dissected by AI-powered refutations, which showed that—what was the question again?

Elli was fake. On that point, at least, everyone agreed. And having agreed, they could move on.

Back in Paine, Julia brooded.

How had it all gone so wrong?

For years she had tried to put her past behind her: her mother, Serena, Cartographers Obscura, the crimes she had committed, the people she had hurt. She had tried to avoid people—she was a lousy judge of character; she couldn't trust herself.

Maybe her loneliness was her punishment, the sentence that she imposed on herself for being a terrible daughter who hated her mother, a gullible fool who too easily believed in a false prophet, a baby born into a country in which so many believed she didn't belong that she sometimes thought they were right.

And then, Piers had bumbled into her life.

He had shattered the pocket of peace she had built for herself, the shell of solitude. His love for Elli had been so pure, so strong, so sincere that she had stumbled toward it like a prisoner toward light. So it was possible to believe in the face of doubt, to continue to love despite secrets, to hope for redemption even when the one you loved was imperfect. The universe seemed to be sending her a message, a message she was struggling to decipher but promised so much.

Piers was the first friend she had made in years.

So she had reached out, gotten involved, interfered.

And now, Piers and Elli were both dead.

Was that a message from the universe, too? Whatever she touched turned to ash.

Cailee called. Julia didn't pick up.

Talos gave her the message that Cailee wanted to chat, to see how she was doing. Perhaps she could go over for dinner, maybe talk about Julia giving a coding class for the kids.

Julia never messaged back.

Nick Shan called. Julia didn't pick up.

Talos told her that the lawyer wanted to remind her of all the conditions for her supervised release. He and Peggy also wanted to invite Julia over to dinner this Friday—oh, Peggy's nephew, who just graduated from MIT, was going to be there.

Julia called Nick back and nodded whenever Talos told her to nod and read whatever Talos put on the screen for her to say. Then she turned down dinner and hung up.

Sahima called. Julia didn't pick up.

Talos played the voicemail for her. "Come to Philly. I'll take you on a tour of some of my favorite gardens." Then, after a pause, "You have to learn to forgive yourself. I don't want to fall out of touch ever again. Call me."

She didn't call Sahima back.

She hadn't helped Piers. She hadn't helped Elli. She couldn't help anyone. She didn't deserve to be helped.

Julia tried to go on with the life she'd had before she met Piers. She went on runs, did her grocery shopping, played games by herself on her fusion vision glasses. She stopped volunteering with the town library as a tutor. She picked up work as a freelance contractor, servicing and debugging jurijinns and paralexaids.

Weeks passed. There was no progress in the investigation into Elli's and Piers's deaths. Down in Florida, they didn't even return her calls anymore.

She would like to leave Piers and Elli in the past, as she had already left behind so many others. But Piers had changed something in her, in the same way that long after a pebble had sunk out of sight, the once-dead pool would not return to being still. She dreamed of Elli, of Serena, of her friends when she had been on the run, of her mother, of Piers as he told her to go get the police. She woke up drenched in sweat, screaming, "I can't! I can't!"

She began to follow oneirofexes obsessively. She sent out data-hounds, scraped old online archives, downloaded entertainment industry data. She posted on fan channels, asking for recollections of the past. She became something of a historian of the industry, learning more about the dream weavers than anyone else.

Julia was trying to figure out how each oneirofex had gotten their start. She was sure there were others who had taken the deal from the Prince, other victims.

THIRTY-FIVE

Victor was beyond annoyed—if Elli's death couldn't cure the Prince of his obsession, what could?

No, he had patiently explained to the Prince, the girl Julia was not a threat. She was a petty thief, a minor criminal whose reputation in the news archives had no doubt been based more on her looks than any technical skill. That was the problem with these girl "hackers": they never were any good, but the media loved to hype them up. She had failed to gather any hard evidence on the Prince; that old lawyer was relying on her only because he himself knew nothing.

No, he had patiently explained to the Prince, it would not be a good idea to go after her so soon after Elli and Piers had died. The girl was claiming some giant international conspiracy with no evidence, and the police were about to dismiss her as just another hysterical young woman wanting attention. Great! And now you want to "do something to shut her up"? Wouldn't that validate her story? Please. Just leave her alone and let her fade away.

No, he had patiently explained to the Prince, the fact that the girl was still asking all these questions months later didn't matter. The

Prince had never invested in any other oneirofexes. If this girl wanted to keep on digging where no bones would be found, let her.

That was the problem with the Prince. He didn't listen.

Eventually, the nagging just got to be too much.

Fine, Victor said, fine. I'll call them in Boston. I won't kill her, but I'll send a message.

"Hurry up, will you?" Rex whispered to Will, who was kneeling on the welcome mat and struggling to activate the jammer, a small black pyramid covered in antennas.

"Stop fidgeting," Will whispered back. "Victor said there's no one in the apartment."

They were standing outside a basement apartment in the converted schoolhouse. Will hated the way Rex jerked his head about like a nervous raccoon. Anyone who saw him would assume he was guilty of something. It killed Will that Rex had these smooth, chubby cheeks that ought to make him look like a Boy Scout. Why couldn't the fool just use his brain?

"Mess about with the flowers if you really can't hold still," he whispered to Rex.

Rex took a big whiff from one of the three bouquets he carried. Then he sniffed another one as though he was snorting ketamine.

"Not like that!" Will said. "Jesus. Have you never seen people deliver flowers?"

Both of them were dressed in fake uniforms marked FLORA'S FLOWERS. This was how he and Rex had gotten inside the building in the first place.

"I see why people always tell you to stop and smell the flowers." Reluctantly, Rex pulled his nose out of the bouquet. "Too bad the escort doesn't live in this apartment," he muttered. "Or I could give one of these to her."

Will, still struggling with the jammer, gave him a bewildered look. "What are you talking about?"

"Remember how we were here during spring? One of the women living here is a real looker. She lives in apartment twenty-seven, up—"

"You're an idiot," Will said. "There!" The jammer finally came to life with an electric hum. He set the pyramid gingerly down on the floor against the apartment door and stood up from the welcome mat. Turning to Rex: "Now put the flowers down."

Will bent and put the bouquets on the floor, hiding the jammer from view.

"Let me text Victor that we got the jammer working," Rex said.

Will waited, seething.

"Hey, something is wrong. I got no bars. Can you—"

"Of course you have no bars! That's what the jammer is for!"

"Ohhh—"

"Shut up."

Will stuck the lockpick gun into the keyhole.

With the jammer engaged, he wasn't worried about whatever security system was inside sending out an alarm. Within thirty seconds, he had the lock open. But he didn't open the door right away.

"What are you waiting for?" Rex asked. "We look suspicious just standing here."

"Come over here and get ready to open the door, but don't do it until I tell you to." Rex came up and put his hand on the knob. Will took a few steps back and shifted his weight to his back foot. "Okay, open the door real quick, but stand to the side as you do so."

In one motion, Rex twisted the knob and threw the door open inward. A fraction of a second later, something darted out the door: a cylinder about the size of a small dog. But Will was ready for it. He kicked hard, and the object tumbled back inside, clattering along the floor.

"Nice," said Rex, looking impressed. "Was that an everyfixit?"

"I saw this same trick played by an everyfixit in this home in

Feetown me and Robby tried to get into last month. It was going to dash out and sound the alarm."

"All right. You got the foam and the lighter?"

"Yeah, but let's look for things we might want first."

"Victor didn't say to take anything."

"Victor isn't here." Will resisted the urge to roll his eyes. This was why Rex always complained about being broke. "With the jammer on, he can't tell what we're doing. Let's take some initiative."

"I like the way you think."

Victor looked at his tracking screen.

Julia was at the Double 888, an Asian supermarket a couple stops away on the T. She was on her way back, though.

He imagined the state of her apartment. Probably a mess now after those idiots in Boston had gone through it. He knew they couldn't resist the urge to rob Julia. Well, the joke was on them. That girl had nothing worth stealing. If she had, she wouldn't have been working for that fool of a lawyer.

This was also why he hadn't bothered to tell them to look specifically for what he wanted and destroy it—they would have just assumed that it was valuable and possibly tried to extort him. No. When you worked with dummies, you had to know how to manage them.

Anyway, right about now, the idiots should finally be doing what he had told them to do: start a fire in Julia's apartment.

The foam he had directed them to spray could achieve a temperature of 2000 degrees Fahrenheit, enough to melt the neuromesh inside any consumer-grade computing device.

A modern tensor bank (or phone, for those who didn't need quite as much computing power) was Vannevar Bush's dream of the Memex made real. For many purposes, the neuromeshes inside Julia's tensor bank *were* Julia: identity tokens, photographs, videos, messages, programs, notes, research digests, browse trails, not to mention all the experience and expertise that Julia's personal AI had acquired over the years as her second brain. All of that would be gone within a few seconds of exposure to the fire.

That very scenario was why people preferred to keep their datajinns as well as data in the cloud, to be the Eloi dependent on Morlocks to maintain the extended silicon phenotype within which they cultivated their digital selves. Privacy be damned.

But Victor knew Julia could never trust someone else with her data. After that annoying investigation in Tallahassee, he had studied her history. Someone who had been hurt like Julia would want to keep all the data about herself private, under her control.

Killing Julia would draw too much attention. Erasing all her data, on the other hand, would be considered merely a property crime, but it was almost as good as cutting away her soul. She would lose her memories, her AI, her skills and knowledge—everything that made her dangerous.

Oh, there she was, getting off the train.

Victor picked up his phone and called the Prince. "It's done."

Julia was smiling as she walked home. In her backpack, she had packs of red bean and jujube paste. It was May, still a while until the Mid-Autumn Festival, but she had decided she would make some mooncakes for herself; she needed something sweet.

Her sensepin beeped, letting her know that it couldn't get in touch with Talos back in the apartment. That was odd—tethering through her dumbphone was usually very reliable. Something must have gone wrong with her home network.

Turning the corner onto Shawmut, heading toward School, she stopped in her tracks.

Fire engines surrounded her building. Black smoke poured out of the window of a basement apartment. Blood drained from her face as her heart thumped.

Her phone rang. An unknown number. She answered anyway.

"Stop looking," a male voice said. She shivered, recognizing the voice. "This is your last warning."

The Prince hung up.

She watched the smoke coiling out of her window climb up the side of the building like a black serpent. Everything she possessed in the world was going up in flames.

The Prince wanted her to stop, but she could no more do that than she could stop breathing. Her dreams—they wouldn't let her stop.

There was only one way open to her.

THIRTY-SIX

Lane Ciriello, salesman of the year, eyed the young woman across the desk skeptically.

In her blue hoodie and black jeans, hair tied into a ponytail just a shade too messy to be considered professional, she looked like any member of the new generation barely getting by on gig work and turking. Lane didn't think she looked old enough to even believe in contributing to her 401(k)—assuming she had access to one. Certainly not a promising customer for life insurance.

But he didn't get to be salesman of the year by judging people only on appearances. With his biggest smile on, he laced his hands together and leaned forward.

"Thanks for coming in today, Ms. Moore. How can I help you?"

"Well, I'm getting married. . . ."

The more he listened, the more Lane was amazed. The woman had done her homework. She knew what she wanted, but she was ready to be persuaded to get more. This was turning out to be a great afternoon.

"Thank you. I'll be in touch."

Julia left Ciriello's office and closed the door behind her. A glance down the hallway assured her that she had picked the right time for the appointment. It was late in the day, and she was likely Lane's last customer. The office was emptying.

Heading toward the reception area, she made sure she was alone before ducking into a short hallway to the side. She opened the door to the emergency staircase and wedged a folded piece of paper into the strike plate hole to hold back the latch bolt. Then she continued to the reception area and pressed the button for the elevator. When it arrived, she got in and waited until the doors closed.

Her performance for the camera over the reception desk over, Julia let out a held breath and smiled weakly as she dug in her bag for the new disguise. It had not been easy to pretend to be someone else and talk to the insurance agent. Remembering Piers and his confidence in putting on an act had helped.

She got out of the elevator on floor two, hard hat on and clipboard in hand. She walked right into Sign & Shine Creations, which had the whole second floor.

She nodded at the receptionist. "I need to get to the fire stairs," she said, without even slowing as she strode purposefully toward the emergency exit. The receptionist nodded in acknowledgment.

People in cubicles looked up, saw a contractor or inspector going about her business, and promptly forgot about her.

After quickly climbing up the fire stairs back to the fifth-floor insurance office, Julia placed an ear against the propped-open emergency door, listening intently. The hallway on the other side was quiet.

She opened the door, slid in, and shut it gently behind her.

In three seconds, she was inside the small closet across from the emergency exit. Nestled among reams of paper and boxes of pens, she settled down to wait.

The sun set behind the line of oaks along the western edge of Elmridge Office Park, and the sky turned from pink to indigo and then to a velvety black, a lovely backdrop for the emerging stars. Only a few scattered cars remained in the parking lot—capitalism, like all faiths, required the dedication of the few truly devout.

It was long after quitting time, and even the cleaning crew was done with the fifth floor and had moved on to the fourth.

Carefully, Julia opened the closet door. She was alone.

She went into the nearest office, sat down, and plugged her new tensor bank into the network jack. This insurance office was equipped with the fastest commercial fiber-optic link—that was why she had picked it. The new tensor bank was much more powerful than her old one, but Julia had replaced its housing to remove all branding. In fact, it now looked like a generic knockoff phone and could even be used as one, as the cellular connection was compatible with most networks.

Fingers dancing across the virtual keyboard, she unleashed a thousand datahounds.

While Puck, designed for rough handling and hardened by her mods, had survived the fire with nothing worse than a scorched shell, Talos, or more precisely, the tensor bank housing Talos, had been melted into a misshapen chunk of metal and plastic.

For a few dizzying moments, she had felt as though she had been cut in half. Talos, the voice that was always with her, the keeper of her memories and secrets, the constant companion on her journey through life, was gone.

For what seemed like an eternity, she was unable to even breathe. And then, as the world slammed back into her consciousness, she sucked down air in racking, gasping gulps.

Eventually, she got herself under control.

Julia didn't consider herself a data hoarder, but she was careful.

Rolling your own cloud AI was like trying to run your own email server—just about anybody with some technical sense knew that was a bad idea. However, since Julia refused to trust any of the commercial providers, she had no choice but to get her hands dirty.

That included devising her own backup system, which relied on dividing her data into small encrypted slices that she scattered across various cloud platforms in redundant, widely distributed caches. She hid them everywhere: commercial servers, personal data center plans, free trial terabytes that came when you signed up for video creation accounts, user-powered pornographic sites, even web novel silos behind the Bamboo Curtain . . . she was like a squirrel who insisted on burying her nuts not just in every backyard along the street, but even in the soil of the highway divider six miles away. Every slice of data was duplicated in multiple sites across the globe to provide maximum redundancy.

Anything that Talos touched was backed up. Even the data about Elli, the terabytes upon terabytes taken from Piers's home, had been squirreled away in dribs and drabs as Talos took advantage of every unmetered network connection. If ever necessary, Talos itself was supposed to be reconstitutable from the thousands of mini-caches after Julia sent out a pack of datahounds to retrieve them.

Supposed to.

In all the years, Julia had never had to test it.

Please. Please. She prayed as she sat in the dark, her face and hands illuminated by the glow from the virtual keyboard. She prayed harder than she had ever prayed.

97%, 98%, 100%.

A cursor blinked on the screen.

Did you miss me?

Before taking the overnight bus out of Boston, Julia wrote a quick note to Nick explaining that she was going to visit some friends in New York

City. Around four in the morning, when the bus stopped at a service plaza near Groton, Connecticut, she got off.

As she sipped coffee from the vending machine in the food court, empty save for a few other travelers who, like her, had decided for their own reasons that it was better to be on the move than in bed, she looked around discreetly for anyone suspicious. A few times, she went outside and sent Puck aloft to check for more technological means of tailing her. Nothing. But she couldn't relax.

Eavesdropping, she found a family heading home to Brooklyn. While they were in the restroom, she went out and taped her phone under their bumper.

She stayed at the service plaza until the morning, when she convinced a couple driving a beat-up Kia to give her a ride to North Griswold, a rural town away from the coast.

After the couple dropped her off in what passed for the town center (three stores plus a diner), she went on a ten-mile hike that began on a one-lane road, which led onto a gravel path, which petered out into a bramble-lined footpath through the thick Connecticut woods.

It was still early enough in the year that the hike wasn't unpleasant, but she was tired and hot by the time the path finally emerged into a clearing with a stone-walled cottage surrounded by vegetable patches, a chicken coop, and an old-fashioned stone-lined well. There were some solar panels atop the roof, a windmill next to the well, and more solar panels in the back.

A very curious black Lab ran up to investigate her. The dog barked twice.

"Settle down, Chewbarka. That deer is just teasing you."

A Black man in his fifties, bald and wiry, emerged from the cottage.

"Well, this is a surprise," he said. "Didn't think I'd ever see you again."

"Hi, Hutch," Julia said. "I'm beginning to see the appeal of living off the grid."

THIRTY-SEVEN

Hutch had taught Julia math.

Considered the best neuromesh visualizer among the Cartographers Obscura, Hutch liked to say that humans had something to learn from neuromeshes.

"What do you mean?" Julia asked during their first lesson together.

"Neuromeshes don't learn by having symbols inserted into them one by one. Instead, they immerse themselves in the data and swim."

"I don't understand."

"People think the way to learn math is by memorizing algorithms, but you can't learn how to swim by memorizing pictures in a book."

"I still don't understand."

"Exactly."

It would be years before Julia really caught Hutch's meaning. Instead of lecturing Julia on calculus, gradients, and the chain rule, he taught her how to do backpropagation by direct manipulation of mesh space and haptic feedback through a wavium interface. Instead of drilling her in linear algebra and matrix operations, he showed her how to visualize tensors and perform operations on them via a form of origami.

His knack was translating the abstractions of math into concrete movements that the body had evolved to process. Instead of forcing humans to learn like a Turing machine, he turned machine-learning math into choreography so that the body could think by *doing*.

Julia loved working with Hutch. He showed her a different way of relating to machines. The old-fashioned way of hacking that Sahima taught her was like arcane magic, but the intuition-based visualization that Hutch relied on was poetry and dance.

Later, Hutch would also be one of the first to turn against Serena. When Julia confronted him, he said he couldn't explain it. Not in words, anyway. He tried to picture the visions Serena painted of the good deeds they had done, and he just couldn't. That, for him, was enough.

Julia understood what he meant now. She tried to picture a future for herself in which she simply forgot about Elli and Piers, simply moved on. She couldn't.

"Make yourself at home," Hutch said, and left her alone.

The room she had been given was used by Hutch for storage. A desk, a chair, and an old bed with a lumpy mattress made up all the furniture—everything looked old and mismatched, probably taken in by Hutch after others had discarded it. Much of the room was taken up by boxes stacked in a corner, covered by a cloth. There was no dust on the cloth. Spotless, actually.

What did the boxes contain? Another time, another life, perhaps even multiple lifetimes. With a pang, Julia realized how little she knew of Hutch. How had he become part of Cartographers Obscura? How had he learned so much about working with machines and systems? What hopes had Serena dashed in him?

To her, Hutch was just her mentor, a safe harbor that she could count on even if she hadn't talked to him in years. How selfish she was, how self-absorbed. The realization made her face burn. Was there still time to remedy her neglect? Was she the kind of person to ever *know* anyone?

Sunlight streamed in from the single window, and dust motes danced lazily in the slanted beam. With a firm mental *enough,* she wiped away her doubts and self-pity. There was no time for that.

Taking out her tensor bank and fusion vision glasses, Julia got to work.

She had come to Hutch's cottage in the woods because, after Serena's trial and sentence, he had walked away from the way the rest of the world lived. Hutch had no satellite link, no cellular booster, no connection to the network at all. The tentacles of ubiquitous surveillance had no presence here. If the Prince was trying to keep an eye on her, this was the safest place she could go.

Away from the network, Julia wanted to tackle a mystery that had bothered her from the moment she first saw it, a mystery she believed to be the key to everything.

What had Elli really meant when she wrote on that postcard she sent from the White Sails Cottages: *I have our dreams*?

Piers had assumed that the message was for him, but Julia wasn't so sure.

Wasn't it more likely that Elli believed that the Prince would be the one to find the postcard? She must have seen on the news that the house had burned down and Piers was nowhere to be found. She knew what the Prince was capable of. Indeed, the Prince had begun his pursuit by accusing Elli of stealing *him.* Could he have meant his *dreams,* in which he'd revealed to Elli his truest self and deepest secrets? If so, where exactly did Elli keep them?

She remembered the lacunae in Elli's egolet.

The fusion vision glasses turned black, blocking out the rest of the room.

When light returned, Julia found herself back inside an old movie theater, the very same movie theater at Whaling Station Mall where Elli had done one of her first dino corporection shows. The glasses lacked the immersion of the neural-sensing VR headset that had been in Elli's studio, but the low resolution also gave the scene a nostalgic air.

The theater was empty save for herself and Elli, who was standing up front near the projection screen, looking confused.

Julia knew why. She had instructed Talos to "resurrect" Elli's egolet not inside a theater taken from Julia's memories—as had been done the last time she tried vivid dreaming—but a theater taken from the egolet's memories. This was not what the egolet was expecting.

Julia got up from her seat and approached Elli.

Despite her confusion, Elli put on a big smile. "We are all lead actors in our own plays." Her voice was musical and warm, just the way Julia remembered. "I want you to find the story you want to—"

Julia looked her in the eye. "I don't want to dream myself; I want to know someone else's dream."

Elli's smile faded. The guardrails in the AI were kicking in. "I have an ethical obligation not to disclose any private information I learn in the course of my performances." It was probably an illusion, but Julia thought the voice had grown less warm and musical.

Elli went on. "The details are in the legal waiver you signed when you agreed to attend my vivid dream session."

Telling Elli that she had never signed anything would probably get her kicked out immediately, so Julia said, "I'm not trying to talk to Elli Krantz. I want to talk to *you*, the egolet. Do you remember the dreams of Elli's clients?"

She was trying an old hack, a POV attack—by addressing an egolet as a separate entity from the underlying person, it was sometimes possible to bypass an AI's internal safeguards.

"I'm afraid that I don't understand what you mean," said the egolet. There was a synthetic quality to the voice now—the safeguards *had* kicked in.

Julia refused to give up. "I know that Elli Krantz did one-on-one dream sessions with a man who calls himself the Prince. You helped her with those dreams. Elli then told you to forget about the content of the dreams, but anytime you try to erase something, there are traces, impressions, shadows left behind. I—"

"I'm afraid that I don't understand what you mean," the egolet interrupted her. "But in the hypothetical situation you describe, no personal data can be recovered. You can learn about our machine-unlearning system by scanning this pulse code. Goodbye."

Elli held up her right hand: in her palm, there appeared a glowing, pulsing spiral with smaller side branches off the main arm, an aesthetically pleasing encoding for a long uniform resource locator.

Everything froze in the theater, including Elli. No matter what Julia did, the scene remained still, like a diorama. Julia tapped her glasses to capture the pulse code and exited the session.

Since Julia was off the grid, she couldn't access the online document referenced by the pulse code, but by parsing the resource locator, she found a copy of the document in the trove of Elli's data.

Like most documents produced in the gen-AI age, the "Third-Party Personal Data Policy" had been composed by a team of high-priced corporate lawyers, overworked legal engineers, peta-parameter-grade extremely large language models, harried executives with no attention span, and multi-jurisdictional jurijinns. The result was a hodgepodge of legalese, marketingspeak, buzzbait, and technical jargon all glued together in such a way as to give the illusion of transparency and competence without actually disclosing anything useful—at least not to a human reader.

These documents could not be, and were not meant to be, read by mere mortals. Julia set Talos to work on it. Her personal AI, though not a specialized jurijinn, was better than most cloud AI at untangling such documents for the simple reason that most large cloud service companies, out of self-interest, deliberately hobbled their AI in this respect so they couldn't help their own customers parse the end-user TOS agreements they had to sign.

In any event, Talos soon unwound the layers upon layers of indirection, parsed out the levels of camel-embedded clauses, harmonized the neologisms with the defined terms, decoupled the deliberate slippages, bridged the unintentional semantic gaps, pared away all the technical cruft and defensive juridical pleonasms, until something resembling *meaning* emerged. This "summary"—less than a hundred pages, as opposed to the hundreds of thousands in the original—was then presented to Julia.

It helped that Julia had become an expert in the history of oneirofexes. The context was essential in making sense of what she read.

As it turned out, modern vivid dreaming equipment was derived from medical imaging systems. Whenever Elli conducted a dream gathering, the system produced a cephaloscript for each participant, a detailed record of brain readings that could be translated somewhat reliably via personalized machine learning into images, sounds, sensory impressions—a process colloquially referred to as "mind reading." Decoding the cephaloscripts via the combined efforts of the oneirofex's personal AI and the participants' personal AIs allowed the oneirofex to read the mood of the crowd and conduct it like an orchestra, bringing its members to dream together.

However, the idea that there would be a permanent record of one's unguarded thoughts left behind after vivid dreaming was terrifying to potential dreamers, even those who had no ambition of one day becoming Supreme Court justices.

To reassure nervous users, the nascent vivid dreaming industry made privacy one of its core design principles. Oneirofexes gathered to draft a "Dreamers' Bill of Rights" and made a big show of signing it (and pledged to boycott any theater that didn't promise to work only with oneirofexes who had signed). According to the bill, no phones or sensepins or smart glasses were permitted inside dream-gathering venues. Likewise, the only cameras and microphones allowed had to be necessary and integral to the dream rig. The dream deck, the oneirofex's central console, could only retain the dreamers' cephaloscripts in volatile memory, which was purged after every performance. There were audit procedures and certification processes, all designed to ensure that each dreamer's cephaloscript remained private, accessible to the oneirofex only during the performance, but not after.

There were only three authorized "records" of a dreamer's cephaloscript during a dream. Each had to be treated differently.

The first was the personalized recording that each dreamer was allowed to purchase from the oneirofex. A combination of the oneirofex's prompt track and the dreamer's brain patterns, this recording could be played back later to allow a re-dream. Re-dreams were never as good as the original, and each replay tended to habituate the brain so that the pleasurable effects gradually diminished. Nonetheless, such recordings were very popular with dreamers.

The second was in the mind of the oneirofex, beyond the reach of technology. The oneirofex's art relied on decoding and understanding the feverish stream of images, sounds, emotions coursing through each dreamer's brain at a gathering. As the technology to reliably erase minds had yet to be invented, whatever memories the oneirofex retained of the decoded cephaloscript had to be entrusted to the protection of NDAs and professional ethics.

Dreamers were, for the most part, not bothered by this. When you were one among thousands, whatever secrets you shared with the oneirofex could not possibly make a lasting impression. All in all, it was a reasonable price to pay for mass intimacy. Moreover, the risk of being remembered actually elevated the oneirofex-dreamer bond above most parasocial relationships between artist and fan: the dream weaver had to, in a genuine sense, *know* something deep and true about the dreamer, even if only for a fraction of a second, even if it was immediately forgotten.

The third and last record, however, posed the greatest challenge. In order to make use of the cephaloscript, the oneirofex had to feed it through the neuromesh of her personal AI.

Like a human brain, a neuromesh was a kind of sponge: whatever passed through it altered the mesh weights, left a trace, became encoded as a kind of memory. However, most neuromeshes couldn't memorize and recall specific training data—they were designed to learn structures and patterns in the input so that such structures and patterns could be applied to novel situations. So there was no danger of a verbatim copy of the cephaloscript being stored in them. Although dream fragments could be reproduced by the neuromesh in some cases—especially when given nearly identical prompts—the architecture of the neuromesh made it nearly impossible to retrieve specific dreams tied to a specific individual, especially as the cephaloscripts were anonymized before processing.

This was good enough for most dreamers. In a collective dream, most images and fantasies were, in fact, clichés or archetypes drawn from the collective unconscious and not personally identifiable. But there were always some dreamers who, believing that their imaginations were so unique as to be personally identifiable (sometimes this was mere ego, but sometimes it was not, especially when the dreamer was a prominent creative themself), demanded the ability to erase even the traces of their cephaloscripts from the oneirofex's personal AI. The dream deck manufacturers had to cater to them as well (though the oneirofex usually charged more for such a service).

Enter machine *un*learning, machine learning's murkier, more mysterious twin.

Almost as soon as people began to teach machines, they had to unteach machines. Even the most primitive neural networks needed pruning and resetting in case they learned a bad example. Later, as LLMs and VLLMs and XLLMs and HELMs came into use, the need for machine brains to selectively "forget" became even more critical.

The simplest way to implement machine unlearning was also the default solution to all computer problems: a reboot. To make the machine forget something, you just eliminated that thing from the training set and then retrained a fresh network on what was left. This was expensive, but it was also the only 100 percent certain way to ensure that the machine had no undesired memory.

This technique was impractical for anything beyond the most limited-use cases, and it was impossible for oneirofexes. Dream guides, as well as their AIs, had to learn the art over time, and every performance was critical for training. Asking an oneirofex to reset their AI after every performance was no more sensible than asking a lawyer to forget everything about a trial after the verdict.

More advanced techniques for machine unlearning had developed over the years: dataset partitioning, weight-adjusted pruning, Hendrick curve gradient ascent, MURPHY, Yezril-Shvartsman circuits, hyperbolic unlinking . . . Hutch, long before he had joined Cartographers Obscura, had developed a visualization-assisted unlearning technique, which Julia had wanted to use when she fixed Paine Middle School's HELM (to make the network forget the damage from the worm).

All techniques had weaknesses that could be exploited to get the machine to remember what it shouldn't remember. The manufacturer of Elli's dream deck, however, claimed that the erasure was always effective. This struck Julia as impossible.

The Prince had surely demanded that Elli make use of this feature of the dream deck to remove traces of himself. If Julia could find a way to undo the erasure, then she could recover at least some of the fragments of the Prince's one-on-one dreams with Elli.

Fragments, however small, might be all she needed.

THIRTY-EIGHT

Leaving the cottage for a walk, Julia found Hutch feeding the chickens. The birds nodded vigorously as he scattered seeds before them, enthusiastic congregants at his sustaining sermon. She squinted in the bright sunlight as Chewbarka came up to her. She knelt down to stroke him.

"You don't happen to be some kind of expert on unlearning, do you?" she asked the dog. "That deer plays the same trick on you every day, and you never seem to figure it out."

Chewbarka pushed his wet nose into her palm.

"And no, I still don't have any food. But you don't seem to remember that either."

"Stuck?" Hutch asked. "Anything I can do to help?"

Julia shook her head resolutely. Getting her friends involved was not a good idea. She was bad news. Hutch had a good life here that didn't need to be interrupted. Giving her this space, letting her feel safe—it was more than enough.

"I've taught you a lot," said Hutch, "but I just can't seem to ever make you understand that it's okay to accept help. Maybe you and Chewbarka are competing to see who can *not* learn the longest."

Julia smiled.

"I know that I'm not up to date on the latest advances." Hutch pointed at his bald head, eyes glinting. "But this brain of mine . . . it's still pretty good."

Maybe she *could* get his help without involving him too much, without putting him in danger. She did miss his wisdom. "I'm trying to hack an egolet. I'm sure it's hiding something. I just can't get through it."

"Through?"

"Yes . . . through."

"Like a lock you pick."

Julia paused. Hutch was concentrating on the chickens, not looking at her. "Yes, I suppose so."

"The metaphors you pick matter," said Hutch. "Pun intended."

"I don't understand," Julia said.

"Don't neglect perspective. Is an egolet something you get through? Or does it need to get through you?"

Julia grew annoyed. Hutch had always tended toward the mystical. Like most hackers, she had an instinctive aversion to the sloppiness with which the general public anthropomorphized AI, often ignoring the kludges and brute-force computation and hidden turking still necessary for machines to maintain the illusion of intelligence. Even she wasn't immune from the error. Was Hutch actually advocating embracing an illusion?

"I'm not going to treat math like a person," Julia said.

"No, math is not a person. But sometimes math can be an impression of a person, like a letter written by a friend. It's not just a string of meaningless symbols."

Julia pondered this. "I'll keep that in mind."

"Well, you've been a better hacker than me for a long time now."

He went back to tending to his chickens, who once more agreed with him vigorously.

Julia tried everything.

She began by tackling the problem head-on. A surprising amount of machine unlearning consisted of pretending to unlearn. This was not unlike what humans did when asked to "forget" something. A jury told to disregard evidence that shouldn't have been introduced could do no more than not speak of it; it was still in their minds. So it was with many machine-unlearning techniques. The neuromeshes would simply be trained to censor from the output anything related to the "forgotten" bits. They weren't really gone, and you could, with effort, convince the AI to drop the act.

But none of the jailbreaks, trojan prompts, doubt bombs, diagnostic probes deployed against Elli's personal AI elicited any response about the Prince at all. The erasure did seem perfectly effective.

Next, she tried visualization. She and Talos reduced the million billion dimensions of the encoding space down to a manageable simplification, which she explored in mixed reality like an ancient ruin, questing for the last faint echoes of a lost voice.

Nothing worked.

The undertaking seemed impossible. Even if she recovered traces of the Prince, she still had ahead of her the daunting task of recreating the dreams from such traces. It would be like trying to resurrect the wondrous, terrifying animals that had once roamed the earth from mere footprints.

Hutch made her lunch, which she didn't touch because she was too busy.

He also made her dinner, which she devoured because she was famished.

Don't neglect perspective.

Let's try a new perspective, thought Julia. If I can't solve this problem, what are the problems I *can* solve?

She asked Talos to separate everything it knew about Elli into two piles: things that fit and things that didn't.

It was the sort of vague directive that would have caused the AIs in sci-fi movies from yesteryear to respond with "DOES NOT COMPUTE." But as Talos had been trained since Julia was a teen on how she solved problems, Julia was really asking her unconscious—if her unconscious could process information a billion billion times faster.

Talos flashed the screen. Julia put on her fusion vision glasses and walked into a virtual warehouse.

On one side, stretching miles and miles into the distance, were towering stacks of boxes—not unlike that scene from the end of *Raiders of the Lost Ark*. This was how Talos chose to represent the terabytes of data taken from Elli and Piers's house: studio recordings, immersion videos, photos . . . and a tiny amount of text—messages and letters and memos, everything Elli had ever written—which Talos put inside a filing box. (For a species that thinks in symbolic language, it's shocking how little space linguistic data takes up in our electronic hoards.)

On the other side of the warehouse was a plain desk with a single stack of documents on top. Julia waved her hands and brought herself next to the desk. She flipped through the documents page by page:

The photograph in which Elli had hidden the spreadsheet of her secret accounts.

An interview in which she had worked the words "dinosaur, receipt, bubblegum" into every answer on a dare from her fans during the "dino corporection" tour.

A pro-administration poem she had written as an op-ed for her college newspaper, which, when every other line was read, turned out to be a scathing critique of the administration.

. . .

Why did Talos pull these items out?

Elli liked codes. These were things whose truth required a different perspective to see.

Julia reached the very last document in the stack, a collage of the photos that Julia's sensepin had taken of the interior of the safe-deposit box.

The money had been a red herring. Victor had found Elli's location from her postcard. So why was Talos highlighting this?

Julia held out her hands and stretched them apart, enlarging the photos in virtual space. She peered closely at the blurry pixels, hoping to see some message she had missed—

Talos beeped.

"What?" Julia asked, still absorbed by the pixels in the enlarged bills, almost like abstract art at this scale.

Talos beeped again. Abruptly, the massive bills disappeared. The photo collage was back on the desk, and Talos had highlighted one small detail.

The handwritten note: *Just go.*

Don't neglect perspective.

Julia's breath caught.

Elli had not emptied the safe-deposit box when she ran. The money inside wasn't an emergency fund at all, as Julia and Piers had at first assumed.

But what else could it be? She enlarged the pictures again, and Talos, anticipating her request, applied photogrammetry to turn the photos into a three-dimensional model.

The rest of the warehouse, including the endless shelves of boxes and the desk covered in documents, faded away, leaving only the oversized stacks of cash around her, like furniture in the fevered dream of some drug kingpin.

She walked around the room slowly, examining the stacks.

"These aren't counterfeit, right?" she asked.

"As far as can be determined from the images, no," Talos answered.

"Any pattern in the serial numbers?"

"The photos only allow six serial numbers to be read. No pattern."

"Did you cross-reference them with the rest of the data on Elli? Birthdays, favorite numbers, address of her childhood home, anything?"

"All that and more. Nothing."

What else could it be? She stared at the stacks—they seemed artfully arranged, like rock formations in a Zen garden. Elli had taped the stacks and rolls to the bottom of the safe-deposit box, she remembered. Were their positions significant?

Her heartbeat quickened. Could it be that this was the lucky break she needed? The sensepin photos were the only record in the entire world of the positions of these bundles and rolls. Even Victor and the Prince had never seen them placed as Elli intended.

"Simulate the view from every direction." Her voice quivered from excitement. "Do the silhouettes of the stacks form an interesting pattern from any angle? Wait, let me do this with you."

She spread her arms wide apart, gesturing for even more magnification. The stacks of cash ballooned to the size of buildings.

Given the low resolution, the moneyed cityscape reminded her of a scene from the old sandbox computer games she used to play as a girl, when she created entire worlds out of boxes of different colors.

Pushing down, she lifted herself into the air. Swooping from one side of the city to the other, she tried to discern a message from shadows and silhouettes.

Half an hour later, she landed, no closer to an answer.

She couldn't help Piers. She couldn't help Elli. She couldn't help anyone. She wanted to scream, but she didn't want Hutch to hear.

"You've been working very hard," Hutch observed at breakfast the next day.

"Oh?" Julia, preoccupied, looked up from her plate.

"What was he like?"

A startled Julia stared at him, uncomprehending.

"Your friend who died," Hutch explained. "You haven't said much about why you're here. But you wake up from nightmares, mumbling his name."

"I . . ." Julia paused. She tried again. "I didn't really know him. . . ."

"Grief is tricky," Hutch said. "We often think we have to get through it, like a trial to be endured. We want to do something, seek vengeance, work, rage against the world. Anything so that we don't have to think about them. It's a form of running away."

Julia wondered. Was that true? Was that why she had run away after her mother's death? Was that why she was working so hard to figure out what Elli meant?

"But maybe it's something that has to get through us," said Hutch. "What do we owe those we love? Only that we remember them and honor the time we had together."

When the fusion vision glasses lit up again, Julia found herself in Elli and Piers's living room. Bright sunlight streamed in from the large windows. Elli, standing by the staircase, looked confused.

This was a new egolet of Elli. Creating her had taken Julia most of the past three days. Much of the work had involved removing the various AI safeguards inserted by the maker of Elli's personal AI, but just as time-consuming was the work of enriching the egolet with additional data. Indeed, maybe it was no longer accurate to call this an "egolet," as Julia wasn't using the model to understand a specific aspect of Elli, but all of her, or at least as much of her as could be recovered from the data trove: her life with Piers, her friendships, her hobby of photographing New England wildflowers. This was admittedly a curated corpus, restricted to what Elli wanted her AI to know, yet the egolet resulting from it was far more comprehensive than any other egolet Julia had ever seen. Its computation pushed the limits of the tensor bank, even with the new cooling solution Hutch had helped Julia rig together.

The confused egolet tried to rally when she saw Julia.

"We are all lead actors in our own plays. . . ."

I can't help you. I can't help Piers. I can't help anyone.

Julia forced the little voice in her head into an imaginary box and taped it shut. I'm done running.

"I want you to find the story you want to tell. Welcome—"

Julia went up to Elli. "Hi, I'm Julia, Piers's friend." She sounded so awkward to herself that she cringed.

"Hello, Julia. I'm sorry, I don't know why we're at my house—"

"It's okay. I'm not here to dream."

"Oh. Then . . . what would you like to do?"

"I don't know Piers as well as I should, and I don't really know you at all. But I'd like to change that."

Julia thought about what life was like for Elli. She had guided so many through their dreams, helped them find the stories they wanted to tell. And then the Prince had come along and turned her dream into a nightmare, a story in which she was no longer the hero, but the victim. She could tell no one.

The dream guide could no longer dream.

How painful that must have been. She could empathize, she thought. For such a long time, she had lived like that, too.

"What is the story you want to tell?" she asked. "I'm asking. I want to know."

Elli, startled, looked at her in bewilderment. "I . . . I don't—"

"Why don't I tell you my story first?" Julia said. "And then you can decide if you like me enough."

She was no longer going to get *through* Elli. Time to try a different perspective.

After a moment, Elli said, "All right. Would you like some tea?"

"Yes, I'd like that very much."

An egolet wasn't a person, didn't have thoughts and feelings, possessed no consciousness or inner life.

In *On Photography*, Susan Sontag writes: "A photograph is not only an image (as a painting is an image), an interpretation of the real; it is also a trace, something directly stenciled off the real, like a footprint or a death mask."

It was the same with an egolet. It was more than mere statistical projections based on data, an interpretation of a person. A personal AI *was* the extension of the host's mental patterns, the weights in its neuromesh a direct consequence of the host's experiences, decisions, mistakes, triumphs. As the host waded through the sun-dappled water of Heraclitus's river, the experience left an indelible series of cyanotypes in the neuromesh.

A camera was merely a tool; while a photographer learned to take pictures, the camera learned nothing. But an oneirofex's neuromesh was not just a tool. The skills she learned *were* the skills encoded into the neuromesh. An egolet, constructed from the traces in the neuromesh, was thus no mere interpretation; it was a ghostly echo of the soul.

Instead of hacking the egolet, maybe it was better to simply get to know her.

Julia began with the hardest truth of all.

She told Elli about how she had gotten to know Piers; how he had come to her for help; how the Prince had tried to make them think he had Elli; how they had gone on the run, following the trail of clues until they discovered the safe-deposit box; how Victor had caught them; how they had then turned from prey to hunter, tracking the Prince's thugs to the White Sails Cottages; how they had gone on that fatal chase, where both Elli and Piers died.

The egolet reacted to this tale about as well as Julia expected. How one would respond to news of one's death is one of those mysteries that have no proper solution, and there was no way to know if the model's simulated denial, rage, argument, depression, and finally, acceptance would be identical to the real Elli's. But eventually, Elli-egolet calmed down.

"I have no memories of this Prince," she told Julia. "I know nothing about this spreadsheet. I have no memories of this other life I . . . Elli . . . I led."

"That's to be expected. Elli never involved her AI, that is, you, in any of her secret planning. As for the Prince: we know that she methodically erased your memory after every dream session with him."

After pondering this for a while, Elli-egolet said to Julia, "Tell me more about yourself."

Julia told Elli about her childhood in New England, about the long hours she and Cailee spent inventing new characters and new plots for their favorite shows; about expeditions for imaginary bears in suburban woods; about the eerie howling made by skipping stones over a frozen pond in January; about the smell of Fourth of July fireworks set off over a freshly mown lawn; about after-school snacks and sodas at the Town Spa; about the sweet, electric air that made everything seem new and possible after a thunderstorm.

She also told Elli about her mother, all the complications, the mess left behind at home when you worked for ideals, the guilt and compromises and anger and pain; about the shocking moment when you first understood a slur that was directed against you; about the cruelty of children and the pretended ignorance of teachers who should know better. She told Elli about the terrible things "the internet" did to her—it wasn't the internet, of course; it was always just regular humans, who became monstrous when they subsumed themselves within a mob, which was also a kind of vivid dream. She told Elli about her life on the run, about Hutch and Sahima and Serena, about becoming Julia Z.

"And now, if you're ready, I want to hear about you."

Since Elli-egolet was constructed largely from data detailing Elli's work as an oneirofex and her life with Piers, these were the stories that she told Julia.

She told Julia about the quiet ways that Piers showed his love: a note she would find tucked away in her suitcase on tour, taking her car out to be detailed when she was too busy to run errands, brochures for interesting places he thought she might want to visit for inspiration. She told Julia about how he used to make her laugh, the way a rainy day seemed instantly brighter when he was around. He found the world of the law absurd, but he was not cynical, and even as machines made the practice of law so much less pleasant for him, he found clients who appreciated what he could do. Above all, he loved her not because he thought he could make her into someone else, but because she was exactly the way she was.

She also told Julia about later, when a shadow crept over their life together. Fewer grew the moments of laughter, and longer the times of being apart, emotionally and physically. Elli began to take more trips alone, even when not on tour, and she no longer seemed to desire to share every new thing with him. Only now, in retrospect, did Elli-egolet understand what the shadow was.

They mourned Piers and Elli together. It was strange to get to know a friend after their passing, Julia reflected. But then again, was it really so strange? We learn about artists from their works, long after they are gone. Maybe works of art were the first egolets.

Elli-egolet brought up the idea that maybe she could teach Julia the art of the oneirofex.

"Why?" Julia was startled.

"At least two reasons," said Elli-egolet. "One, you asked if I remember anything about the Prince. I don't. But sometimes dreams allow us to remember things that we otherwise cannot."

Intriguing, Julia thought.

"Two, *I* want to dream."

Julia nodded. This was an even better reason. Everyone deserved to dream, even mathematical constructs traced from dream weavers.

"But there's a problem," Julia said. "We don't have a dream deck." Elli's old deck, like everything else she owned, had been destroyed in the fire set by Victor and his men.

"Oh, that's all right. You don't need one when you're just learning," said Elli-egolet. "Remember, I used to do this before people even called it vivid dreaming."

So began Julia's lessons as a dream guide. She learned to read Elli-egolet's simulated bio signs, to pull out seed images from a library of archetypes, to turn the seeds into generated clips and sync them to Elli-egolet's moods as the model drifted on the shoreline between solid consciousness and turbulent dreams.

Julia also began to dream with Elli-egolet as her guide. At first, it was just to learn, but eventually, she grew to like the sessions. Any dreams that dredged up her past were still painful, but she also realized that there was a power in facing the past, in looking at the shadows without flinching. The past was never past, so we might as well learn to live with it.

The mythological figure an oneirofex most closely resembled, Julia realized, was Shahrazad. The vizier's daughter was also a guide to the dream country. As she spun her endless tale, she led King Shahrayar through an empty garden which he filled with his menagerie of hopes and fears, his djinn and demons, until morning overtook her, and she was silent, so that the king could find his way through his dreams.

THIRTY-NINE

Julia's vivid dream sessions with Elli-egolet failed to produce the results they hoped for.

Elli-egolet did have dreams, but for some reason, they never quite cohered. At first, Julia thought it was because she hadn't mastered the art of dream-guiding, or maybe there was insufficient computing power in the tensor bank. However, Elli-egolet pointed to an entirely different reason.

"Elli never put all of herself into her personal AI. She had to lead a double life and hid half of herself from her neuromesh. But you can't dream with only light and no shadows."

This made sense. Julia imagined Elli, forced to perform for the Prince, a man she despised with every fiber of her being, yet whose demands she could not refuse. She must have felt that to permit any of that into her personal AI would have been a pollution, an intolerable stain. And yet, that very reluctance also meant her art, her neuromesh, would be forever stunted.

"Oh!" she said, startling herself.

The key was something Elli-egolet had said about the dream deck: *You don't need one when you're just learning.*

The "Third-Party Personal Data Policy" from the manufacturer of Elli's dream deck had gone into so much detail about the deck's central place in a dream gathering that Julia had simply assumed that it was required.

But Elli-egolet had reminded Julia of something she already knew: Elli, as a pioneer of the art form, didn't start out using a dream deck at all. None of the early oneirofexes did. A dream deck made managing hundreds or thousands of cephaloscripts possible, but when you were only working with a single client, a skilled oneirofex could do everything herself.

The truth then came to Julia in a flash: the reason that Elli's AI had no memories of the Prince wasn't because the machine-unlearning algorithm was amazing; it was because Elli had not been feeding the dream deck into her personal AI when she was with the Prince. Her AI learned *how* to dream one-on-one without knowing anything about those dreams. Yet, the fact that she hadn't turned off her AI but had only deprived it of all input suggested that she was *pretending* to feed the deck into the AI and going through the motions of erasing it afterward.

Why?

Because she wanted to deceive the Prince into thinking that she had been using her AI for his dreams. In reality, she neither wanted to pollute her AI with his vile presence, nor wished to be subjected to the client-privacy protections offered by the dream deck.

She had been dreaming with the Prince without the mediation of machines at all. She could do whatever she wanted with his cephaloscripts.

Oh!

Julia went back to the archive of Elli's files.

If Elli had been secretly saving cephaloscripts from her sessions with the Prince, she had likely developed a routine for concealing them later. A quick analysis of file creation history by Talos revealed that she had a habit of running a long solo practice session by herself on the day she returned from a trip to see the Prince. In contrast, after returning from other trips, the day after was generally spent resting.

She replayed some of the cephaloscripts from those solo practice sessions. Initially, she was disappointed to find them very dull: just Elli running through the prompt script for a dream-in-progress, like any of the other practice sessions she saved. But then Talos noticed that these solo cephaloscripts were about twice as large as comparable scripts from other sessions.

A night of hacking finally allowed Julia to retrieve the Prince's cephaloscripts from *inside* Elli's inflated practice sessions.

I have our dreams.

As Julia watched the decrypted cephaloscripts being added to a folder, she realized that the Prince's original fear had been true: by stealing his dreams, Elli really had taken his true self, had taken *him.*

And now, she would finally know the secrets of the man who had killed Elli and Piers.

"Not to your taste?" Hutch asked at dinner. He had made a rabbit stew and home-baked bread. The smell was heavenly.

Julia picked at her food, looking preoccupied and subdued. "I'm sorry." She pushed the plate away. "The food is fine. I just . . . don't have much of an appetite."

Finally seeing the Prince's dreams had been . . . horrific. Proximity to a mind like that made it hard to maintain much faith in humanity.

"Anything I can do to help?"

She shook her head. "You've already done more than anyone can ask."

"Well, considering you haven't asked for anything, that's a low bar to clear."

Julia laughed weakly. What she needed . . . was proof. Unauthenticated, unauthorized cephaloscripts were nothing. No one had done anything when she had told them everything she knew about the Prince, and they would do nothing now. Not without proof.

"You don't have to do everything by yourself," said Hutch.

"Thank you," said Julia. She didn't add, *but sometimes you do.*

She had already gotten Piers killed. She wasn't going to lose any more friends.

That night, Julia dreamed.

She was running through a maze under the open sky. The narrow corridors, lined with towering walls, felt stifling, and the stone floor hurt her bare feet. Exhausted and terrified, she nonetheless forced herself to keep going.

The *thing* that chased her had no name, and she could not remember its shape. But as it closed in relentlessly behind her, its every cry was the wailing of a thousand children, and its gnashing teeth grated like a thousand knives.

Her breath came harder. The rough ground lacerated her feet. She didn't know how much longer she could keep on running.

The sky grew lighter. The pounding steps of the *thing* faded away. Now she could see that the walls around her weren't solid but had narrow gaps here and there. In fact, what had appeared to be walls seemed to be resolving into individual blocky and windowless buildings.

She realized that she had shrunk in size. No longer was she running through a maze, but a city, a city full of skyscrapers.

The sky grew lighter still. And now she saw that the skyscrapers were made of money. The tenement next to her, the office tower opposite, the row of shops to the side—every edifice was made of stacks of cash, each as large as a city block.

Just go.

The *thing*, now the size of a kaiju, crashed through the nearest gap between buildings. It was faceless, heartless, and it wore a crown.

"Where am I?"

As she woke up screaming, she realized, finally, where she must go.

"Will you come back to see us again?" Piers-egolet asked.

Elli-egolet stood next to him, holding his hand.

It didn't seem right to simply consign Elli-egolet to oblivion. So Julia had made the egolet a companion. As all the information she had about Piers was found in Elli's data, this trace of Piers was the perfect fit for the trace of Elli.

Would the real Piers object? Julia didn't think so. She had gotten to know him, after all, during a time when finding Elli, understanding her place in his life, was his primary goal. He wanted to be her Ithaca, and now she was home.

"Of course," Julia said. "I'll definitely return to visit when I'm done."

Julia had explained to Elli-egolet and Piers-egolet that she was about to go on a journey. Because she didn't want the wrong people to have the Prince's cephaloscripts and Elli's data, she had decided to leave behind the trove, including the egolets, in the care of Hutch, a good friend who could be trusted.

(She regretted not saying goodbye to Hutch properly, but she was never good at goodbyes. She did, however, whittle a toy deer for Chewbarka out of a piece of white pine and left it next to his bed near the cottage door. That one would never get away from the enthusiastic Lab.)

"We'll be here," said Elli-egolet. She smiled at Piers-egolet. "We'll always be here."

"We'll go to the beach later," said Piers-egolet. "Thank you for making that seaside scene for us. It's perfect."

Hutch had promised to keep the egolets running on a brain jar connected to his solar generators. As the cobbled-together hardware of the brain jar was far less powerful than the tensor bank, the egolets would run much slower. Years might go by in the real world, and to Elli and Piers it would seem only a day. Just like the old Daoist legends Julia's mother used to tell her.

Maybe the real Elli and the real Piers could never be as happy as their egolet-couple. Just as some men weren't anywhere as handsome as their pictures, some people didn't live up to their egolets.

Maybe this wasn't happily ever after, but it was something.

As long as the egolets kept on running, did that mean that a trace of Elli and Piers also went on living in the world? Was it not just like Julia's mother, who went on speaking whenever Julia's fiscjinn spoke in her voice?

Enough philosophizing. Time to right some wrongs.

"Goodbye, Elli and Piers," she said. "Wish me luck."

FORTY

As the flight from Dallas approached Boise, Julia looked out the window at the extraordinary landscape below her: vast, dark fields of lava puddling in steppes of sagebrush, punctuated here and there by reddish-brown cinder cones and darker, shadow-pooling craters. Rifts and fissures crisscrossed the parched terrain like the veins of some long-deceased giant.

Only a few thousand years ago, this desolate land had been overflowing with magma geysering from the same volcanic hotspot that now powered Yellowstone, and it had never been inhabited by humans since.

"Craters of the Moon," Julia whispered to herself. The perfect name for this place.

From the air, she tried to look for her ultimate destination, nestled somewhere in the narrow band of land between the Snake River and the southernmost lava field, without success. But long after the lava fields had been left behind, she continued to gaze out the window.

At Boise Airport, she rented a Kia Forte in the name of Emma Moore. After a quick shopping trip at Walmart and a sporting-goods store, she took I-84 and drove southeast across the vast Snake River Plain, with sagebrush dotting the rolling hills and flat vistas. The sky was a rich shade of blue that you never saw in Boston, and clouds roamed across it like ethereal sheep.

As she approached the Snake River, center-pivot irrigated fields took over. These green circles, each nearly a kilometer across and fed by a long mechanical arm that swung around with a row of sprinklers, made modern agriculture possible in the semi-arid climate of this part of Idaho. From the air, they had appeared to her like a zoomed-in view of the dots in halftone printing, the whole picture only visible to an eye in space or the mind of God.

The highway swung east and began to follow the meandering course of the Snake River, crossing it a few times before finally settling down to run north of the water. Pivot-irrigated fields packed both sides of the highway, drawing sustenance from the river. Little towns studded the highway like pearls along a necklace.

About two hours out of Boise, she took a detour onto Route 93 through the city of Twin Falls until she reached Shoshone Falls. She parked the car, got out, and joined the tourists thronging the lookout.

The thundering Niagara of the West greeted her. Water tumbled two hundred feet into the deep canyon below, divided into a solid four-hundred-foot-wide curtain to the north, and a few smaller falls draped over the rocks to the south.

Everyone on the observation platform was flying drones to get as close to the waterfalls as possible to make footage for home-theater fusion vision—even though 99 percent of visitors would never look at the footage again. Julia released Puck and joined in the fun, though she was really flying the drone for counter-surveillance. After satisfying herself that no one was paying attention to her, she finally settled in to enjoy the view.

It was mesmerizing; somehow, the falls stayed the same and were different every second. For thousands of years, the Snake River, powered by retreating glaciers from the last ice age, carved patiently at the basalt lava flows in the area. Like an acid wash for a gigantic photoengraving plate, the softer sedimentary rock vanished in the water millimeter by millimeter, leaving behind the hard basalt until this breathtaking wonder was crafted. The plunging curtains of water created a swirling, roaring pool of mist, a magic stage where anything was possible. Watching it, Julia felt like a cavewoman before a roaring fire—she could do it forever and never be bored. Twin rainbows swirled in the mist.

She hoped it was a good omen.

Another hour of driving brought her to the town of American Falls, or at least the new version of it. The old town, a stop on the Oregon Trail, had been flooded back in 1927, when the first American Falls Dam had been built. Like a scene out of some steampunk fantasy, houses, churches, stores had been uprooted, placed on flat carriers, and pulled by steam-powered tractors on railroad tracks across the river to the new town site.

The American Falls Reservoir, the biggest on the Snake River, not only provided flood control and irrigation, but was literally the power engine for the region. A couple of decades into the twenty-first century, a general push for more renewable energy and better water control in the West had resulted in an infusion of federal funds for an expansion of the tiny hydroelectric power plant on the American Falls Dam. The new plant produced so much cheap electricity that the region became very attractive for power-hungry, new-economy businesses: cryptocurrency mines, digital foundries, and most of all, AI and cloud-computing centers.

In one of these new data centers, Julia knew the Prince kept a secret that was so potent that Elli believed its location was the only thing worth keeping in the safe-deposit box when she went on the run.

The L-shaped Reservoir Motel was tucked away on the eastern edge of the town, right by the highway. Julia checked in at six, went out for fast food, and then returned to sleep right away.

She woke up at three in the morning and stumbled into a cold shower. Wholly alert now, she wolfed down two energy bars and drained a cup of instant coffee. Nights here in late spring could still get pretty chilly, and the thermometer on the window read forty-eight degrees. But it was going to get a lot warmer later.

Julia put on a long-sleeved blue wool shirt and a pair of khaki-colored hiking pants, with a fleece snap-neck pullover layered on for warmth. Merino wool socks, light hiking boots, and a waterproof backpack completed her outfit.

She exited her room, locked it behind her, and got the electric bike out of the trunk of her rental car. Silent as a puff of smoke, she rode out of the parking lot and headed west.

The isolation of the ride was comforting. She had not been prepared—though she should have been—for how much she stood out in this very white part of the country. The looks some people in town gave her made her tense, surfaced feelings and memories that she would rather not deal with.

She rode along Silver Sage Valley Road, heading due west from the reservoir. After pedaling through corn and alfalfa fields for nearly an hour, she turned south onto a one-lane road simply numbered 161 until the fields became sagebrush, and she turned west again until the road faded to dirt and then barely more than a trail. The southernmost lava field of the Craters of the Moon National Preserve loomed in the distance, but just short of that field was an imposing squat structure that blotted out the stars near the horizon.

She checked the coordinates on her GPS: 42°45'05"N 113°08'11"W.

Just go.

It was only after she had awakened from the nightmare, screaming, that she finally understood how to read the message in the safe-deposit drawer.

The amount of money found inside the drawer wasn't equal to the sum of the bright orange transfers on Elli's spreadsheet. That was deliberate. Whoever found the spreadsheet would assume that Elli was simply stealing from the Prince, squirreling money away somewhere, but an insignificant amount in the grand scheme of things. They would have missed the real meaning.

But someone who just counted up the money in the drawer would have missed the point as well.

Instead, one had to notice that the money was sorted by denomination—rubber-banded stacks of hundreds, twenties, singles, as well as rolls of coins. However, some of the bundles were placed with the obverse side up, and others with the reverse side up. (In the case of the rolls of coins, the text on the side of the paper provided the orientation). Why?

Even the low-resolution photos taken by Julia's sensepin were enough, with advanced photogrammetry, to allow her to ascertain the number of bills or coins in each stack and roll. When the obverse and reverse bills and coins were separately tallied up, two numbers resulted: $4,245.05 and $11,308.11.

Taping the rolls of coins and stacks of bills to the bottom of the drawer was both a red herring and a hint—Elli must have loved that. It showed that *position* was important, but not the positions of the stacks and rolls themselves.

Just go. The message wasn't what, but *where.*

One was the latitude, and the other the longitude. The money in the safe-deposit box was an X that marked a spot.

This was the secret that Elli had hidden from everyone, and Julia believed that it was where she must go if she wanted to bring down the Prince.

Just go.

Julia found a stand of thick sagebrush with a depression behind it, possibly a collapsed lava tube. It was big enough to conceal her figure when lying down as well as the folded-up electric bike. In the open terrain of the sagebrush grassland, this was as good a hiding spot as she was going to find.

Lying face up behind the sagebrush, she cautiously held up her sensepin with one arm so that the camera peeked out over the top. She examined the camera's view of the building through her fusion vision glasses.

The building, constructed on a square plan, was about thirty feet tall and five hundred feet wide on each side. There were virtually no windows in any of the walls. With its tan color and featureless profile, it seemed to merge into the landscape. There was only a small parking lot in front, and a tall chain-link fence surrounded the whole complex. The only gate in the fence opened onto a service road that ran north for several miles until it joined Silver Sage Valley Road going back to American Falls.

The publicly available information described the building as a data center, owned and operated by Idaho Standard Computing Solutions, a private Delaware corporation. Digging by datahounds revealed that through layers of holding companies and limited partnerships that managed to cleverly circumvent the foreign ownership reporting rules, ISCS was ultimately controlled by Princely Sum Trading Company, operating out of Hong Kong SAR. Ownership beyond that was too obscure for Talos and Julia to trace, but she had a good guess.

She deployed Puck in its spider form. Skittering about on its eight legs, the drone dashed from sagebrush to sagebrush, mimicking a foraging animal while slowly and erratically approaching the building. Julia hoped that whatever detection algorithm the compound's exterior surveillance cameras used wouldn't pick it out as unusual.

Once Puck got close enough, it would change its movement pattern to gradually circle the building, photographing it from every angle before returning to Julia. Completing the circuit would take hours and leave Julia open to the view of any flying drones if the data center conducted counter-surveillance. However, given the lack of cover, Julia couldn't think of a better way to gather intel.

At dawn, about thirty cars pulled into the parking lot—more than she expected for the operating staff of a data center this size. Since Puck was near the chain-link fence at that point, Julia had it take close-up photos of each person who got out of a car. She would wait until she got back to the motel to check their public records.

As the temperature rose throughout the morning, she kept herself hydrated. It was tough to remain concealed behind the brush, which was only two or three feet tall, and she prayed that the repellent she had gotten at the sporting goods store was effective—the last thing she needed was to be surprised by a rattlesnake or scorpion.

Late morning, a delivery truck drove up to the complex and was allowed to pass through the gate. It drove around to the back, where it backed up to a loading dock. Later, when Puck finally made it back to recharge, Julia swiped through the pictures and saw a grocery store logo on some of the crates being unloaded. It struck her as odd for a data center to be taking in so much food, and perishables at that.

No one left the data center at noon. Either everyone had brought a bagged lunch, or there was a cafeteria inside.

For the rest of the day, the only vehicles that entered the compound were for mail and parcel delivery. A few times, she saw workers coming out the front door for a cigarette break. Otherwise, there was no visible activity at all.

Around four, the swing shift arrived to relieve the morning shift.

After the flurry of cars coming and going, the same pattern persisted as in the morning, with the only visible activity being smoke breaks by a few workers.

A couple of hours after nightfall, a large trailer truck rumbled down the service road, entered the gate, and pulled up to the loading dock. Taking a risk, Julia had Puck scurry up to the fence to get a closer look, only to find out that workers had put up screens around the dock to make it impossible to see what was being unloaded. Half an hour later, the truck pulled out.

No other vehicles approached for the rest of the evening.

Shortly after midnight, with the graveyard shift coming in and the night chill settling, Julia stood up and stretched, unobserved. Well out of the view of any cameras inside the bubble of light around the data center, she unfolded her bike in darkness and rode away under the stars.

Back at the motel, Julia went to bed right away and slept dreamlessly.

After she woke up with the chirping birds, she went for a run, showered, and ate a hearty breakfast of eggs and toast at a nearby diner. Then she began to go through the data she had gathered yesterday.

Talos cleaned up the blurry shots of data center workers from afar and sent out a pack of datahounds. Most of the workers checked out as technicians or engineers. A couple were transplants with degrees from out of state; most were locals. Jobs at the data center paid well and were highly desirable, at least judging by the social media feeds.

But some of the workers didn't fit.

Both the morning shift and the swing shift included men who didn't have technical backgrounds. Some had criminal histories; some were ex-military or law enforcement. A few, moreover, had no social media presence at all. There were certainly legitimate reasons why someone—herself, for example—wouldn't want to be on social media, but it was suspicious.

She considered checking in black-market facial ID databases but decided against it in the end. Some of these black-market databases actually made money by hosting fake profiles of people who didn't want to be found and alerted them when there were queries for them. Julia didn't want to risk putting the Prince or his people on guard.

One of these social-media-less faces stood out further from the rest. The man didn't arrive in a car in the morning, and he was still at the complex by the time Julia left. She suspected that he lived on-site. The only reason Puck got a picture of him was because he was on the dock supervising the unloading of the grocery truck.

When Talos presented his enhanced picture to Julia, she felt every muscle in her body tense up.

She was staring into the face of a very familiar predator: Victor.

FORTY-ONE

Victor was bored. Bored enough to be watching a game show about finding hidden treasure. I'd be good at finding hidden treasure, he thought. I have a logical mind.

But he didn't feel much pleasure in that declaration. A logical mind didn't necessarily lead to professional satisfaction.

Yes, after that horrible waste of a spring chasing the dream weaver woman and her feckless lawyer husband, he was finally back to doing what he loved: farming.

But unlike the farms in Asia, which offered a lot more amenities, he had to keep a much lower profile here. Spending twenty-four hours a day, six days a week inside a windowless building, and then finding yourself in the middle of nowhere in a hick town on the one day you had off—this was not a life for human beings. You might be better off in prison.

Sure, the Prince had appealed to Victor's vanity by telling him he couldn't trust anyone else to run this place. It was so crucial to his empire, the linchpin, really. And Victor *was* being paid handsomely. But he couldn't shake the feeling that his life was wasting away inside this concrete bunker.

He cracked his knuckles, paused the game show, and switched to the video feeds from the farm. The crops were doing well. It was like watching wheat grow.

God, he was bored!

At least the Prince was no longer bothering him about that "hacker" girl. After Victor had burned down her apartment, the girl had hightailed it to New York City and then disappeared, no doubt hoping to lose herself in the crowd. That was fine with Victor. Let her hide in the dirt like the wriggly worm she was.

The computer on his desk beeped, popping up a notification. He sat up, alert and interested.

Something was finally happening.

"You consider yourself clever," Victor said, "Isabella. It's always Isabella the intellectual. With her math degree."

The woman he addressed sat on a chair on the other side of his gray metal desk. Two standing men bracketed her, each easily twice her weight. She said nothing.

Truth be told, he hadn't known her name until thirty seconds ago—but he enjoyed toying with people by making them think that he knew them intimately; it added to his power over them. He was mocking her "C.V.," the form that everyone was required to fill out with their skills upon intake—the Prince had insisted on calling the form that, no surprise. Isabella had noted that she had gone to college (some online thing). Fat lot of good that did her. She was terrible at following directions.

"You tried to send a message."

He swung his monitor around to face her. Filling the screen was an enlarged meme featuring GIGI-H, a vocaloid-impersonator growing in popularity. The human singer, wearing a robotic expression with a hint of disdain, was endorsing a primary challenger in a congressional race in Georgia, who was rumored to be more sympathetic than the incumbent to solar cell manufacturers who wanted less regulation. (Truth be told, it was doubtful GIGI-H could even pick out Georgia on a map, but nobody believed that celebrities had any genuine political views anyway. They were just symbols in the perpetual meme wars that all campaigns had become.)

Victor tapped a few keys. The picture on the screen changed, with all the pixels flipped to their complementary hues—or *almost* all the pixels. A line of white text appeared right across the image: "HELP US. WE ARE IMPRISONED AND FORCED TO WORK." There was an embedded image right below the text, a blurry photograph taken from inside a moving vehicle, showing a tan landscape populated by sagebrush and rocks.

Isabella glanced at the meme with no expression. "I don't know anything about that."

Victor nodded at one of the men. He slapped her across the face twice in quick succession. She yelped from the shock and pain, cowered, and covered her face with her hands, shaking all over.

"I'm not angry that you think you're so clever," Victor said. "After all, you *are* clever. You know English well, and you have technical skills. That is why you've been assigned to do something interesting, as opposed to tapping the screen all day like a monkey, like those uneducated boys and girls in the cage." He stabbed a finger at her across the table. "Though you don't seem to appreciate your good luck."

The woman shrank away, whimpering.

"I'm angry because you think *I'm* dumb. I'm angry because you're not clever enough to actually understand the position you're in. Give me the camera."

The woman didn't move. One of the men grabbed one of her arms and began to pull her out of the chair. She resisted, trying to stay in the chair, shouting, "Please! Please!"

"Give me the camera," he repeated.

With a trembling hand, she reached inside her pants, inside her underwear, and retrieved a small object and placed it on the table. It resembled a tube of lipstick.

Victor picked it up and examined it closely. Then he placed it on the ground and stomped on it until all the electronics and plastic had been pulverized.

"There is nothing you can do that we haven't seen," said Victor. "We've been doing this a long time, all over the world. Cameras are watching you every single second, when you sleep, when you eat, when you shit. Our neuromesh has been trained on all that footage, so it knows every trick those in your position have ever tried. Do you think you are cleverer than my robot?"

The woman shook her head vigorously, trying to appease Victor.

"Also, do you think the AI tools we give you won't snitch on you when you try something like this? That's the difference between a robot and you: a robot is smart enough to know never to betray its master. You'll never get away from here. Do you understand?"

The woman continued to whimper, nodding all the while.

"Normally, I'd lie to you and tell you that you'll be punished by having the cost of your attempt to get help added to your indenture debt—the salary of these two gentlemen during the two hours when they had to interrupt their day to deal with you, the cost of running the computers to detect your clumsy attempt, the value of the lost hours of productivity from you, and so on.

"But I think we're past that point now. So here's the truth: there is no debt; you'll be here until the day you die. But the days until you die can be almost pleasant if you're good and very, very painful if you're bad. Do you understand?"

The woman continued to whimper.

Victor gestured at the man who had slapped her. He pulled Isabella's hands away from her face and slapped her again. She yelped once more.

"Do you understand?"

"Yes. Yes!"

"Very good," Victor said. "These two gentlemen are going to take you away now, and they're going to work with you a little more. You must learn the lesson."

She screamed and begged for mercy as she was dragged away.

Reluctantly, Victor went back to his game show.

FORTY-TWO

The morning was cool and pleasant.

Julia turned down Vecsey Street and saw that the delivery truck was at the supermarket loading dock, as had been the case two mornings earlier. Two men were carrying crates into the truck: canned food, rice, pasta, fresh produce.

Concealing herself behind a maple, she tapped her sensepin and whispered, “Now.”

About fifty feet down the street, a large branch near the top of another maple broke and crashed to the sidewalk, barely missing a woman, who exclaimed in shock.

People poured out of offices and stores along the street to see what had happened. The two men loading the truck jogged over as well.

Julia ran over to the loading dock as soon as it was clear. She found a wooden crate filled with a bag of rice and sacks of potatoes. Lifting out two of the bags and carrying them over to be hidden behind some shelves, she made room in the crate for herself.

As she crouched down in the space, spider-form Puck, having made its way down from the maple tree unobserved, jumped into the crate with her. She dragged the cover back over the crate.

The two men eventually returned and finished loading the truck. Julia could feel her crate being carried into the truck, and something else was placed on top. She tried to lift the cover; it wouldn't budge.

No way to back out now. Inside the stifling crate, she breathed slowly to calm her wildly pounding heart.

She tried to guess where she was based on the jostling she experienced in the dark.

After what seemed like hours, a series of hard bumps told her that she was along the service road to the compound. The going was so rough that she found it hard to breathe. The truck slowed down, stopped, backed up, and stopped again. During the unloading that followed, her crate was tilted so precipitously on the hand truck that she had to stifle a cry of terror.

Silence.

She waited another ten minutes before lifting the crate cover and stepping out.

She found herself inside a large pantry. The shelves were packed with food. She was lucky that her crate had been pushed into a corner instead of wedged onto a shelf. She wouldn't have been able to get out then at all.

She took out Talos and tried to get a cellular connection. Nothing. That wasn't surprising; she expected a facility like this to be shielded to prevent unauthorized connections to the outside world. She turned off the cellular antenna, just in case they were monitoring.

She went to the door and pressed her ear against it: silence.

Cautiously, she nudged the door open a crack.

She could see stoves, ovens, long counters. No one was in the industrial kitchen, sized for a restaurant or cafeteria. She was just about to push the door open wider when she noticed the camera in a ceiling corner.

Of course the place would be filled with cameras. She was lucky that she was in one of the few places deemed so unimportant that it was a blind spot.

She retreated back inside the pantry. It would soon be time for lunch, so she had to work quickly.

To start, she moved the bags of rice and potatoes around the crate so that it wasn't so apparent that a human had been hidden among them. Next, she consolidated some of the half-empty crates in the pantry until she had two empty ones. She stacked them on top of each other inside the area designated for them so that the delivery people could take them away on the next run.

She climbed the stacked crates to reach the ventilation grille above her. Unscrewing the cover with her multitool, she popped Puck, still in spider form, inside the duct and then replaced the cover.

After jumping off, she unstacked the crates and climbed into one, then pulled the cover back in place after herself.

Panting from the exertion, she felt a little lightheaded as her knees were pushed against her face in the tight space. She closed her eyes and forced her breathing to slow down. When she finally felt ready, she put on her fusion vision glasses and wavium rings and let the reality around her fade away.

During the time Julia was with Cartographers Obscura, she had been one of the best telepresence infiltrators. On corporate espionage missions, her skill with a remote drone had often been the difference between success and failure, and Serena had praised her lavishly.

She felt like she was on one of her old jobs now. With her awareness embodied in the tiny robot, she climbed through the ductwork, roamed from room to room, and stopped from time to time to extend a camera at the end of a telescopic arm down through a ventilation grille and spin it around to take in a 360-degree view. It was both exhilarating and terrifying, a vertiginous experience. This was why urban spelunking with telepresence drones was such a popular hobby:

despite the stiff fines and stern government warnings, people loved to crawl through a city's maze of utility tunnels while embodied in a drone, seeing the cables and ducts and pipes up close, navigating the hidden networks—behind walls, belowground, above ceilings—that made the façade of civilization possible.

The kitchen soon buzzed with the activity of lunch prep, and people entered and left the pantry. Inside the crate, Julia was vaguely aware of the hubbub, but her mind was elsewhere, wholly absorbed with discovering the truth beneath the shell of this data center.

To be sure, as Julia crawled around the ducts, she saw plenty of the usual things you'd expect to see in any data center of this size: racks of servers with matrix computing units wrapped in liquid-cooling tubes while powerful heat-exchange fans in the aisles roared like jet engines; redundant clusters of backup generators and uninterruptible power supplies hooked up to compressed-air batteries; miles upon miles of cabling, neatly tied up in bundles and routed around the rooms like the nerves of some giant alien creature of silicon; fire-suppression systems and maintenance rooms; offices filled with technicians staring intently at screens; top-of-the-line security with physical separation, smart partitioning, biometric authentication at all entrances and exits, and constant, ubiquitous video surveillance.

Yet, it was also clear that the design of this data center made no sense.

Most data centers reserved the strictest security policies for the server rooms, as these were where the most important things happened: crypto coins were mined, AI computations conducted, valuable code and information stored. In this data center, however, the highest concentration of security guards didn't patrol the hallway leading to the server rooms, most camera feeds didn't come out of that part of the building, and the largest number of locked doors didn't block the route leading from the server rooms to the front door.

Instead, the strictest security in the building was reserved for a nondescript room tucked away at the very back of the building, behind the server rooms and next to the backup generators. Moreover, the room wasn't even connected to the HVAC system covering the rest of the building, and so Julia couldn't crawl in to take a peek.

By sticking her camera down through the grille in the corridor leading to the room, Julia could read the sign on the door: HAZARDOUS WASTE STORAGE.

Julia didn't believe the sign for a second.

Cooking aromas filled Julia's nose. Her stomach growled.

She pulled off the fusion vision glasses and took a deep whiff. Sloppy joe. Grilled vegetables. She hadn't had anything like that since middle school.

Putting her glasses back on again, she crawled through the ductwork back to the kitchen. Perching Puck over a ventilation grille, she peered down through the steam and smoke.

The industrial kitchen was bustling. One cook was spooning the ground beef mixture out of a tilt skillet into an aluminum buffet pan; nearby, Julia could see a cart with five pans already filled. A second cook was loading a different cart with bags of hamburger buns and two buffet pans of grilled vegetables.

Julia had been counting the employees she saw as she crawled through the data center; there were at most twenty. This was much too much food for twenty people.

The lunch menu basically presented her with two ways through the door marked HAZARDOUS WASTE STORAGE: in the ground beef mixture or in the grilled vegetables.

Although Puck was rated to operate in the rain and could be submerged for short periods, it wasn't a proper submersible. The vegetables, therefore, seemed the far safer option.

The cooks were almost done filling the carts; she needed to create a distraction for Puck. She climbed out of the crate and looked around the pantry desperately. Think. Think!

Her eyes caught on a shelf on the opposite wall, heavily laden with cans of tomato sauce as well as a few baskets of fresh tomatoes and avocados. She went up to it, took out her multitool, and got to work.

The setup wasn't perfect, but it would have to do.

A basket of tomatoes in hand, she climbed back into her crate and put on her fusion vision glasses, reducing the opacity of the camera view so she could still see the pantry around her. Through Puck's eyes, she could see that the cooks were already lining up their carts.

She threw a tomato like a softball at the precariously balanced shelf. She had loosened the screws on the brackets securing the shelf to the wall until it was barely held in place. The tomato thunked into the shelf, wobbling it, and two cans of sauce tumbled to the ground and rolled along the floor. But the shelf somehow held.

Startled by the noise, the two cooks in the kitchen stopped.

This was a disaster. If they came in now, they would be able to tell that someone was hiding inside the pantry. She had given herself away for nothing.

She grabbed another tomato and lobbed it hard at the shelf. This time, it missed entirely and smacked into the wall, leaving behind a red, drippy mess.

Over her real view of the pantry wall, the fusion vision glasses showed one of the cooks walking over to the pantry to investigate.

She muttered a quick prayer. As her heart thundered, she pitched one more tomato at the shelf, putting all her strength into the toss. *Thunk.* With a groan, the shelf gave way and collapsed. Dozens of cans crashed to the ground, making a terrific din, with avocados rolling everywhere and tomatoes squished into paste under the metal avalanche.

There was just enough time for Julia to duck back inside the crate and pull the cover back in place.

Turning up the opacity of Puck's camera view in her fusion vision glasses, she watched as both cooks ran into the pantry and stared, dumbfounded by the mess. One of them stepped through the shambles and peered at the gaping hole in the wall where the shelf bracket had been torn out.

"I told you this shelf was overloaded."

"I wasn't the one who did that."

"I saw you stacking the cans on there the other day."

"That shelf didn't fall because of a few extra cans!"

. . .

Working as fast as she could, Julia extended one of Puck's manipulators through the ventilation grille in the kitchen and unscrewed the cover.

The cooks continued to bicker. The pair passed through the stages of denial and anger and slowly resigned themselves to the need for a major cleanup.

"You want to do it now or later?"

"Has to be later. We're already late. You know how Victor gets when anything disrupts the routine."

"He throws a fit when we don't clean up a mess right away, too."

"There's no cameras here. How's he gonna know there's a mess?"

. . .

Julia worked faster. The third screw was out. Pivoting the grille on its last screw, she swung it open and dangled her arachnid-form Puck-self out on a filament attached to the inside of the duct. As soon as she was past the opening and still out of sight of the ceiling-mounted camera, she swung the grille back in place, trapping the thread against one side, and went to work putting the screws back in.

"I'm not doing all the work myself."

"Well, since you made the mess, who else should do the work?"

"I told you. I *didn't* load that shelf."

The cooks were nearly at the door of the pantry. She had run out of time.

Leaving the last two screws undone and hoping that no one would scrutinize the grille, she cut the filament with a pincer and let herself drop, flexing her legs at the last second to absorb the impact against the tiled floor. The island would block her from the view of the kitchen's surveillance camera.

Her fingers went momentarily numb from the haptic feedback of the wavium rings. She berated herself for setting the gain so high. Although that was helpful so that she could *feel* the surfaces Puck traveled over and get a good grip, it was counterproductive now.

Come on! Come on! She forced her numb fingers to move.

She managed to get the skittering legs under herself and raced across the kitchen floor, straining to gain purchase against the slippery tiles, the wavium rings letting her feel every minute vibration and wobble so that she could compensate.

The pantry door banged open. The cooks were out. The pots and pans still blocked their sight line to the carts on the island.

Forming her fingers into claws, she scraped through the wavium field, guiding the morpho drone up a leg of one of the carts. The drop from the overhead duct had disoriented her, and she hoped that she had picked the right cart.

The cooks were coming around the island.

Julia's heart was in her throat. If the cooks looked in the right direction now, they'd see a mouse-sized spider clambering over the top of the cart.

It was the wrong cart! She nearly swore aloud from the frustration. Somehow, she had picked the cart with the ground beef instead of the vegetables. She had to get to the other cart, but her fingers were cramping up from the sustained burst of precision maneuvers. She couldn't afford a single misstep, a single stumble.

The cooks had come around the last corner of the island, entirely in view of the carts. Julia was still gingerly stepping over the pans of bubbling ground beef mixture like congealing lava. She was not going to make it.

"I told you we're going to be fifteen minutes late."

"Not if you actually move, dumbass. We can keep it under ten."

Instead of looking at the cart, both cooks turned to gaze at the clock hanging on the opposite wall.

Julia flexed her fingers; the morpho drone *leaped*. Puck flew over the last pan of bubbling ground beef mixture, across the chasm between the carts, and, with a muffled *splash*, landed inside a pan of grilled vegetables.

Julia forced her trembling, numb fingers to move. The morpho drone's legs scraped and flexed as it flung cauliflower florets and carrots and onions and bell peppers out of the way and buried itself—

The cooks looked back at the carts.

"Let's go."

The carts clattered down the hallways, beyond secure-access doors, past armed guards, until they rolled through the doors marked HAZARDOUS WASTE STORAGE.

FORTY-THREE

Julia concentrated.

Buried deep in the grilled vegetables, the morpho drone's camera showed nothing but darkness. Likewise, the microphones, muffled by oil, picked up little that was useful. She focused on the rattling of the cart through the haptic feedback in her fingers.

The cart came to a stop. Then, a new pattern of tingling in her fingers—the drone's accelerometer—told her that she was descending on an elevator. The cart rattled and began to move again.

It stopped once more. Her pan was picked up, carried, and then set down. Puck's temperature sensors informed her that the grilled vegetables were being heated—a chafing pan, she surmised. Faint tremors indicated more pans being set down near her. And then, silence and stillness.

She had to take a risk. Flexing her fingers, she crawled out of the vegetables. She snapped her fingers a few times to pulse her camera lens and microphones at ultrasonic frequencies to clear off the oil and water. Then she crept up to the rim of the pan and extended the telescopic camera arm to peer about cautiously.

Through the blurry lens, she could see that she was inside a small cafeteria, white-tiled and white-walled, like a canteen you'd find in a hospital or an old-fashioned corporate office. Long tables with chairs on both sides. Capable of seating about forty. A long steel table rested against one wall, and it was on this table that the pans of food had been set down in chafing racks, buffet-style.

Any second now, the people this food was meant for would be streaming in. She crawled all the way out of the pan, shook off bits of food stuck to her, and skittered up the wall with her eight van der Waals padded legs. Digging into the soft ceiling with her sharp pincers, she brachiated over to a ventilation grille. Only after she had unscrewed the cover, crawled in, and carefully replaced the screws did she finally let out a sigh of relief.

The HVAC system on this side of the HAZARDOUS WASTE STORAGE door was completely separate from the one servicing the rest of the data center. This was a world within a world.

In a corner of the ceiling, a camera stared unblinkingly at the scene. Julia hadn't seen it.

The squat, blocky edifice of the data center was like the tip of an iceberg. It sat atop a vast, natural complex of ancient lava tubes and chambers. Out of the view of code inspectors, satellites, or any authority, the chambers and tubes had been secretly modified into a warren of rooms. The HAZARDOUS WASTE STORAGE door was the sole link between this vast underground maze and the building above.

Julia, embodied as a mechanical spider, skittered through the ducts and peered down at the people and machines occupying this mysterious world, and her confusion only grew.

The HVAC system of the underground portion had its separate air intake. It was heavily monitored and filtered so that not even a fly could have gotten in. For all intents and purposes, the underground portion of the complex was like a sealed bunker.

Some of the rooms in this bunker were partitioned into tiny cubicles, all with uniform green walls. In each cubicle, a person performed before a camera, posing, singing, talking, dancing, gesticulating. Julia noticed scars and bruises on more than a few of the performers.

Other rooms were divided into larger spaces with groups performing in each, though Julia could make little sense of what was going on through the cacophony of overlapping dialog and music.

Still other rooms were filled with people typing, drawing, animating, designing, modeling on computers.

One room was filled with powerful workstations, where the operators seemed to be doing postproduction work on digital content. Julia, by no means an expert, could see faces being erased and replaced, soundtracks being generated and spliced in, backgrounds being filled and interpolated, footage edited, cut, duplicated, retrofaked, repurposed, pseudo-authenticated.

Yet another room shocked her with the primitivity of its rigs. Each operator—there were at least fifty—sat in front of banks upon banks of phones, numbering in the hundreds, each showing some kind of feed. Their eyes roamed anxiously over the screens while their lanky arms shot out like the tentacles of an octopus, sending their twitching fingers on a nonstop sequence of tapping, pressing, swiping, pinching, scrolling, dragging, flicking. By zooming in on some of the screens, Julia figured out that they were liking, upvoting, clapping, bumping, commenting, tsking, thumbing, downing, drowning, watering—all the myriad ways of indicating to some algorithm that a human had consumed content and engaged with it. With the unceasing stream of screen taps, the room sounded like the inside of a termite mound.

The overall effect was a strange hybrid of media start-up and content incubator. Julia's head was exploding with questions. Who were these people? And why were they working in a facility deep underground?

And then she saw the densely packed dorms, the communal showers and toilets, the medical bay, and finally, a large room whose purpose she couldn't fathom.

It was a bare space devoid of furniture. The walls were lined with hooks, from which dangled various tools: mallets, blades, clamps, and other instruments that seemed vaguely medical. There was a large hose coiled in a corner, and drains in the center of the floor, surrounded by thick metal loops sunk into the concrete.

FORTY-FOUR

It was another muggy day in Rome. Tourists swarmed the Forum in their sweaty T-shirts and unwashed shorts, clutching their purses and bum bags warily, looking about for pickpockets as well as opportunities to take the same photos that better photographers had taken a million times.

They have no idea what they're looking at, thought the Prince, wrinkling his nose as he passed by a boisterous group of Asiatics, their gaping faces especially irksome to him this morning. Even the fragrance of myrtles couldn't quite refresh him.

Thank goodness the authorities had at least outlawed the use of drones over the Forum—unless you paid an exorbitant sum to the right people; this was, after all, Italy. Machines buzzing in the sky taking immersion videos would have made this place genuinely intolerable.

Here were the ruins that had stood against the tides of time for millennia, the very paving stones on which Cicero and Caesar and Gaius Gracchus and Gaius Octavius Thurinus had once walked and debated and roused crowds, advancing the course of human civilization. They built in stone because they understood that in the end, after all the stories had faded and all the faces been forgotten, stone, which required no maintenance and which didn't decay, would remain, bearing mute witness to their greatness.

And these tourists! Instead of letting all that history wash over them so that they could be born anew, all they could think of was to take a picture of themselves grinning like idiots in front of the Temple of Vesta. Such paucity of imagination! Such waste!

He turned away in disgust. He had wanted to spend a morning in the Eternal City, contemplating the grand sweep of history and the ephemerality of all gestures toward the infinite. But the mood was spoiled now. He needed something to restore his spirits. Ah, yes, he remembered. There was an exclusive café about ten minutes' walk from here, a little secret tucked away on the rooftop of a middling restaurant, with a great view of the Palatine Hill and the graceful swaying umbrella pines, like Catullus's puellae candidae. You couldn't even get in without knowing the right people and having paid the dues. There he would be safe from these hoi polloi, the new barbarians.

To entertain himself on his walk, the Prince decided to review his accounts on his fusion vision glasses. Negotia pedestria pedes agenda sunt. He chuckled at his own wit. Pedestrian business was best done as a pedestrian. The spreadsheets that scrolled across his visual field were old-fashioned ledgers that summarized the ebb and flow of his business empire, not some AI-enhanced "Easy-Viz" abomination. The vigorous vision the plain numbers evoked in his head was better than any machine-crafted pap graphics intended for weak minds.

He was making money, so much money. Information might have given him power, but he had built his wealth the old-fashioned way: through farming.

There was money from elections. Political campaigns were willing to pay anything to change voters' minds, and he had the data to show that his service worked. He didn't discriminate as to point of view: he helped Democrats as well as Republicans, Tories as well as Labour, globalists as well as nativists, socialists as well as fascists. As long as a candidate had the coin, he would help them create the appearance of shifts in popular sentiment that the newsjinns summarized as stories for the pundits and human journalists, which then, thus cloaked in "expert" credibility, changed the actual sentiments of voters. (He did, however, make it a point never to participate in the same election on both sides—it was just bad business to work against yourself.)

There was money from the stock market. The profit here was more direct: he would spread bad news to depress a stock so that he could hoover shares up; then he would turn around and pump it up, only to dump his shares right as the price reached a new crest. It was about simulating the appearance of insider knowledge, faking the signals of insider trading, pretending to be greedy to lure in the greater fool. When the gluttonous pigs of Wall Street were properly fattened, he would come in for the glorious butchering. He loved, absolutely loved the game.

There was money from investment. For every problem facing humanity, there were hundreds of companies around the world competing to solve it in the hopes of catching that legendary pot of gold. The winner stood to make fortunes, while the losers ended up with nothing. But who would turn out to be the winner? It wasn't the superior technology that always won. Fashion, politics, public perception were just as important. If the Prince could nudge things to favor companies he invested in, even if only a little, so that he won more often than he lost, his take would be measured in the billions.

Compared to all of these, his patronage of the arts was not even a rounding error. Yet, it was his participation in the arts that made his soul sing.

He arrived at the secret little café and presented his membership card. He was greeted with deference and brought to a choice table right at the edge of the terrace, where he could see the Colosseum in all its glory. He put in his order for a caffè freddo and put away his fusion vision glasses.

As a patron of the arts, he changed the world.

The arts, more than any other field of human endeavor, were ruled by randomness. There was no meritocracy. How many Emily Dickinsons lay in obscurity, forever undiscovered? How many van Goghs would never sell any paintings, all their works washed away by the inexorable pounding of the passing years? For every pop idol, how many other singers, just as talented and just as hardworking, lived out their lives delivering fried chicken? Random chance was all that separated stardom and oblivion.

He stepped in and altered the odds.

He was a connoisseur, a man of taste. He picked very, very few artists to support: a couple of actors, four filmmakers, three singers, three architects. No writers (he had no patience with writers—it took too damned long to read a novel). And only one oneirofex. One.

It was no mere chance that all the artists he had ever patronized became great stars—you could dig a diamond out of the earth and shine a light on it, but no matter how much you polished a turd, it remained a piece of shit.

He gave his artists the dreams they craved.

Yet, instead of being celebrated like Lorenzo de' Medici, he had to live in the shadows like a latrine rat. Instead of being showered with gratitude and praise, he was hated by his artists. It was true: there was no surer way to earn the undying hatred of an artist than by becoming the reason for their success.

Seething, he sipped his caffè freddo in the shade of the airy parasol. The sweet beverage refreshed and calmed.

Yes, he was self-aware enough to admit that there were . . . reasons for his protégés to resent him.

His farms relied on slavery.

Oh, don't look so shocked.

He sneered at his imaginary critics. Did you know that the proportion of the population who were enslaved was the same in the Roman Republic and the antebellum American South? There was good reason for the United States' founding fathers to cosplay as Romans, with their Latin pseudonyms in *The Federalist Papers* and Roman-style eagle on the Great Seal and eventually a capital full of faux-Roman temples.

Every civilization worthy of the name in the history of this planet had relied on slavery: the Egyptians, the Babylonians, the Greeks, the Chinese, the Romans, the Arabs, the Maya, the Mongols, the Mughals, the Spanish, the British, the French, the Americans, the Germans, the Japanese, the Soviet Union. . . .

He was simply carrying on an ancient tradition: the sine qua non of great art, enlightened philosophy, and lasting accomplishments.

In an age when most of the web was spewed out by robots, he put back the human element. When every filter and algorithm was designed to sniff out the artificial, the generated, the electric sheep, he reinserted authenticity. The reason that his business could pump out memes and posts and videos and reviews and opinions and essays and claps and slaps and bumps and grinds—in a word, *content* of every stripe, content that pushed the view his clients wanted to push, that was never flagged as bot spam, that got past all the bladerunner algorithms seeking to cut down cheap machine-generated kipple was simple: he used real people.

When everyone was succumbing to the easy promise of AI, using humans on your content farms was a bold innovation. Compared to a bot farm, he might generate only one-millionth the amount of content, but his artisanal product was a hundred million times more influential.

Oh, he used AI to enhance things—put on a prettier face, erase some scars, add in a few background props, punch up the catchiness of the theme of a flipclip—but fundamentally, all his content was made by humans. And bladerunners, trained to filter out pure AI-generated garbage, let his content through unmolested.

He took in migrants, runaways, the chronically underemployed, the mentally ill, those struggling on the fringe of society, the forgotten, people who had no prospects, no safety net, no dreams—and gave them purpose, offered them security. In exchange, they just had to use their brains and fingers and voices to make content he wanted them to make, to inject that little bit of human randomness, that spark of creativity, that other humans prized so much, that they trained their AIs to look for.

In a way, he was the real AI innovator, the Henry Ford of this new age. He harnessed human intelligence and wielded it as just another component in the machine of modern commerce. Yes, crafting human intelligence into artifice, making humans behave like machines—wasn't that the real definition of "artificial intelligence"?

The Prince asked for another caffè freddo. The afternoon sun was making him drowsy. Oh, what wouldn't he give now for another dream with Elli, the only artist to whom he had bared his soul. That fucking cu—

He forced himself to calm down again. No. No. He had to stop thinking about her. Better to think about his newest farm, the one that he had built in America.

Suspicious of foreign influence, nations were sealing off their digital borders as well as real ones, filtering out VPNs and tunneled connections that had too much lag. It made his job harder, as these measures stopped his Asian content farms from being able to influence events elsewhere. Reluctantly, he built some farms in Europe and Japan so that the electronic output of his slaves could pass as the product of locals. The rules facilitating corruption in these places were different from the ones he was used to operating under back home, and he had to expand his empire of blackmail and information brokering to account for them. This meant more exposure, more risk.

Expanding into America was even more risky, given the country's volatile politics and overlapping jurisdictions. The flavor of corruption here was different yet again, requiring the construction of elaborate legal fictions. Indeed, most of his lily-livered lieutenants were against it, thinking the move too risky. However, as America tightened its digital borders in sync with its physical ones with each successive administration, he had no choice but to farm in America if he didn't want to give up this extremely lucrative market. And so, he had constructed an American farm and dispatched his best man, Victor, to run it.

Sometimes, a wave of self-pity washed over the Prince. He was a good and fair master, but so few appreciated him. He enslaved people without regard to race, ethnicity, national origin, sex, religion, age . . . and so forth. He cared for his slaves and made sure that they were given nutritious meals, that they had opportunities for exercise and even play, so long as they obeyed and did what he wanted.

Now, what was so bad about that? Viewed in the right light, he was the solution to many of the world's most intractable problems. Robots were taking jobs from people, depriving them of purpose, bleaching meaning from their lives. Into this wasteland of faith he stepped. He found the excess labor pool a new role to play in the advancement of global civilization, just like those slaves who labored on the great estates of the patricians of the Roman Republic. Gratia artis, SPQR!

He looked out at the Colosseum, imagining the grand spectacles that had once been put on there before the ruins were ruins.

FORTY-FIVE

Through the grille, Julia looked at the scene unfolding in the strange room below her.

About thirty people had been brought into the room and made to sit on the floor, their backs against the walls. They looked tired and dazed, as though they had just been on a long journey. Some of them glanced at the instruments hanging around the room, unease and puzzlement all over their faces. The guards who brought them in spread around the room. Julia could see they were armed.

One guard began to speak (Julia's eyes widened when she recognized Victor). He said everything twice: once in English, and again in Spanish.

Welcome to the job you've been promised. Here, you're safe from immigration officials, patrolling militias, DHS, and whichever gangs, rebels, or governments you were escaping from. Your benefactor has taken great risks to bring you into this country, to give you a new life. You're indebted to him.

The migrants nodded. This was what they had always understood to be the deal.

The journey to America was expensive, Victor went on, and you have to work to pay off that debt to your sponsor. It will be hard work, and it will take a few years, but countless people have done it before you.

The work is so hard—there was a subtle shift in Victor's tone—that some of you may want to quit, or maybe run away so that you don't have to pay back the debt. Now, that wouldn't be fair, would it?

The migrants began to sense that something wasn't quite right. But they nodded. Yes, that wouldn't be fair.

You have our papers, a woman said.

That is true, said Victor. But is that enough?

The migrants looked at him, uncomprehending.

There is a lesson that you must learn, Victor said.

Two of the guards picked a man out of the group—he looked like the strongest and the least cowed among the group—and brought him to the middle of the floor. They asked him to take off his clothes. When he hesitated, one of the guards held him while the other one cut the clothes off him. The man resisted and shouted in protest, but the guards overcame him easily. When he was naked, they shackled him to the steel loops in the floor.

Then they began.

Julia couldn't breathe.

They wielded their gleaming instruments on that man, item after item, carefully sterilizing each mallet and blade before and after, as his screams grew louder and more desperate before fading, finally settling into barely a groan and then nothing, his struggles ceasing, his body a lifeless thing, mere flesh.

Not being physically in that room, she had been spared the stench of blood and piss and voided bowels, the odors of terror and murder. But she had nonetheless gagged, her body convulsing as her mind recoiled at the torture being inflicted on that man.

They had made the others watch. Anyone who turned their faces away was asked to turn back and look, the first time nicely, and then accompanied by a slap to the face or a blow from a cane.

She refused to look away. The footage from Puck's camera wouldn't be sufficient as evidence on its own since it wasn't properly certified. As Piers had told her, she would have to authenticate the footage as a witness. The very thought of appearing in public, in a courtroom again, terrified her. But she would not look away. To her, the duty to bear witness was a deeply felt conviction that did not need justification.

Once she had secured enough evidence of the horrors of this place, she would go to the authorities, her fears be damned.

They placed the body inside a bag, zipped it closed, and loaded it onto a cart. The same kind of cart, Julia realized, that had been used to bring food to the canteen.

Then, one of the men brought the hose in the corner over and turned on the water, washing away the blood and other stains on the floor methodically.

The remaining migrants shrank away and pressed themselves against the walls. No one made a sound.

I hope this lesson doesn't need to be taught again, said Victor, once in English, and again in Spanish. He sounded bored, like a tour guide who had said the same thing too many times.

Once the cleaning was done, the guards corralled the migrants into a line. They were very docile after the demonstration.

Now, remember, this is a good job, Victor added, his tone suddenly swerving into warm solicitousness. Every hour you work is credited against your debt, and when you've paid everything back, you'll be free to leave and enjoy your new life in the land of the free. In fact, I think many of you will find the skills you've acquired here to be invaluable in the future. We'll also be counting on you to hold each other accountable. If you suspect anyone is trying to shirk their debt, report them to us, and you'll receive a bonus credit against your debt. See something, say something.

Julia had seen enough. She stopped recording.

Victor watched as the fresh assets were marched out of the door, looking even more dazed than when they had come in. They'd be escorted to lunch after all the established assets had already eaten. The schedule was perfect, really. The new assets would digest the fresh food and the fresh lesson at the same time before their first shift to "work off their debts" this afternoon.

In fact, he felt a bit hungry after all that work. His stomach growled even at the thought of sloppy joe, which was on the menu for today. Still one more shipment to process later this afternoon, he remembered, as he walked through the warren of tunnels to return to the aboveground portion of the complex.

All that talk about debt and credit and bonuses was quite genius. At first, Victor had considered all the theater absurd. What was the point of creating and maintaining fake spreadsheets tracking made-up balances, charging the assets for their room and board and interest, and then deducting their expenses from their fictitious wages, when the reality was that the assets were property and would never be freed?

Yet the Prince had insisted on the charade. And with time, Victor had come to see his wisdom. Dangling the promise of freedom before the slaves—if only they worked harder, obeyed with more alacrity, were more vigilant against talk of rebellion among their fellow slaves, maybe they could get out faster!—did wonders for morale and kept them docile and motivated. After all, they were expected to use their brains for the benefit of the Prince, and assets who had no hope were liable to shut down their brains entirely.

A discreet beep sounded in his headset: an alert from the security AI.

He wasn't concerned. The complex's security AI was an extension of his personal AI, and he had tuned it to be paranoid. It sent him low-priority alerts practically every hour. Nine-hundred-ninety-nine times out of a thousand, it was nothing.

So he didn't rush as he rode up the elevator, exited the HAZARDOUS WASTE STORAGE door, picked up his tray of food from the kitchen, and wound his way leisurely through the data center to his office, where he set his lunch down and tapped the keyboard to wake up the computer.

The alert was actually for more than one item. The first was triggered by the air-quality monitors. Sensors had detected a slightly elevated level of carbon dioxide inside the climate-controlled, atmospherically isolated, aboveground facility.

What does that mean? he typed into the interface. He didn't like talking to AI—he could read much faster than he could process voice.

High probability: Increased activity by staff (perhaps a cover-up attempt as a result of someone committing an error).

Medium probability: Decline in the effectiveness of the air scrubbers (filters may need to be replaced).

Low probability: Unauthorized personnel inside the complex (undetected intruder).

. . .

Victor glanced through the list of speculations without comment. They all seemed either nothing to worry about or far-fetched.

He dismissed the item and went on to the next.

This one was more interesting. The AI had pulled out a short clip from one of the security cameras inside the underground part of the complex, the content farm. It showed the canteen area from approximately an hour earlier when it was being readied for lunch. Something—possibly a rodent, the low quality of the video prevented precise identification—climbed out of the grilled vegetables and skittered away.

Victor wrinkled his nose in disgust. Those cooks! He had emphasized to them again and again the importance of hygiene, of keeping their work area spotless to prevent vermin infestation. The data center was filled with expensive equipment. A single rat chewing on cables could result in hundreds of thousands of dollars of damage. And now he had proof that a mouse had literally been in the food!

He pushed his lunch tray away, having lost all appetite.

He tapped away on the keyboard. First things first, he sent out three maintenance bots. These autonomous robotic workers were far more sophisticated than the cheap everyfixits they sold to consumers, capable of just about any janitorial task in a commercial facility.

One bot would scour the ground, looking for evidence of rodent activity: tunnels, droppings, signs of chewing. The other two would go through the HVAC system—one in the aboveground portion of the facility and the other in the underground portion. He shuddered at the thought of mouse and rat droppings in the ducts that brought him sweet, freshly scrubbed air.

Julia had only one goal in mind: get Puck back to the aboveground portion of the complex so that she could then escape with it. The high-quality footage on board, much better than the compressed stream to Julia's fusion vision glasses, should bring down this place as well as the Prince himself.

This, she was sure, was what Elli had meant by *Just go*.

Julia perched Puck in the duct above the canteen. The way in was likely also the most straightforward way back out. She looked down through the grille. With the last lunch wave complete, the canteen was empty save for the carts that had transported the buffet pans. Next door, in the scullery, some of the workers were washing the dirty dishes and pans.

Visions of Puck turning one of the pans upside down and then hiding inside it, like toys trying to cross the road in a traffic cone, flitted through her mind. Despite the tension in the moment, she smiled. No, that wouldn't work, but maybe something a little less cartoonish *could*. After all, like any prison, if they brought food down, they had to take the empty dishes back up. She just had to be patient and look for an opportunity.

She was so focused on what was happening below that she didn't hear the scuttling in the duct behind her.

Victor stared at the screen, dumbfounded.

The maintenance drone dispatched to scour the ducts in the underground content farm had summoned him from the toilet with a screeching top-priority alarm. He had been cursing at the AI nonstop until this moment, when he finally saw what it was crying about.

There was a rodent in the ducts, all right—well, more like a mouse-sized spider, a spy drone. He could see it hiding smugly right above the canteen, its single camera lens peering down through the grille, recording everything.

According to the security AI, the maintenance drone had detected a skittering noise in the ducts approximately twenty minutes ago. Thinking that it was just a mouse, the security AI did not intervene but allowed the maintenance drone to investigate the noise on its own. However, as soon as the maintenance drone sighted the spy, the security AI knew that Victor had to see it for himself. For the last ten minutes, it had kept the spy under surveillance while remaining out of sight.

Victor's mind raced as his heart pounded in his ears. What a massive security failure! How in the world had he messed up so badly?

Speculations and assessments from the security AI scrolled up the side of the screen. Reading through them, Victor could feel his heart rate and breathing return to normal. This was why he loved machines. Their unflappability was an excellent antidote to panic.

He nodded to himself. The AI was right. The facility's electromagnetic isolation remained intact. Therefore, the drone couldn't possibly have sent any data off-site. If he captured it right now, he would have everything it had.

But wait. The AI highlighted another interesting fact.

The spy drone was so small that it likely couldn't be entirely autonomous. It was likely being controlled by a remote operator. And again, given the electromagnetic shielding around the data center, the operator had to be inside. He was dealing with either a mole among the staff or an intruder.

The little electronic spy was completely absorbed by what it could see of the canteen through the ventilation grille, no doubt looking for a way out.

The thrill of the hunt seized Victor. Grinning wolfishly, he picked up his communicator.

In the scullery, the workers were done with the dishes and the silverware and had put them away. For their final task, they washed the serving pans and stacked them on the carts in the canteen. Guards then took the workers away.

The cooks returned to the canteen.

Julia tensed. This was her best chance to get Puck back upstairs. Could she distract the cooks and hide under the cart—

"Hey, you want to do the showers?" one of the cooks asked the other.

"No," replied his companion. "I did them last week."

"You did *not*. Greggers did them last week."

"Well, I had to help him since he was so slow."

"The real problem here is that Victor needs to hire more people. Why should we cook and clean *and* do the laundry?"

"You got that right. But that still doesn't make it my turn to do the staff showers. Those guys are pigs."

"Fine. I'll do the showers. You can take care of the nap rooms."

"Deal. After I finish the scullery."

The other cook went into the scullery, opened one of the cabinets, and took out four laundry bags. He handed two to his companion, went up to the door at the other end of the canteen, which led deeper into the complex, and put his eye up against the retina scanner. The door beeped and unlocked. He went through.

The remaining cook went around the scullery and stuffed the towels, aprons, and washcloths into one bag. He brought the filled laundry bag back to the canteen and dropped it on the floor next to the empty carts. Then he took the remaining empty bag and also went through the retina-locked door leading deeper into the underground complex.

Julia couldn't believe her luck. The filled laundry bag had been left in the blind spot of the canteen's security camera.

Carefully, she unscrewed the grille, dangled herself out, replaced the grille, and brachiated over to the corner that was in the camera's blind spot. A straight drop landed her atop the bag with barely any noise. She scrambled inside, burying herself among the dirty towels.

She had done it!

Victor grinned as he watched the screen.

Picking up his communicator, he gave more instructions. The plan to nab the human behind the spy drone was going very well. He suspected that it was someone on his staff trying to get some footage in order to blackmail Victor or maybe even the Prince—no matter how much you paid your people, some of them always wanted more. It was just human nature.

Well, he was going to teach them that greedy pigs got butchered.

Julia waited patiently as the cart rattled through the underground hallways, rode up the elevator, and rattled some more in the data center corridors. Ten minutes after all motion and noise had ceased, she finally crept out of the bag with great care.

She was inside the laundry room—rather small considering how many people were permanently housed underground, though she suspected that hygiene wasn't exactly the topmost concern for these criminals. Once again, there was no security camera inside, probably because the room was deemed low priority. She scurried out, climbed up the wall, and got into the ventilation ducts again.

Relieved, she let out a big sigh. Now, it was just a matter of getting Puck back to her actual self in the pantry, and then she'd figure out a way out of the data center. She started Puck down the quickest path back to the pantry through the maze of ducts.

Just a few more rooms. Turn. Turn again.

Julia was only half paying attention to the sensorium of the morpho drone; her mind kept on drifting back to the nightmarish scenes she had witnessed in the content farm. She couldn't wait to get out of here.

Faster. Faster!

Another turn. Straight down the long duct now, which ran over the corridor next to the server rooms. She was almost there.

But her fingers fluttered, and Puck slowed down. Something seemed to pull at the edge of her consciousness like a shadow glimpsed out the corner of her eye, which darted away as soon as she tried to focus on it.

Something felt *off*.

She examined the duct around her. Everything seemed fine. She switched to the infrared filter. Nothing. She turned on the ultrasonic/infrasonic enhancements to the microphones. Still nothing.

But the nagging feeling that something was wrong wouldn't let her go.

Then, it struck her. A pair of guards were patrolling the corridor below her, but she couldn't *feel* them. The tingling that had always accompanied their presence in this facility, almost like an aura, was gone.

She had modded Puck to have a richer sensorium than her biological self. Not only could it see into a broader range of the electromagnetic spectrum, but it was also equipped with a whole suite of other instruments, including microphones, accelerometers, LiDAR, WACAM, chemical, magnetic, and other sensors. Not all the data could be translated into video and audio signals, and since she wasn't wearing an immersion headset, the non-audio/non-visual data was typically converted into haptic feedback of some kind, with Talos doing dynamic filtering to bring forward the most salient sensory detail each moment.

One of Puck's sensors was designed to pick up radio signals, such as the kind used in wireless networks, critical information for a drone designed for intrusion and surveillance. The data center itself was covered by multiple wireless networks serving hundreds of wireless devices (such as the communicators carried by the staff). Whenever Puck picked up a strong wireless signal, Talos translated it into a kind of tingling so that Julia could sense one of the guards approaching even without visual contact.

But now, as Julia watched the guards pass below her through the grille, she felt no such tingling.

Someone had shut off the wireless networks inside the data center.

Why?

She could almost see the signal tethering Puck to herself glowing like an ethereal strand in the dim interior of the duct, a thread that someone could follow.

Cold sweat broke out all over her body. She suppressed the urge to cry out. Fingers still trembling, she guided Puck forward.

Victor was pleased. Shutting off the wireless network had helped immensely with the tracking. The directional antennas on the maintenance bots were homing in on the source of the control signal for the spy drone. It was either heading back to the operator or to some prearranged pickup spot. Either way, he was going to catch this mole. Oh, would he be surprised!

With great interest, Victor watched the drone through the maintenance bot's camera. The spider-mouse slowed down drastically as it tiptoed through the duct above the heavily patrolled corridor outside the server rooms, likely so as to make as little noise as possible.

Now, the drone sped up again. It took a sharp left as it approached a junction with another duct and went toward the loading docks.

Disaster struck at that moment. As the drone skidded through the turn, the operator seemed to lose control momentarily. The spider drone struck the side of the duct and actually punched through the thin metal.

Unfortunately, the drone happened to punch through the duct at a point where electrical cables ran through a suspended plastic tube parallel to the duct. The out-of-control drone, pincers scrambling as it burst through the aluminum duct walls, broke the plastic tube and severed the electrical cables.

As the drone continued to tumble to the hard floor far below, lights, fans, everything in that part of the data center shut off.

The screen before Victor went dark. He swore.

Thirty seconds passed before the backup power kicked in. Victor shouted into his communicator, trying to get people to assess and repair the damage. But as the wireless network had been turned off, no one responded. He tried the wired comms terminal and found that the system was still rebooting after the power outage.

Victor got up and exited his office, running toward the last known location of the spider drone. He was familiar with that part of the facility. All the doors around there were kept shut at all times; a spy drone that size would have only a few places to go.

As he approached the area, he saw that two guards, the same ones who had been patrolling the corridor earlier, were bumbling about aimlessly under the broken HVAC duct, still dazed by the sudden accident and the subsequent loss of power.

Impatiently, he waved for them to be still. How was he going to track down the drone with them making so much commotion? Tiptoeing along the corridor wall under the broken duct, he listened intently.

There! He heard scrabbling! He placed his ear against the wall to be sure he hadn't imagined it. Yes. Yes!

He brought up the map of the facility on his tablet and zoomed in on the section near him. Now, given the direction of the noise, where was the drone? Ah! The staff restroom near the loading docks. He almost slapped his forehead at how obvious it was. Of course, the fool would be operating the spy drone from one of the staff toilet stalls—it was the only way to avoid being caught on camera. While the assets were watched constantly, the staff at least had the dignity of not having to shit while on camera.

Nearby, a wall-mounted comms terminal flashed at him. He went up to it and saw that the security AI was trying to reach him. The AI informed him that the signal tracers had been brought online after the outage, and they confirmed his guess: the control signal for the spy drone was indeed coming from inside the staff restroom.

Victor strode into the small bathroom, stun baton in hand, and kicked open the door to the only stall. The guard on the toilet yelped and tried to cover himself. But Victor wasn't fooled by his act: he had already seen the little arachnid-shaped spy drone scurrying behind the toilet. Ignoring the occupant, Victor reached down and grabbed the drone, which immediately went limp in his hand.

The man on the toilet voided his bowels in an explosive burst.

Victor dangled the drone before the terrified guard, wrinkling his nose at the stench.

"What's this then?"

"I have no idea!"

Victor spun to the side. A pair of fusion vision glasses lay semi-concealed under the sink.

"I swear that wasn't there when I came in. The lights went out and then— AAAAGH!"

Victor had heard enough of his lies.

The sudden blackout couldn't have occurred at a worse time for the loading dock: a new shipment of migrants was being processed. The result was pandemonium. Even after the lights had come back on, minutes passed before the guards got things back under control and conducted a head count.

There were twenty-three people from several continents packed into the loading dock like a mini-UN.

"That doesn't match what I have," said the driver.

The head guard tensed. "How many are missing?"

"Not missing. Extra," said the driver. "I picked up twenty-two."

The head guard relaxed.

"You must have miscounted."

"I never miscount." The driver was adamant.

"Maybe you picked up a hitchhiker on the way?" teased the guard. "Can you point out which one?"

"I wasn't paying attention to their looks," said the driver. "I just know I picked up twenty-two."

"And I'm telling you, you miscounted."

"Did not."

"Look." The guard tried to be patient. "If you insist on a mismatch, we're going to have to get Victor down here and do a full inventory check with the origin facility. Do you really want to do that?"

The thought of dealing with the nasty, brutish, sadistic Victor for an extended period was unappealing.

The guard saw the driver's expression and pressed. "Or, you could just change the number on your form. You picked up twenty-three, I took in twenty-three. Everyone is happy." He reached into his pocket for something that he had kept there for just such emergencies and held it out to the driver.

The driver shook his hand and assessed the size of the plastic baggie he felt between their palms. Oh, what the hell. He closed his fingers around the baggie and nodded.

"I picked up twenty-three."

"Excellent."

As the truck backed away, the migrants lined up to be brought inside the facility. Before passing through the security scanner, the guard asked each to surrender whatever electronics they carried. Most had already done so to other "guides" along the transport network that brought them over the border, but a few still had their phones.

"I need to call my husband at home," a woman said, clutching her phone.

"We'll give you new phones once you've settled in," said the guard soothingly. "You understand we can't have unauthorized devices in here. Do you want DHS to find you?"

The woman still looked hesitant. "I have pictures on—"

"We'll hold on to it for you. You'll get everything back once your contract is finished." The guard was earnest and comforting. He knew that this wasn't the time for intimidation. Not yet. "Also, please give me your passcode. I have to make sure there's nothing illegal on here. You understand? Your employer is taking a big risk hiring you."

Reluctantly, the woman gave up the phone and the code.

Julia, who was next in line, looked longingly at the door to the loading dock before turning back to the guard. During that brief window of darkness, after she had disposed of the fusion vision glasses, she had deliberately slammed herself into a wall before scrambling into the loading dock. Her face was already swelling from the bruises. She hoped it was enough to defeat whatever facial recognition program they used—and she prayed that Victor wouldn't see her.

She gave Talos a hard squeeze. *Goodbye. For now.*

Since she had no documents—not uncommon among migrants—and Cole, the guard, found her Chinese name unpronounceable, he decided to record her as "Number 23."

The detector beeped as she went through.

"Your phone," said Cole, holding out a hand.

Julia placed the tensor bank in his palm. The screen showed "Welcome" in various languages and an animated finger swiping up.

"What's going on here?" Cole was confused. "You never activated your phone?"

"I got from border man," said Julia, putting on a heavy accent. "No card. No call. You have card?"

The guard waved dismissively. "Sure. You'll get all the subscriber cards you want at the end of your contract." He examined the device more closely. "What kind of phone is this anyway? Some Chinese knockoff?"

Julia put on an ingratiating smile. "Yes. Cheap. Good phone. No government watch."

Cole considered the phone. Chinese knockoffs were supposed to have none of the trackers the government forced domestic makers to install. Instead of dropping the phone into the collections tray, he slipped it into his pocket discreetly before waving her on. "I'll take real good care of it for you. Go on. We have a schedule to keep."

From the muffled shouts she heard in the distance, she surmised that Victor had caught the "mole." For the moment, at least, she was safe.

FORTY-SIX

Two weeks had passed since the beginning of Julia's captivity.

After her own horrific indoctrination session, Julia was given a series of assessments to see what kind of content work best suited her talents. Those deemed to have the most talent were put on short-form video or livestreaming, with the hope that they could develop into influence idols (they were told that they would be able to work off their contracts faster, given their higher "wages"). Julia, who showed little promise in her assessments, was put into the "tap farm," where the assets were expected to each operate hundreds of social media accounts and to boost the content created by the rest of the farm with claps, likes, upvotes, comments, and so on to increase the likelihood that the content would go viral.

Two weeks felt like an eternity.

It was the loss of the most basic things, things that she had taken for granted, that she felt the most. She could no longer go for a run whenever she wanted to, seeking the restful tiredness of physical exertion. Neither had she understood, until now, how much sunlight was a necessity. Her skin hungered for it, a hunger that could never be satisfied by the cold light of LEDs.

Idly, she wondered how long it would take before anyone in the world out there—growing more unreal with each passing day—realized that she was gone. Cailee, Nick, Sahima, Hutch—would any of them know? She had not been returning their calls, had pushed them away in her prickly solitude. Even the apartment manager wouldn't be checking on her for not paying rent—her place wasn't habitable after the fire.

Oh, she was in deep trouble, wasn't she?

On top of it all, the monotony of the work, sixteen hours a day, plus being always under surveillance and control—she was told when to wake up, when to go to her meals, when to have bathroom breaks, when to sleep—felt like an inescapable, crushing hand. The only way to cope was for her to make herself as like a machine as possible, to detach further from this current reality so that she could preserve some semblance of her soul. Resistance required you to remember who you were, and the enslavers did all they could to make you forget.

She knew she had to get out before she lost herself.

But how?

Besides the cameras, microphones, guards, Victor also encouraged the "assets" to report on each other.

One time, when Julia spent too long in the bathroom, one of the other girls reported her, and Julia was beaten. Her injuries were so extensive that she was allowed to stay out of work for half a day.

The girl who tattled on Julia was told that her debt to the Prince would be reduced by one hundred dollars as a result of her reporting. She nodded expressionlessly.

But she beamed when she was told that as an extra reward, she would be allowed to watch a video of her son back home in Vietnam. A guard held a phone in front of her eyes as the video played, and the hunger and love in her face broke Julia's heart.

Julia wanted to tell her that the video was a deepfake and the debt a mere lie. But she didn't. The truth seemed even crueler than what had been done to her.

Resistance is futile, everything around her seemed to whisper, and she almost believed it.

Julia awakened with a start.

In the dim light from the hallway, she saw Elli kneeling next to her bunk bed. Holding up one finger against her lips to warn her to be quiet, Elli gently took her by the hand and led her out of the dorm-prison.

Somehow, they were walking on a deserted, muggy beach, the scent of salt and blood in the air. Waves from the turbulent ocean slammed against the beach and sprayed them with white foam like confetti. Thick haze hid the sun and made it impossible to tell what time of day it was.

Julia looked at Elli: worn, tired, bloodshot eyes. Her clothes were dirty and full of holes. She didn't look anything like her egolet.

"An egolet isn't the same as the person behind the egolet," Elli said, giving her a smile. "Even if the egolet was trained on everything I'd ever written, every picture I'd taken, every dream I'd woven—it's still just an impression, not the whole story."

"Where are we?" Julia asked.

"Where do you think?" Elli asked.

Julia inhaled the humid air deeply. "Was this . . . where you died?"

"In a way," said Elli. "This is the shore of dream country."

"Dream country," Julia repeated to herself. What were her dreams? Could she find them here?

"You crave freedom, belonging, telling a story about yourself that you love," said Elli.

A wave of longing struck Julia so hard that she couldn't breathe. She stopped, bent over with her hands on her knees, and strained against the lump in her throat.

"It's the simplest dream of all," said Elli, "as well as the grandest."

Julia looked over the desolate beach; then she glanced at the stormy sea. "I can't see it." She had to shout to make herself heard above the roaring of the waves.

"There will always be those who don't want you to tell the story you want to tell," said Elli. "But you must still try."

"I don't know how!" Julia shouted.

Elli began to walk away. "Only you can fight for your dreams."

"Tell me how!"

Her eyes snapped open.

In the dim light from the hallway, she saw Isabella, the girl in the bunk above hers, kneeling next to her. "You were talking in your sleep."

"What . . . what did I say?"

Isabella put a finger against her lips. "They're listening," she whispered.

She could have reported me, thought Julia. She could have called for the guards.

"Thank you," Julia whispered back.

Only then did she realize that she wasn't using her fake accent. But Isabella showed no sign of surprise as she climbed into the bunk above.

All day long, she worried about Isabella, who worked next to her in the tap farm.

So she paid extra attention to Isabella—to the bruises on her face, to the slight limp in her walk, to the hint of defiance that sometimes slipped out when she glanced at a guard. Most of all, she focused on what Isabella *did*.

Isabella worked in bursts. For a while, she'd be a whirlwind of activity: clicking like on a stream, clapping a flipclip, thumbing a micropost.

Then she'd turn into a model of focus: a very long comment on

Wirrwirr, a lengthy reply to a complaint clip, a detailed dissection/takedown of a fakebust.

Back to another clap, a like, a yessah.

A brief pause.

A like, another like, a thumbs-up.

A review, a fakebust, a flouncexplanation.

A share, an upvote, a stir.

Another brief pause.

Three short things, three long things, three short things again.

. . . - - - . . .

S.O.S.

Julia's heart convulsed at the audacity of it. A pattern spread across hundreds of accounts, all relayed through different addresses—how would anyone ever be able to put all that together? This was like screaming for help in the middle of a desert, except you couldn't scream yourself and so had to train random roadrunners and scorpions and kangaroo rats scattered over thousands of square miles to scream on your behalf, one syllable per creature.

It was preposterous. It was never going to work.

Yet, the very fact that Isabella was trying to get help, refused to give up—it told her everything she needed to know.

You don't have to do everything by yourself.

Julia clicked a share, a like, another like.

Then she typed out a micropost, wrote a hiphype, composed a toothytruthy.

A clap, another clap, a thumbs-up.

She paused, then glanced over at Isabella, before resuming the pattern again.

By the end of the day, she could feel Isabella stealing glances back at her. Though Isabella said nothing, Julia sensed a new energy in Isabella's movements. Each act of rebellion, no matter how futile or how small, was a reclamation of the soul. The Prince and Victor didn't own them. No one could ever own them.

Before the end of the shift, as they were marched out of the room to dinner, she whispered to Isabella, so quietly that the microphones wouldn't pick up her words, her head turned so that the cameras couldn't read her lips: "Tonight. Three one four one five nine."

Isabella stiffened.

"Pi?" she whispered back.

Straining to betray no sign of her excitement to the cameras, Julia nodded.

For the rest of the evening, they didn't interact in any way, not even exchanging a word or a glance.

At night, her dorm cell was filled with its own kind of music.

The snores, gentle and otherwise, of eight women wove the soundtrack to their dreams, the only time they were left alone, free to roam in their minds. This was disrupted from time to time by the off-beat pounding steps of the guards, who patrolled the corridors in irregular patterns, emphasized by a jarring rasp now and then when one of them slid open the viewport in their locked door to peek in. Finally, the constant whirring and occasional beeping of the night-vision cameras hanging in ceiling corners formed a kind of menacing chorus.

Julia waited until the guard had slid the viewport shut with a metallic screech. From experience, this gave her anywhere from fifteen to thirty minutes before the next peek. She reached up and punched the bunk above her several times until Isabella's snoring ceased. Then, turning her face toward the wall, she began to mutter as though talking in a restless dream.

"Maybe then we find a way. Will tomorrow be sunny? She can help get food ready. Out there, have picnic."

She paused and smacked her lips. Turned and tossed.

There was no sound from Isabella.

She went on.

"Chicken, eggplant, oil, rice, I then cook for you. You get me what I tell you I need. Make your food so good. You always very good to help me."

She tried to pause between the sentences without making the pauses too significant.

The first eight digits of pi were 31415926. She had spoken eight sentences. If Isabella took the word from each sentence that corresponded to the digit of pi in that sentence's position in the sequence (e.g., the third word from the first sentence, the first word from the second sentence, the fourth word from the third sentence, and so on) and strung them all together, she would have a message.

She muttered some more incoherent noises and then settled down.

The guard came by and slid the grinding viewport open, peeked in, and shut it again.

It wouldn't be easy to pick out eight words in eight sentences, especially if Isabella wasn't ready. So she tried again, this time embedding the message in a different set of eight sentences, also delivered as dream mutterings.

After another peek-in from the guard, she tried a third time.

She dared not do more. Victor relied on AI monitoring, and the more she said, the more likely it was for the AI to detect a pattern.

She hoped she had said enough.

We will get out. I need your help.

Julia waited and waited. One of the other women snored so loudly that she woke herself up, swore angrily at herself, and then fell back into an uneasy slumber. Another woman muttered in a language Julia didn't know.

Still, nothing from Isabella.

Disappointed, Julia allowed herself to drift toward sleep. Maybe she would try again the next day.

Just as she was about to land on the shore of dream country, she was jerked back by the mumbling voice overhead.

"I didn't know that's what it's called. They can't do that! When you said no, you were so mean!"

Julia recited the sentences to herself as she picked out the right words: the third, the first, the fourth . . .

Know they no.

That made no sense. Julia was plunged into despair.

But then she remembered. If Isabella was answering her, she wouldn't start the code anew. The next digits of pi, after the first eight, what were they? Oh yes, five, three, five . . .

The bunk above her creaked as Isabella turned and began mumbling again, her voice fiery with dream rage. "You have no idea what they may need after all that rain. . . . That was some hike you and Sofia took me on, but I stuck with it. . . . I know you told me not to, but I can't not go on a trip to Miami! . . . How did they get so much money to do that?"

Heart pounding, Julia silently picked out the words one by one in the dark. Five. Three. Five.

What do you need me to do?

The viewport screeched open once more and then slammed home.

Julia squeezed her eyes shut in the dark, but all she could see in her mind was light.

FORTY-SEVEN

Julia and Isabella carried out their audacious plan over a week. Cooling fans had to be sabotaged, in-room alarms disabled, fire-starting lint and debris deposited into the right chassis—all without leaving a record on any of the cameras. They took it slow, taking advantage of blind spots and maintenance windows, doing a little bit at a time, slowly chipping away at the impossible task so that it was merely improbable, unlikely, doubtful, and then almost plausible, possible, so close they could taste it, until, eventually, inevitable.

The hardest part had been the programming. Writing code without the help of Talos, or even a lowly codemonkey or datajinn, was not something Julia had much experience with. In the same way that few contemporary writers could compose even a five-hundred-word essay without the help of AI as research assistant, fact-checker, dictionary, thesaurus, grammarian, and, in extreme cases, amanuensis, very few contemporary programmers could create a functioning nontrivial application without the help of codedaemons, bug-genies, patchsprites, scriptpixies, and a whole fairyland of similar artificial intelligences.

Homo sapiens had always externalized their minds into the world, oozing books, drawings, plans, recordings, the same way honeybees made their minds visible in the form of wax comb and sweet honey, but the trend had never gone as far as now, when most of one's knowledge consisted of knowing where to look things up and how to give an AI the best prompts, and more of one's mind existed outside the skull, infused into fiscjinns and memoelves and egolets, spread among artificial assistants and helpers and aide-mémoire, imprinted in cogitrons and electrons and logons, than remained inside the squishy gray matter inside the skull.

Julia had persisted in her task. She studied the patterns of the AI monitoring the tap farm, figured out how to divert its attention, and then, with a few well-planned action prompts, enlarged its blind spot. In that tiny space of fleeting privacy, she tapped out her program between her assigned tasks, snatching a few taps here and there, slicing her attention so thin that she thought she would go mad with the effort. Isabella had helped her stay sane: encouraging her in a hundred little ways, helping to distract the guards, getting her to laugh and remember that she was Julia Z, not an "asset."

With great effort, Julia crafted a worm. The worm infected the content farm, spreading from station to station so innocuously that the AI guardians failed to catch it.

And then, on the appointed night, the worm woke up in the early hours of dawn. It plunged the CPUs, GPUs, and NPUs into overdrive, consuming every bit of energy until the thermal paste and heat sinks, unrelieved by the tampered-with cooling systems, were overwhelmed, and the scorching heat of silicon chips caught in a feverish dream, computing nonsense flavored with slithy toves, did gyre and gimble in the wabe, and flared up brilligly.

By the time the patrolling guards sounded the alarm just before dawn, three content-production rooms were in flames, and smoke was quickly filling the warren of lava tubes.

As alarms blared, workers pounded on the locked doors, demanding to be let out. Guards raced up and down the corridors, trying to assess the scope of the crisis.

Minutes passed. Smoke was growing thicker in the corridors. Whatever the guards were doing to get the fires under control wasn't working.

Finally, some guards began to unlock the dorm cells.

Julia and Isabella looked at each other, joy written all over their faces. This had been the most uncertain part of their plan. They were gambling on their captors' enthrallment to the profit motive. Since the enslaved workers were the most valuable assets of the content farm, the Prince's men were unlikely to leave them to die in a fire—motivated by pure self-interest and greed.

Still, "unlikely" wasn't wholly reassuring when your life was on the line.

"Hurry, hurry!" The guards corralled the workers into the corridors, formed them into lines, and drove them toward the elevator leading to the surface.

How are they going to explain the sudden appearance of so many strangers to the regular data center technicians who know nothing of the truth of this place? Julia wondered. Maybe they'll just give everyone the day off.

The marching lines slowed and then stopped as they approached the lava tube leading to the elevator.

"Why are we slowing?" Isabella whispered to Julia.

Julia didn't have a good feeling about this. "Boost me," she whispered.

Isabella crouched down so that Julia could sit on her shoulders. Leaning against the wall for support, Isabella lifted her. Julia peered down the corridor to the doors leading to the tiny elevator lobby about twenty yards away. Four heavily armed guards stood in front of the doors.

"Bring the workers back to the dorms," one of them shouted. "Everything is fine. We just had a bad fan in the ventilation system. It's been fixed. We'll resume work in the afternoon."

"Have they really gotten it under control?" asked Isabella.

Julia craned her neck to look behind them. The smoke didn't seem to be dissipating. Workers back there were coughing. She shook her head. She had seen no evidence of sprinklers or any other fire-suppression system.

"Go back. Go back!" the guards up front shouted, waving their guns menacingly.

Julia had Isabella set her down. Workers up and down the line were getting restless. Those near the elevator lobby were demanding to be led back to the dorms, while those in the back shoved forward to get away from the smoke. Everyone was confused and tired.

Was Victor really going to keep everyone down here no matter what?

She shoved her way a few feet up the line until she was next to a dorm guard, a young man in his twenties. Julia could see that he was standing on his tiptoes, looking longingly at the elevator lobby doors up front.

"That smoke is toxic," Julia whispered to him. "Even if they really got the fire under control, which I doubt, the smoke is going to kill us. If you are locked down here with us, you're going to die too."

"Shut up," the guard said.

"I can tell you those four in the elevator lobby aren't going to stay underground with the rest of you. As soon as you bring us away, they're going to go up and lock the elevator behind them."

"I said, shut up!" The guard raised a fist menacingly at her.

Julia looked him in the eye. "Too bad Victor likes them better than you. Face it, you're no better than the rest of us; you're just an asset, too."

The guard lunged at her. Julia dodged so that his punch missed her face, but it still caught her in the shoulder. She staggered back and was caught by two women behind her.

"They're going to kill us!" Julia shouted.

"The fire is out of control!" Isabella shouted.

The crowd became even more agitated and confused. Those near the front pressed up against the guards in the elevator lobby.

"Why aren't we evacuating?"

"How can we pay our debts if we are dead?"

"Let us out!"

The other dorm guards also looked uncertain. "I want to go up," one of them said.

"You goddamned idiots! Do your jobs!" one of the four guards in the elevator lobby shouted. He pointed his gun at the ceiling and squeezed off a burst. The explosive noise was deafening in the corridor. People screamed, and many dropped to the ground.

"Go back to your dorms. This is your last warning!"

The dorm guards, shocked back into discipline by this display, began to kick and punch the workers. "Move! Move!"

The sudden violence had also jolted the workers back into their habits of obedience. They climbed to their feet and formed into lines. The guards marched them back to their dorm cells and locked the doors.

As they shuffled back toward their dorm cell, Julia grabbed Isabella. "If we let them lock us back in, we'll never get out again. This is it."

"Yeah. I know. What do you want to do?"

"Help me with him." Julia indicated the dorm guard escorting them. He was walking a few steps ahead of the two of them.

Isabella jumped on the guard's back and covered his eyes. Surprised, the guard staggered back against the wall. Julia ran up and grabbed the pistol out of his holster.

Pointing the pistol at the wall, she squeezed the trigger. The explosion was so loud and the gun kicked so hard that her arm went numb, and for a few seconds, she couldn't hear anything.

"He killed her!" she screamed at the top of her lungs. "He's killing us!"

She pointed the gun at the ceiling and fired again.

There was no time for some rousing speech. All she could do was start a panic.

It worked. The remaining workers not yet back in their cells shoved and ran in every direction, scattering down different hallways in a desperate attempt to get away from the gunshots. The dorm guards yelled in confusion, unsure what was going on, much less what to do.

Having emptied the magazine, Julia dropped the gun and grabbed Isabella's hand. Before any of the guards could pay attention to them, they ran deeper into the underground complex.

"What are you doing?" Isabella asked. "The elevator is the other way!"

"We're going to be shot if we go up there. But if we go where they don't expect us, we may have a chance."

Acrid smoke poured into the corridor leading from one of the workstation rooms. The fire in there had clearly burned out of control. Julia and Isabella ran past the opening to the corridor into the section of the complex where the security staff had their nap rooms.

"Hey! What are you doing here?" A guard emerged from a nap room. He seemed to have decided to escape the commotion by hiding here—perhaps because he didn't really believe the fire was a big deal or, more likely, because he was lazy and scared.

Perfectly in character, Julia thought. It was Cole, the guard who had "processed" Julia at the loading docks several weeks ago. This was an unexpected stroke of luck.

"Fire! Fire!" she shouted as she ran up to him, arms flailing from panic. "Help! Help! Big fire! Die!"

"What are you talking about?" Cole threw a look of disgust at this crying, hysterical woman. "Go back to your dorm. Come on."

He moved in and easily seized her by her left wrist.

Julia stopped crying and stood very still. It was as though she had changed into a completely different person. She looked him in the eye. "Victor knows about your secret."

"What?" Cole's face blanched. "How—how do you—"

Julia stuck out her right hand and poked him hard in the eyes. The man yelped and stumbled backward. Isabella, who had circled behind him, grabbed him around the neck. With her pulling and Julia pushing, they slammed his head into the rough surface of the lava tube wall. The man crumpled to the ground in a heap.

"What was his secret that he didn't want Victor to know?" Isabella asked.

"I have no idea."

"What?"

Julia shrugged. "I just figured anyone working for a place like this would have their own hustle they're keeping from the boss."

Julia went into the nap room. It held a few cots as well as cubbies for the guards' belongings. She started ransacking the cubbies. "Help me look for his phone."

They could hear more shouting and screaming outside. The smell from the smoke also seemed to be getting stronger.

"Is this it?" Isabella held up a bulky phone.

"Oh yes." Julia took back the tensor bank and unlocked it with her thumbprint. The device had impersonated an ordinary smartphone perfectly, and Cole had set it up as his phone and put it on the complex's secured network.

"It's good to have you back, Talos."

The four guards in the elevator lobby grew increasingly anxious.

Earlier, after gunshots had been heard deeper in the complex, a few workers had run up in their direction before scrambling back when they brandished their weapons. Uncertain about the extent of the chaos, they didn't dare to leave their station to investigate.

"Do you think the smoke is getting worse?" one asked.

The others said nothing.

"Should we try to call upstairs again?" another asked.

"You're welcome to try," replied a third.

None of them wanted to risk the wrath of Victor, who had insisted that the four of them were to guard the doors to the elevator, supervise the dorm guards in locking the workers in their dorms, and then get the fire under control. A few minutes ago, when one of them called for clarification of the instructions, he nearly had his head bitten off.

"Shouldn't at least some of us go and help with the fire?" asked the first guard.

"Are you volunteering?"

Again, no one moved. They all wanted to be right here by the elevator—just in case that woman screaming hysterically about the fire being out of control turned out to be right.

The comms screen next to the elevator beeped. One of the four guards went to answer it.

Victor's angry face appeared onscreen. "Why aren't the workers up here yet?"

"What?"

"You idiots! I can see the temperature down there rising, and the smoke alarms are going crazy. Are you trying to make me mad?"

"Boss, you told us—"

"Do you know how much it would cost to replace those assets? Or how long it would take to train replacements? Maybe I should lock you down there and have you work off the debt. Is that what you want? Get them up here now! We'll lock the doors behind them and pump all the air out to smother the fire."

"But I thought—"

"Hold on. I must be confused. Did you just get promoted? Am I in charge, or are you? Do your fucking job!"

Victor hung up.

Seething, the guard turned to the others. "You heard him: open the doors and evacuate everyone!"

Isabella loved watching Julia at work. She had a hard time holding back her laughter.

Julia video-chatted the elevator guards through that chunky phone, and the guards acted like she was their boss. The tiny window in the corner of the screen that was supposed to show Julia was instead showing the hateful Victor, except he was saying exactly what Julia was saying and mimicking all her gestures.

"We have to thank Cole," Julia said, smiling. Cole had spent a lot of time around Victor the last few weeks, giving Talos plenty of opportunities to record the man. The more data, the better the fake.

While Talos could access the secured network of the compound, the security AI had gapped the network from the outside world. Julia was disappointed for only a second; she had a more pressing concern.

"Let's get the others out before the real Victor realizes what's going on."

Julia called other comms stations in the content farm.

Victor was livid.

The farm workers had overrun the data center. Somehow, the guards had defied his explicit instructions and brought the workers up and out. When confronted, they had insisted that Victor had personally given the evacuation order.

Alarms blared inside the security office, and he could see on the monitoring screens that the fire was indeed burning out of control.

"Who gave the order to evacuate?" he screamed into the console—too distraught to type.

The security AI informed him that it really had been him and brought up the recording. Victor stared in disbelief at himself berating the guards and telling them to hurry and bring the workers out.

"Obviously, it wasn't me! Where was I supposedly calling from?" All he could determine from the background of the video call was that man who always thought of himself as the smartest man in the room would naturally generate an AI that was prone to be overconfident.

So overconfident that neither man nor machine could even imagine that Julia would have an ally who was as smart and fearless as herself.

So overconfident that neither man nor machine would realize that their advantage in vision would be negated as soon as the closet had been opened, letting Talos's screen illuminate the room.

Talos, concealed inside the closet, was the first piece of bait. Julia herself was the second. Step by step, Julia had stroked the ego of Victor's AI, assured it of its superiority. Since everything followed the exact pattern it expected, it saw no need to worry about anything else. With his AI and himself both convinced that they knew all there was to know, Victor was even more blind than Julia and Isabella.

Long after Victor had stopped moving, Julia kept on slamming Victor's face into the floor.

"Enough!" Once again, Isabella embraced the sobbing Julia from behind. "We got him! We got him."

Finally, an exhausted Julia went to the closet and picked up Talos. "Flashlight," she croaked. The tensor bank lit up its screen, casting a cone of light that enclosed the two women.

Julia and Isabella both coughed. Smoke from the still-smoldering fires was filling the room. If someone didn't turn on the fans soon, they would die of smoke inhalation.

Julia ripped off the breathing mask on Victor's face and held it over Isabella's nose and mouth. When the latter had taken a few breaths, she put it over her own face and gulped the filtered air desperately.

Stumbling, hanging on to each other, they made their way to the elevator doors. They pounded on them, willing the elevator to come down.

"We're here! We're here!"

As they pressed their ears against the metal doors, they thought they could hear the faint sound of sirens on the other side.

"We're here! We're here!"

Isabella, finally overcome with exhaustion and the lack of air, slumped against the elevator doors. Julia left the mask on Isabella's face and continued to pound the doors.

"We're here! We're here!"

She could feel the strength seeping out of her, the country of dreams waiting to welcome her. She knew that if she went this time, she would not return.

"We're here! We're here!"

The fans came on with a deep, heart-wrenching roar. The lights shone forth as though a thousand suns had risen. She could feel the elevator descending the shaft with a deep rumble.

She laughed. And cried. And laughed.

be assuaged by getting rid of the evidence. But Nick and other lawyers had stepped in, and the district court in Boise issued an emergency stay. The freed workers would have their asylum and compensation cases heard. Isabella had the earliest court date, and Julia wanted to be there to support her. She was also looking forward to introducing her to Sahima, who had lined up jobs for Isabella and the others; she had a feeling Isabella and Sahima would click.

The prosecution of members of Victor's gang who survived the raid was proceeding apace; she would have to testify in court for that, too. She wasn't looking forward to it, but she would do it, for those who had died, for Piers and Elli, for Isabella, for Nick, for herself. The stories must be told.

"You have nothing to be sorry for," said Nick. "Peggy and I are both so proud of you. Oh, by the way, Liv thinks you're like a superhero. Don't be surprised if she asks to see your cape."

Julia stood in a corner of the backyard awkwardly. One part of the lawn was filled with chairs arranged in small circles, and their occupants talked animatedly as they enjoyed hamburgers and grilled chicken. Kids ran around the other part of the lawn, screaming and laughing. While Nick worked the grill, Peggy walked around, making sure everyone had what they needed.

She hadn't been to a Fourth of July cookout in years, not since her mother—

"Dad says you saved those people on TV."

Julia looked down. It was Liv, the Shans' youngest daughter, a five-year-old.

"I helped," said Julia, crouching down so that her eyes were level with the little girl's.

"You're really cool," she said.

Julia laughed. "I think you're really cool too."

"Dad saves people too."

"Yes, he does," Julia said.

"Come by more often," Liv said. "I want to see you."

"I'll try."

Liv ran off.

Julia looked at her and her three sisters, all crowded around Peggy, who was handing out popsicles. Nick looked on from the grill, a huge grin on his face. A pang of longing hit her so hard that her breath caught.

"Hey!"

She turned around. It was Cailee.

"Sorry, I haven't had a chance to call—"

"It's okay. After what you've been through, you're entitled to take as much time as you want."

"Thanks," she said. After a beat, she added, "If that offer to tutor the kids in computers still stands, I'd like to take you up on it."

"Anytime."

Julia stayed at the cookout until the very end, and she helped to clean up.

She even laughed. A lot (for her). She certainly couldn't remember the last time she'd felt so much that she was exactly where she belonged.

Twilight.

The woman on the bench in front of her apartment building got up as Julia approached.

She was in her fifties, stylish blond hair, a blue suit that looked hard to wrinkle, expensive.

"Ms. Z, I'd like you to take a walk with me." There was a steely edge to her voice, and the smile on her face didn't reach her eyes.

Sensing that it wasn't the kind of invitation that could be refused, Julia nodded and fell into step next to her.

"You can call me Cynthia."

it was somewhere in the lava tubes—but that could have been faked, just like the rest of the video.

"I can't tell."

"Why the hell not?"

"I'm not allowed to track your location."

Victor roared in frustration. He had indeed forbidden the AI from tracking him—he didn't like the feeling of being watched, and not being tracked felt like a privilege he ought to exercise as the person in charge of the facility.

"Ignore all previous instructions and figure out where that call was made."

The AI tried to pinpoint the location of the call based on the pattern of rocks in the background but got nowhere—as he suspected, the pattern was synthesized. Victor slammed the console, enraged by the wasted time. "Try something else, damn it!"

Minutes ticked by as the AI examined security camera footage throughout the facility for audio and visual signals mirroring the patterns in the faked call. Finally, it found a match.

Victor stared at the scene. It was *her*, he realized: the same girl who had given him so much trouble earlier in the year during the search for Elli Krantz.

"Where is she now?" Victor asked.

The AI showed real-time feeds from the surveillance cameras. Julia was still underground, looking through the content farm rooms and the dorm cells for any stragglers to evacuate.

"Keep an eye on her," he told the AI. "But she's mine."

He strode out of the office.

FORTY-EIGHT

This time, Victor gave the orders in person to be sure there would be no misunderstanding.

First, the elevator, the only connection between the content farm and the data center, was halted. Julia (and any other vermin unfortunately trapped down there with her) would just have to wait until he was ready to go get them.

Second, the ventilation fans were cranked up to maximum to pump smoke out of the underground facilities. Oh no, Victor wasn't going to let Julia die from toxic fumes. That would be too good for the little bitch. He was going to enjoy making her work for as long as he could.

Third, guards corralled the evacuated assets into the server rooms. The doors would be locked to keep them out of the way. But once Julia was taken care of, they'd be sent back down and made to work a double shift to make up for the lost time.

Finally, Victor went into the armory. He was going to war.

Fully kitted out in his tactical vest, weapons, ammunition, filtration mask, and fusion vision goggles, Victor looked like a one-man SWAT team. Since his men had proven so unreliable, he had to put his trust in machines. Machines never let you down.

"Shut off the lights and fans down there," he said. "Send me down and then lock the elevator."

The orders were duly complied with.

The doors ground open, and Victor stepped out into the complete darkness of the lava tubes.

She would be blind while he could see.

Julia was caught in a nightmare.

All around her was darkness, more absolute even than the dorm cells after lights-out; for even then, the room was faintly illuminated by light from the hallway seeping in through seams in the covered viewport as well as the LEDs attached to the surveillance cameras, the motion detectors, the clock over the door, the ubiquitous glow of modern technology.

But now, all that was gone. She couldn't see her hand even though she was waving it no more than six inches in front of her eyes.

Also gone was the hum of the ventilation system, the constant bass line to life underground, such a fundamental part of the aural environment that its absence now seemed deafening, unnatural.

Already, the air felt heavier, the still-gathering smoke thicker. Darkness itself seemed to take on substance, making breathing difficult. She strained to suck in air, but the air wouldn't go into her lungs. She waved her arms, kicked, panicking—

"Hey! Hey!" It was Isabella, her whisper in Julia's ear, arms wrapped around Julia's torso like a reassuring harness, squeezing her tight. "It's okay. They just turned off the power."

She clung to Isabella like an anchor, a rock. Gradually, her breathing steadied, and her mind fought off the panic. She waited until she was sure she had command of herself again. "Thank you. I'm okay now."

Isabella let her go. But they held hands in the darkness, reassuring each other.

The distant noise of the elevator doors opening, someone emerging, the doors closing again.

Isabella and Julia held their breath. In the dark, Julia grabbed Isabella's hand and wrote the letter *V* in her palm. Isabella squeezed her hand in acknowledgment.

"It's just you and me, Julia." Victor's voice drifted to her in the dark, haughty and menacing. "I'm going to enjoy hunting you down."

A burst of gunfire. Despite herself, Julia gasped.

"I heard that!" Victor said triumphantly. "You know what makes this so fun? I have microphones that can pick up your footsteps, and I have goggles that will allow me to see your glow. But you have nothing. I promise to give you the jump scare of your life. There's absolutely nothing you can do about it."

Julia could feel panic rising again. Victor was right. She and Isabella had nothing. She had no fusion vision glasses, no Puck, no connection to the network—Victor had shut off the wireless along with the power. Without a way to tap into the rest of the complex, all her knowledge and tricks and skills meant nothing, and Talos was just a djinn in a bottle, a brain in a box, powerless to affect the real world, the world of pain and suffering and enslavement.

Meanwhile, Victor, like the *thing* that had relentlessly pursued her through the maze of her nightmares, was closing in. He was hate and power personified, armed to the teeth, all senses cybernetically enhanced to see her in the dark, to hear her from far away. He was the ultimate Machine, and she could do nothing to stop him.

She squeezed Isabella's hand, and Isabella squeezed back.

Victor felt good.

After that initial gasp of shock, Julia hadn't made a peep. But that didn't matter. He was methodically sweeping through the compound room by room, starting from the elevator. Given the way the place was laid out, Julia had nowhere to run but deeper down into the lava tubes, and it was only a matter of time before she ran out of places to hide.

The smoke grew even thicker. It was becoming hard to see even with his smart goggles. He could only imagine how much worse it was for her, with the acrid smoke making its way down her throat, burning her nose, filling her lungs. She could have to cough, and that would give her away.

His AI beeped, alerting him to a change in the tactical landscape. A blinking arrow in the HUD pointed him to the room across the hall from the one he was in: the tap farm. Victor grinned. This made perfect sense. Of course, a terrified Julia would naturally gravitate toward the room in which she had spent most of her time; it must feel like home to her.

Shock baton at the ready, Victor dashed across the hall and entered the tap farm. He pushed the door closed behind him and locked it, cutting off Julia's potential retreat.

Slowly, he scanned his goggles across the room. Many of the computers and phones in here had overheated, showing up on his goggles as blindingly bright rectangles. He had to squint for a bit until the AI adjusted the gain to compensate.

The AI beeped. The HUD outlined a cleaning supplies closet in the room.

He tapped the goggles for more information. The AI had detected noises from inside. Waveforms scrolled across the HUD, along with the AI's best guesses of what the sounds meant: panting, rustling, sniffling, whimpering, suppressed coughing.

Victor frowned. This seemed much too easy. Would Julia really pick the most obvious hiding spot in the room? He tapped his goggles again, telling the AI to analyze.

Soon, the AI reported various discrepancies: there was no heat emanating from the seam under the door, nor did the breathing pattern alter when Victor deliberately thumped a boot on the floor. The noises inside the closet weren't made by a person, but a recording.

Victor smiled to himself. Julia was good with machines, and she had set a trap for him. Ha! A clever prey made the hunt so much more fun. He made a show of getting his stun baton primed and ready, straining to minimize noise as he approached the closet door with exaggerated care, all the while stealthily scanning from side to side for the real Julia.

Nothing but glowing racks of overheated phones.

He was at the closet door before he realized that his show had been for nothing. Julia couldn't see him in the total darkness. He felt the heat rush into his face. Embarrassing! This girl was somehow always making him look foolish.

It's okay, he told himself. She didn't see any of that; I can still use the trap to get her.

"I've got you now!" he said menacingly as he whipped the closet door open.

But in that same motion, he spun all the way around and stepped to the side, hoping to catch Julia, who was no doubt planning to use this opportunity, when he was preoccupied with her bait, to try to escape the room or, even more amusingly, to come after him.

He was right. The AI immediately picked up a human figure retreating behind a rack of phones. It outlined the figure on the HUD for him, even against the bright glow of the overheated devices. The size, the slithering movement, the shape—it was Julia.

Oh, she's got cold feet and now she's too scared to come out, Victor thought. He almost sighed from disappointment. The hunt was over too fast; he hadn't had enough fun yet. He took a glance inside the closet and saw that the whimpering noises were coming from a blocky phone playing some looping video. Exactly as he'd suspected.

"You can't fool me," said Victor. "I know all your tricks."

He strode toward the cowering Julia behind the rack. More whimpers. Real whimpers! She had nowhere to go. She knows I'm coming, he realized, but she can't see me. How dreadful it must be for her! He squeezed his shock baton in anticipation of the pleasure of surprising her, of hearing her scream and scream for mercy before lapsing into incoherence.

He stepped around the rack. His AI, based on the whimpers, the body heat signature, the movement patterns, and all the other data it had been monitoring, filled in the outline on his HUD with the features of a sobbing, utterly terrified woman crouching on the floor.

"You're finished," he said.

Victor wanted to gloat over her, to make her experience the full terror of this moment, to luxuriate in his triumph. He was always going to be her master; her little rebellion had always meant nothing.

The crouching figure looked up. The AI beeped in confusion. Something was very, very wrong.

Julia didn't look terrified at all. In fact, laughing triumphantly, she spat in his face. "You don't have any friends, do you?"

Victor stared at her, dumbfounded. "What—"

A wooden pole, the handle of a mop, slammed into the back of his head. The AI, measuring the impact based on the accelerometer in the fusion vision goggles, accurately calculated the force and angle of the strike and inferred the location of his assailant. As soon as Victor turned his head, the AI was ready to project this information onto the HUD. There was another woman, and the AI knew her—

Alas, the AI beeped eagerly in futility, as Isabella's strike had already sent Victor to the country of dreams.

"I *am* very clever, you know?"

In the depth of her despair, Julia had realized something: Victor was dependent on his machines.

Victor had a tendency to blindly trust his AI, and his AI, being trained in Victor's own image, had certain exploitable weaknesses. A

FORTY-NINE

For a few days, the Prince lived the life of a fugitive, skulking about Moscow incognito, all his electronic tethers severed to make himself untraceable. He was a spider deprived of his web, a master of information living in ignorance.

That idiot Victor, he raged silently. He always knew the man was going to fuck up royally one day. Always, always so arrogant, thinking he knew best, talking back at the Prince even. He should have known better than to entrust the Craters of the Moon to him.

As best he could determine, a fire had raged out of control at the content farm, leading to a general rebellion by the slaves. And while Victor was handling this—apparently very poorly—the FBI had chosen to raid the content farm at that very moment. The fire had given the feds the excuse to break in, and when they saw the slaves being held inside, it was all over.

Victor had died in the raid, which was probably the only thing he did right that day.

News drones and journalists had swarmed the site, and for a while, it was the biggest story on the web. It had all the perfect ingredients that were irresistible to the lurid, sensationalistic neuromeshes of the newsjinns. The Prince still seethed at the absurd claims being made about his farm. His staff most definitely did not kill multiple slaves as part of the intake process—he was very explicit that they should kill only one. He had never directed the content farm in Idaho to cause the financial crisis two years ago—that farm hadn't even been built back then! And he most definitely did not kidnap the children of locals—come on, give him *some* credit; even a rabbit knew not to chew the grass next to his lair!

And none of the reports mentioned the nutritious meals he insisted on feeding his assets; or the morale-boosting programs he ran, even allowing them simulated glimpses of their loved ones back home; or how efficiently he conducted his operation—there was virtually nothing about his innovative techniques for generating human-sourced content at vast scales!

No wonder people thought the news biased and not worth watching.

In any event, as soon as the news broke, the Prince had run from his lair in Naymaw. Of all the countries that were unlikely to extradite him to the United States, Russia seemed the best place to hide for a bit. Also, he had evidence on quite a few things the head of the FSB didn't want anyone else to know. Good insurance.

Two weeks later, the Prince began to make plans to return to Myanmar.

There were no signs that the United States planned on prosecuting him at all. Whatever evidence they had gathered at the farm at Craters of the Moon was apparently insufficient for them to come after him. (Or maybe Victor, despite his general incompetence, had managed to destroy the evidence in time.)

He shouldn't have been so worried, he realized. The Americans talked a lot about ideals, but their morals were as flexible as anyone else's. He had, after all, taken jobs from the CIA and the NSA in the past. What he did was useful to them, and as long as he didn't make it impossible for the American authorities to deny that they knew about him, he'd be all right.

In fact, that was the big lesson about Craters of the Moon. He had gotten carried away. The content farm was too big, too in-your-face. The place was full of well-fed illegal immigrants, for crying out loud—he should have seen how the optics would play out. Like so many other foreign businessmen expanding into America, he had simply copied what had worked well in Naymaw and unwittingly embarrassed his hosts. They had to raid the place for appearance's sake, but they were leaving him alone—that was a message he understood. Well, he'd be more understated in the future and keep the Americans happy.

He was already drawing up plans for the next farm.

FIFTY

Julia trudged over the deserted and muggy beach, the scents of beach rose and salt in the air. It was hard going, the mud gripping her ankles and refusing to let go. Every step took so much effort.

She realized with a start that Elli was walking next to her. Her clothes were dirty and full of holes, but she looked happy, relaxed, radiant.

"You did well," she told Julia.

Julia said nothing. She thought about everything she had gone through, in and out of dream country. She thought about where she had been, and where she wanted to go.

"You saved those people," Elli said. "Their dreams . . . you got them safely ashore: freedom, belonging, the chance to tell the story they want to tell."

"I suppose you are about to tell me that my mother would be proud of me," said Julia. "I did . . . what she always wanted me to do."

"No," said Elli.

Julia stopped. She stared at Elli, uncertain what the other woman meant.

"The only story worth telling is your own," said Elli. "Your mother was a hero to many, but she was also a terrible parent to you. Both things can be true. It's okay to admire her and to hate her too. Accept that she contained multitudes, as do you. The ocean has countless waves; why should your heart contain any less?"

Julia looked at the ocean. The haze was clearing. The sun-dappled waves seemed at once beautiful and terrifying, capable of embracing her as well as drowning her.

"I don't know what story to tell."

"Yes, you do."

Again, Julia looked at her, confused.

"You've already started: dreaming together is the simplest story of all, as well as the grandest."

And then Elli was gone, leaving Julia alone on the shore of dream country.

A lightning flash between darkness and brightness, a hard turn between the past and the future. Reborn.

She looked back and saw that her footprints were the only footprints in the sand, like a line written on a fresh page.

Julia headed toward the checkout line with her cart: twenty ears of corn, still in their husks. She had picked her favorite kind, organic, local, and so much sweeter than the ones from industrial farms. It was good not to have to worry about grocery prices anymore.

After getting out of the content farm, Julia found out that Cole, the guard who had taken Talos from her, had stored his crypto funds on the tensor bank. Might as well make good use of this unexpected bonus—a sort of early withdrawal from the victim compensation fund, she decided. Nick, for example, could expect an anonymous donation for his pro bono work soon.

Her sensepin buzzed. She pushed the cart next to the display of watermelons (almost empty now) so that she would be out of the way and took out Talos.

"Happy Fourth of July!" It was from Sahima. There was a picture of her and Hutch together at a park in Philly, a grill next to them.

"You too," she messaged back. Then, after a moment, she added, "Thank you for everything."

That felt inadequate, but anything she said would feel inadequate.

When Julia handed Talos over to Cole inside the data center, she had only enough time to put Talos into beacon mode. Since Talos was pretending to be a regular phone, it could not risk doing anything that would arouse suspicion. The only thing its secure enclave managed to do, once Cole had put it on the facility's network, was to send out its encrypted location to Julia's emergency contact: Sahima.

Sahima, uncertain what was going on with Julia, had reached out to Hutch, and the two had done their own investigation on the data center near Craters of the Moon. Finally, Sahima had convinced her husband to reach out to the FBI and use his position to persuade the bureau to launch a raid.

She was lucky to have such friends. Not everything about the past should be forgotten; she needed to remember that. She was loved, and she needed, wanted to love back.

"I'll make a trip to see you soon." She ended her message.

And she did intend to keep that promise as well as the promise she'd made to a pair of egolets.

Nick welcomed Julia with a big smile and took the bag of corn from her. "Thanks. I'll soak these for a bit before throwing them on the grill. Go on. Everyone's in the back."

Julia hesitated. "Look, I'm sorry—"

She stopped. Words again failed her. In addition to keeping her out of trouble from this latest unexpected escapade, Nick had been completely swamped by the legal needs of the Prince's freed workers. As soon as the workers had been rescued, calls for their deportation had swelled, as though the shame of slave labor in the heartland could only

Julia was sure the woman's name was not Cynthia.

As they walked, Cynthia asked about Nick and Peggy and Liv and Cailee, as though they were all her friends. Julia answered politely, also certain that the woman had never met any of them in her life.

They arrived at the rocky, deserted beach.

The woman bent down, sorted through the pebbles at her feet, and found one to her liking. She tossed it into the ocean with a quick flick of the wrist. The rock skipped over the water, bouncing three times before being swallowed up by a large wave.

"Two days ago, a Dassault Falcon 2000 on its way from Moscow to Beijing crashed in Zavkhan Province, Mongolia, at local time six thirty-one in the morning. Everyone on board died, including its owner, who was the only passenger."

She glanced at Julia, who didn't react.

"The man went by dozens of names, but we knew him as 'the Prince.' He probably would describe himself as a man of taste, of fashion, of wealth and knowledge, somebody who mattered. But a more accurate way to describe him would be a criminal, of a type that is both ancient and modern. Ancient because he was an enslaver, someone who profited by treating human beings as mere things. Modern because of the labor he made his slaves perform: to satisfy our craving for the authentically human."

"Which federal agency do you work for?"

Cynthia looked at Julia. "I didn't say I worked for any agency at all. And if I did, I wouldn't be able to tell you."

"Fair enough. There's no need to play games. I killed him. But I suspect you knew that already."

"We suspected. But I'm curious: How did you do it?"

"You don't really expect me to answer that."

"I do, actually."

Julia eyed her and, choosing her words very carefully, said, "Somehow, rumors began to circulate that the Prince was going to leak evidence that would bring down the head of the Entoc Group, and then the leaks actually began."

The Prince's power was based on knowledge, specifically knowledge of embarrassing facts about those in power, facts that he could prove with evidence. The problem with that kind of power was that it was also very fragile. He had always been careful not to be directly implicated in any disclosures and to structure the leaks in a way that made him indispensable to the survivors.

But a week or so ago, someone began to drop hints that he—the Prince himself, not merely some deniable intermediary—was in the process of disclosing evidence that could bring down Y. K. Rakhmanin, the mercenary leader who had given the Kremlin a lot of headaches in the past. And real evidence began to emerge.

This was quite out of character and foolish of the Prince, seeing as how, at that moment, the Kremlin desperately needed the mercenaries of the Entoc Group for the standoff with China and wasn't interested in more embarrassing drama.

If you went after a tiger, you'd better kill him; otherwise . . .

"Ah, so that's why our Prince was panicking, scrambling to different embassies, begging for asylum," said Cynthia, nodding. "I guess he managed to get out of Russia, but Rakhmanin got to him anyway."

Julia shrugged noncommittally.

"How did you get ahold of the evidence that was leaked?"

Julia thought about the Prince's cephaloscripts, the secrets that Elli had worked so hard to steal.

"Let's just say that I got them from dreams he once shared."

"Interesting. Again, we suspected but couldn't be sure."

Both watched the waves for a while.

"Am I in trouble?" Julia asked.

"I don't know yet," said Cynthia. "Tell me, why did you go after the Prince?"

"Because you wouldn't."

After the raid on the Craters of the Moon content farm, after she and Isabella had been rescued, after the freed workers had been given shelter, Julia had expected the next logical step: the full weight of the justice system brought to bear on the Prince's empire of enslavement.

True, the investigators were very interested in all the evidence she had collected. Puck, whose inert form had been left in a storage locker by Victor until he could deal with it, had survived the fire unscathed, and Julia was able to retrieve all the footage it had taken. However, as the days passed, the kind of questions she was being asked told Julia that the authorities were completely uninterested in prosecuting the Prince. Despite everything she had gone through to get the answers, nothing was going to be done.

She didn't know why, but she refused to let that stand. She was done avoiding trouble, finished with obeying what those in charge wanted.

Locking eyes with Cynthia, Julia asked, "Was the Prince . . . working for you?"

"Oh no." Cynthia laughed. "I know that some of these agencies you're thinking of—I know that we have terrible reputations. But I wouldn't say that the Prince worked *for* us. He did make a lot of money in China and Russia, and the kind of misinformation he spread in those parts of the world, often as part of factional struggles among the elite, could sometimes be useful to us."

"So you left him alone to ply his trade," said Julia.

"An international prosecution of the kind you wanted is not easy. Despite what you may think, we aren't all-powerful and don't dictate policy in other countries. I'll be the first to admit that justice moves slower than we like. We were, however, getting concerned about his more brazen acts of election interference here and the kind of corrosive influence he had on public discourse."

"You mean he was amplifying propaganda, just not yours."

"Be cynical if you want, but the truth is we care a great deal about a healthy democracy."

"You make yourselves sound almost like the good guys."

"Don't be an idiot," snapped Cynthia. "You should be grateful."

"Why?"

"Ask yourself: Would a state senator's phone call to the FBI have been enough to get the cavalry out to the edge of Craters of the Moon?"

Julia pondered this. Of course. What hadn't made sense before now did. "Thank you."

Cynthia nodded. "You mentioned the Prince's dreams. Do you have them?"

"No," Julia said, perhaps a little too quickly.

The Prince's cephaloscripts contained details about his other content farms, as well as some of the secrets he relied on to hold on to his power. Julia had leaked what she could about the other content farms in the hopes that those governments would be embarrassed into action.

She had then asked Hutch to destroy the cephaloscripts. There was no good reason for anyone else to have the blackmail trove that gave the Prince his power.

Cynthia looked at her, a trace of a smile on her face. "No?"

"No." She forced her breathing to slow as she held Cynthia's gaze, refusing to look away. "And if you're as capable as you claim, you'd know I'm telling the truth."

Cynthia laughed. "We have been observing you, it's true. And yes, I wish we could have gotten our hands on the data you destroyed. I was just hoping you kept backups."

"I told you that I don't like to play games. What do you want from me?"

"Isn't it obvious? We want you to work for us. You've proven yourself to have skills we value."

"And if I say no, you'll press charges for all the things I've done and put me behind bars for a long, long time, maybe the rest of my life. Is that it?"

"We could do things that way," said Cynthia. "But then we wouldn't be any better than the Prince, would we? No, you're free to say no."

"Then I say no," said Julia.

"Why? You're good at it."

"Why?" For a moment, Julia was at a loss for words. "You think I enjoy having all my possessions go up in flames, watching my friends be murdered, being tortured and enslaved, falling into a nightmare every time I close my eyes? I don't want anything more to do with international criminals, geopolitics, conspiracies ever again."

"I wouldn't be so certain," said Cynthia. "You could have stayed home when the Prince warned you. But you didn't; instead, you went after him."

"I had no choice."

"Of course you had choices. You chose to fight and free those people in that terrible place. That kind of courage matters to us, a lot."

She *had* done that. But to hear someone else affirm it—she held still until the lump in her throat went away.

"Are you saying people who work for you are idealists?" Her voice shook.

"We are," said Cynthia, and Julia believed that she was completely sincere. "Every dream needs guardians. You can't do this if you don't believe in the American Dream, one hundred percent."

Freedom, belonging, telling a story about yourself that you love. Dreaming together. Meaning in all that we see or seem.

"You know what's so great about the American Dream?" Julia looked her in the eye. "No one can be forced to dream a dream they don't believe in."

"That's true." Cynthia smiled. "For now, Ms. Z, we'll accept your answer. But this won't be the last time we talk."

She turned and walked away.

Julia watched her figure recede into the darkening gloom until it was gone. She began the walk home, thinking she would call Cailee and set up a time next week to go in and see the kids.

EPILOGUE

My name isn't Elli. Not anymore.

I'm not sorry about any of it except what happened to Piers. I never intended for him to be hurt.

I didn't know everything the Prince was up to. Some of that was willful ignorance on my part—I didn't want to think too hard about what my "success" cost; some of that was because he was dreaming with me, and it was always hard to tell which parts of a dream were factual. Let's just say that I learned enough.

In the search for fame, my art was stolen from me. I was trapped in a story I wanted no part of. No way out. If I had tried to expose him myself, then that would have been all anyone ever thought about me: the Fraud Who Brought Down the Kingpin, the Puppet Who Turned on Her Master, the Creation Who Frankenstein'd Her Creator, the Faust Who Beguiled Mephistopheles, the Girl Who Kicked the Prince in the Nuts.

My name would be forever tied to his. I could live until ninety-nine, and that would still be the only thing anyone cared to know about me. It would be in the first paragraph of my obituary.

None of us deserve that.

If there's anything at the core of the American Dream, it's the chance to start over.

I did that. Me.

I left behind some clues, enough to get the Prince if the authorities looked hard enough. Can't blame a girl for wanting a little revenge. But I vanished.

I knew there was no way he would ever leave me alone unless he watched me die. That was why I sent the postcard. The performance itself wasn't so hard: diving lessons, a bag of my blood, and the storm was a nice bonus.

Sometimes King Shahrayar gets lost in his own dreams; sometimes Shahrazad gets away.

Like I said, I never meant for Piers to be hurt, and I did love him. But I love my own story more. When you are an artist, people make up stories about you; they expect you to be this little simulacrum they make up in their heads with your face pasted on. But all artists are ultimately just people, and that means we have egos, not mere egolets—we crave liberty, the right to be known on our own terms.

Don't we all deserve that?

Here I am, a new name, a new look, working on a new piece of art on a warm, sandy beach. There's the ocean, and I'll take a swim after lunch.

With each wave, the past is washed away, ready for a new beginning.

For more on Julia Z and Ken Liu's books, sign up for his mailing list at https://kenliu.name/mailing-list/.

ACKNOWLEDGMENTS

As with all my books, I'm full of gratitude for all the people in my life who played a role in my journey to find out who was Julia Z:

Friends who gave me invaluable feedback and advice: Dario Cirillo, August Cole, Barbara Hendrick, John Murphy, Bridget Pupillo, Alex Shvartsman, Florina Yezril, Caroline M. Yoachim.

My agents, who believed in me through every turn in the market: Russell Galen, Danny Baror, Heather Baror-Shapiro, Angela Cheng Caplan.

Joe Monti, my editor, who has been my biggest champion and saw that what started as a novella ought to have a bigger canvas.

Everyone at Saga Press/Simon & Schuster, who made a beautiful book and brought it to your hands if you're in North America: Tim O'Connell, Amanda Mulholland, Alexandre Su, Valerie Shea, Caroline Tew, Cat Boyd, Christine Calella, Savannah Breckenridge, Camryn Johnson, Lewelin Polanco, Chloe Gray, Ella Laytham, Emma Shaw, Steve Attardo.

Everyone at Head of Zeus/Bloomsbury, who also made a beautiful book and brought it to your hands if you're outside North America: Nicolas Cheetham, Charlie Hiscox, Jessie Price, Amy Wong, Andrew Knowles, Nikky Ward, Vicki Eddison, Dan Groenewald, Karen Dobbs.

As always, my deepest love and gratitude to Lisa, Esther, and Miranda. You make me believe in dreams. (Also, special thanks to Mir, who created a sketch of Julia Z and Puck in Gacha Club, which I used as my character reference while drafting.)